A Christmas Killer, Comfort & Joy

Doug Booth

Chapter One
Jed, Rosemary's Treachery & Charlie Wicker

May 31, 1865 began a long-awaited and fateful journey for Jed Wicker, little did he realize. He was going home to his wife in Tennessee, to the alluring young bride he married a week before April 12, 1861 when the Confederate's General Beauregard rudely awoke enemy troops at Fort Sumter, South Carolina with cannon fire that signalled four years that would forever be the nation's worst war.

At long last the strife, devastation and killings were over. The hour had come for healing deep wounds, of understanding and forgiveness; he was returning home across state lines without fear, or so he hoped, of being killed by some itinerant Johnny Reb. Unless, of course, Johnny was a little pissed for having lost the war. Or somehow suspecting that Jed was, in the narrow minds of many, a traitor to the South. With that in mind, wishing to increase his chances of a prolonged future, he had borrowed some less conspicuous clothing than a Union soldier's blue broadcloth and cap from the clothesline of a darkened home he had been passing one evening near midnight.

He hadn't stopped thinking of her while on the march, or dreaming of her during each night's restless slumber that would repress the more violent images indelibly logged with countless others in his mind from the most recent day he'd survived. Most of all he was grateful to his father for taking her into his home despite Jed's determination to fight for what was right, to free the South's Negroes from their chains and shackles and misery. Which didn't mean he wasn't walking closer each day to a hornets' nest of recrimination and rejection from his father, his friends and his neighbours, the many sons of whom would not be making Jed's difficult journey home.

Before the war, as with many of his peers, Jed had scarcely travelled twenty miles from his family home on horseback or by carriage. Now, since first tugging on his Union boots, he had marched and trudged and run and climbed hundreds of miles in what he believed would be his life's single greatest adventure. He wanted never to walk again, anxious for the luxury of his well-worn saddle.

His final solitary march lasted all of nine days, mostly on foot, often aided by the kindness of strangers no longer his enemy, arriving home on June 08th. He was starved for a proper and home-cooked meal, eager to soak in a real bath that wasn't a bucket, an icy brook or a stagnant pond; he was anxious to lay under a late-day sun in the hammock he remembered on the back porch. Most of all he longed for his wife to lay by his side so that a warm and gentle breeze might sway them from side to side as she kissed him and soothed his troubled mind. He had killed countless men, some so close that too often he would see the shock in their eyes transmute from the terror of being killed to the disappointment of not going home. So many Southern men and boys whose families would never understand, forget or forgive him. It was their way: arrogance disguised with a false sense of honour, gentility confused with pomposity. Even men of modest means, clerks and storekeepers and other common folk pretended such superior airs that they could more easily believe themselves better than they were.

He was neither. He had left to fight as a privileged young man, foolishly idealistic and self-righteous in everyone's mind but his, for several weeks spurned by his father who bore the brunt of his family's shame. His new bride, however, did understand. Or so she thought, or so she believed, at first caught between her loyalty to her brother who had refused to attend her wedding, and the life she had always known, and to her new husband whose persuasive conviction was that a man's worth should never again be measured by his colour. She wanted very much to understand, to the extent that a woman was able, more adept at reading and writing poems and letters of the heart, to piano recitals and singing and tea parties, and to one day being a good mother with the best governess and nanny her husband could afford.

Worse, Jed knew by way of reading her fifth and last letter near the end of the first year that her brother, the last of her family, had fallen to a Union bullet. At least he could truthfully say 'not his' if she would care to listen. He jumped from the wagon unashamed of his lie, saluting the kindly man who had crossed his path early that morning, who had travelled miles from his intended course to repay the brave young Confederate soldier for all he had done to preserve what every decent citizen of the South, man or woman, held dear: Slavery.

He was expected, he supposed, that day or some other not far off, since armies never thought to inform a soldier's next of kin of his survival, particularly an opposing army. And neither had he. He hadn't thought to send a telegraph message, not certain why. Perhaps he was fearful of his father's vivid threat to never again allow him into his

5

childhood home, to ban him from the estate he would never inherit the very moment he passed through the doors on his ill-intentioned way to murder and maim his neighbours and friends. Without whom, the father reproved his son as he would an undisciplined child, the Negroes he was so concerned about would have no one whatsoever to care for them.

He stood between two wooden pillars marking a long and well-trodden path to the home, the paint flaked and faded, the gate between them broken. He felt curiously shaken, uncertain what to expect when he should have known. The large two-story home, once stately, was no longer painted bright white with windows trimmed in a pastel rose and the grass where he expected to see horses grazing was more yellow than green. Most curiously, not a single soul, Negro or white, was anywhere to be seen. Why were no Negro children running and playing, why was his wife not waiting expectantly for him on the veranda, sipping lemonade on such a terribly hot day? Or his father sitting with her, smoking his pipe with his carbine cocked and ready in his lap?

The closer he went, all the more threatening was the bile in his throat, the young man partly relieved to see the front door and windows opened behind dark screens giving access to a mild breeze that would do little to tame the sweltering heat.

He hesitated, pondering for a moment the last ten and twenty miles, his smiles and the happy waves of his hand that the passing Negroes and their Negresses had not repaid in kind, making him sad, making him wonder why so many men had lost their lives and limbs. For what, if not the thank-you of a simple smile? Then again, he wasn't wearing his traitor's blue uniform. They didn't know he was different from the others, that he was a better man in his thinking, that he didn't believe a man or a woman should be beaten or sold. Or that, unlike his father, he had never believed three meagre meals and a straw bed to sleep on were by any means a reasonable day's wage.

He was in no particular hurry to reach the veranda, to climb the warped steps, to call her name through the open door. He was afraid. Not of him, rather of what he might find. The old man would be forty-nine or fifty, no match at all for a young soldier made fit by war and the privation of simple luxuries. In spite of such confidence, however, he would not step past the door.

He called out, controlling his fear. "Rosemary! Come to the door! Your husband who chose not to be killed in a filthy war has come home to you. I'm at the door, Rosemary. Please, come to me quickly." He paused, his every sense on alert. "Rosemary, dear, can you hear me? It's me…Jed."

He retreated to the veranda's railing whose paint was peeling and washed-out by the sun, waiting, crossing his legs at the ankles, his arms across his chest, needing to appear more relaxed than he felt. He didn't doubt his father's threat, half believing the old coot would blow off his head with his trusted carbine for how he had disgraced the family name, rather than see his son walk through the door unscathed.

He sucked in hot air, forgetting the sweat on his brow, thinking 'what in hell's damnation!' She was twenty-three, not forty or fifty. What had she done to herself? The lustrous raspberry blonde curls he remembered were gone, her short straight hair streaked with dull strands of grey. Her face was gaunt, her once bright blue eyes sunken and unsmiling. The slender body he had dreamed of lifting into his arms was too thin, her slumped shoulders making her appear frail, her skin dry from the neglect of protecting herself from the sun. Her hands by far were the worst of her. No longer smooth and white, they were chafed and raw as though she had toiled all her young life as a scullery maid.

The shock of seeing him drained all colour from her already pale face. The anguish in her eyes was real, the tremor in her usually gay voice alarming. "You should not have come back, Jed. I truly believed you would understand my changed feelings for you when I no longer wrote my letters. You should not be here. This is no longer your home. We are no longer your family."

"Rosemary, what in hell's name…?"

"I prayed to the good Lord each night that you should be dead and never come home, like my brother. I prayed with those very words each night since the day we heard he was taken." Her eyes spoke volumes. The hate he saw was tangible, chilling him to the bone. "Truly, I could never help wondering whether you took his innocent life, whether you killed a man who loved you like a brother before you disappointed him so profoundly." She sneered. "Did you, Jed? Did you take him from me? Were you the one?"

Jed Wicker lurched forward. "No! I would never. Better he would have killed me."

"Our friends and neighbours, the few we have left, don't want you here, Jed. They have not forgiven you. I believe they never will. What you did has made life different and difficult for us, your father and me."

He stepped forward, reaching for the door handle, jerking to a stop. Her palms were pressed hard against the screen, commanding him. Her eyes were dry and lifeless, when for countless days he had imagined himself wiping away her tears of joy.

"You are not welcome here, Jed. Your father has never pardoned the shame and the pain you brought upon us. He would rather see you dead, buried in a nameless grave."

He hadn't expected any less from the old man, standing firm, convinced that a man must do what's right. And what he did *was* right. His father was wrong, the entire genteel South was wrong. And if brothers could fight brothers on a battlefield for what they believed in their hearts, why not fathers and sons at home?

"There's no need for us to stay, Rosemary. I'll stand here while you pack your clothes and necessities." He snorted. "If he won't lend or sell me a horse and wagon, I'll steal one. Let him dare to stand in my way. We'll leave this very afternoon. We'll head north. It's truly a better place, Rosemary, I promise you. I've seen much of it with my very own eyes. Everyone is free and happy. There's no slaving. There's no name-calling, simply good-hearted Christian folk like you."

She stood in a daze, slowly shaking her head. "I did not want you here, Jed. Not ever. But since you are I have more to tell you. Not a word you will want to hear, and nothing that makes me proud of what I have done. God knows that and He forgives me even if you will never."

"Can't say God's got much to do with my current life, Rosemary. Shooting first with a better aim and ducking into holes did more to save my useless hide than anything He cared to do on my behalf," he paused, crestfallen, inhaling a deep breath, "which doesn't mean I wasn't doing His work for those who had no reason to believe in Him...until now for those who choose to."

Her eyes glared. "And my brother, his murderer was doing God's work?"

9

"He and I chose different paths. I wet my britches more than once, Rosemary, and not from any particular urgency. Just my nerves letting go, pure and simple."

She dropped her head against her hands. "You did a terrible and reprehensible thing, Jed. What could possibly be worse than killing your own kind?"

"Slavery. I fought to make things as clearly they should be between us white folk and the Negroes, like I told you before we married, which you thought then was compassionate and noble. What has he put into your head, the old bugger? He's a bigot, Rosemary. He's cruel in the narrow manner of his thinking, in the harsh treatment of his people."

"They're all gone. Or haven't you noticed? They left many months ago, went on their merry way one day without so much as a single word, without the slightest gratitude for the good life we gave them." She couldn't disguise her disgust. "Good riddance to them. They'll discover soon enough and, truth be told, our situation is better for their leaving. We had no work for them and precious little food for ourselves, let alone the ungrateful likes of them. You did that, Jed. The crops that weren't burned, no one wanted to buy. We sold our cattle. And the horses? What horses? We have a single one left, and far from the finest. Go ahead, step around the back. See the black rot for yourself, then tell me about you doing God's work. "

"Crops grow back, Rosemary. And they will with the hard work of men, white or black, willing to work for a decent day's pay. What's he done or said to taint your always kind ways? How has he treated you so badly? I see clearly on your face that he's worked you hard…treated you meanly and not as a precious daughter." He pounded

10

the railing with his fist. "Damnit to hell. I should never have given you into his care. His mind's twisted, Rosemary. Always was, a fact no intelligent mind would too quickly dismiss. He belongs in a darker world, a netherworld where he can dwell with his own kind. He ill-treated my mother to such an extent that she gave up living. Nothing was ever properly done, not in his view. And he's done the same to you, the bastard."

She dropped her hands to her side, shuddering, her entire body racked by a sudden deep chill. "I couldn't help thinking all these years that you might have saved my brother, Jed, if you had been by his side. Instead you helped in his murder."

"He was a good man with different notions, free to think for himself, as am I. Although I doubt a Negro would ever have given much consideration to saving your brother's skin, despite his being a fine officer. Yet one saved mine, Rosemary. Me, a simple private without the advantage of horse or sword the many times I ran short of powder. Or haven't you read my letters?" Her eyes opened wide. "Held the man dead in my arms not an hour later. His eyes were so white, wide-open with shock, Rosemary. White like you've never seen against the blackest skin. Black like coal. His name was Jerimiah, preferring that we call him Jerry. He was a good man and, like you, he believed God heard his every word. I made his face wet with my tears, Rosemary. The last thing he felt. I whimpered like a fucking baby with a dead Negro held tightly against me." He clamped a hand over his mouth harder than he wanted, smearing the sweat. "Now, if there isn't anything worse coming to your mind, what has you so vexed and fearful of properly greeting your husband as any

11

good and eager wife would after these many years apart? Or must I remain standing here all night?"

"I never took you for a liar, Jed. I received one letter. One. And not from you. I thought for a while that I might cry, or that I should cry, but I had no tears left for you after my brother." She cautioned him again with a firm open palm. "Stay here. As I said, I have more to tell you and your father's got his gun ready. He has for days for reasons he's keeping to himself, and he's emptied more than one bottle of whisky since hearing the South will never again be the same. I wouldn't do anything to set him off. Ruminating over what you have done for no good reason, and the war being over with all hope lost to us, has made him crazy. He's not thinking straight and seeing you here will make matters worse. He's not in a fit state to see you."

"For no good reason, Rosemary? With all hope lost to us? Can you possibly be serious? The war was not about you or me or him, with our fancy clothes and our grand homes. The war was not about the likes of us losing all hope. It was about them, the Negroes, having hope."

"What hope did they require, Jed? We cared for them."

"No. We owned them, to our eternal disgrace, never caring to change our despicable habits, no less guilty than the many others of us who owned so many more of them. Four million, Rosemary, all in the South. That is why you lost the war. That's why I left, to fight for the greater cause."

She walked away, disgusted. Jed let her go, unconcerned, nevertheless fingering the grip of his gun. When Jed Wicker exchanged his threadbare Union uniform for a famer's fresh work clothes, he didn't leave behind the Army-issue six-shooter he had wisely chosen not to return upon his release. They owed him that much, and he wouldn't think twice.

When Rosemary again grew larger into the door's screen Jed stood straight, deliberately, his lips tightly pursed, his eyes unblinking.

"Jed," she choked, "this…"

He cut her off. "Is not many days older than a year or two, Rosemary. What…?"

"She's mine, Jed. A daughter born to me nearly two years ago. Her name is…"

"I don't care a good devil's damn what its name is. The name I need is the father's. A man should know who he's about to kill." He couldn't look at her, or the girl, searching past them. "Not on a single occasion in four years did I think to bed a whore. Not one. I was too busy killing, too busy sleeping to dream of you when I wasn't." He spun in a tight circle, wanting to scream. He wanted to kill someone. He had been there on the porch, with her, standing for ten minutes or more and hadn't yet felt her warm skin or kissed away the tears he hadn't yet seen. "Who was he, the one you whored with? Tell me the name. Or is he dead by my father's hand? Tell me the hateful old coot was that much of a gentleman at least."

She was trembling.

"I am no longer your wife, Jed. I'm legally free of you and the girl is not the result of my whoring. How dare you? I needed a man's comfort when hearing the most horrible news, knowing you were dead, yet holding off for as long as I could. He's not as bad a man as you're thinking, Jed. He's just hard in his ways. It's his nature to be strong."

Jed gripped his gun. "You're talking foolish talk, Rosemary. Speak plainly and calmly. Decent women do not carry around a stranger's progeny. So, because I won't ask

13

again, who took you as a whore? Who do I kill, and where will I find him if not under a tombstone?"

"We received news that you were killed, your father and I, not many months after my brother...when I stopped writing letters, thinking you might have killed him yourself. Your father showed me the letter, comforting me. We truly believed you were dead. That was my one letter. I received no letter from you, not a single one throughout the entire war, and that you would tell me such a terrible lie is despicable."

"That's as far from the truth as can be. I bought paper and ink whenever I could, when others bought whisky and tobacco and women and, as you can see, I am very much alive. Although I must admit I do find myself sincerely wishing that your brother had killed me. Who is the man, Rosemary?"

"He's my husband, legally joined with me by God. I truly believed you were not coming home to me, not wanting you back; despising the thought of you for what you might have done. Your father, Jed... he's the one who made me his wife and gave me a pretty little girl."

The words assailed him worse than a bullet piercing his heart, causing him to lurch. Jed Wicker drew the gun from its holster. "Rosemary, stand outside here on the porch. Or I swear I will kill the brat's shameless mother before I do likewise to a whore's spawn. Now stand here and step aside. You did wrong, plain and simple." He cocked the gun, pressing his thumb against the hammer, swinging the door open with his other hand. "Get out here woman."

She stepped past him, too numb to cry.

Jed Wicker was no murderer. The men he killed in countless bloody battles knew he was facing them and why. Fair was fair. Now so did his father who had committed an

14

abominable crime worthy of his killing that no Southern court would view as murder. He'd stolen a man's most prized property in a place where men frequently found themselves unceremoniously swinging from trees for stealing another man's horse. The war had claimed 620,000 men, maiming 50,000 others. What did one other of the enemy matter to anyone?"

His father was sitting in a rocker, a whisky bottle planted between his legs, a crystal glass in one hand resting on one arm of his seat, his breach-loading carbine resting on the other with the hammer pulled back.

"I'm not accustomed to speaking with a man I can't see, boy. Have the guts to stand where I can see you."

"Good afternoon, father," Jed called from the edge of the closest corner. "It's been a while, and no doubt not long enough from where you're sitting. I hear you've been busy with my wife."

"I did the right thing by her, boy, after we received news of your deserved passing. Admittedly not the worst news I ever heard. That's the truth. Still, I gave her time, letting her grieve for the brother. Taking on a woman isn't something a man hurries into. Not twice in his life."

"She asked what was worse than killing my own kind. I said slavery, not thinking to say a whoring father fornicating with his son's wife."

"Thing is, you are not my son." The old man chuckled. "Could be you never were."

"If such a letter exists you should have set her free, doing what was proper for once in your life. Not this. If she wasn't a whore before, she's certainly one now with a bundle of proof I don't mean to take on."

"No need. We're legally bound. What else could be done with a traitor's wife, which is a damn sight worse in

15

these parts than a leper? You should be thanking me for taking her in, for giving her a home. Who else would? No respectable family."

"I got her five letters. They came late, but I got them. Where are mine? Where's the one telling you I'm dead? Could keep you breathing awhile longer, father."

"Made into ashes, as were yours." He snickered. "What's the use in reading good news twice? How would that make the words any better?" The older Wicker drained his glass. "Killing one man from hundreds to choose from in battle isn't the same as a squirrel's head from a hundred feet or more. Be very sure about yourself, boy. No judge in these parts will see anything wrong in my killing a turncoat."

"Or the likes of you." Jed's first shot tore into his father's shoulder, old Charlie's aim shy by a foot, burying the lead ball into the wall a second before Jed stepped calmly into view, free of worry for his life. "You look unwell, father. You disappoint me. I was truly hoping to send a strong and healthy man to his grave. However, and not sadly, I see you're well on your way to Hell by your own hand."

"If that's where I'm headed, boy, that's where I'll meet you soon enough."

"I never did take much to drinking, not the best prescription for staying alive in battle. That could possibly be how the Union won the war." He cocked his gun. "I never did take pleasure in killing good and otherwise innocent men. Never cared to brag at day's end about how many. Sadly though, eventually killing comes too easily. You put them from your mind. You stop seeing their faces, you stop hearing their shouts and their screams." He raised the gun. "There was no letter. You wrote the words and you

16

walked to the gate without her seeing you, deceiving her for the sake of your own vile needs. You burned my letters meant for her eyes from the very first, all the while scheming to take her for yourself, believing you might punish me by making her into a whore. That God she seems particularly friendly with is not about to welcome you into His loving arms for conniving your way under her frilly petticoats. I truly hope you enjoyed her while you had her, until you made her old many years too early. The devil's house is where your headed now…father."

The man shrugged, dropping the useless carbine to the floor. "I've been with a few women in my day, boy. Some good, others better. Whores mostly, your mother somewhere between the first and the last of them." He pointed toward the porch, smirking "A gentleman has certain needs despite ruination and war, though my money has recently been better spent on more practical supplies. I must tell you though, her, the wife, she was the best I ever paid for. So warm, smooth and willing. I always did have a craving for the young ones. Sweet as freshly jarred honey. Still, I had no choice except to put her to real work after the girl." He snorted. "Truth is, she didn't take very long to forget you. She'll do well without you…now that she's been properly broken in."

He died that instant, his forehead shattered by the bullet's intrusion, blood exploding across the narrow gap between them to splash against Jed's boots and britches.

He left his father alone, retracing his steps to the porch, telling the dead man's wife to put the girl on the ground and to hitch the horse to a wagon. Then, when she was done, if she was of half a mind to, she was to pack the finest clothes she had. A Sunday dress if she still had one, since she would very soon want to make her very best first impression. And not for God. She might also want to rummage through her husband's pockets and drawers for whatever money she might find to sustain her in the short-term. She was to work quickly, as they would soon be on their way. He said not another word, striding ahead of her to the barn.

An hour later, the sun still bright, his work was done. The entire house was carpeted with hay made wet with kerosene. The defeated woman stood gaping midway from the broken gate to the house, cradling the girl, watching as Jed Wicker flicked a match with his thumbnail. He tossed the first past the front door, beginning his father's lone journey into Hell, the second onto the porch before disappearing, running to the back porch and then to the barn where he threw the last.

Then she saw him sauntering towards her, grinning, not taking his eyes from her. He stood by her side, pleased with his work, asking her whether she had thought to search through her dead husband's desk for his will and proof of their wedded bliss. When he heard the answer he was hoping for, witnessing the palpable distress in her eyes and on her face, his laugh was real, raucous and derisive. What did it matter, he consoled her, barely able to contain himself? Kept women were not expected to consider such legalities. She was not to blame herself too harshly. Besides, she was young and, he had heard very recently, as sweet as honey. He was certain she would not be without company for long, possibly even her third suitor, notwithstanding his firm opinion that she would be wise in her current state not to imagine that any gentleman of means would beg for her hand on bended knee. As for work, he would do what he could to assist her in a finding an appropriate position, one in keeping with her station and current abilities. He would not leave her in a lurch, he assured her. She was family, his widowed step-mother.

The barn was the first to collapse, red-hot cinders exploding into the air providing a spectacular backdrop to the engulfed house ablaze inside and out with wildly raging orange flames roaring and blowing out window panes that, to Jed, was a magnificent symphony.

She was sobbing, begging him to leave; pleading with him in vain to take her away, to forgive her for being a foolish woman and thoughtless wife. Jed, though, was puzzled, not understanding her disquiet. When would she ever again be as close to such a dazzling spectacle, he answered? She felt weak, sick to her stomach, loathing him for what he was doing.

Within the hour the high walls swayed for long, indecisive moments before buckling and crashing to the ground, the instant squall of searing orange embers causing them to mask their faces and retreat. Jed Wicker turned his back on the inferno, content that what remained of the old man would continue to burn and smoulder throughout the evening and night.

He strode to the wagon, leaving her to follow with the girl, not thinking to help either onto the rough wooden seat. He could no longer consider himself a gentleman of means; that was his past that would quickly fade from memory, happily renouncing his birthright and ensuring her future with the strike of a match. Nor could she ever again pretend a superior air. The old man had aged her, stolen her beauty, rendering her passably handsome with little trace on her face or her body of an earlier privileged life when she was endlessly striking and carefree.

He had no idea what lay ahead of him, nor was he of a

mind to care. Although he could well imagine the unkind and deserved future that lay in store for her. Their ideal and idyllic life together that he had longed for and dreamed of throughout the war had been cruelly and abruptly stolen from him by a cheating wife and a whoring father. Though of one thing he was adamant: He was no longer a Wicker. That tainted bloodline was staunched forever.

Chapter Two
Jed & Margaret

They travelled throughout most of the evening in relative silence, notwithstanding her constant snivelling and the girl's incessant wailing; the woman at last coming to realize that all was lost to her, that her pleading for a new and better life with him was futile. He was as deaf as he was blind to her.

In fact Jed was pondering his new name, not worrying over what his father's neighbours would care to suspect about the old man's damaged remains and the current condition of the house. Most, he rightfully believed, would suspect a band of marauding ex-Union soldiers who had burned the house out of spite after killing the man to eliminate his interference, taking the woman for as long and as far as they cared to for the sole pleasure of her womanly charms and companionship. Which would certainly become the common belief before those same men, distraught by the senseless murder and heinous mistreatment of the woman, would hurry to the Land Office to research Charles Wicker's deed that would with any luck end in a sale to the highest bidder. Such was the human condition: Love thy neighbour with all thy heart, unless he contrives or threatens to impede your gain.

Nodding pensively, glancing at the woman curled into

21

herself atop a bed of hay behind him, the girl cuddled in her arms, he decided on Billows. He would from then on be Jed Billows, a peaceful and unassuming man from somewhere his genteel accent would not belie.

He wanted her out of Tennessee, particularly as distant as possible from war-ravaged Chattanooga, from those who might remember her, possibly and perversely believing her and taking pity on her. He had often dreamed of travelling to Atlanta before the war. Then, as fate would have it, managing to fill a modest number of unnamed Confederate graves there during the civil conflict. However the city had already begun aggressively reconstructing, modernizing and steadily growing. Not what he had in mind for a recently widowed mother, a woman with few qualities beyond those of a pampered sister, wife and adulteress. She would be out of her element with but one skill to fully, or in part, sustain her.

He believed Huntsville, Alabama would be a more ideal choice: His solution to her dilemma. The town was much less populated than Atlanta, less intimidating to a widowed mother where she could establish herself with greater ease and less anxiety. He'd heard tell of men flocking in droves to find work in the burgeoning cotton mills. What better place, he believed, for her to begin a new and more fulfilling life?

He stopped the first night, in the dark and near a farm, to let the horse graze and drink from a bucket he'd filled from a roadside brook, scooping handfuls of the chilled water into his own mouth. From the home's garden patch he borrowed carrots and potatoes and a sugar pie they had left to cool or had forgotten on the porch. Then he was on his way.

The 100-mile journey continued over three agonizing

days and nights, Jed stopping for short intervals to stretch his legs when he felt the horse needed rest, not giving much thought to her needs. He made fires and cooked their meagre late-day meals while the sun was lingering bright and warm, using his skills learned from the army, not the least tempted to hunt for fresh meat not yet curing in someone else's smoke hut. He never dallied, continuing on each night, managing after dark to replenish his supplies from a similar source in a manner more furtive than when he was emboldened by his blue uniform.

She had not uttered a word since the first night, fearful he would cast her aside, scarcely bothering to coo over the girl who was giving Jed second thoughts about planting his seed in any female worth his continued attentions. He wouldn't deny that a man's need for a female was natural enough, much preferable to the hard-sought privacy he seldom achieved to any satisfactory extent in the army-issued canvas Dog Tent he was forced to share with another who, likewise, would do his best to stifle the peak of his rare fulfillment midway through the night. Yet he couldn't help pondering for the first time he could recall that most families were, in fact, consequences of pleasant intimacies ending in tragedy more than any mutual desire. And that any such intentional conclusion was more a result of social expectation than personal want.

Either way, that many days with a loathsome woman he could no longer abide was more than any man should bear, particularly since he had kept himself faithful to her in war while she was freely giving her entire person to the worst of men. He would wait. She was no longer remotely appealing to him. In fact, driving the blade of his distaste all the deeper, he had offered her during the second day a can of balm meant to soothe the sore parts of animals so that she might coat her body from head to toe in the hope of restoring her smooth skin if not her lost beauty.

Adding insult to injury he turned his back to her as she stripped off her clothing, remaining unaffected as she stood brazenly near to him and naked for the better part of an hour as she massaged the balm into her body in order not to stain her dress or make her dress unpleasant to wear.

On the third day he suggested that she do likewise by tossing her the can, speaking not a single word. And she did, for an hour, glistening under a warm morning sun, wishing with all her heart that he would take notice of her and want her. He did not.

Now he was hours away, strangely elated. He would spend what he could afford on a room and a bath; he would eat the long-awaited proper meal that her actions and her husband's death had precluded, and he would find a pretty whore very near the beginning of her profession, if possible, whose expectation of payment would be in keeping with her unskilled ministrations.

He arrived past the dinner hour: the real beginning of his journey as well as the end of hers. The main street was paved with packed and dried mud and lined with horses, awash with men and women strolling side by side who were watched by old men bent over on benches and smoking clay pipes. The town wasn't a new experience, just another town no different from all the others he had marched into five feet behind the tip of his bayonet. He guided the horse from one end of the street to the other, passing a general store and a bank, a barbershop and hotel, a saloon and a whorehouse where men gathered near the doors appeared either very eager to fill the heated voids left ready by their predecessors, or very satiated. Whatever the case, he was about to join their numbers.

He reined in the horse some distance farther on, beyond earshot of the coarse banter and unpolished humour of uncouth men too filled with ale and whisky. He knew what she was thinking, that they would spend the night before continuing on to somewhere more civilized such as Louisiana or Texas.

"Rosemary," he began, his first words spoken to her all day, "I'm taking a room this evening, for my use alone, after which I intend making myself appear more human than I feel and attend to my empty stomach. This is where we part company. As I view your present situation, you have three options. There is a saloon where you might find employment as a scullery maid, honest if not enviable work. Or a man to supply you with a meal either by way of his generosity or in return for your later compliance towards him. Unfortunately, with her in your arms you should more likely expect that latter. Or you might speak with the manager of the hotel, to propose the exchange of a day's worth of menial chores for a roof over your head and a meal while you collect your thoughts. Or, which I see as a far more equitable solution given your recent and apparent proclivities, I believe your best interests would be served well and better by forging a path through the happy mob at the whorehouse to speak with the madam on the subject of your longer-term and more beneficial employment. I have not the slightest doubt that she will see past the decline of your natural good looks, which are somewhat improved since yesterday, and quickly restore you to a passably desirable woman."

"No, Jed. No. I beg you." She could not believe what she was hearing, too stunned to shed a single tear. Yet the mounting terror in her eyes was unmistakeable.

"There's no shame in such work, Rosemary. Those who

say otherwise are either liars to please their peers or women who have lost their charms with nothing left to them if not to envy young whores like you. You have already been with two men that I'm aware of, Rosemary, one of them young, the other old. It's a good beginning and, I would suggest, much preferable to a woman of your previous existence to cleaning the filth of others from dishes, floors and toilets. You'll see. One or two more this evening won't make a difference and by this hour tomorrow you'll be eager for two or three more. You'll make a good life for yourself, Rosemary, and" he hesitated, "my little half-sister. You'll do well for yourself, and when you're at last proficient in the intricacies of what best pleases a man, you'll most certainly become the most sought after diversion in town. Your late husband assured me as much before he died. You have him to thank for the idea. Though make no mistake, this evening I will not be your first visitor." He dropped the reins, leaping onto the street. "Stay here for as long as you believe prudent, while you decide what is best for you." He glanced across to the whorehouse. "Not too long, mind you, and don't think to steal my horse. The sorry beast won't get you very far and I will not hesitate to put a permanent end to your current misery."

"Jed, please…"

He tugged a gold ring from his left hand. "This alone should buy you a good meal, Widow Wicker. I have no need of trinkets that will forever evoke unhappy memories of your cruel deceit and the most abhorrent of treacheries. In actual fact, if you are not yet aware, I, your brave and loving young husband, was mortally wounded in battle while fighting to preserve all that was precious to your and his ancestral homeland. After which, fleeing your home burnt to the ground by a callous Union foe, you sought safe refuge at a farmhouse where you came across a young couple, brutally murdered by the same men, and their baby girl that you took to love as your own." He dropped the ring into her lap. "Were I not so intimately acquainted with the players in such a sorrowful story, Widow Wicker, I would without question beg that you sit at my table or pay as high a price as required for the pleasure of your physical charms. Good evening to you."

He spun on his heels, striding directly to the livery stable to arrange for the horse to be fed since he had better use for the little money in his pockets than a stable. Then to the doors of the hotel from where he took notice that she was no longer seated on the wagon.

Jed Billows paid an extra two dollars for his room to have a view of his horse and the convenience of bathing in private in a cast-iron tub the housemaid would fill with steaming water for him and no one else within the half-hour. He'd had enough of bathing in the company of other men over recent years, those same pockets not so empty that he couldn't afford a second tub full when the first would begin cooling, telling the housemaid as she emptied the last of several buckets that she had thirty minutes at best to boil several more.

He figured she must be of an age to know her own mind, perhaps as old as twenty; she was covered with sweat, her cheeks smeared with grime, her person not the least bit fragrant.

He suspected her possibly endowed with tolerable good looks whenever she might choose to cleanse herself and comb through her tangled hair. She appeared well-formed with adequate breasts, as best he could determine, straight girlish hips, and quite possibly she would not require much convincing to soak her tired and aching body for a short while in his tub with a dollar in her skirt to boot for her amenability. Or as high as three, were she of a mind to save him the trouble of crossing the street to something decidedly more sweetly scented and decidedly less fresh. Whether she was pure of heart, her misery a by-product of the war, or two-faced, catering to the urgent needs of men for whatever she was able to negotiate from their pockets, was not his concern to worry over or lament.

Her name was Margaret. Her dark hair was knotted into a tail of sorts, her brow wrapped with a bandana to soak up her sweat. Her white blouse was a coarse shirt, loosely fitted, stained with sweat and buttoned to her neck; her woolen skirt was thick, too thick for the season, and fell to her ankles. Her shoes were hard, clacking loudly on the wood floors with each step made heavier by her unsteady load, Jed thinking she would be much better off with her feet bare.

Jed Billows was, as a man in search of a woman, no different from any other of his kind. Despite his bedraggled and unenviable appearance, he wanted a woman superior in her design and abilities to what he would offer her in return. Jed Wicker had gone to war as a clean-shaven, well-attired and educated young gentleman, standing five feet and ten inches tall in his socks. Now he was Jed Billows and he had no socks.

He was road-weary and dirty. His long, brown hair was thick with dust and hung matted and heavy in a tail tied with a leather thong. His body was lean and sculpted, as much from army food as from living four years as a common man deprived of fine wines and delicacies; his arms and face, his chest and his back were burnt by the sun, whereas what lay beneath his britches was pasty white.

By the time she came in again without the courtesy of

knocking he had washed and shaven, having vigorously scrubbed his body from head to toe to the extent that he believed in certain parts he had rubbed clear through his skin. Soaping his hair as she stood waiting behind a row of steaming buckets, he fashioned the wet mass into a tail that had become so much a part of him. He was a new person.

He raised his knees, covering his privates with his hands as she worked the drain at his feet and emptied the water that was grey and littered with islets of lather and froth into a noisy vortex. He was as certain as he could be that she had seen that much of a man often enough before, and that his first of two proposals would not be the first of such invitations she had ever heard or entertained.

When finally she emptied her last bucket, he asked her, "Margaret, I've got a silver dollar for you if you would kindly agree to soak with me for a while and lay gently against me." He waited. "To lay against me, Margaret, nothing more. On that you have my word. Or two-bits if you would rather leave me alone and disheartened."

She wasn't surprised, not startled in the least by his brazen effrontery. "I'm a decent girl, mister." She eyed him closely, figuring his brashness gave her the right. "As plain and as soiled as I am, what normal man would content himself with a soak and nothing more? I can tell by your manner and your speech that you're accustomed to much finer women than me, despite the poor condition of your clothes. I'm sure you'll find what you need and more to your liking across the street."

"I disagree entirely, Margaret. I believe I would pay a good bit more for a good bit less than you. I mean you no insult. I've been four years without anyone as lovely as you, keeping myself for another who recently passed on to a better place before hearing the words I held so close to

29

my heart."

"You're a soldier, mister?"

"I was a soldier, one who bears the unspeakable shame of having lost what we all held dear, and then to hear of my sweetheart's unfortunate and early demise."

"A likely story to lure a young woman into your tub, mister."

He nodded to the table by the chair where he had draped his britches and shirt. "There you'll find a dollar and two-bits, two dollars more if you would care to remain in my tub awhile longer. I'll be tender with you and thoughtful of your feelings, because didn't you just say that by my manner and my speech I'm more than what I appear?" He added, "Or is it that I would be your first and not in the least way the man of your dreams?"

"Not the first to ask, mister. The first with all his teeth and the youngest by far. I suppose the others of your breeding prefer the prettier whores who smell sweeter than me. Anyway, would you believe me?"

"I would. And does the question encourage me to believe that you will join me before I shrivel beyond any use to either of us and likely die from the chills?"

She stood silent, staring at him. He could read in her eyes each word of her debate, until at last she nodded matter-of-factly that she would, as if surrendering, taking a moment longer to examine him further before walking to the table to take his money and slip dispassionately from each piece of her wretched clothing as she would in her private bedroom.

Much to his amazement she wore no undergarments at all, which he felt no right to question since neither did he. His had weeks earlier sunk lazily to the bottom of a forgotten pond where, decidedly failing in their sole purpose, they had not survived their final washing while still on his person. Since then he'd bathed naked where and when he could.

"How old are you, Margaret?"

She thought for a moment, coming closer. "Young enough to cause that reaction, mister. Old enough for you to pay me the money I took."

"Did you take one or three dollars?" he enquired with a smirk, admiring her, his eyes travelling across every inch of her that was much lovelier than he imagined.

"I took your three dollars and the two-bits," she replied, her deep green eyes sad and dark, "that I'll share with the first man who comes through the door if you think to hurt me. You're not my first, mister. I was betrothed to a man awhile back who, unlike you, was killed in the war. He was loving and caring. He taught me how to pleasure a man as much as he took care to pleasure me. But now I work here by choice and not across the street as a whore."

"A gentleman can only ever be a gentleman, Margaret. He knows no other way." He made a twirling gesture with his hand. "I wouldn't for a moment think to hurt you or question your character. Now show me the rest of you before you climb in as slowly as you can. With such an uncertain future ahead of us, I will very likely have to remember and relive this moment for a very long time."

She was as tall as Billows, her hair as black as a midnight sky, falling halfway down her back when loosened. She was slender and toned by harsh labour, her small breasts in complete conformity with the rest of her. Her buttocks were firm and well-shaped, her belly flat and firm, the downy patch of black curls which most distracted him a perfect accent which did nothing to conceal that which was the most delicate part of her.

When he had seen all of her in slow motion, she stepped closer to the tub, letting him caress and squeeze the smooth flesh of her buttocks. "What's your name, mister?"

"Jed Billows, at your service. Formerly a learned gentleman of leisure, now a lost and wandering soul in search of his true destiny."

She raised one leg over the edge tub's edge, deliberately, splashing a foot into the heated water. Then the other, the way he wanted. She squatted, facing away, forcing from her mind that she was naked and vulnerable, letting her body ease against his, sighing a deep guttural groan despite herself.

Her mind was a whirlwind of emotions. She had lied, in part. Her promised beau had indeed been killed in the war, by her dear father's side who fell with him, never having touched her more than to hold her hands or to put his lips lightly to hers until next they met. She had no idea whatsoever how to please a man. Still, a hot bath with steaming clean water was impossible to refuse and, she reasoned, eventually some man, somewhere, was bound to take her either for love or for money. She was an orphan, never knowing the loving mother who died bringing her into the world nineteen years earlier.

She was to have become a devoted wife that very summer, a caring lover, and soon after an adoring mother. She was certainly old enough with the natural curiosity and yearnings of any woman her age, and Jed Billows was as good a man as any she could hope for.

He was young and handsome. He did seem kind and he was clean. What's more, the money was much more than she earned in a day and she did believe that he could have been a gentleman before. He wasn't like the others who came to the hotel and when else would she ever know a man as loving as her betrothed or her father? Who, save the most loathsome of men, would ever wish to marry a woman whose hands were forever chafed from washing the clothes of strangers, her body and clothes forever smelling of sweat from hauling pails of water to the baths of rude men whose minds and words were as unclean as their bodies?

"First things first, Margaret. Let's see how lovely you truly are beneath this thick layer." She thought he would put his hands to her breasts or immediately bring a hand to between her legs to probe and poke her that way first. He did neither. Instead he began washing her hair. "How are you feeling, Margaret? Are you afraid, are you nervous?"

She didn't know what she was feeling. She was certain that she wasn't afraid, yet how could she not feel nervous with her chest pounding so? She sank deeper into the water, pressing her hands infused with heat against her face. "I think I feel… wonderful." She thought a moment longer. "Yes, I do feel wonderful."

"Then we both do. And allow me to say as a simple matter of truth that I cannot imagine any woman with a more magnificently sculpted backside. Truly a captivating marvel to any man's eye." He eased her gently forward, splashing water onto her back, white froth bursting from the soft bar of soap. Easing her backward, he washed her shoulders and her arms with long tender strokes before daring to lather her stomach that was smooth and her breasts where he paid more attention, smiling at her unconscious reaction. "As best I can tell, Margaret, the only thing plain about you are your clothes on the floor. If I were not such a vagabond myself in appearance I daresay I would beg you to consider my deepest and heartfelt feelings towards you."

"If he hadn't been killed I would soon become a respectable wife. His dream was to be a school teacher. Now I'm being washed by a stranger in his tub who seems to want my breasts to become the cleanest he's ever touched. What do you think he would say about that, mister?"

"That life continues on. That perhaps with a few more dollars in your pockets you can leave here and be another teacher's wife. No one need hear of your clean breasts."

"I haven't been this clean since I can't remember and I sleep at night with three others in a room at the back. We share a tub of cold water each week and eat our meals when we can from food left over in the pots and skillets. My monthly pay won't buy me a new skirt or a shirt or new shoes, so I don't see how I can pick up and leave. Not like a man who can work at most anything. This is where I'll be for a long time, mister."

"Then do what you must, perhaps with more men like me who would never refuse a pretty girl in their tubs. Not after seeing you this way, I daresay. There's no shame in wanting a better life when our lives change for the worst through no fault of our own. No one has to know the number of baths you take, Margaret, and who's to say your next suitor won't have had more than you?"

"Would you want a whore for a wife, even a clean one?"

"If I caught her eye early on and she wouldn't take offence to a man without means. Yes." He passed her the soap. "Do the rest yourself, Margaret, unless you want to face me."

She took the bar, leaning away from him to begin at her feet. "I think he would hate me very much, and when would I know to stop? Where would I go without knowing how much I would need to get there, and then what would I do? Four years ago I left school with my papers to become a piano teacher, that's how we met. Then he went to war where he died and I came here searching for work when my students fled with their parents, or left to fight, or decided that filling their stomachs was more important than my music."

"You're an educated woman as well. Good. That's more than any whore can say, and frankly I don't see the difference in explaining to your next suitor that you were once betrothed with full carnal knowledge of the man, if you care to extend the truth, or keeping to yourself the fact that you will have been with however many are required for you to leave here and find yourself new students. It's your body, after all. Use whatever you must to set yourself free."

Margaret dropped the soap into the water that was clear and hot, a tattered blanket of foam clinging to their legs. Her face and shoulders were beaded with sweat from the steam, her stomach and legs tingling, turning a deep shade of pink. She truly did feel wonderful, and clean, yet she was becoming nervous. He wouldn't sit talking much longer, any minute he would want what he paid for.

She had no good reason to wait. "Should I turn around, mister? Or do you want me this way?"

"I want you to stay with me throughout the night, Margaret, when we're finished in here. I can manage another dollar without starving myself tomorrow to help you on your way. And yes, please face me, not that I don't like the feel of your backside against me. I do. However I would also enjoy seeing your face. How else will I determine whether I've pleased or upset you?"

He helped her manoeuvre, to straddle his legs, holding her at her waist.

35

"Is this how they do it, the whores?"

"I have no experience with whores, apart from a night or two with my wife before I went into the army. In fact, I'm very likely on the verge of disappointing you, Margaret, for which I apologize in advance of my inept actions."

She took a deep breath, leaning closer, staring into his eyes. "If that's true, I'm glad. Furthermore, I won't know the difference."

"A strange thing to say. I would think you would expect the same fervour and expectations of your first passionate love."

"I lied for the money. I've never been touched, not ever before. Could be, if he had, I would have crossed the street. Instead I work here, taking my bath with you, waiting for you. Still, I won't stay with you longer than you need to finish with me and the water to cool. That's what we agreed. Then I'll leave with the pails. I would lose my employment if the owner discovered I was doing this with you. He's likely already thinking that I'm shirking my duties."

He smiled, pulling her closer. "Might I suppose that, in spite of our mutual lack of experience, that you are acquainted with the fundamentals?"

She nodded, closing her eyes. She had always imagined that she would be with her husband in their bed, with the lights put out, under their blankets, his warm and tender hands pushing up her nightgown; never had she dared to imagine herself taking her bath in a tub with a complete stranger, naked in a fully lighted room and nestled snugly into his lap.

"I know the first part. Anyway, the money's mine. I never promised anything good, mister."

She raised her body, waiting until she believed him properly centred, lowering her weight as deliberately as she could, her first sensation of him causing her to jerk, the second evoking the faintest gasp. She was no longer nervous, no longer afraid of thinking herself a whore. In fact she believed she was actually happy she had met Jed, and now somehow her hands were clasping his face.

She assumed that he must be well-made. He seemed very comfortable being naked with her and he was more handsome than she first believed, particularly after his first bath. His body was lean and muscular. His appendage that she saw growing firm before joining him, and had thus far felt pressing against her back, seemed to her too impossibly big to fit inside her tiny opening. She couldn't imagine how such a thing could possibly not hurt her, yet it didn't.

Her eyes were tightly closed, feeling not the slightest sense of shame or guilt. She was committing each pulsation to her memory, at first raising and lowering her body in accordance with the upward-downward pressure of his hands, thankful he wasn't talking. She was in another world, a better place, her arms wrapping instinctively around his neck, her body rocking freely in concert with his, her mind oblivious to the hectic water splashing around them. She had never experienced a man's hands exploring her body anywhere near as shamelessly, kneading her buttocks and pressing their bodies closer, fondling and kissing her breasts until the force of their combined climaxes jolted them apart, Jed's still ready member the focal point between them, swaying in the water like some curious pendulum.

She was breathless, gulping more than breathing. "It wasn't what I thought. Was I worth your three dollars and two-bits, mister?"

"You were, and you are. The water may have cooled, that which is not covering the floor, not that you seem to have noticed. Nevertheless my offer stands. In fact I believe I could well forego a meal tomorrow. I would much rather remain with you and selfishly advance your newfound cause."

"I cannot. He would dismiss me at once." She turned her attention to her clothes, sighing. "We wash our clothes when we're finished our baths and hang them to dry while we sleep." Tears welled in her eyes. "This was never to happen. Me working here, him dying, you paying for the use of my private body."

"That we both enjoyed."

She hesitated. "Yes…that we both enjoyed. Were you the gentleman you possibly formerly were, with more in your pockets than three dollars for a whore, I believe I would stay with you for an entire week and earn enough with one man to leave this place with nothing worse to explain than had I truly been married."

He eased her weight from his legs, her words chilling his mood as much as the water.

"You are no whore, Margaret. You're not. I've seen many of them from the least costly roaming our camps with their raw parts barely refreshed, to the best of them in proper houses where I went strictly to win at cards, and you are not one of them by any measure." He cupped her breasts, thinking he wanted to kiss her. "And what is so wrong with a gentleman appreciating the obvious beauty you keep too well hidden beneath your soiled clothes?"

"I'm cold. Are we finished?" She shrugged. "I suppose that's up to you since I'm not in any position to refuse if you want more of me."

"I do want more, in the bed, not that I'm complaining.

To say the very least of our" he grinned, "intimate closeness, you are breathtaking, delightfully lovely and incredibly animated. For a brief moment I believed we were ardent lovers newly found. Truly, I did. I cannot possibly envision a more desirable woman and I believe without any expectation that you will change your mind."

"So I can get out?"

"Yes. If our delightful bath is at an end I would prefer seeing you stand first as a matter of dignity and not a fixation on any lovely part of you."

She stood, bracing herself on the edge, raising one leg then the other, stooping to reach for her shirt, bringing the fabric to her nose, pausing, facing him as he stood reaching for the towel.

"How many baths would I need to leave here, do you think?"

"Enough for a ticket on the train, a meal or two in a rooming house, a new dress and shoes. No one has to know you're naked underneath if the savings will get you out from here that much faster."

He passed her the dry towel, intrigued, watching her bend and stretch and ponder.

"Or I could give my body freely to one man for a short while in exchange for the use of his wagon and a meal each day while he goes in search of his true destiny. I don't eat much, Jed," she nodded shamelessly at his privates, "and you do seem very smitten with what you see of me unless it's pointing its way past me to the whores."

"You want to travel with me, a man with very little to offer other than a bed of straw? Margaret, the food I've eaten since the war's end, I've stolen. The clothes you see on the chair, I stole. No one is hiring. No one's got money to pay for work they can manage themselves."

"We can work together for our meals and to feed the horse, to sleep in a barn, and maybe for a dress no longer wanted." She waited, unblinking, beginning to feel uneasy standing naked before a man she'd known for an hour, beginning to feel as though she was begging. Finally she threw the towel at him. "And don't say anything your stiff cock will make into a lie, Jed. The thing hasn't stopped staring at me since it watched me undress."

Jed stepped from the tub, going for his britches. "A music teacher and housemaid never figured into my plans, Margaret. We had a deal, you and I, agreeably honoured by both parties."

"Nonetheless, a woman of your own did figure into your plans, until she did something to make you call her a whore. I can replace that loss until we are both properly settled." She tossed her clothes into the tub. "You're right. I am not a whore, but since he died, and until our bath, each day I've smelled worse than one. I don't want that anymore." She sauntered to the bed, throwing back the thin cover, crawling to the middle, stretching out on her side across its width. "We're leaving here together, Jed Billows. Tell me I'm wrong. Tell me you don't want me. And, if you don't mind, I'll first take that other silver dollar."

Chapter Three
Jed, then Margaret

Words were not needed. He tossed her the dollar, adding his britches and shirt to the tub. Then he was at the foot of the bed watching her, grinning, "A dollar richer, Margaret, and apparently no longer cold."

Stepping from the tub Margaret decided then and there, standing fragile and naked in front of the first man to see her that way, this one a complete stranger, that she would do whatever she must to improve her condition, that she would escape from the bitter work and her pitiable circumstance that she had succumbed to out of desperation. Jed Billows had come to her not a day too soon and she could do a lot worse, she believed, matching his appraisal of her with a critical eye of her own.

He was certainly not a man lacking in manners or education; he was no hapless vagabond content to travel along country roads drifting from one menial task until finding another. She had known men like him before. Whatever ill-fortune had befallen him because of the war would not endure forever. He was better than most, a gentleman with no wife or family to burden him. He was healthy, strong, and seemed correctly built, although she had no means of determining to what extent as a whore might. More to the point, she must have pleased him

41

because he clearly desired more of her, standing so near to her in a manner that not very long ago would have horrified her. In addition to which, she confessed silently, the experience was not remotely unpleasant.

They were each other's solution. He had little or no money left in his shallow pockets to afford the worst whore available to his sort in a brothel or saloon, while she was young, clean and perforce willing with a body he clearly enjoyed; whereas she had no money for a train or a meal, while he had a horse and was unafraid to beg, borrow or steal what he needed to get by.

What's more, he was right. A man or a husband, what was the difference if one could very likely lead to the other? She would simply tell any future suitor the horrible truth: Her young husband died in the war, leaving her to fend for herself.

Jed Billows somehow persuading her into his tub had transformed her as much as saved her. That she had given her body for payment would trouble her mind not at all, the hotel paid her much less for much worse. She placed the coin by the oil lamp on the bedside table and rolled onto her back with a smile that was not the least bit timid.

"As well, I will take an equal part of whatever we can earn together, given that I will likely do the washing and cooking in addition to what you see here."

"Agreed, given that the cost of satisfying my foreseeable cravings with one such as you would be considerably higher and presently beyond any reasonable expectation." He crawled onto the bed beside her, resting a hand on her belly. "Had we met years ago, when I had land, a home, and a future laid out, I can see that I could have married you first. Not that I wasn't once enamoured of my departed wife. I was, for as much as I believed I knew of her. Yet now I believe I would have endured an unhappy life. Whoever finds you next, Margaret, will truly be the proudest and most fortunate of men. If he hasn't already come upon you."

"Easy enough to say when we're like this. However, as often as you will require the use of my body, or I yours, I have no particular need to hear what you are thinking. No such man has yet happened upon me. I believe that had we met years ago, and he hadn't been killed in the war, I would have invited you to my wedding. I'm doing this for me, for a new dress, for a train ticket and a piano, which has nothing to do with what you did with me in the tub that nearly threw me onto the floor with the water. I never expected that such a thing would happen, which gives you no reason to expect more than you would after feeling yourself satiated by a whore."

"We both got more than we expected, and when better than now to stop talking, Margaret?" He leaned over her, cupping a breast, daring at last to kiss her lips. She gave him no reason to probe, to test that she was ready or to arouse her beyond her present state. She was as ready as he, and agreeably receptive, parting her legs without as much as a whimper or a whisper. She would not ruin her one chance to run from Huntsville and to put her past behind her as quickly as she could.

Margaret came away from him breathless and exhausted. She had never felt so exhilarated and never so enraptured; he drew away depleted, collapsing onto his back, drawing the bedcover to his waist while choosing to leave her exposed.

He propped himself onto an elbow, admiring her contours, tracing them with a finger. "We'll be an unusual sight crossing the street to the wagon tomorrow, Margaret, in our dripping wet clothes. I believe our second union of body and mind was as good as any handshake, and a deal is a deal."

She had a more pressing dilemma, she had her own water to pass and no clothes to wear to the outhouse at the back of the hotel. He didn't appreciate the quandary. The tub had a drain that emptied into that very space by the miracle of brass piping, Jed suggesting that the quicker she got to it, the faster they could relieve their present and separate discomforts. He rolled her away, smacking her backside, remaining as he was to watch her and to study every compelling inch of her.

Many of the whores who followed soldiers from camp to camp were potted and bruised from so many gruff hands and heedless demands. Even the more expensive women whose single purpose was a man's ephemeral pleasure were often imperfect, disguising their natural and man-made flaws with thick creams and unnatural scents. But Margaret was flawless. Her beauty was unspoiled, her scent delicious and natural, her excitation and eagerness to please him were real.

He had no timepiece, having lost his gold watch in a card game to a man whose luck that night was more lucrative than his. A preferable loss to his hard-earned pay since soldiers were very seldom interested in what hour of the day they would kill or be killed. She must have stayed bent over the tub five minutes or more, and from his perspective she was a marvelous creation. That she believed herself plain was too difficult to imagine.

When she was done with her washing he sprang from the bed to help her wring the clothes that would dry wrinkled and fresh by the open window, Margaret next filling a pail from the tub before stepping in to pull the plug from the drain and squat. She cleansed herself of him first, enjoying the coolness of the water against the pleasant discomfort that was foreign to her, well-past any previous shyness and too relieved to care that he was by her side waiting his turn.

War made men indifferent to their surroundings, to death, injury and destruction. On more than one occasion he'd pissed by the side of a whore squatting with her skirts held high to avoid smelling worse than she did, or possibly attracting beneficial attention to herself. He helped her out, not bothering to step in as the water drained, talking with her as though waiting to take their seats at the theatre or deciding what provisions they should purchase at the general store whenever they might have money to spare. Between the hardship of her workday and the little energy left in her body that he hadn't yet sapped, she was barely able to stand, too fascinated by the force of his stream to move or fall down.

When he was finished she went to the bed, her mind reeling, slipping under the cover, surprised that she had not yet fainted or dropped dead from everything she was seeing and doing since coming into his room. Yet despite her newly discovered emotions and her desire for more of him, or for more of the frenzied state he had twice stirred within her; despite the reality that she was no longer decent or pure and had taken money in exchange for her body, she fell asleep quickly, contentedly oblivious to his tender caresses and hot breath.

She hadn't slept as soundly in a very long time, not that she was cognisant of her peaceful euphoria or angelic purring as he kissed every inch of her, fondly, trying his utmost not to wake her. Rosemary, in the short while she had been his loving wife, had never remotely provoked that much arousal in his mind or in his body.

He sat against the wrought-iron headboard staring at her. Never in his life had he felt as invigorated. Not when he took Rosemary as his own, not when the Confederate lead ball blew his Union cap from his head, which, sadly for the other fellow, gave Jed ample opportunity to repay the gesture in a more meaningful way.

He went to the window, the yellow sun was rising. After four years of camping in fields and forests, he rightly deduced the hour was very close to five o'clock and that the early hour promised a warm and pleasant day. Not far from when she would normally wake, he thought, clambering into his damp britches and wrinkled shirt. At least she had him for one night, with a clean bath and a private room to boot. He would miss her, for a while, or the thought of her, or the smell and the taste of her until all that would undoubtedly fade.

For her part, she would loathe him. She would curse him and cry until she would at last come to understand how he had helped her. She was schooled more than the average woman, skilled in music, and he wasn't the last gentleman who would wander through Huntsville for whatever his purpose. Many would follow. She would do very well for herself and before very long she would have her new dress and train ticket without the need to travel along dust-covered roads begging for work and staying awake to steal the food of honest folks while they slept.

He left without the temptation of touching her, fearing she would open her eyes and alter his future. He gave her a meaningful glimpse into a much better life, a way out for which she was now abundantly well-equipped to see through to fruition. Life did go on, and would for each of them. He had already proven that truth to her beyond question.

He reached for his boots, padded to the door in bare feet and left her behind. At the stairs his pace increased. The horse and wagon were as he left them; the feedbag was gone and he wasted no time leaving the town behind without too much disturbance from the horse's hooves and the grinding squeals of ungreased wheels. The town was soundly asleep, even the drunkards and those too poor to afford a room remained slumped and unconscious against lampposts and doors.

He didn't look back, travelling for a few days, working when he could, mostly for his meals and enough water at day's end to last him through the night as he searched for farms along his journey whose windows and front porches were darkened. Life was increasingly unkind, clearly and justly punishing him for his cold-hearted treatment of Margaret, his previously shallow pockets at present serving no practical purpose whatsoever. He had not a single sou to his name with which to cleanse himself, or to pay for a winning seat at a gaming table with likeminded past or present gentlemen. He was in the truest sense a vagabond.

By the end of June he had little choice but to rethink his mindset. He was better than what he had become. Or, for that matter, reduced to. He was a gentleman and should be regarded as such, not looked down upon and spurned by those he passed each day in the guise of a homeless wayfarer.

The last afternoon of the month was pleasant enough, Jed not bothering to coax the horse past an amble. He came to an old man standing at the road by his gate outside Montgomery, hopeful the man would have work for him in exchange for a meal, when to his surprise the man raised a palm to halt Jed. He had been standing at the road most of the day, expecting that a fellow such as Jed would eventually pass by. He had done about all the hard labour he could manage at his advanced age. He was willing to pay a good wage for good work, about a week's worth if Jed had a need that was as strong as his back.

Jed assured him that such was indeed the case, and would the man have any use for a sturdy wagon and quality harness for whatever honest price he would care to attach to a week's pay? The old man nodded. Jed nodded, and the two shook hands, the old man climbing up beside him.

A week later Jed Billows' pockets were sufficiently full to afford him a bath, a new pair of britches and a shirt, with sufficient funds remaining for a good meal and the assurance of another winning seat whenever he might arrive in Mobile where he planned to remain until either his luck ran out or he was run out by disgruntled losers.

That journey lasted ten days on the back of his horse that was tacked-up with only a bridle and reins, Jed not the least inclined to beg for more work, stopping often to walk and refresh the beast as much as himself. The hotel he came upon, for there was no other in town, was grander than Huntsville and family run, leaving Jed with a predicament to which he had not devoted a moment's consideration.

The innkeeper's daughter was much taken with him, particularly when hearing he would be their guest for several days. She was young and pretty and flirtatious, curvaceous and well-endowed with much of her pinkish white swells at the edge of her bodice begging his favour as she leaned over the counter to stare shamelessly at the buttons on his britches and offer to pour him a bath. She was bored, in search of excitement and adventure, Jed very much of the opinion that she might actually teach him a good deal. She was his for the taking, he was certain, and well within his means since she merely wanted to improve upon the monotony of her days and not her personal wealth.

Her pa was gone most evenings to the saloon, she assured him, when he wasn't with his favourite at the brothel to assuage the grief he felt at losing his wife and her mother. Leaving her to attend to his guests, and Jed's was the last room she rented that day. They were young and could have as much fun as he wanted with her each night in his bath or in his bed or in hers, she tried her best convincing him outright as if pointing out the more exquisite features the hotel had to offer. He wasn't to worry. She had her majority and would expect nothing more of him. So, please, could she pour him a bath? She promised he would like her very much. And, best of all, she tried with a bright smile, because she would be with him in the tub, there would be no extra charge.

As much as he desired and felt the urgent need of a woman, and could clearly envision an agreeable few evenings with the girl, believing she would taste as sweet as what he was seeing of her, and that the thought of engaging a proper whore was decidedly distasteful to him after what he had savoured of Margaret's sweet charms, he declined her offer very much against his will. He hadn't spent a single night without Margaret crowding his thoughts and dreams.

More pragmatically, from a gentleman's perspective, he would not in consideration of his life, bed the daughter of an innkeeper inside the man's very own establishment. They were, after all, in the Deep South and very few fathers would take kindly to a stranger taking advantage of their innocent daughters whether or not the girls were cute and all too tempting coquettes.

Disappointed and pouting, her cheeks flushed, feeling slighted since she was so young and appealing, she cupped her breasts, squeezing them and pushing them higher to tease and torment him. She scolded him that he was too unkind to rudely and without reason hurt her feelings and that he should never for a moment think to approach her with a change of heart, no matter how desperate his condition.

He understood. He would never again think to injure her sensibilities, yet would she please instruct a maid to prepare his bath. After which, bathing alone once the woman left his room, he hurried to the general store where he purchased new britches, underpants, socks, and a shirt. He left his rags on the floor and went directly to the saloon for a well-earned dinner, a single whisky, and to sit with the pretty coquette's father and a half-dozen others who had been sitting there long before him.

From the moment he joined them he held the best hands, his sombre expression never changing as they began folding and grumbling. To a man they wished none had set eyes on him, their week's wages resting in neat stacks in front of him until he left the table with sufficient funds in his new pockets to support him a month or more without the strain of physical labour he had come to abhor. To the point where, come morning, he went first to the bank to make a deposit.

His good luck endured the better part of two weeks, taking in more than he lost, until midway through July when his luck gave out to someone many years his senior, a man stylishly attired, manicured, and professional in his demeanour.

The next morning the innkeeper's daughter, aware of his financial distress, dressed for the day in her most flattering bodice, pampering herself with beauty oils and perfume. She hated him terribly and sat in her parlour waiting, impatient and more intent on scorning him with each passing moment. When at long last he came in to settle his account, she was haughty with him, sneering at him for daring to intrude upon her privacy as she was adjusting her garters and hose with her skirt pulled indecently high. He was no gentleman at all, and should immediately express his regret at mortifying her in such a horrible way.

He replied with a smirk and his fullest attention that he did not regret. He was appreciative and very pleased with how she had chosen to show her forgiveness for his previous ill-treatment of her and his complete disregard for her urgent feelings towards him. Only a true gentleman could rightly appreciate such bare and slender legs…which, he could not help but remark, she seemed in no particular hurry to conceal.

Jed Billows left town with a smile atop the back of his horse with not enough in his pockets to allow himself the purchase of a comfortable saddle, fully convinced better days lay ahead.

He tossed a coin: East or west?

He headed west to Louisiana, to a place he had never seen, to a place of saloons and brothels and men like him. He had no choice that he could figure. He had no home and no skills other than killing and gambling, decidedly more expert in the former given his current privation. He had led a privileged early life, when his most arduous endeavour was riding into the fields to inspect the work of his father's Negroes, choosing to abandon that life to fight a war against his Southern brothers, divorcing himself entirely from his advantages with the flick of a match and the difficult choice not to kill the harlot who was formerly his wife. Perhaps, for a moment consumed by the lament of retrospect, he should have killed them both and made himself the rightful landowner.

He was debating one day, often silently, often talking aloud as he rode towards New Orleans, whether he should reverse his direction and return to Huntsville as quickly as the beast could carry him, to beg her forgiveness and to start his life over with her. Yet so many weeks had elapsed, he fretted, searching his conscience for what he should do. He was certain she had truly loved him that one night together, adamant she would one day soon become a respectable woman again with his help. To that end he failed her beyond any reasonable expectation that she would forgive him, which mattered not at all. He loved her, he was certain he did, certain he could reignite her love for him. His thoughtless and cruel actions, driven by whatever misguided thinking had clouded his judgement at the moment could be undone because they did love each other.

He damn well loved her. His left hand jerked hard on the reins, his body flung violently to the ground before the horse could react to the command. The man coming towards him kicked the six-shooter from Jed's hand, forming a thin, toothless grin from the centre of a gaunt and grey face.

Jed snorted. Why in damnation wouldn't he, or shouldn't he? As far as he could figure he was dead either way, whether he did or he didn't. The hole in his gut spewing blood told him that much. Each night throughout the entire war he swore that, when killed, he would die properly with the dignity of a gentleman.

"You sure as hell didn't have to kill me for my money or my horse, mister. I'm as poor as you and the horse is as dead as me."

"It'll get me as far as I need, friend. Fact is, I saw your boots first."

Jed clasped a hand hard against his wound. He saw no need to gasp, or groan, or lament his current situation. At scarcely twenty-five he was twice the man most men twice his age could claim. "Union boots, mister, with a good bit of history in these parts." He coughed a laugh, spitting blood. "Guess I should have stayed with her, my Margaret. Pretty as an angel. Soft as cotton and a mite kinder towards me than you. So I rightly figure you owe me a favour or two, friend, if you're of a mind: If you ever come across a certain Rosemary Wicker, would you kindly kill the whore for me and tell her who sent you? As for me, I would be greatly obliged if you would put an end to this acute misery you have unduly caused me, and quickly. I can't see that we have much else in common to talk about, you and I."

His killer shrugged, the shirt was already ruined. Jed lay back and closed his eyes. An instant later the stranger put another bullet into Jed's chest.

Jed's pockets were empty, the stranger contentedly continuing his journey having earned for himself a sturdy pair of boots, clean britches, a well-oiled gun, and a horse that would, if nothing else, make his journey to New Orleans easier on his feet and a good bit quicker. All for the cost of two bullets.

*

Margaret Wallace woke much later that next morning in June than her usual hour, with a smile wider than she could ever have imagined. She was leaving at long last with a man. She was elated, even when she sleepily rolled over to face the window and realized Jed had gone. She stretched, moaning deeply, her entire body shuddering. She sat, kicking the cover free of her legs, seeing her body differently, seeing a truly beautiful young woman.

They had much to discuss, so much to hear about each other's plans. So, yes, she admitted to herself, why could she not be more than simply an accessible release for him? They were young, smart, with their entire lives ahead of them. He had come to her when she was at her most wretched, she mused dreamily, hugging her knees, how wonderful would they be together as a proper couple for everyone to envy?

She remained as she was for an hour, naked, eager for him to return, dreaming of her better life, yet increasingly worried. She didn't know. He wouldn't possibly do such a horrible thing to her. He couldn't, not after all they said to each other, promised each other, Margaret reluctantly less certain and more fearful with each passing moment.

She saw the silver coin on the table, scrambling from the bed to her clothes by the window. The horse and wagon were gone, though he hadn't taken her money.

She dressed as quickly as she could and hurried downstairs, ignoring her manager's ranting accusations. She went directly to the livery stable, enquiring about the man who the night before had paid for his horse to be fed and watered across from the hotel. When she heard the worst she collapsed against the nearest wall and wailed.

Composing herself, she dried her face and went to her manager to confess that she had slept in, even though he could clearly see otherwise by her clean hair, her fresh scent and her freshly washed clothes.

"You're a bold and brazen liar, Margaret. You passed the entire night with the drifter you delivered the water to and stayed with him in his bed to fornicate with him with your legs spread wide open to snare him, doing God knows whatever else to ensure more silver coins in your skirt. I'm not operating a common whorehouse," he yelled. "This place is a proper establishment for decent folks. Perhaps you should cross the street to a place where your loose ways will bring more to the whores' mistress than you bring me."

Margaret crumpled to the floor, distraught, sobbing copiously. "I don't want that. Not ever in my life, sir," she pleaded. "I am not a whore. I was feeling poorly, too easily swayed by his kind words and gentle behaviour towards me."

He learned forward, his full weight on his elbows, leering at her. "I understand, I do. You're lonely, in a town with no friends. I understand your feelings; I've often felt the very same way myself since the wife's passing." He reached out to her, compassion in his eyes. The grandfather clock in the narrow lobby read 10:30. "Guests seldom arrive before one or two, Margaret, which allows us to speak privately in the office. We're not done here, you and me. We need to talk about what you've done to dishonour yourself as well as your continued employment with me."

Her chortle was guttural, abrupt and raw, thinking she could easily kill Jed Billows for what she was about to do. Albeit never again in her life without mutual gain, she promised.

He was no Jed Billows, if that was ever his real name. He was twice Jed's age, his arms sagged where Jed had firmly defined muscles; his head was practically bald, where Jed had brown hair and lots of it; and his belly protruded well over his belt. Jed's was rippled and lean.

In that instant Jed gave her strength. Without a hint of forewarning she stood briskly by the desk, making herself fully naked within seconds and not the least bit bashful or coy, succeeding at making him all the more eager and ensuring her employment for as long as she needed. Her face was dry, her mind in full control.

"Let's have one thing understood and clear right now. This is your first and last time with me. We have nothing to talk about. This is what I willingly gave to Mr. Billows twice for me being foolishly smitten by his charming ways and convincing words. He paid me three dollars and two-bits, then a dollar more because he was keen to enjoy more of my open legs. I could very well be a whore for as good as I discovered I am. He said as much after first poking me in the tub and before our second and more ardent on his part in the bed. This is what you really want. The question is: How much are you willing to pay in cash, and for me to maintain my employment, in exchange for amusing yourself with me right here and now and not for a long duration? In fact, I would very much prefer that you work hard towards your conclusion as soon as you're fixed inside me. Or do I dress to cross the street and begin this very day taking business from your register? Plenty of men will want me in their beds the moment they become aware of me. Or do we agree, you and me, that five silver dollars is reasonable payment for a young girl who's only been sampled twice, since you're far from the man he was and you are not likely for as long as you may live to have anything near as good as me?"

He was gaping. "You can't be serious. I don't have five dollars to spare."

She thought as much. She reached for her skirt, pausing, not intending for moment to cover herself. "Then you will pay me one dollar more each week for a year." She smirked, bringing a foot to the waist of her skirt. "Very fair to my mind, though I'm not the one to decide. Do we have a deal, or do we not, particularly since you will have something special to remember whenever you see me? Or should I leave here this very moment to find and please much younger men who will gladly pay me what I am worth? I won't stand here any longer without being paid."

She stepped partway into her skirt, ignoring him.

He was visibly taken aback by her candour. His breathing was rapid, Margaret confident at seeing the thing pushing at the inside of his britches that he would agree with her terms. "Alright, we have a deal. A dollar more each week for a year."

"Very well. I'll lean over your desk with my backside towards you, since I have no desire to see you that close to my face, me, or to see you excite whatever it is you have to push into me through your britches." She dropped her skirt to her ankles, leaning forward over the desk, her breasts pressed against the varnished top and unreachable, bracing herself. With her legs spread far apart so that the least of him would touch her, she waited. "Get to it. I won't remain as I am much longer while you gawk at me to excite yourself. That's not what you're paying for. You either can or you cannot. Also, I will require a heated bath to cleanse myself without your company when we are done."

His breathing was loud as he fumbled with the buttons on his grey flannels, tugging at his shirt, struggling with his underpants to free himself from over the waistband to expedite matters.

Margaret shut her mind to how much of her body he was ogling, to his hands groping her buttocks until at last he pushed his way into her. He was urgent and aggressive, pounding her hips into the edge of the desk. She pushed towards him, to save herself from injury and ensure that he would finish with her quickly. With Jed she could scarcely stop herself from screaming, thinking herself on the verge of damaging herself or him, were they to clash together any harder, their bodies as soaked with sweat in the bed as they were with water in the tub.

This was nowhere near the same. If not for the violent pounding and his coarse grunts, she could barely feel him and, when he concluded, as quickly as she had intended, she knew by the touch of his indelicate hands travelling quickly to her shoulders that she should twist away from him.

"We're finished. You had sufficient opportunity to feel my parts." She reached for her clothes, wasting not another second before stepping into her skirt. He looked ridiculous standing there with his flannels stained, his flaccid member choked by the waistband of his underpants and peeking at the ceiling.

"You weren't any help. I can't fathom for a moment that you would make much of a whore. I've taken longer to piss." He stared at her breasts. "Again, with your back on the desk. You owe me that much. I had no little chance to get to your fine tits."

She shrugged into her shirt, crossing one side over the other, tucking the ends into her skirt. "By the sounds you were making I would say I did well enough for you."

"I said again. I'm craving a good sense of how your tits feel."

"Mr. Billows told me they feel exquisite, the best he has ever held in his hands or put to his lips." She paused, reaching for her shoes. "Very well, again, and on my back…one year from this day when you've paid me in full. Then you can sense them for as long as you last. I never said not to touch me there first. You seemed content enough with squeezing and bruising my backside."

She went to the door and walked out. In the kitchen she boiled water for her bath while she wondered where Jed could possibly be, and why he had treated her so cruelly after loving her more passionately than she believed most men loved their wives.

She would never discover the reason. In spite of which, one year later, in a new dress and shoes, with a train ticket and a goodly sum remaining in her new purse, Margaret left Huntsville without leaning again over her manager's desk, her breasts untouched by anyone's hands except Jed's. She wasn't a whore, despite what he was yelling at her from the main doors of the hotel for everyone to hear as she stepped into the coach that would deliver her and her son to the station.

They were going to Charleston where refinement and gentility had survived the war. She had written a letter to a school there, requesting a position, and they replied that, indeed, they were very much in need of a capable person with her knowledge of music.

One day years later her son would learn from his mother all that Mrs. Margaret Wallace remembered or made real in her mind about her first husband, Jed Billows, who was killed in the nation's worst war.

Chapter Four
Marcus Simms & Sheila

New Year's Eve in Manhattan was indeed for everyone. In particular those polished and sophisticated gentlemen whose credit levels were pronounced in titanium, or those of a gentler nature whose youth and superbly good-looks would complement such a man's most exceptional and long-anticipated evening of the year. Marcus Simms possessed one of the requisite attributes, what he needed was the other with every confidence that he would succeed once again.

He never drove in Manhattan, he taxied. Or, on rare occasions, he did the limo thing. This New Year's Eve he walked. He was staying on Madison Avenue in a five-star for the simple reason that, apart from his wealth, people unquestionably perform better, appear more successful, and *are* more successful when they maintain or improve upon their standard of living when gone from home on business. They begin each day feeling good, feeling inspired, feeling better than the guy who paid 89.95 for a dank room and a shag carpet with more DNA pressed into its matted fibres than a shelf in a fertility clinic. Such was his oft repeated axiom at the office and he lived by the rule.

He also maintained with good reason that people perform and achieve in accordance with their respect of self. In a word: How they dress, given that their industry knowledge is unrivalled and their ability to communicate conveys with certainty that they know what the hell they're talking about. Or, as all members of Southeast Consulting understood, not dressing to enhance one's performance, one's pride in oneself and Southeast, meant not coming to work the next day. No gentleman would ever consider barbequing in a three-piece suit, French cuffs and a silk tie, nor would any lady clean her oven in a silk blouse and linen skirt. The message was simple and clear: Dress for success.

Marcus Simms was visible proof. Stepping through the revolving doors onto the wide pedestrian thoroughfare that was a Manhattan sidewalk, he caught everyone's attention. He smacked of subdued elegance, erudition and achievement. His body and his mind felt exactly as he appeared. He was confident and very much in control.

The restaurant was several blocks from the hotel, his corner table reserved for seven-thirty. The evening was mild and clear, his cashmere coat required strictly as a fashion accessory. He strolled, pondering, smiling at the few who smiled at him. Mostly chic young women walking in second place to their boyfriends' iPads, and middle-aged women strolling on the arms of envious older men who were not smiling.

Excluding raspberry blonde, a familiar colour he found distracting, her hair colour was not an issue. Everything else about her was: She would be an inch or two either side of 5'10", slim and shapely, smiling with bright teeth because she was happy and wanted his company, not because she was getting an expensive free meal in a posh restaurant. He wasn't into big-breasted women or those whose asses were intentionally made larger than required for comfortable sitting. Big was not always better. He wanted successful; he wanted poise and self-assurance, which was a given since the restaurant, whose staff were wary of anyone asking prices, catered to a particular thirty-something clientele who understood and embraced the requirement of a strict and fashionable dress code.

Arriving precisely on the half-hour, the lady at the lectern made a check-mark by his name and table and draped his coat over her arm. Another lady, as young and as pretty, also with legs to her neck, also dressed in a short and eye-catching cocktail dress and low-heeled pumps, escorted him to his table for two and noted his drink order. A moment or two later, a waiter dressed in a tux came with his Johnnie Walker Blue, neat. Niceties were exchanged, the snifter was placed in the centre of the simple yet tasteful setting, Marcus suggested he would order in due course, and the man left with a polite nod.

Marcus took a moment, letting his mind drift, letting the dazzling sparks dancing on the sleek crystal contours under the halogen spots mesmerize him. Certain luxuries must never be hurried, never taken for granted. He reached out, cupping the snifter in his warm palm, swirling, breaking the spell. He brought the sharp aroma to his nose, inhaling deeply; liquid gold, never intended for the common or undeserving man's palate, developed and achieved uniquely for the most discerning of gentlemen, such as the one he had become. Then to his lips, burning his tongue, its heat bringing a glow of satisfaction to his face and a warmth to his body.

Such a delicacy was not to be gulped and reordered by the impolite snapping of one's fingers. Nor would he. One was expected to linger, allowing the rich character of the aristocratic spirit to meld with one's own.

The timing was deliberate, the ideal hour for his purpose. Single women, in particular the more desirable women, inevitably dined early, especially that festive evening, preferring corner tables to avoid appearing as desperate and incongruous centrepieces.

He snorted into his glass, congratulating himself. She arrived at 7:45. Or such was his fervent wish.

He put her at five-eight or nine in her patent leather stilettos, three inches less standing or laying naked beside him. Her sequined off-the-shoulder dress was mid-thigh, deep emerald, her glimmering stockings, he visualized, were attached to silk panties or a teddy that would make undressing her later that evening a delightful highpoint of the year. He smiled faintly, at no one in particular and for no apparent reason. She was late twenties, none of the men openly gawking at her seeming to care that she was sauntering into their thirties retreat a few years ahead of schedule.

When she was seated, her vodka, gin or rum served to her on the rocks, he was pleased at seeing her shake her head 'no' to any waiter's initial question. Although no waiter worth his twenty percent would think to humiliate a woman sitting alone by clearing the unneeded half of her table. He waited until her first sip, discreetly raising his glass to signal the waiter. When the man returned with the JW Blue they spoke in furtive whispers, Marcus watching intently as the waiter went to the young woman.

"Madam, the gentleman attired in the black tailored suit and red tie is dining alone this evening. He wishes to enquire whether you would allow him the pleasure of joining you for dinner. His name is Marcus Simms. He has dined with us on previous occasions either in the company of business associates or alone. I believe him to be well-intentioned and of the highest calibre."

She was visibly shocked, if not utterly surprised. She had noticed him first, pretending otherwise when he first saw her. She had nothing to consider, already determined that he would join her were he to approach her. Besides, she had little or no choice in the matter. Not accepting would be discourteous. Making eye contact or sending the waiter to his table with her refusal would make her evening and her meal alone uncomfortable.

So she did. She made eye contact, returning his smile. Any attractive woman living and working in New York could spot a real gentleman in a blink because they were such a rare breed. Most her age were arrogant and self-centred, more interested in getting her naked and laid than maintaining a conversation that wasn't all about them.

This one was the real thing. She figured about a grand for the suit, a hundred for the shirt, another hundred for the tie. He was clean-shaven, not the least full of himself, and not a newbie with an expense account. Simply…she didn't know. She would find out.

"Please tell Mr. Simms his suggestion is very gracious. Yes, he may join me."

Marcus Simms stood as the waiter reached for his Blue, walking together to the young lady's table. When introductions were made, the man left them.

"Please sit, Mr. Simms. Thank you for thinking to join me."

He did. "Thank you, Ms. Banks. However, I would prefer Marcus."

"And I, Sheila."

"Let me say first that I adore your gown. The green is perfection, an impeccable choice to complement your dark brown eyes and lustrous hair. And now that I've gotten that out of the way, Sheila, which has been mesmerizing me for the past several minutes, tell me everything about yourself that is harmless and safe. Or we can talk about travel, our work, the theatre, art."

"Nice suit," she smiled with her eyes in concert with her full, prune-coloured lips. "Please, nothing about work, Marcus. I'm an environmental theorist. Unless, of course, you really want to fall asleep at the table."

No. Not at the table. Later, in your bed. "I'm the CEO of a Brooklyn accounting firm, which compels me to agree with you. No work. Nothing to spoil what has metamorphosed from yet another boring meal into an unexpectedly lovely evening."

They spoke about art and the theatre, worlds that for years he had been relentlessly coerced into discovering. And, more to his liking, fashion and travel which honestly amazed her. She fully agreed with his work ethic and workplace philosophy. Men in the 00s had lapsed into a wretched state of disrepair, becoming too casual. Casual meaning sloppy, sloppy meaning 'get lost'. Modern-day Neanderthals in sweats with caps on backwards. And women were no better. In her office they wore jeans or shapeless slacks with drab cotton tee-shirts, hoodies and runners. Worse yet, six-to-a-box white or beige briefs and bras better suited to post-operative recovery. She didn't.

She wore fitted dresses, skirts and silk blouses. She preferred stockings and garters to pantyhose. And sensible briefs? Not a chance, not even on bad days, which addressed two of his curiosities, and camisoles to her designer bras except on special occasions. At home she wore silk and satin regardless of weather. She did have a thermostat after all.

"I'm mean, really." She sipped her wine, taking a

breath. "Sorry, Marcus. You set me off. It is so absolutely frustrating." He was grinning. "What?"

"I don't wear briefs either. Italian silk, and I don't wear caps. Thought you should know."

"I think I did already. And since we're being unequivocally honest, this is a special occasion. I thought *you* should know." She glanced at her watch as the waiter approached with their desserts and digestives. Coffee was not on the evening's menu. "I would have gone by now, probably in bed reading reports. Thank you, Marcus, for saving me."

"Very much the opposite. I thank you." He saw the wheels grinding. "Now it's my turn. What?"

"I haven't been on a real date in months. Now I'm sitting here with you, each of us dressed to kill, and I want to go dancing." She sliced into her mouth-watering grilled peaches with honey chevre.

"I'm forty-three, Sheila, until midnight anyway, and a bit over the edge for flailing arms and thrusting pelvises. My heart is already beating at full capacity sitting here with you. I believe dancing would kill me, thereby ruining my entire evening."

She giggled. "I know CPR. Besides, you look thirty-something and I'm twenty-eight. I don't flail, or thrust, and I like you. So what is your point?" She gave him a moment, fitting a tiny sliver onto her fork, allowing the indulgence to melt in her mouth. "Please tell me you are not married. That isn't a wedding band adorning your hand. What, something to keep the girls from closing in?"

"I'm not married. I was thinking of you, not to embarrass you. And this trinket, by no means what you suggest, certainly not to precipitate an early end to such a lovely evening."

"I don't embarrass and, since you're not married, and I don't believe you're a sociopath, I wasn't necessarily talking about noisy clubs that will be jammed to the rafters this evening. I do like dancing though, if not by myself, and I do have a fabulous collection of easy listening." She rested her fork on her plate, her hands in her lap. "Life really does suck, Marcus, both of us young and attractive coming here alone on New Year's Eve, in New York of all places. How sad is that?"

"Pretty sad," he agreed, grinning. "Regrettably somewhat of a tradition in recent years."

"And you're celebrating your birthday tomorrow, Marcus. What more reason do you need to dance with me?"

"Am I getting this right? You're inviting me to your home?"

"Yes, since you're not gay and you like me or you wouldn't be sitting here. And I do like you, or you certainly would not be sitting here."

"You won't hold me for ransom? I'm very important, you know." He sipped his Rémy Martin Louis XIII. "I will be free to leave at will."

She put another morsel into her mouth, letting him wait. "Who says you'll want to?"
*

The New Year with Sheila began with the predictable flow of alcohol into the nation's bloodstreams. Police sirens were blaring, spears of electric red and blue lights deflecting wildly from the steel and glass walls of high-rise towers. They had no interest in Time Square or a crystal ball inspiring the usual empty promises for better everything to come, the excitement of booze-facilitated love that would last until otherwise unacquainted lovers would wake groggily from shared stupors to a late morning sun and the accepted reality that nothing whatever would change anytime soon in their predictable lives.

That's not what Sheila wanted. She wanted to dance and that's what they did, intermittently sipping a very palatable Moët until well past midnight when they lounged on her sofa and kissed until he swept her into his arms and carried her gently to her bedroom where he undressed her tenderly and in accordance with her precise and inaudible commands.

She faced away, lacing her fingers, sweeping her hair high to bare her neck, letting him undo her emerald pendant. He cupped the chain in a hand, tugging as slowly as he could at the zipper of her gown, stopping, slipping his hands between the skirt and her hips, kneeling, breathing in her perfume, gliding what little material was left to the floor, thinking he might well go insane. Her ass was firm and smooth, he mused, a sculptor's fantasy, the most exquisite to enchant him in a year.

Standing, his hands reluctantly leaving the silky sensation of her nylons and the warmth of her flesh, he unhooked her bra, a deep green, three-quarter and satin, putting his hands between her warmth and the bandeau strap to push the thing gently away. He cupped her breasts, kissing the nape of her neck and her delicate shoulders, trailing moist kisses down her back as he sank to his knees.

If ever he would die, at least he had passed through the gates of Heaven this once, when suddenly Sheila seductively twirled as though she were a statuette mounted on a plush carousel. Rosemary Sandra had not thought to entice him into their bed or anywhere else with nylons and garters in what, years? The unquestionable loss of an unquestionable bitch. Yet Sheila, an inexplicably exquisite stranger, a divine angel by anyone's high expectations, stood gazing at him, her breasts bare, as though she would never again be with a mortal man.

He ran warm palms between her open thighs towards high-rise silk panties that he, against his better judgement, took too long to slide to her ankles, faced at last with the most inviting and moist aperture he could remember since…he didn't care. Their evening wasn't about his faded memories. She was young, and she was remarkably stunning, the heat of her hands against his face compelling and irresistible. He breathed her in, clutching at the warm mounds of flesh he could not see.

He first unhooked the feathered clip at the front of her left thigh, then, with equal dexterity and determined expertise, the right. He guided her gently, facing her away, paying equal attention to the delicate clips behind her, kissing her soft cheeks and the small of her back. He slid one nylon to her ankles, then the other, sliding each one in turn from perfectly formed feet. She was finally and fully undressed, in no hurry for him to stand, taking his hand when she was ready. Already weakened, helping him to stand, and with a fingertip to his lips, she began her reciprocity.

Marcus Simms was forty-four when he woke in a cold sweat from his vivid New Year's dream. He stood six feet. His hair was black and flowing, his skin always deeply tanned, his teeth bright white and straight, his eyes a deep green and warm that could without warning be cold and piercing. He was slim and toned, not sculpted. Athletic, yet not imposing. Not to himself. He might have been a star athlete, though being a jock was never his thing.

He preferred fine dining and quiet nights, emphatic since graduation from college that he would never threaten his future success with kids. Such was the unfortunate lot of others. Neither did he like crowds, attention or confrontation, maintaining a subdued presence no matter the circumstance. He was suave and sophisticated, well-travelled and erudite. His female employees adored him. Married, attached or single, he was their workweek mission in life, particularly since his increasingly difficult marriage to Rosemary Sandra was beginning to show signs of irreparable fatigue. Which was also the basis for his particular dislike of raspberry blonde heads that would instantly provoke invasive thoughts of yet another impending inquisition.

For that reason and more the men envied him, albeit never in a hurry to challenge his decisions without first thinking things through. For despite his dislike of confrontation, he inevitably enjoyed the last say when his warm eyes turned cold, which was seldom a pleasant transition.

The young woman lying beside him whose name he couldn't recall at the moment, Margaret was as good a name as any, was sleeping, her breasts rising and falling with breaths that were sensual groans more than purring, her face every bit as captivating as eight hours earlier when she brought him into her home, or into his dream. Certainly a good choice. Not that he cared because he never stayed with one longer than he dared. He couldn't, even if he wanted to. He was afraid of interminable questions. Or, better said, he was afraid of potential webs woven with lies. Women, particularly women on the fringes of new relationships, were unrelenting inquisitors constantly marauding into the personal lives, invading the most private thoughts of their newest acquisitions and she showed no promise of being any different.

He lit a cigarette, his last he promised, brightening the

ember with a deep breath as he drew back the covers seeking confirmation, studying her, pleased with every inch of her. Searching for flaws was pointless, remembering his dream as clearly as though he had actually lived as that Confederate traitor who was killed for the want of his Union boots. And her, the remarkable young girl in his tub, Margaret.

He always dreamed of her a week later, or someone like her. Never twice. The dream was not recurring, never repeated, never a haunting reminder of what he had done, the vivid scenes immediately put from his mind, never consciously melding his reality with his delusion. He had drifted into many such dreams over the years, re-enactments of real events with different players and different faces set in different locales and epochs that somehow mitigated the fact that he was, apart from how favourably he regarded himself, a sociopath and serial killer.

Their faces were never familiar to him; like their names, they were fabrications of a wandering mind and never important to him. And that he woke to remember he had been killed for his boots did not matter. His death was a constant, always anticipated and embraced. An eye for an eye: His absolution.

What did matter was the comfort and the joy of closure each one brought to him. The women he could easily lure into his dreams, and others more real like the one laying naked by his side, her a complete stranger, their tender warmth combined that would allow him each time to dream in peaceful slumber. She was requisite to his well-being since, the day before Christmas one week earlier, he willfully and with the utmost conviction successfully killed one Charles Wicker for reasons the State of Tennessee had determined twelve years earlier were insufficient to warrant the death penalty.

Simms believed differently, he supposed, very much like the parents of the young girl Wicker had kidnapped and kept captive to abuse at his leisure for several weeks.

*

Wicker believed he could escape what awaited him as a newly freed ex-con in small-town Tennessee by fleeing into the anonymity of a blind, deaf and mute society too preoccupied with self and selfies to notice anyone else or remotely care. What better place on earth than New York City? That's what he told Marcus Simms moments after he walked into his one-bedroom Brooklyn apartment, not believing for a moment that someone as elegant and out of his element as Simms could or would kill him.

He had lived there for a few months, Simms doing what was required to track and establish a pattern of Wicker's movements. His was a vile creature of habit, most like him were: down and out with no inherent value, not worth saving, not worth keeping alive. Very much the opposite was true. They were prowlers, parasites constantly searching for the easiest and weakest of decent people on whom they could breed and survive. They had no real reason or need to exist. They were losers, unwanted company to anyone save the lowliest whores who would as soon settle for a few swigs from a bottle or a shared joint whenever a sufficiently desperate john would swear to have no cash to offer in return for five quick minutes in an alley or a backseat.

He lived alone in a two-story tenement, he ate cream of wheat for breakfast with bacon bits and maple syrup, and, according to his fridge and garbage pail, he packed never-changing lunches consisting of pastrami sandwiches laced with sauerkraut and mustard on white bread laced with butter. A real epicurean. Shit in shit out, and sure as hell he wasn't washing it down with milk, Simms figuring that even a bottom feeder like Wicker wouldn't waste perfectly good half-bottles of vodka, albeit not premium, with two or three beers each night. Not a chance. The man was drinking on the job.

He worked as a courier, driving a plain white van between eight AM and six PM, wearing a uniform of black jeans, a black tee-shirt and black windbreaker. The kind of guy everyone wants ringing their doorbells.

From what Simms had observed over several weeks, Wicker got home near 7:00 each night to an apartment sparsely furnished and passably clean, although Simms never removed his coat or gloves. The entire building smelled worse than food rotting in a green bin.

As with Wicker's predecessors, Simms had complete surprise on his side, to a man all of them believing themselves paid-in-full for their atrocities. They were also, to a man, suspicious, forever looking over their shoulders, for which reason he never relied on them opening their doors to him because they never expected company. They were not social animals. When a meeting between them was required for the purpose of something insidious, dingy bars or abandoned buildings that were homes to the disenfranchised and homeless were the preferred venues.

Simms glanced at his watch: 6:55 Christmas Eve in Brooklyn. He was already in Wicker's apartment, not a big deal, peering from the frosted window and realizing he was not seeing anything Christmassy. No trees flickering blues or reds or greens from behind other windows, no carols being sung from street corner speakers, no revellers or shoppers rushing home with last-minutes gifts to wrap. All

73

that heralded Christmas was a light snowfall.

He hunched his shoulders, adjusting his coat. Christmas was overrated. The root cause of Christmas-everlasting was women and kids. In his case, not disappointing the woman he suspected of cheating and the kids neither he nor she ever wanted.

He hated Christmas as much as he disliked celebrating his birthday and, recently, shopping to surprise Rosemary Sandra with original gifts and stocking stuffers was a completely unpleasant and disagreeably time-consuming process. Marcus certain he would from then on pass that marital duty onto his secretary with carte blanche since Beverly Benton knew everything there was to know about Rosemary Sandra Simms.

Seven PM, like clockwork, with the bedroom door half-closed to conceal him. Simms reached into his cashmere coat, gripping the gun, thumbing back on the hammer. Seconds later Wicker was inside, lighting the apartment with a bald 100-watt bulb hanging from the centre of the living room, tossing a package-store paper bag onto the couch, shrugging off his windbreaker that he hung on a hook.

"Good evening, Mr. Wicker, and a Merry Christmas to you, sir."

Wicker swung so quickly that he flung his weight against the door, slamming it shut with a bang. Simms already knew what he was facing. Wicker was not a man to get close to. Despite being shorter he matched Simms in weight, far surpassing him in muscle mass. The man was a threat. He was a brawler, a down and dirty streetfighter hardened by twelve years in the prison's gym.

"Who the fuck are you?" He lurched forward, stumbling at seeing the gun. "You ain't a cop. No way. Not in that getup. How'd you get in? And why?"

"Please stay as you are. I won't stay long. I picked your lock, as a successful graduate of a DIY internet course, proving the adage that practice does indeed make us perfect. And I do apologize for my enviable appearance, I came from a business luncheon that required proper attire. Whereas I do normally dress appropriately to fit in. As for the why, I'm here to kill you, Charles Wicker, for what you did to the girl throughout all those many weeks at the farmhouse. Personally, I would have burnt the place to the ground and you with it."

Wicker coughed a laugh. "No you ain't. What I did or didn't do ain't your affair. This ain't even Tennessee. How'd you find me anyway, when there ain't a better place anywhere to get lost and start over than here? You a private cop or somethin', someone pay you for this?" He stood straight, Simms reading his eyes, choosing not to answer. Wicker was talking too much. "Listen, let's not cause each other no grief. I'll even step aside nice and slow and you can fuck off out of here right now. No hassle. That little thing of a gun ain't about to stop me."

"Your starting over is precisely what concerns me. And, yes, this little thing will. Watch this." Simms squeezed the trigger, the dart's one-inch needle piercing Wicker dead centre of his chest, the impact slamming him again into the door. "I see by your expression that you fully appreciate our situation, not unlike those who came before you." Wicker was buckling at the knees, sinking to the floor. "A sedative, 1.5cc's Wicker, more for me than for you, recommended for primates and the like. Like you, albeit not meant to kill. I need you conscious for what comes next." He replaced the gun into his coat, reaching into another pocket. "This however will kill you, and not very nicely. Pentobarbital, Wicker, very effective and usually pain free when used for euthanasia of unwanted animals like you. Or, I suppose, assisted suicide. Which is why, in varying degrees, depending on my frame of mind or the matter at hand, such as a girl kept hidden and abused for several weeks to satiate a deviant compulsion, I add sulphuric acid to eliminate any possibility whatsoever of a decidedly undeserved peaceful crossover to the dark world that awaits you. In other words, Charles Wicker, enjoy your few seconds of pleasant stupor. You are about to suffer immeasurable agony that I cannot adequately put into words. Would that I could show you imagery. I daresay your heart would stop prematurely which, of course, would not do. Despite this not being the highest dosage I have ever administered, my thinking being that you should at least suffer in minutes what the girl did in weeks, you will most assuredly regret not having any quicker method at hand with which to self-administer your demise."

The "Fuck you," was weak and slurred.

"Indeed." Marcus Simms went to kneel by Wicker's side. He raised a limp arm, first removing any possible air from the syringe's barrel that would serve to hasten Wicker's death, proceeding to break the skin with the needle and quickly thumb the plunger to empty the barrel. Timing was important. The full effects of the lethal injection would take roughly four minutes; the effects of the acid were immediate.

They all whimpered at first, crying, twitching, wrongly believing that was the worst, within a minute discovering their false hope as the gagging and coughing and choking quickly stifled their wailing and muted their screams. The absolute terror in their eyes and distorted mouths brought him the most satisfaction. Within two minutes they would tear at their arms and chests and legs with hands smeared with vomit and blood, their eyes bulging, their bodies twisting and jerking, convulsing into the most improbable configurations. And then too quickly they lay dead, as did Wicker. Far too soon, he supposed, in the minds of a devastated girl and anguished parents who would forever continue reliving their worst nightmare.

Simms retrieved the dart from Wicker's chest, stepped over the corpse and left. Wicker wouldn't be thought about or found until his boss would tire of calling, at first to ask what the hell was going on, then to terminate his employment.

Marcus Simms walked several blocks, stopping at a corner to flag a cab, stepping out several minutes later to wait and hail another, stepping from that one several blocks from his Manhattan hotel. He dropped the gun into one storm drain as he ambled along in no particular hurry, disposing of the hypodermic syringe into another several hundred feet farther on.

From the hotel he went by cab to the airport, and from there to his home in Charleston, South Carolina for a late dinner and an argument with his wife of eighteen years. The next morning they would open their gifts with hot toddies and gasps of wonder. They would dress and visit her best friend, Wendy Brighton, bearing gifts. After which all three were expected at the Rothstones for a traditional family dinner.

On the 27th he would return to New York and remain in the city until his much reviled birthday, very much in need of the comfort and joy that was his requisite closure.
*

She was without question several notches above attractive, the Margaret lying beside him, he pondered; mindful that rousing her to false expectations for the sake of ephemeral gratification would be a terrible mistake on his part. How he had savoured undressing her, ever so slowly, meticulously removing each piece until she stood naked and he lifted her as he would a down-filled pillow to lay her upon the bed. Yet allowing her to waken to anything except her empty bed would be difficult to undo in the short-term. She would want him to stay, to see her again. And then what? Disaster, when he had simply come into her home to continue welcoming in the New Year with something new and younger, for high-voltage sex and champagne, to celebrate his birthday with someone who knew nothing about him other than he was unattached, a good dresser and charming, a passable dance partner, successful in business and potentially a good catch. Or soon could be.

He couldn't deny that thoughts of divorce were beginning to tamper with his thinking, as were vivid thoughts of Beverly Benton.

Whatever her name, the one sleeping naked next to him, her wide brunette locks plastered to a pale face as smeared with prune and black as her satin pillow, she was twenty-eight, she lived in Manhattan where he didn't, and she worked as an environmental theorist. Whatever the hell that was, Marcus thankful she had spared him a detailed explanation. Above all she served her purpose and served it extremely well, he granted. She brought him comfort and joy and closure after he returned to the city for long days of soul-searching and entertaining his clients, laying in her bed one week after surprising Wicker with an impromptu visit. And that he was elevated to the city's final and top-rated news story of the year was a bonus.

He believed in his heart that with each one he had done the right thing, his dream absolving him of all guilt, regardless of which he would not cross her path again or remember her.

He would return to his own life sentence in Charleston. He didn't have friends, which he viewed as the sacrificial lambs requisite to his success. He preferred his own company to others constantly needing or wanting something from him, including the woman beside him and her gorgeous clones whose names he'd forgotten, their shapely and lithe bodies primed and ready for the price of a fancy meal, incongruously not comprehending the concept of one-night trysts when that's what they habitually were. He wasn't ready for another Rosemary Sandra in his life; he wasn't ready for any Rosemary Sandra including his original raspberry blonde.

His free time and sole focus were directing his energies into the funnel that was running a corporation, preparing for the year's first round of high-level meetings which he would preside over personally. Yet ever ready when the opportunity would arise, never knowing when to adjust his hectic schedule in order to rid the world of another deserving Charles Wicker, from then until the moment at hand meticulously researching the crime, the punishment and the criminal. Only then creating a plan and time-frame that would end with his comfort and joy of closure. That's what she was, this Margaret, his comfort and joy. His closure.

He didn't keep records, mementos, personal agendas or diaries. He simply acted with as much preliminary work and preparation as his workflow would allow, doing what he felt he must while providing a public service before returning to his favourite city after another round of successful business meetings. Not realizing until a few years earlier that he had evolved into an expert in two professions.

Marcus Simms travelled frequently across the country to personally express his appreciation to new and old clients whose pockets were sufficiently deep to pay for Southeast Consulting to make them appear, in the eyes of public opinion, better than they were. He wined and dined. That's what he did, from the very moment his underlings dropped another signed contract onto his desk.

He lived and led a good life to the exclusion of excessive liquor most weekdays, drugs, and self-importance despite his achievements. He was owner, president and CEO of Southeast Consulting; he was unassuming and quiet, giving thanks each day that he had no children to forever share with the woman he was beginning to suspect was the worst whore he had ever slept with.

He dropped the butt into a half-empty champagne flute, easing from the bed and padding to the bathroom. He reeked of her perfume and her body. He needed a shower, believing he smelled too pungent even for the thirty-minute ride to his hotel in a cab that would likely smell worse. He didn't need snide side-glances from a smartass driver, and certainly not the superior smirk of the female elevator operator who would immediately recognize the familiar fragrance.

Stepping from the bathroom into her bedroom he saw her. She was awake, rubbing her eyes, bringing her knees and satin sheet to her chest. He smiled at her, raising a forefinger, a moment later reappearing with fresh fluted stemware. He came closer, for an instant regretting he had placed the opinions of lesser mortals, who would forget him in a blink, ahead of his own urgent need. He stood before her naked, holding out a brightly coloured mimosa to her, feeling somehow foolishly vulnerable despite their mutual and heated welcoming in of the New Year.

"Good morning. My name is Marcus Simms," he reminded her, his smooth Southern accent diluted from the sleepy drawl of his fellow Carolinians by years of travel. "You invited me into your home last night. I hope you remember that, darling."

"God, I absolutely reek." She sipped the effervescent eye-opener, moaning. "Delicious. Thank you."

"For medicinal purposes, though I didn't feel comfortable snooping. However perhaps now you will allow me to prepare a breakfast? I'm rather good in the kitchen, not so good with dishes."

"Yes." She sat, tousling her matted hair. "Is that your real name, Marcus? Marcus from Brooklyn? And, please, do not call me darling. We are way too new for that sloppy lovey stuff." She giggled. "At least not until tomorrow morning."

Precisely. "Yes, I am Marcus, and I am from Brooklyn. That said, you don't reek. You smell wonderful, enticing. But I did. I hope you don't mind me taking a shower." He reached for his Italian straightbacks, drawing an invisible circle around his face. "I love your scent. Really, I do. The make-up thing, that's another matter. It's a little scary, what with the hair and all." She grimaced at that, he chuckled. "Kidding. I'm kidding. But, listen, you take a shower and I'll lose myself in your pantry. Deal," he wasn't at all sure, "Sheila?"

She nodded, swinging her legs over the edge on her side, smiling because he was smiling. He liked what he was seeing, and she liked that. "We will have a tomorrow morning, won't we?" She yawned. "God, I'm so tired."

His long gaze spoke more than words. "I certainly hope

we do, and more."

"Good answer. Then I'll do breakfast both days, after I pee and take a shower. Sorry, I don't have anything for you to wear."

"Not a problem, I'll dress."

"Now, you see, that is a problem. I want a repeat. I really need to know I wasn't dreaming, though by what little missy down here is telling me, very puffy and pink, I probably wasn't. Wow."

"Make that a double wow, and I would suggest avoiding really hot water. Little missy there might wince a little."

"Not an issue. You can dress before you buy me lunch. I don't do lunches. Agreed?"

Marcus from Brooklyn nodded, frankly bewildered as to why such a ravishing girl had no one to eat breakfast with each and every day, content at the moment that he had somehow recalled her name. "Agreed. After we drop by my place for a fresh change."

She went to him, wrapping her arms tightly around his neck, kissing him, slightly swaying and peering into his eyes. She hadn't stopped smiling. She was happy, her face flushed. She felt blissful. He didn't.

When she disappeared into the bathroom, he dressed quickly. He had come to her home as he was, with nothing to burden or delay his escape. When he heard the toilet flushing, then the shower hissing hot water she seemed to delight in, he chanced a final and lingering glimpse of Sheila Banks bending and stretching and paying particular attention to her little missy.

She was Margaret in every way. Or he had made her so in his dream, except for her hair that was as long and lustrous and brunette, and her eyes that were liquid brown and not green. Her body was no less exquisite. She was flawless, without a mark on her, and far from unique. They all were, and he would meet others equally as lovely; he would need others equally as flawless to aid and abet in his closures. And he would leave them, as he was meant to and wont to.

Without question they would at first loathe him for his masterful lies and manipulations, until reliving him in their eternal dreams of him with the fondest affection for what he brought to their empty lives for too fleeting a moment, unaware that he did truly and deeply love them for as long as he needed them, for what they had brought to him and the reasons why.

Men of his calibre attracted such women wherever and whenever with little or no effort. When she pirouetted, humming, her face cleansed of garish colours and incredibly pretty, her sweet lips pouting into a luscious kiss, Brooklyn's Marcus Simms hurried in a heartbeat to break her fall.

She was fragrant and smooth, her body beaded with water and oil. He kissed her, laying her gently onto her sofa that wasn't stained with the damp imprints of their passionate love. He knelt by her side, kissing her face, her lips and her breasts. He stood for a long moment absorbing her beauty, fascinated by her shallow breathing and serenity.

Finishing his mimosa, leaving her home as orderly as possible, he strolled several blocks before hailing a cab that would take him first to the hotel, then to the airport and a first-class seat that would carry him to a house, two cars, a wife and a mortgage in Charleston, South Carolina.

Chapter Five
Jed, Rosemary's Fib & Mr. Wainscot

May 31, 1934 was a miserable day, the worst in three years that he could remember. The heat was oppressive, the wind searing. All Jed Billows wanted was a bath, at the very least a handful of water that wasn't fetid to splash onto his face and cracked lips. The one good thing about the wind was that with each stale gust his own insufferable stink was swept far away.

He had been walking the roads for days, heading for California like the many others devastated by the drought that was the severest yet known with no indication that nature would resolve to show its kindness anytime soon. Two years he had gone without steady work, standing in food lines the days his stomach suffered the same unenviable condition as his pockets, which occurred often, when he would sleep in parks or whatever unlocked and darkened doorway seemed inviting.

His life was in ruins, he was convinced, his previously bright future decidedly bleak at best. His life was supposed to have been wonderful. Two years earlier he was well established as a capable bookkeeper with his completed high-school education assuring him of unlimited success in his career; as well, he was affianced to a strikingly fetching girl who loved him dearly, with no greater expectation for herself in life than to please him as a cherished wife and to bear him good-looking sons and daughters. Until his superior called him in one day, until day by day thereafter he became increasingly familiar with the unpleasantness of privation and hunger, of sharing his room at the boarding house with men previously unknown to him, men he had no good reason to trust. All this while stubbornly pretending his situation and future were not irreversibly grim so that he might afford the rent from what little remained in his account. Until late one day not very long after the commencement of his misery his beloved Rosemary thought to shatter his heart when he chanced to witness her cruel and blatant debauchery where she oughtn't to have been.

He had spent the long day interviewing for work without success, deciding in desperation to explore the possibility of a more modest and affordable accommodation which, at the very least, would allow him to sleep alone in his room until such time as his prospects improved sufficiently to support a wife and family. His hopes were at the highest point, elated to hear of the vacancy from the lady of the house and of the monthly rate she was proposing. He would not be late, he promised her. Nor was he.

He arrived at the boarding house promptly at five o'clock, weary from a day of disappointments, yet eager to inspect his new room and later to tell Rosemary that he could now invite her to a nice lunch given the recently improved state of his finances.

Then came the cruellest of blows as he stood frozen, his heart impaled, no longer counting down the addresses from door to door. He recognized her dress and her umbrella instantly, in spite of the raspberry blonde curls hanging from under her most favourite bonnet to conceal her face. She was wearing her best Sunday clothes and standing on the stoop of the very house whose address he had circled in red on his folded newspaper. She was locked in a mutual and tight embrace, her mouth crushing hungrily against a stranger's whose hand was wickedly concealed between them at the height of her breasts, who by his fancy style of dress was not from Oklahoma City.

"Rosemary!" he blurted, mortified.

Rosemary jerked backward from the shock of hearing his voice, her crystal blue eyes so wide-open that for an instant he believed he could read the workings of her mind. Yet within a second at most, that for Jed seemed an eternity, she was composed and stood facing him completely unperturbed. "Good evening, Jeddore. The gentleman with me is Mr. Wainscot. He is a dear and close friend," she said coolly.

Jed thrust a rigid finger at the ground. "Rosemary, come here to me this very instant. Stand away from him."

Instead she took the man's hand. "I cannot, I'm afraid. We were this very moment stepping out. Mr. Wainscot has invited me to dinner, Jeddore. Please don't be upset with me."

"What are you saying, Rosemary?" His mouth was dry. "A dear friend? For how long a dear friend, and by dear you mean to imply to what degree exactly?" He twisted from his hips, searching this way and that along the empty street for no apparent reason. "How is it that you come to be here, so far from your room, with him, and so shamelessly entwined? Never in my entire life have I thought to imagine you behaving so brazenly."

The stranger was fully ten years Jed's senior. He stood quietly poised, relaxed and in control, not the least bit intimidated.

That he would dare to impugn her character made her angry. "I might ask you that very question, Jeddore Billows," she scolded, leaning forward from her cinched waist, jabbing the air between them with her umbrella. "How is it that you come to be...?" She stopped herself, noticing the paper, pressing a palm to her cheek. "You're the one who's pledged to rent her room. You're the landlady's new tenant."

"For how long, Rosemary? Tell me. I demand to know the truth. And to what indecent extent has this lout coerced you?"

"Do not be rude to Mr. Wainscot, Jeddore. He has always conducted himself towards me in the most gentlemanly manner."

"For how long, exactly, Rosemary, has this Mr. Wainscot conducted himself in a gentlemanly fashion towards my fiancée...exactly? I insist that you tell me the entire truth at once."

"For a good while now, I'm afraid," she answered, her voice softening. "Quite some weeks."

"For a good while? Is that so? Quite some weeks, by which you mean to imply well before the termination of my employment."

She nodded. "Mr. Wainscot comes to the city often from Louisiana, when we meet here discreetly to delight in each other's company for as long as we are able. Oh, dearest Jeddore, we did meet very much by the happiest of accidents, I assure you. I meant you no intentional harm, Jeddore. You must believe me."

"In the most loathsome secrecy, while betrothed to me!" he accused. "What must I think? What must I feel?"

"I *was* so very content with your company and your

affections towards me, Jeddore. Truly I was. Nevertheless, and in all honesty, you are an unemployed clerk with no immediate prospects, which does leave me very little reason to suppose your present condition will soon improve when everyone else is fleeing to the coast to better themselves. Look around you. The sidewalks are empty. The times are difficult. We are in the deepest depression, our countryside covered with black and grey filth from these hideous storms. Can you for a moment blame me for wanting to improve my station with such a good and kind man as Mr. Wainscot? Can you, Jeddore?" Jed Billows stood mute. "No, you cannot. How can you possibly expect that any reasonable woman would want you as you are? How could you in good conscience possibly think to properly afford a good wife?" She waited. "We soon would have become completely unhappy together, Jeddore. Unkind to each other. This is for the best. This way we shall remember each other as the dearest of friends."

"You misled me, Rosemary, with your smiles and your sweet words. Tell me, what words do you say to him, this Mr. Wainscot, when you're in his room for the night?"

"I did not mislead you, and you have Mr. Wainscot to thank. I was uncertain whether I should tell you at all, until this very afternoon when we discussed what I should do about you. I truly hated the prospect of injuring your feelings. However I do believe in my heart I would have confessed to you very soon, Jeddore, even without Mr. Wainscot's impressions. I would not simply run off with him without telling you. I couldn't possibly."

"Confessed to what? Run off to where, and to what extent has this fellow beguiled you with his sophisticated ways?" He smacked an open palm with the folded paper. "Leave his side this very instant, Rosemary, while I am still able to forgive your disgraceful flirtation. While you are still able to forgive yourself for wounding me so terribly."

"Jeddore, I cannot. However much I care for you, my feelings toward Mr. Wainscot are beyond my control," she declared. "I must also be considerate of myself and of my future family. Mr. Wainscot has come to know me very well, to a far greater extent than you and I were ever able as the dearest and closest of friends, and I will return here with him by my own choice to end our evening together. Do you understand, Jeddore? Please tell me that you do. I could not bear to know that you hate me."

"Friends, Rosemary? Is that what I am? Is that my reward for resisting my every urge to touch you? At least I would have had the right, which is more than this vile fellow can claim. I saw how boldly he touched you."

"An expression of his ardent feelings toward me, and mine for him, with my fullest and willing consent." She led Wainscot to the street, standing eye to eye with Jed, unwavering. "We are, the two of us, very near to agreeing on terms for a wonderful life together, Jeddore, in New Orleans. I shall be leaving with him very soon." She raised a hand to touch his cheek, causing him to flinch and retreat several steps. "He has the deepest affection for me, Jeddore. Please be as happy as you can for me."

He felt his entire body imploding. "You did mislead me, you did, in the most horrible and unforgiveable way." He assessed Wainscot more closely from where he stood, sneering. "I can't help wondering what your dead mother and mine would think of your unseemly antics; and I can certainly imagine that our fathers are very likely pleased that they lay dead and buried beside their loving and devoted wives. Without question they would stand here as fiercely angry with you, as ashamed of what you have become as I am. You are the worst harlot, Rosemary."

She put out a hand to halt Wainscot. "Please understand, Jeddore. This is hardly the place for civilized gentlemen to be unkind to one another."

At a much later date he would easily have beaten Wainscot to within an inch of his life. As it was, Wainscot was taller, more solidly built and, no doubt, more endowed with physical prowess. Conversely, and much to his shame, life had not yet instilled in Jed Billows a sense of pride or any discernible strength of character beyond his expressions of indignation which many older and wiser men would consider a weakness. All that he possessed had come to him too easily. He was, in point of fact, innocent in mind and body, if not entirely blind. Which can hardly explain or defend why he stood there visibly defeated with slumped shoulders. Before their very eyes he transformed inexcusably into a pitiable spectacle teetering on nervous legs at the very precipice that was his future, dropping his weight forlornly onto his knees, distraught and muttering as Wainscot, unable to tolerate anymore, gave his arm to Rosemary and led her in the direction of their meal.

Jed Billows saw her twice more within a matter of days. On the second occasion she was leaving for the train station, wearing on her finger vivid proof of Wainscot's promise of much brighter circumstances, without the slightest suggestion that she would return Jed's. Nor did he have the good sense to insist that she treat him fairly, as she would a dear friend.

He remembered the day, the hour, the very instant he believed himself wanting to strike the harlot for her blatant treachery. However, she wasn't wrong in her estimation of him. He was a clerk, unassuming and between positions, meek and unaccustomed to altercations, brawling or unseemly outbursts. He had already humiliated himself sufficiently in public for one lifetime.

That was two years earlier, Rosemary coming to him each evening as he ate whatever meagre sustenance he could beg from a kindly farmer's wife or steal from an unlit porch, and every night when he would invite her into his dreams. In fact he refused to let her go. How else could he loathe her more each day? Imagine, he mused, if she could see him now alongside the dandy she had chosen to carry her through life. He was no longer that clever bookkeeper whose good manners and promising future had caught her eye. Or so she had previously led him to believe.

The parts of him that people would see were dark brown, burnt by the sun. His dark brown hair hung to his shoulders for he had no money to pay a barber, and his person, which he had supposed in his past required a tailored suit to enhance his appearance, was chiselled and hard.

He might now have been married a year or more, content in his mended heart that he was not. If she was being a whore for Wainscot for however long behind his back, what might she have done to deceive and betray him in marriage? Whose child might now undeservedly carry his name without his knowledge?

Instead he was day after day down on his luck and in no way irresistible to the lowest breed of women, for which reason, each evening and every night, he wished upon Rosemary the worst possible outcome in hers.

He spent his days from dawn till dusk walking along westward roads, wandering aimlessly towards yet another farmer's wasted fields where the only work left to any willing man was digging out from incalculable tons of black blizzard dirt and sand that was six feet deep and more.

Chapter Six
Jed, Charlotte & Sam McKinnie

That Rosemary was a loose and wicked woman for however long a duration, which caused him to believe the worst, and for her personal convenience, was now a matter of little importance to him. He would allow her the benefit of his doubt that she was at the very least Wainscot's private strumpet. Unless, of course, which was entirely plausible, the old man had tired of her. Or, as was more likely the case and his most heartfelt desire, Wainscot had discovered her lewd duplicity while standing on another sidewalk, straightaway discarding her so that she might make the best use of her youthful charms as an honest and forthright whore in a house better suited to her purpose than his. We are, after all, what we are. As was Jed Billows.

He had no recollection of when he last bathed, or shaved, or gazed into a mirror to see how greatly he had metamorphosed into a determined man no longer suited to keeping ledgers and balancing monthly accounts. Why he ever thought himself privileged to labour in a windowless corner six days each week for others who dwelled in grand and spacious homes while he slept on a furnished bed in a room that was not his, was a question he discarded with Rosemary.

What he might do had not yet become a burdensome

question. That he woke each morning to a day that was unremarkably the same as the day before was burden enough. Two years and he had achieved no greater distance than midway through Texas. He was nowhere near the West Coast, nowhere near the end of any road worth travelling. He made his days tolerable by creating fanciful imagery in his mind during his most capricious and lonesome moments, daring without consequence to imagine a few dollars to spare in his pockets, or that he had altered the direction of his travels and found her in a New Orleans brothel as an affordable diversion to the average man. By which he meant the man he had become, impoverished through no fault of his own, a man who in better days would not have considered for the briefest moment stealing a meat pie to survive another day without the slightest concern that he was, by his selfish act, depriving others no less needy of a meal.

No one believed the drought would soon end. He certainly did not. Nor did those fleeing to whichever coast was closest to their ruined fields and ravaged homes, simply to discover the devastation of one interminable plague had gone with them into another that would persist with equal ferocity in defeating them. The entire country was trapped in the throes of financial collapse.

At some point he stopped counting the empty homes he passed, or going into them for that matter. Nothing was left for the taking, nothing a man on foot could easily carry. Whatever the owners had not taken, those before him did. Where he did stop he begged for a cup of water to drink before asking for whatever honest work they could give him in return for a sandwich or a slice of pie.

They never kept him on longer than a day or two; the era was too desperate for acts of kindness to exceed the most basic decency.

Near noon the air was even more heated, making Jed wonder whether he was walking too quickly into June since he was no longer very much acquainted with which day he was living in any particular month. He stopped by the side of a road to rest his feet, instantly regretting that he did, dust and grime sticking to the sweat on his face and clogging his beard like a thin irritating paste.

Birds in flight were a rarity in times of drought, yet those he saw circling high in the air not a mile from where he sat were cawing loudly, Jed praying that he would finally discover water and not another carcass picked clean to the bone. He was gritty and soiled far worse than his usual state, the powerful stink emanating from his soiled britches and stained shirt quickly enveloping him like a toxic cloud, making him nauseous and forcing him onto his aching feet.

He stood watching them for a while, in part containing his exuberance for fear of being needlessly disappointed, at last urging himself toward the rise in the road. He reached the low summit an hour later, the highest point that he could see on yet another nameless and winding path stretching into a colourless infinity. He was alone in the world. Shielding his eyes he saw not a single body, nor any reason to expect that he would fill his stomach that evening with anything more than the sandwich decaying in his pocket, the sound of the birds and the wind suddenly very annoying.

Leaving the road he ambled in no particular direction past emaciated thickets and shrubs and low trees whose branches were devoid of leaves, watching the birds, believing he could smell water, telling himself that, fresh or foul, clear or thick, he was going in fully dressed. Instead he stopped dead, squatting close to the ground where he could not be seen.

Wandering men had senses most other men had no need to develop. They could sense the slightest danger in the least likely places or for the most unlikely reasons. He was in danger, despite his disadvantaged circumstance. The man ahead of him, upwind of him, was crouched facing into a row of shrubs, peering at something or someone with no good purpose in mind, leaving Jed with little choice but to close the distance between them.

From what he could assess of the man Jed was superior in his build if not his height, which increased his chances, Jed supposing the fellow had arrived there from an opposite and southerly direction. For who, in his right frame of mind, would willfully walk into the nation's Dust Bowl? Better to face a foe head-on than to expose your back.

"Good day to you, stranger," he whispered, crouching.

The man twisted violently and fell backward, sprawling. "Who the fuck are ya?" he grunted in a harsh whisper. "And what do ya mean sneakin' up on a man from nowheres? Ya scared the shit from me."

Jed gave him somewhere near fifty. He was dressed in the ragged and unclean fashion of the day and, from what Jed could discern, he had been intimately familiar with the difficulties of an unenviable common life most of his years. He was not a victim of the drought, depression, or hard labour. He was a drifter and a ne'er-do-well. Any man's body would take years to degrade into such a poor state. His yellow-white hair, the little he had, sprouted from his head in thin patches; his one eye was coated with a layer of some grey mucous; his other, whether he had it or not, lay behind a loose-fitting flap tied to his head with twine.

His complexion was ruddy, not burnt from the sun,

covered with sores he apparently picked at regularly with the yellowed and fungus-packed nails he had not chewed on in weeks. His teeth, the ones he had, were chipped and of a colour one could only achieve with rot and, even if he had shit himself, he wouldn't smell any worse than he did.

"I don't see that names matter," he answered, thankful the man was wearing shoes. "I'm a stranger who means you no harm. I left the road hoping to find water," he pointed at the birds, "and you?"

The man scrambled onto his hands and knees, raising a finger to his cracked lips. "The same, never expectin' to find her here." He pointed to the separation he'd formed in the shrubs. "There's water alright. Plenty of it, and as fine a specimen as I ever did see all by herself makin' good use of it. A real beauty, that's fer damn sure, and buck ass naked to boot. Go ahead, take yerself a good peek. Just don't go spoilin' a good afternoon of humpin' for us. Or the evenin' fer that matter. Where's she got to go? And fair's fair by my way of thinkin', ya hear? I'll toss ya what's left when I'm done with her, cause I got here first afore ya." He spit into his palm, holding out the bony and gnarled hand to Jed who chose instead to nod his agreement.

Jed Billows peered into the shrub expecting to see an undressed woman of passable good-looks knee-deep in water washing her clothes. What he saw to this greatest surprise was an oasis of soft green grass bordering a pond of clear and sparkling water, its surface barely touched by the wind, and the head of a woman seeming to float in the centre of concentric circles spreading out from her swaying arms that he could tell were smooth, lightly tanned, and leaving him no choice whatsoever.

The man on his knees beside him was snickering. "Not a day over twenty, that's my guess. Ain't never poked nothin' that skinny and sweet, not a single time. Me bein' here is God's work. That's fer damn sure. Been watchin' her an hour or more, strippin' from her clothes nice'n slow afore swimmin' and splashin' and makin' herself clean as a whistle. The blackest hair ya ever did see, as black at her privates as at the top and not a smidgen bigger than the patch ya see over my lost eye. Sweet as candy, she'll be." He crawled closer. His breath smelled of rot and liquor. "And I means to take my sweet time with her."

"She's alone? Are you certain?"

"She's alone. That's a fact, fer as long as she takes to show me her feet. Never been much good in the water." His groan was sickening, not that Jed could take his eyes from her, silently beckoning her into shallower water so that he would then see all of her. "Yessiree, I expect ya gonna be waitin' a good while fer what's left of that sweet treat. Gonna have me a good time."

"If she doesn't die first from fright."

"Don't much care, less'n she does and cools a mite too quick. Expect she'll kick a bit though, do some squirmin'."

"She'll scream. Someone might hear her from the road and come running to see whatever's amiss."

"A punch to her pretty face'll stop that right quick. Expect she'll whimper a mite, and what's left for ya to pick at after ain't fer me to be care'n about."

He had to admit, the water was much more inviting with her in it. He had never been with a woman, never saw one fully naked, and the ones in the parks and hallways at night with their skirts pulled up for a few coins or in payment for a plate of baked beans and stale bread would never be as costly in any daylight. In his other life he had always behaved in a proper and courteous manner towards Rosemary; and, thus far throughout his renaissance, which was not entirely to his liking, the women he had encountered were either too attractive and superior in their comportment to consider relieving a dishevelled beggar or too expensive for the beleaguered condition of his pockets.

He was picturing how frightened the girl would be, whether she was familiar or not with men, already hearing her screams resounding in his mind. He was resolved. That he would stand by and willingly witness any young girl rudely taken by such a revolting troll of a man was beyond the range of his imagination.

"Friend, take another look at her. I see what you mean. She *is* truly wonderful." He blew a long breath through pursed lips. "She's incredible. She's wading to the shore for you to poke her good and hard. I believe she must have heard you. She does seem very excited."

The man pushed Jed aside, burying his head into the shrub then scrambling backward, cursing. The girl hadn't moved.

"Fer that cheap trick I'll keep her to poke all the night by myself, boy. And if I was you I'd be on the road right quick, cause I'm thinkin' if she's no good or gets worn too quick I'll be afflicted with a yearnin' ya can likely cure as good as her."

Jed chortled at the thought. "Then I should at least know your name. Don't you think?"

"Sam McKinnie, fer what it matters to ya. Now piss off."

"The recently deceased Sam McKinnie is what you mean."

The heavy rock smashed into the side of McKinnie's head, throwing him sideways to the ground. A second blow destroyed his skull with a loud thwack, the third made certain he would never harm any girl.

99

Jed Billows collapsed onto the ground to calm his breathing. He had killed a man, or the wasted likeness of one, the very proof lying somewhat damaged at his feet. He wasn't certain how he felt, good or elated for what he had done. Confident he didn't feel ruthless or wicked or guilty of a man's murder. He could scarcely be accused of killing another human being.

He raised himself onto his knees, crawling to the portal in the shrub, fascinated. She was washing her hair, a cloud of white foam erupting from her head. He couldn't exactly stay as he was with a corpse that would never smell worse that it did, especially since the girl had a bar of soap. Besides, had he arrived first, she would have most certainly and innocently intruded upon his solitude.

After a moment's reflection, he proposed a solution with which his good conscience readily concurred. He would simply approach her and call out to warn her, to offer her two choices: If she declared herself alarmed at the thought of seeing a naked man, she could merely face away. Or, were she to declare herself fearful of him seeing her naked, he would likewise be courteous towards her.

She wasn't 100 feet from him when he stood to strain his ears for the slightest sound, a whisper, a voice defiant or threatening. How could such a comely girl possibly be alone in the middle of nowhere? He heard nothing at all, even the birds had ceased their cawing. No doubt anxious to feed on the newly delivered carrion.

He stepped into the open, tugging at his shirt, padding as he did to within a few feet of the water's edge where he dropped his weight lightly onto the grass by her carpet bag, her dress and her underthings all neatly placed like a drab canvas to dry. He was alone in a private world with her, where he pulled off his shoes and tugged away his britches while wondering what he should say first to her.

She disappeared for long seconds, a thick carpet of white spreading over her. Surfacing several feet farther from shore to press her long black hair into a headdress, she shrieked her terror when she twirled and saw him. She must be the most beautiful girl he had ever seen, he was certain, fully cognizant that her current state of undress and his forthcoming proposal made him somewhat biased.

Then: "The best I can determine, miss," he shouted, "is that your choices are twofold. You can sit here with me to warm and dry yourself with the sun. Or you can stand where you are until your legs give out, in which case I, being a gentleman, would feel obliged to rescue you since I can see by the poor condition of your shoes that you have walked as far as me, if not farther. Truly, I have very little desire to stand or walk farther than need be to save you or to borrow your bar of soap. Either way, I stink to high heaven and firmly intend to correct the matter before I wash my torn clothes, rest awhile, and be on my way. I expect I shouldn't be more than four, possibly five hours at worst."

She was horrified, yelling at him to face the other way. Instead he stood without the slightest shame, standing there naked with a smirk on his face and his arms akimbo for a short while before reaching to the grass to gather his clothes in a bundle and tossing the heap into the water. That Rosemary had never seen his former or remade person as complete was her great loss.

He waded directly toward her, dunking first to wash his face and beard as best he could before halting an arm's length from her, the swirling water reaching his chest. She had nowhere to run. Besides, what made her predicament any worse than his?

101

"My name is Jed Billows, a gentleman walking the byroads searching for honest work while maintaining the highest expectation that I will, and one day soon, begin to live the life I earlier envisioned. What's yours?"

She waded backward, her arms firmly crossed over her chest. She was terrified, beginning to cry.

"As delightful a surprise as you are to my eyes, miss, and you are very much that, you have no reason to fear me or to cry. Believe me, you are much safer with me than five minutes ago. However our current situation does appear to have presented us with the dilemma or the pleasure of properly acquainting ourselves with one another." He waited. "Miss, a man as tired and as dirty as me is not necessarily a bad one. As I have mentioned, as soon as I'm cleaned and fed by the meagre sandwich I have, which by some miracle I have managed not to eat until now, I will be on my way." He grinned. "If you can wait that long with your skin all pimply and your teeth chattering. And, if you're of a mind to join me, I will gladly barter half my sandwich for a minute or two here with your soap. I didn't see any lunchbox by your clothes and we're a good distance from the nearest farmhouse. I promise the transition will surprise you."

She gulped, cupping a handful of water to her lips. She needed moisture in her mouth and her throat. "You have food?"

"I do, enough for a bite or two if your teeth are strong and sharp. It's been with me awhile."

"My name is Charlotte Higgins."

He held out a hand. "I'm pleased to make your acquaintance, Miss Higgins." She remained as she was, staring. "If you won't take my hand as a welcoming gesture, won't you please pass me your soap as an indication of your good intentions to share my evening meal," he chuckled, "and not consider harming me in my vulnerable state?"

That she was afraid didn't matter. She was the vulnerable one, naked and helpless, though her tears were drying. What would be would be, she told herself. She was no match for him. He was taller and bigger by fifty pounds or more. He was fit and lean from hard labour, his arms and face darkened by the summer sun and the harshness of winter winds, his fists scarred from conflict or survival. Which one, didn't matter. He would do whatever he wished to her. And she would submit to him, to save herself. Whenever he was finished bathing she would go with him to the shore, what choice did she have? And then he would be gone like the others to take whatever he pleased from another helpless girl. Then again, the soap smelled of pine and her belly had not been full for a week. She passed him the soap, thinking that, at best, whenever he would decide to hurt her, he would be clean.

Jed wanted very much to see all of her, expecting or hoping that she would wade to the shore while he bathed, since the water was refreshingly cool and her shivering was intensifying into spasms. She didn't. Instead she remained as she was and watched as he proceeded to bathe; Jed somewhat surprised, choosing not to turn his back. Nor did he feel any further obligation to explain his motives or give her the privacy she was for some reason denying him.

If she was adamant in her thinking to remain as she was, he most certainly had the right to bathe as he wished, for which reason he dunked himself within a few feet of her to briskly rinse his hair and his beard.

She was enticingly shapely, despite her young age that he supposed must be nineteen or twenty, her body many shades lighter than her face and her arms. When he surfaced, he wore the widest and silliest grin, taking a moment to ponder the extent of his rinsing before disappearing again to ensure that his hair was thoroughly clean, since he had no idea how many days or weeks would pass before his next bath.

When he surfaced again he returned her soap, grateful, Charlotte ignoring his thank-you. She wanted to smack the silly grin from his face for how he was thoughtlessly humiliating her, and she would have with all her strength in the days prior to the downturn in her circumstances. She knew very well what he was doing under the water.

For his part, Jed saw nothing of what she was thinking betrayed in her eyes. He spun around and strode away from her, paddling with his arms. She would follow, or she would not. He waded to shore, kneeling by his clothes, swirling them in the shallower water and silt to dislodge what he could before stepping onto the grass to lay them out by hers and sit cross-legged to watch her until he would inevitably be called upon as a gentleman to rush in to save her and the soap.

"Fair is fair, Miss Higgins, now that you've seen the best of me, or the worst if you regard yourself as a more discerning woman. Please do not worry on my account. I've seen enough of your fair breed to understand what I like and what I do not. You'll be very safe here with me...and your clothes will not dry before you drown."

Charlotte Higgins inhaled a deep breath. She didn't believe him. She had no reason. She was accustomed to men and their ways. He would not be her first, nor her last; she had submitted to unkind men the few the times her empty belly perforce led her astray. She waded confidently from the water, her body petite and perfect and glimmering under the sun; her mass of obsidian hair glistening, clinging to her shoulders and her breasts, lending the effect of fired coals struggling not to fade. The other, sparkling with droplets of water, with which he was most concerned or preoccupied, of which she was fully aware, provided her no more modesty than a dead man's patch.

She walked to the far side of him, in her mind completely alone, to her clothes where she sat with her damp dress draped over her raised knees, to wait.

Jed brought his knees to his chest. Reaching to the side of his soaked britches he took his sandwich and tore the stale bread and slice of pork into uneven halves, offering Charlotte the larger piece. Then he began the story of his travels, and when he was finished Charlotte began hers.

She was closer to twenty than nineteen. She was an orphan, her mother long ago deceased. Her father, not much of a man, had also passed on, abandoning her in the most despicable fashion without saying goodbye when times had become too difficult to manage without work. He'd made himself sufficiently brave with liquor one evening a year earlier, pulling the trigger that woke Charlotte with a start.

He had nothing to leave her save the scars of horrible memories. Then came news that the shop where she worked could no longer afford the luxury of a talented seamstress. She was, after all, a junior. Though she was gifted with needle and thread, which gave them the highest hopes that she would do well for herself very soon.

That didn't happen. No one in the cities was hiring, all of them telling her to head west. And she did, spending the past year visiting farms to mend and transform clothes and blankets for the few coins anyone could afford, or a meal, or a night in their barns when, on occasion, the man of the household would visit with her. The worst were the few times her needles and threads were inadequate to sustain her when, desperate for food so that she would, if nothing else, have the strength to reach another farm, cold-hearted strangers on the road would take her in trade where they stood for a drink from their canteens and a mouthful of beans or nuts or dried meat.

She had survived one year, and she would survive another, and another after that. She would do whatever she must, for she was certain she deserved better in life, a shop of her own and a good husband who would forgive her weaknesses.

Young Billows hung on her every word, as she had listened intently to his sad tale. Until what she said out of the blue truly shocked him.

"Thank you for sharing your sandwich, and for taking the smallest portion for yourself. And now that we've eaten I would as soon get the matter of payment over and done with. What will you do with me? Should I lie flat on the ground or do you want me on my knees?" she asked matter-of-factly. "You can't think that washing yourself with my soap is a fair price. Can you?" He didn't answer, Charlotte taking for granted that his smile was selfish and mean. "Very well, I won't put up a fight, not unless you're cruel to me. I've had worse than you, much older and on my knees if you must know. On my knees by choice, not to remember their faces and to hasten their conclusion. To which I have nothing to add. Do whatever you want to me?" she practically snarled. "At least since your bath you're not the least handsome."

She was done speaking. She had nothing else to say. She was naked, young and appealing, slender and well-proportioned, her skin smooth and clear, her sad eyes searching his. Her shoulders slumping into her knees, waiting to hear what she should do next.

He sat pensively for a moment, coughing a laugh for the first time he could remember.

"In the first place, Charlotte, you haven't yet called me by my name. Secondly, I'm twenty-five, nowhere near as old as the face you see behind a sparse beard and unjustly ravaged by these difficult times, a stranger's face I see in each of the doors I've knocked on hoping for work. Or in this calm water where I was hoping you would swim with me before leaving. Nor can I deny enjoying the day's dress code of this exclusive eatery, Charlotte. You know very well, as well as I can see for myself sitting here, how pretty and desirable you are. Yet despite the temptation that is very real to me, I cannot for a moment think to make your current life even less tolerable than the story you told. Naturally I want to lie with you, especially since I'm at long last fresh and clean. I do very much want to enjoy a young woman who otherwise would never give me a second glance. I'm not that much of a fool. However, if you're not inclined to swim with me, at whatever safe distance makes you comfortable, I'll give you my back while you put on your dress. The choice is yours, whether or not the soap was a fair price."

She was visibly stunned. "Jed…you're saying that you will let me dress? Truly?"

"You've been through enough. I can't possibly expect to mistreat you for the sake of a stale sandwich."

"But I thought…"

"I know what you were thinking." He pivoted to face her. "You've paid that high price far too often for such a young and pretty girl, although, if you don't mind, I would like my clothes to dry awhile longer. I'll do my best to maintain a little modesty as I sit here." He spun around again, giving his back to her, pausing. "I must say, Charlotte, hearing your story, I find myself severely troubled about leaving you vulnerable to the further dangers awaiting a young and compelling woman wandering alone, particularly since we're travelling the same roads and considering our recent history. What do you think of me being your protector, Charlotte…until we find our separate ways safely?"

If she had shocked him earlier, he was absolutely flabbergasted when she sank to the ground behind him, her arms wrapping tightly around him, her breasts pressing into his back as her bare legs framed his. "Thank you, Jed. I would like that very much." He let her cry, her warm tears trickling onto his shoulder. He'd never felt anything as soft or as warm against him.

He chuckled. "I certainly do already. If you want to thank me awhile longer, I don't mind at all, Charlotte."

She giggled, wiping her face. "I suppose, given that we've seen each other already and know what we do of each other, we could swim together while the sun is still warm."

She stood, reaching for his hand. She led him into the cool water where they swam and waded and talked until they somehow felt awkward that he hadn't yet pulled her into his arms. Which is what he did, happy when she clung to his shoulders, swaying against him like an exotic pendulum, his body speaking volumes while his expression left her no doubt whatsoever that the next choice was hers as well. By that same expression conveying that he would appreciate a prompt decision. Charlotte chose well from Jed's perspective, praying with all her heart that she had not misjudged him.

That evening under the stars and her blanket, Jed Billows, despite his unpolished techniques and ineptitude with tender words spoken to a woman naked and entirely captivating beneath and beside him, made Charlotte Higgins feel safe and secure in his strong arms. She drifted into a blissful sleep she hadn't known for a very long time, dreaming, as young women are wont to do, of a true and lasting love that would surely come later, content for the moment not to be alone.

The next morning they bathed their bodies freshly coated and perfumed with their sweat, laying together on the soft grass to dry. They had nothing to eat, which seemed not to matter, filling their stomachs with water from the lake before they dressed.

As they were leaving, Jed, taking charge of her carpet bag, Charlotte shrieked at noticing several birds feasting frantically on the dead man lying behind a curtain of shrubs. Her father's irreparable body was the first corpse forced upon her, the stranger's damaged head flooding her mind with frightful visions and memories.

Inching closer, she clutched her stomach with one hand, clasping the other to her mouth to muffle a high-pitched squeal. The cadaver was utterly repulsive. Its good eye was gone, the socket as black and as vacant as the one next to it whose patch the birds had pecked at in the hopes of exposing another moist treat. The gaping mouth had no tongue, the grey and whiskered cheek exposed to the sky picked clean through to a toothless jaw.

"He's been here with us all this time, Jed. How do you think he came to be here?" She was scared, hugging him tightly. "Who do you think killed him, and when?"

"Don't be afraid, Charlotte. It's me who killed him, yesterday," he told her, "with the rock by his head, not five minutes after coming across him crouched where you see him. He was not a very good fellow and, in all truth, he appears not much worse to me now than he did then. He was spying on you in secret while you were in the water, very eager to hurt you throughout the entire day and night, waiting for you to settle yourself on the grass. That was his plan. Then when I saw you, I could not let that happen. The rest, however, I was not expecting."

Tears welled in her eyes. So many nights she had dreamed of seeing them lying dead at her feet, the ones who had treated her so shamefully, tossing her aside like scraps from a plate when they were done with her. "You saved me, Jed." She pressed a warm palm to his cheek. "Thank you. And thank you."

"You thanked me nicely enough yesterday as I recall. For what now, exactly? I did what any decent man would do."

"Yes, for him, who I'll forget the moment I can clean him from my nose. I don't care about him, or any of them. Not anymore. I believe I would have found the means to kill myself before letting anything as foul and disgusting touch me. I mean thank you for yesterday. I'm certain now, standing here with you, seeing what you did, that you would have hurried into the water to save me from drowning because I was terribly afraid of you. So you see, you saved me twice. You *are* my protector."

They walked to the road, the first leg downhill, neither Jed nor Charlotte with anything in their minds to say. Neither one had anything to offer but themselves to each other, each day becoming closer until, not very long after, Charlotte's fanciful dream of falling in love came true and they married.

For almost a year they journeyed along rural roads

finding work with whoever happened to require his strength of body or her skilled hands. Until not far from their twelfth month together Jed found the work in California that Charlotte had promised he would, for she couldn't possibly imagine her man as a clerk. He was taken on full time, at first picking grapes, learning all he could about the making of wine, and by the winter of 1941, at the age of thirty-two, he was the manager in charge while Charlotte spent her days making dresses in the shop that she owned, excited about the news of their first baby.

That would prove to be their last Christmas together, their last Valentine's as lovers the day before Jed Billows shipped out as a sergeant with his platoon to the fields of France. Six months later Jeddore Billows was killed in action early one bright and sunny morning. Fallen, closing his eyes and feeling at peace, he whispered her name, a gentle breeze melding with his final breaths to deliver his promise to never leave her alone. At that very moment, an ocean apart, Charlotte howled his name, her body at once contracting into a difficult and premature labour, frantic with what she felt deep in her grief-stricken heart was true. Her darling Jed was not coming home.

What should have been Charlotte's and Jed Billows' most glorious moment deteriorated quickly into hours of feverish agony and mournful anguish for the despairing young wife and mother until at long last, as darkness prevailed, sapped of her will and her strength, Charlotte fell into a deep sleep, she and her unborn son floating into her husband's waiting and loving arms to fulfill their true dream: To be forever together.

Chapter Seven
Marcus Simms & Leona

He felt her invisible weight bearing down hard on him, pushing him deeper into the bed. She was rocking, annoying him. Her thighs were warm against his skin, her moist lips between them too warm. He felt barely able to breathe, his heart scarcely beating as though broken. He felt incredibly deep sorrow.

"Charlotte, my darling," he blew a breath tainted with the previous night's scotch from the half of his mouth that was not buried into the pillow, "I am so sorry you're dead."

The sharp pain at the back of his head startled him. He jerked. He wanted to move, unable to budge from under her weight, his arms pinned to his side.

"I am not dead, asshole, and I am not Charlotte. I'm Leona. Remember me, the stunning and breathtaking Leona, exotic Leona and Happy New Year, kisses and candles, good wine and steamy sex, lots and lots of hot sex? And calling me Charlotte is not cool when I was about to give you your fifth best piece of tail you'll get this year, asshole." She clambered from his back, naked and lovely and scowling. "So who the hell is Charlotte?"

Oh, spare me! Why did so many of his comforters want complete ownership of him? The female condition. They couldn't simply have sex, a good time, roll over and get on with life. He tested one eye, then the other. The first of January of any year was never particularly good, not for him, and this birthday was no exception given his rude awakening. The one good thing about the day might possibly be the absolute beauty whose green eyes were digging into his that were half-open and blurred. Or perhaps that, eight days earlier, he had killed the son of a bitch whom the State of Illinois had failed to put down years earlier for brutally stealing the innocence of two young nuns he later murdered for showing him the kindness of stopping on some backroad or other to offer him a ride.

A meaningless eighteen years later, not yet forty, he was a free man released from a state-run psychiatric facility and declared fit to re-enter society, which did not sit well with Marcus whose favourite diversion was finding people like Sam McKinnie.

*

The weather was hellish, had been all week. He hated Northern winters; he hated snow and ice pellets bombarding his face. He hated frozen ears and having to constantly wipe his nose and comb his hair. He hated wearing hats, for which reason he didn't. In fact he hated most things northern, inclusive of its ill-mannered and ill-proportioned population.

He hated how his balls had shrunk to the size of peas as his rental had leisurely careened into the car in front of him the previous day. When, shortly thereafter, in spite of his sincerest apologies and concern, he was informed that he was, in fact, "a complete fucking idiot." This by some boorish, 300 pound troglodyte who had no idea whatsoever that Marcus Simms really and truly felt the urge to stick a needle in the fellow's flabby neck. Or how fortunate he was that Marcus' true purpose for being in Chicago was Sam McKinnie.

McKinnie was pure scum, an irredeemable deviant. He was the worst example of human evolution: a species not fit to live. That Illinois had not executed him when they had the chance was a despicable miscarriage of justice. Because he would kill again, and again, not caring about prison because he was a loser and Illinois six years earlier had gotten religion. They put forth a bill that, thereafter, would prevent the extermination of human vermin like McKinnie.

At any rate he didn't run far, making him easy to track. He fittingly worked in a pork abattoir, mopping floors and cleaning vats in the Kill Room from four PM until midnight on the outskirts of Chicago. He lived in a one-room apartment that took most of his minimum wage that he would earn until his three months were up, when he would either be good enough to join the union or, before then, be back in custody for finding another girl to rape and kill. Neither of which would occur.

Marcus Simms had planned a year-end trip to Chicago to wine and dine clients until the twenty-third. The next day was his and McKinnie's whose apartment Simms had been into one late afternoon a few days earlier.

The place was dingy and dark, with a bed better-suited to a landfill, a chair, a table, a television, a VCR and a stack of porno flicks. The bathroom was off limits, decorated with crust, smears, rot and mould. There was nowhere for him to hide. The best Marcus could hope for was that McKinnie would get in and close the door before shitting himself.

McKinnie walked into his private filth each night at thirty minutes past midnight, and he would that night as well. Christmas meant nothing to his kind. He had no friends and, with no money to spare and a wardrobe of sweats, coveralls and work boots, he had nowhere to go. Nowhere anyone would want him.

Simms didn't have long to wait, nor did he allot much of his time to worrying how the meeting would play out. He had size and surprise on his side. He was also very fit and accustomed to facing off with scum. At 12:30 Christmas Eve morning McKinnie pushed his key into the lock. Seconds later he was inside, flicking the light switch, the door slamming shut for him, his face smashing hard into the wall. Much harder the second time.

The two-foot steel bar crashed into his kidneys, then his head, then into each knee. That's when Marcus Simms calmly stepped aside, tossing the bar onto the bed before reaching into his coat for his gun.

"Good evening, McKinnie. That isn't the worst you'll feel, I'm pleased to say."

McKinnie was on all fours, struggling for breath, coughing phlegm onto the floor. "Who the fuck are ya? Jesus Christ!"

He looked and carried himself like a con. Hardly debonair. His skin was tinted grey from years of smoking in an airless cell, his hair was greasy and slicked back, his neck tattooed, his face scarred from brawls or worse and his yellow teeth would cause any dental hygienist to shriek from fright. Marcus not failing to notice that his eyes were already dead.

"Jesus Christ? Seriously? A strange thing for you to say given your proven dislike of nuns."

"Who sent ya? What the fuck! I've only been out a couple of weeks."

"A couple of weeks too many in my view. And this isn't a prison thing, not really. I'm simply someone who, very regrettably, corrects wrongs after the fact. When I would much rather have killed you before you raped and murdered those two innocent girls."

"Like I told the cops and the judge. They wasn't dressed like no nuns, sashayin' the way they was, wigglin' their little asses'n gigglin'. All pretty like when I come across 'em. And they was just as nice'n pretty under their skirts. Not like no nuns would ever do."

"You left them naked and dead in a field by a lake, their young bodies badly scraped and bruised. You had no reason to murder them. None whatsoever. What you did to them first was sufficiently horrific, which I believe makes the trial judge as guilty as you."

"Couldn't play with one without makin' the other lay still for a bit. The bruisin' came from their kickin'n scratchin'. Two hellcats if ever there was." He snickered. "Had me a good afternoon. Gotta say, had some certain difficulty leavin' 'em, them little bodies all soft and curvy and warm. They went quick, mind, and I done my time." He tried standing, falling. "And now yer thinkin' yer gonna kill me?"

"I believe the term is damn straight, which will require some cooperation on your part, McKinnie." Simms waved the gun. "Get yourself into the chair. My gloves are new, I want to keep them that way. Go."

McKinnie did, slowly and painfully. "Now what?"

Simms chuckled. "You know what."

"Bullshit, that there's a toy shooter."

"No. It's a CO_2-powered dart gun, and very effective. The tip is a needle. It will hurt like a bitch, but won't kill you." He fired, hitting McKinnie in the neck. "Here's the thing, what I tell all my account people: Know when to stop talking. Do not oversell. Do not talk yourself out of a job well-done. Know when to leave. That's a sedative, McKinnie, sufficiently strong to make my work quicker and easier, albeit nowhere near enough to diminish the best part of this meeting, which is your very unpleasant departure from this crippled world." He put away the gun, reaching into the other inside pocket of his coat for the syringe. "This on the other hand is pentobarbital. It's used for putting down animals mostly. In this case a rabid dog, very soon. You did very nasty things to those girls, McKinnie, horrible things, for which reason I particularly delighted in adding sulphuric acid. My highest dosage to-date, in fact, for the girls. Two equal parts. You're sort of a test, as much as you are a Christmas gift. They're dead, they won't benefit from your agony, but their parents will. I do hope so. You should expect a good amount of vomit, convulsions, unbearable pain and blood, copious amounts of blood from the mouth, the nose and, yes, you will royally shit yourself. They all do. No doubt the ones who find you will contribute to the mix."

"This ain't right, not after eighteen years. I paid fer what I done. "

"You merely had a reprieve. You're paying in full now." Simms stood and walked behind McKinnie. "If you don't mind I'll wait until you're dead to extract the dart. A question of hygiene, nothing personal." He pushed the needle into the jugular. "With this dosage I'm estimating something less than four minutes before lights out, one minute before you seriously begin jerking and crying, two before the blood and the puke. By three you won't care. You'll be in another place, which should not encourage you to expect a reception of angels or nuns. Not you. And now I'll stop talking, my work is done."

117

Marcus Simms pressed his thumb against the plunger, emptying the barrel. Replacing the protective sleeve he stood in the middle of the small room to wait, watch, and retrieve the dart.

Sam McKinnie died badly, as expected, as intended, Simms leaving him as a twisted corpse with wide-open eyes and a gaping mouth, splattered with vomit and blood, his stench polluting the air.

He left the steel bar he hadn't touched with bare hands and walked out, satisfied with the new and improved results. His work was done. All he could hope for was that the girls' parents would learn of the event and find their own sense comfort and closure. He would return to Chicago in a few days as Rosemary Sandra would expect of him, to continue his year-end thank-you luncheons and dinners with his premier clients in the city as well as to recover his civility and find his requisite closure that was critical to his continued success.

In the meantime he would fly home to South Carolina, first dropping by his pied à terre that she knew nothing about, his personal and private getaway since realizing years earlier that he needed balance in his life, that he needed to meld his past with his present and his future, that without question he had committed an unfortunate error in judgement by marrying the pampered by-product of Mr. and Mrs. Roger Samuel Rothstone. His single and arguable solace derived from within his own mind: She was, in the continued short-term, convenient.
*

Her name was Leona, he remembered, whom he had recognized immediately the previous evening as his enabler, his source of comfort and joy.

She sauntered into the hotel lounge across from where

he was seated for Happy Hour to relax in the quiet and dimly lit ambiance after a day of meetings and a luncheon that concluded his year. She was tall and slender, her auburn hair bouncing at her shoulders with each step. Her leather skirt was short and oxblood, showing more of her thighs than not. Her tights were a pale shade of burgundy, her crossover blouse sheer, a deeper burgundy, silky and billowy, the hint of a darker designer bra showing through. Her purse dangled from a shoulder, her arms slightly swaying, making her impossible to ignore.

She had no coat. Possibly she was a guest wearing knee-high boots that matched her skirt to achieve a compelling allure, the wow factor most Northern females had for too long deemed not worth their effort, preferring to settle for second best rather than striving for the attentions of discerning and deserving men such as Marcus Simms.

Or she had left her coat and her hat with the coat-check girl in the lobby. Women of her apparent quality would never venture out in such nasty weather without the indispensable fashion accessories. And she was coming closer, toward the only other banquette that was empty and next to his. She wouldn't sit at the bar. Not her, not with men on either side of her hunched over their shirt sleeves, or slouching, or half cut. Out of shape men twice her age, Northern men, or just plain obese with their ties loosened and their guts about ready to explode past a threatened barricade of buttons.

Marcus was dressed in a dark blue suit, a fuchsia shirt with French cuffs and silver links, a Mediterranean blue tie and oxblood loafers. They already had something in common and she was making eye contact. Not 'buy me a drink and you might have a chance' contact, more like 'you won't know if you don't try' contact. She wasn't timid, that

119

was obvious. She was accustomed to losers ogling her, stripping her naked as she sauntered past them; she had heard all the lines and was probably a little jaded, probably wondering how long before one of them at the bar would hit on her, offering to buy her drinks and dinner.

She disappeared into the booth, Marcus noting the time: 6:20. She was served a few minutes later. A glass of red wine.

He wondered what she was thinking, expecting. Did she think he must be meeting someone? Or that he would introduce himself? Or was she waiting for someone? More to the point, what could he possibly say that she had not heard before?

6:40: No movement, no whispers into a cellphone. No one at the bar brave or drunk enough to chance humiliation and ridicule. Who would possibly keep such a disarmingly attractive woman waiting? What he read in her eyes was absolutely correct, his catalyst into a wonderful evening. He would not know without trying.

"Excuse me, miss." He had never seen greener eyes or more exquisitely sculpted lips. "My name is Marcus Simms. I could not bear the thought of you sitting here by yourself a moment longer, vulnerable to any number of dangers. Any rogue daring to mistreat such a lovely lady in such a despicable manner deserves the severest punishment. May I, in any small way, hope to serve as your protector until this thoughtless fellow arrives, particularly since we seem to have so much in common?"

She was neither surprised nor perturbed, neither smiling nor reserved. "Have you spent the last twenty minutes rehearsing that line, Mr. Simms? And what exactly do you believe we have in common?"

"Your boots are the colour of my shoes, and we both have the deepest green eyes."

She chuckled, her voice sensually guttural. "I'm wearing a skirt as short as this and you noticed my boots? How very gracious of you, I think."

"Whatever else I may have inadvertently noticed is truly exquisite, a wondrous gift to any man's eyes. Searching for a more appropriate word is futile. None exists in our current era to properly describe what I behold. I was fearful of destroying any chance of sitting with you. Forgive me."

"How could I possibly refuse your company, when we share so much in common? Please do join me. My name is Leona Wright."

He sat across from her. Lying beside her would come later, and not much later. "I am the envy of every man at the bar. Are you a guest at the hotel, Miss Leona?"

"I have a condo at lakeside, near the university where I teach Humanities. I'm here for an early dinner against my better judgement because they have an excellent chef. Against my better judgement because I hate dining alone when everyone else is hooked-up. Especially this of all nights. And you, Marcus?"

No diamond ring. No ring whatsoever. Excellent. Her hands, delicate and smooth, were tipped with a deep violet lacquer.

"We're practically neighbours. I live in Highland Park and I'm not a very good cook. I was in the area this afternoon with clients, I own a plastics moulding company. Anyway, some fellow, who's not remotely as happy as I am right at the moment, decided to collide with my car. For which reason I decided to dine out and let traffic die down before hailing a cab."

"My goodness, you aren't hurt?"

"Invincible. Unless any possible injury would induce you to join me for dinner, Miss Leona."

"What, no champagne at midnight?" She beamed.

He coughed a real laugh. He loved her voice. "I absolutely love your voice, Miss Leona. Spending the entire evening listening to you would be a delightful gift to my ears. Moreover, we're both here and dining alone after meeting you would be too painful." He paused, ordering another wine for the lady, which he discovered was an '89 Margaux, and a JW Blue. Each one impressing the other.

When the waiter was gone Marcus raised his glass discreetly. "May I be so bold as to toast an unexpectedly pleasant evening?" She tilted her head, quizzically. "You must, Miss Leona. My injuries are becoming more apparent, my legs are weak, my eyes blinded by dazzling beauty."

She hesitated a moment for affect, not uncertainty. She liked him. "That being the case, I don't see how I could possibly leave you with such severe injuries. I couldn't live with myself." She sipped her wine. "On condition that, until dinner, we do not sit here like you're selling me something. Or, worse, that I'm selling you something. And that you drop the cutesy Southern 'Miss' thing."

"I most selfishly concur with all stipulations."

He stood, sliding in beside her, making no secret that he was entirely captivated by her body, bringing a wider smile to her lips. Not being captivated by her was impossible when seeing that what he thought were tights for a skirt that daring were nylons accented with tantalizing lace trim and a daring hint of bare flesh.

In the dining room they took turns listening to her life story and his fabrications. After dinner they returned to the lounge where they spoke in quieter whispers, where Leona let him kiss her hands, where she guided his hand to her thigh that she crossed over her other, where she rested her head against his shoulder. She saw no reason whatsoever to deny herself. She wasn't a slut by any means, or a whore, or a money-chaser. She didn't need him; she wanted him, whether for a night, or a week, or a month. Or until, as predictably happened with each of her past lovers, the novelty of their shared intimacy eventually waned, supplanted by the mounting stresses of divergent expectations.

Love and marriage would or might come later. Not a big issue. She was too young for marital bondage, devoting her youth entirely to her career. Everything and everyone else were fleeting diversions.

"Marcus, however tonight happened and why, who knows? Which is why if you don't come home with me this evening, I'll never know."

"Never know what, Leona?"

"Whether what I'm thinking is absolutely right, or completely wrong. Either way, I want you to come home with me. I like you, Marcus. I like you very much and I have no one to answer to. If I'm making a mistake, if you're a prick, my illusion or my delusion, that's on me. But I am not making a mistake. I know I'm not." She nestled closer. "Am I?"

"No, Leona, you're not. I feel the same way. I've wanted since dinner to express those very hopes and fears. Thank you for being more courageous than me."

They drove to her condo soon after in a Jag XKR-S convertible with the top up, to a designer-decorated penthouse boasting a bedroom and closet that left no doubt in his mind that she was a sensual and sexual woman. Or that she didn't believe in wasting time. They could drink champagne later, she told him, in the same breath telling him where to sit and watch. She wanted to gauge his reaction. She was familiar enough with men to distinguish between their bullshit and candour, short-term lust and genuine quests for love. Candour and love were possible long-term goals, not requisite in the present. At the moment, seeing him sitting there, his body relaxed, his eyes sparkling and keen, she absolutely needed to get laid.

Her blouse came away first, floating in the air until coming to rest on the floor like a sheer stain. Then her skirt, pushed seductively to the floor in a deep bend, Leona coming up slowly, throwing back a wave of lustrous hair, standing in a laced bra, G-string and stay-ups. When other men would be ripping at their own clothes, she remarked, Marcus was sitting with his legs crossed, quietly appreciating, not assessing, his gaze travelling from her bra to her panties to her stockings as though deciding which should come off first.

The choice wasn't his. Like a man putting on his slacks before his socks and his shirt, there was a procedure to follow. Her bra was three-quarter and deep blue, that she opened as enticingly between her breasts with her fingertips as she would an exotic drape concealing a rare wonder.

He approved. Good. Better yet, he hadn't budged. All she needed to know she could clearly read in his eyes.

Lightly cupping her breasts, squeezing gently, she faced away, scarcely moving her feet. Her stockings were next. First the left, slowly, excitingly for her, painfully for him; then the right with the same deep bend from her waist, her deliberate return his agonizing torment. Her G-string was the same deep blue, the silk ribbons at one side pulled to their limit and left dangling against her bare thigh. She turned again, slowly, deliberately, although he could easily tell her heart was racing. Tugging at the other ribbons she parted her legs, staring down, letting her hair cascade, letting the satin patch stay in place for long seconds until its delicate weight fell to the floor and time stood as still as Leona's breathing.

Okay, alright, someone had to say something. Standing naked at arm's length while he leaned forward planting his elbows on his knees, cupping his face in his hands and smirking contentedly without saying a word was a little one-sided. "Okay, don't tell me you do not like this. I know you do." Nothing. A stupid grin. He was teasing her. She hunched her shoulders, hugging her elbows to her sides, raising her palms upward. "Duh, man-person. Hello. Naked woman standing here. I believe this where you're supposed to say something nice and sexy, get naked with me, and carry me to my bed."

That was an hour or hours ago. Now she was poking and prodding him.

"Hello...You...In there...Hello." He groaned. "Who the hell is Charlotte?"

He hated anyone poking him. You are. You're Charlotte, or you were until you cracked open my fucking skull. "She's the last wife of a good friend who visits with me on occasion, or she was. She died."

"Oh, my God. How terrible for you." She reached out to touch him, the way women instinctively do as if possessing rare curative powers. "Of what, Marcus, and when?"

"She drowned, which she never believed would happen. Recently, and I'll miss her. She helped me when I most needed her. So does Jed very often. I've known him a good while and I'm certain he'll marry again."

"You said his last wife. How many has he had?"

"Fourteen, including Charlotte."

"What!" She lurched forward, pushing against his dead weight, trying to budge him.

Marcus rolled onto his side. "Yeah, fourteen. It's sort of a thing with him. They somehow come along when he needs them most, and then, well…In any event, not to worry. I'm not that needing of variety. I prefer women who stay with me longer than my next credit card bill."

She smacked his arm. "That is such a horrible thing to say. Don't you dare say anything so insensitively chauvinist when you're looking at me, Marcus. I don't need any man's credit card, yours or anyone else's for your information." She leaned forward, kissing his arm, repairing the hurt. "However I do have to admit one of you staying around long enough to celebrate my birthday, which, by the way, is in three months, would be a pleasant change. So, Mr. Marcus Simms, if that's who you are, and if you're really not married, do you think that is even remotely possible since we've only known each other…?" She glanced at her wrist, "Oh, shit. I must be a frigging whore. I am a whore." She tapped the crystal face of her Movado LX. "Maybe it stopped. Do you think so, maybe?"

No. "The best twelve hours of my life and I would never sleep with a whore. I do however, and very selectively, occasionally make love to a breathtakingly beautiful woman."

"I'm sorry, Marcus. I should not have said that about my birthday. I'm really not a clingy female. I'm not, and I do like my freedom. Anyway, we haven't even peed together, or taken a shower together, or any number of things a girlfriend eventually does. The key word being 'eventually'."

He propped himself onto an elbow, grinning. "That is

true, we do have a few things to discover. In addition to which, I'm seeing you this early in the morning and I am not the least bit disappointed. That must count as a good beginning. It does for me, and by all means you can pee while I shower if that's what you want. As for your birthday, I don't even know if you're legal. Or, for that matter, how can I be certain you're not the married one?"

"I'm thirty, not real happy about my upcoming thirty-one, and I'm not married because for some reason I only meet jerks who can't deal with independent women. The last of which, for your information, was six months ago and not very good."

"That's difficult to believe, which doesn't make me unhappy. Selfish, yes, but not unhappy. You are breathtakingly gorgeous, perhaps too breathtaking. You are certainly stealing mine. In addition to which you are smart, successful, a professor no less, and you live in a penthouse. That scares lesser men."

"I didn't scare you, Marcus."

"That's precisely right, you did not. That said, don't believe for a moment that my stomach wasn't churning when I introduced myself. And, being honest, your legs…keep me after school any day, Prof. And this," he caressed her with gentle strokes from her shoulder to the small of her back, pulling her closer, "all of this, this is a gift to all mortals from some higher power. You should be in a magazine."

"Last evening was a first for me, Marcus. The stripping thing. I have never done that and I don't do this, bringing a man home after one dinner. I don't. But I'm not sorry. There was something about you, there is something about you." She giggled. "Or I was simply frigging horny after such a long dry spell." She kissed him, lightly. "I was really

127

beginning to despise my fingers."

"Your striptease was exotic and spellbinding, as you are now." Her brow wrinkled. "What?"

"Seriously, Charlotte was Jed's fourteenth wife?" He nodded. "So why were *you* calling her darling? What's up with that? Did you three have a thing going on?"

He shrugged. "No. I had a secret thing for her, a short-lived infatuation. Nothing happened, nothing ever would. I respect Jed too much, which doesn't mean I couldn't fantasize or dream about her. That's legal, or was. Anyway, I'm over it. I'm thinking I've got another dream girl"

"So you live here in Chicago, you're not married, you don't have a girlfriend, we've had four rounds of hot sex without saying anything stupid, we're still very naked, and I have to pee…by myself. So what happens next? Or does anything happen next? And don't tell me you're not thinking about it. I'm not expecting you to move in after twelve hours, but if you are not staying long enough for dinner with me here this evening, this should be about when you tell me before my newly activated vagina begins making me feel like a slut. No hard feelings. No regrets. In which case you can shower at your own place, or you can shower with me if you can be honest with me."

"That's right."

"What's right?"

"I'm staying for dinner, actually taking you to dinner since I didn't see a turkey in your fridge. Besides, it's Sunday. I'm free until tomorrow morning. I've got a noon flight to LA, which gives us twenty-four hours to discover whether last night was our shared destiny or opportune damage control for your vagina and my ego. Mutual gain or mutual loss when we'll kiss as more than friends or kiss goodbye with no regrets. I'm forty-five today, Leona. To some women that's over the hill. Are you good with that, Leona?"

She straddled him and kissed him, bouncing from her bed and striding to the door where she stopped and leaned into the frame to create what he saw as a purely fabulous nude. Not an ounce of fat spoiled her contours, not a dent. Her breasts were firm and full, her belly and arms slightly sculpted from too many nights alone in her home gym and, he acknowledged, giving credit where credit was most certainly due, her esthetician was exceedingly good at her job. Leona was picture-perfect, though picturing her in a tweed suit with her hair styled into a severe knot was impossible. She was all woman, 100 percent female. He reached to her side table.

"Yes, I am good with that," she answered. "Dinner, then back here for your birthday gift…or gifts, if you're up to it. There's a brand new cozy robe in the closet, a washer-dryer in the powder room, and if you're thinking of smoking that cigarette, I don't think so. If you're that desperate you can freeze your parts on the patio at minus ten. Good luck with that."

"Don't need it." He dropped the packet. "You've got five minutes, then I'm coming in. Ready or not."

She giggled and sauntered from sight. If he believed she was gorgeous the night before, and he did, she was that and more in the daylight. More importantly she had brought him closure and he was grateful.

She would for a short while loathe him, for all the right reasons, as would he of necessity forget her. For the moment, however, he would make the most of what little time he had with Leona, make the most of his well-scripted lies and practiced ruse she would never condone or forgive in a hundred lifetimes. Such was his penance for doing

129

what no one else would dare, such was his need for closure.

Moments later, hearing the water running, he padded into her kitchen searching the fridge for any juice that was chilled and refreshing before joining her. She was a mystic beauty shrouded in steam, her body and the longing in her eyes beckoning him closer. That she was alone in life was inconceivable, definitely somebody's loss and certainly a deplorable waste of a gorgeous, smart and sexy lady, which was never his problem. He could not stay with her, not for as long as she wanted. Impossible. She was his comfort and joy, in return for which he would make her feel special for as long as he deemed wise. He would kiss her and caress her passionately without saying anything cutesy, leaving her in peaceful slumber to explore a new frontier, a new and more wonderful beginning. The most he could allow was an hour, or two, and then he would leave.

Besides, scent of a woman was a very appropriate cliché; she was literally caked all over him.

He stepped in, passing her a patio glass, entwining their arms. Marcus downed his juice thirstily, Leona drained hers in three or four gulps, kissing him with cool lips. Placing both glasses onto the caddy, she passed him the soap, instructing him not to miss an inch. He, of course, happily obliged wearing an impish grin. For what else was a gentleman to do?

Standing behind her, he began at her shoulders, inhaling the fresh fragrance of her thickly matted hair as his hands went lovingly first to her breasts, lingering at them before kneading downward in wide and concentric circles to the curves of her hips, her belly, and her waist.

Leona turned, facing him, staring into his eyes. Feeling euphoric, she hugged him and kissed him, placing her hands on his shoulders with a commanding pressure.

Sinking deliberately to his knees, leaving a trail of wet kisses from her breasts to her belly as he gently caressed every inch of her legs, and sensing that Leona parting them was yet another clear and silent command, he dug his fingers into the firm flesh of her buttocks as he pressed his mouth lightly against her lips to teasingly pry for any young and sensual woman's primary jewel.

She was delirious, her legs trembling, her hands clutching at his head, her throaty moans arousing both ardent lovers until her violent shudder and raspy yelp left them depleted, her entire body trembling as she sank dreamily into his waiting arms.

Marcus carried her into her cinema room, laying her tenderly onto a soft and comforting daybed, intrigued by the angelic innocence emanating from her.

He was fairly certain that one day he would leave Rosemary Sandra, that he would find someone new, someone better who loved him for who he was and start over. Just not with Leona who lay peacefully in her sleep, who would never realize the extent to which he was grateful.

He glanced at his watch. He would leave her home as pristine as possible, doing his utmost to erase hurtful memories all too briefly shared, above all removing his condoms and their implicit memories from her trash.

The timing for them was not right. Instead he would fly home to Charleston where he would call Rosemary Sandra that evening from his private condo after dropping off his week's wardrobe at the corner cleaners where often he left his shoes for polishing or repairs.

He would promise to come home to her from the airport within the hour, often arriving with flowers or jewellery or something sexy that never seemed to matter. The lament in his voice was difficult to disguise, the indifference in hers very clear. He wasn't returning home to a loving wife, but to an ancient argument over New Year's, his birthday, and the misery of her privileged and near-perfect life.

The heartless and cold bitch was becoming more insufferable than her incessantly arrogant father with each passing year.

Chapter Eight
Jed, Rosemary's Spite & Sarah

May 31, 1888 was the worst day of Jed Billows' young life since the day his unwanted birth eighteen years earlier stole his mother's life. He was miserable, forced by his master to leave behind the girl he loved with such passion, convinced in his heart he should have died in his mother's womb, never to have known her, rather than live without her for what remained of his life. Though possibly he would have thought differently had he ever discovered the truth: that the Billows woman had not wanted a child, him or any other.

But her husband was often belligerent in demanding his rights. She was weak and sickly as she was, in no fit condition to spew a child from her loins, even if by God's grace she were to survive such a burdensome weight through a harsher than usual winter and into an ungodly hot Charleston spring. Which she did, each day her fragile faith waning more, her last months and weeks painful and fraught with worry for her life, with her last breaths crying out in anguish to her midwife that, had God been truly gracious, He would have killed her outright and not have filled her last minutes with such frightful terror. And then she died, buried early that same afternoon and forgotten.

His father was a labourer of the lowest strain, boorish

and unskilled if not for the strength in his arms. He could read no book, nor write a simple letter. He was big and brutal and mean, many nights earning enough for a few ounces of whisky by stepping into a ring to smash his fists into the faces and heads of willing opponents who believed themselves the better man until the loss of a tooth or an eye proved them wrong.

His father didn't want him. A man's life was plenty hard since the failed war without the added troubles of a motherless boy who would not stand on his own for a good dozen years. And what if he came out from her crippled or not right in the head? Say what ya will, he often bitched and griped with a drink in his fist, things hereabouts are sure enough all rosy and bright for the high and the mighty fancy folks like the Abercorns. Not for the likes of us, not since the Union came to burn our crops and ruin our homes.

He wanted nothing to do with the boy, spending his nights for the last month of his wife's unbearable life as far as he could from her to figure out what he should do to fix the mess she was leaving behind.

A Negro passing him by one night gave him inspiration. Young Abercorn, the master of the plantation where the sweat poured from Billows' burnt skin twelve long hours each day, was paying his Blacks a goodly sum less each year than if they was white, he reminded Billows. Abercorn's missus always smilin' at 'em like they *was* white when givin' 'em water and fruit to keep 'em on their feet like she was makin' things right. They was young, the master and the missus, the master not yet doin' a proper job on her when she was as ripe for the pluckin' as she ever would be, makin' folks talk that could be the young man's spigot was broke. Could be he'd be doin' 'em a good deed, he figured, raisin' a white boy proper-like as their own or keepin' him to toil in the fields.

The day his wife died Billows was in the fields, Abercorn the first to advise him without the slightest emotion of the anticipated event and of the boy-child, excusing him from an afternoon of toil and offering him the use of a wagon to promptly remove the remains from the property.

Billows nodded, returning to their cabin where his wife lay under a damp and soiled sheet, the foreign midwife sitting by her side and cradling the hollering new-born. He carried the dead woman from her bed to the wagon, not bothering to gaze upon her face or touch her lips before the chill of death consumed her. From there he went to town where he paid to have her buried, leaving her as she was on a carpenter's table, returning to his ramshackle home to a meal of hot pork and beans made for him when at last the weary midwife was finished timidly suckling the infant.

With his stomach full he sent her home, grunting at her, making her understand with unkind gestures that she was no longer required. When she was gone from sight, cradling her new-born Sarah asleep in her arms, he went to the stables to return the horse and the wagon. With it he delivered the boy into the care of a mother and father who, within the same hour, hurried from their parlour see what the fuss was about.

Master Abercorn went hastily with field hands he trusted, each one sturdy and strong, to Billows' cabin expecting to soundly berate the man and cause him to take back the boy. They found the place empty, lit by a candle or two with no sign of the man inside or out.

"The blasted bugger, be damned," was all Abercorn could mutter, spinning on his heels and striding toward the mansion in a black mood, the men following silently to

135

their shacks.

The next morning at their breakfast, "Dear husband, the boy's name should be Jeddore. It's what the mother decided, according to the other women such as herself in your employment. And I wonder, would you also be agreeable to the boy residing in our home and in our care, since we have not yet achieved a child of our own?"

"Dearest Lily, have you completely lost your wits? I will not for the duration of a single breath consider such an eccentric folly. My decision is made and firmly set in my mind." Abercorn, anticipating this moment of his wife's inherent feminine frailty, had searched his mind and his conscience without cessation since the previous evening, peering into the future, finding solace in his reasoning and his beneficence. He could not, in any way, deem to lend the boy the Abercorn name. "I cannot, dearest Lily. He must forever exist as a Billows. We will without question ensure the boy a decent home, unquestionably. Simply not our own. The implications are simply too far-reaching to not boggle even the most superior mind."

"Have you considered a suitable arrangement, husband?"

"We will give him into the care of the woman who, in my view, is best suited to the task. And at the considerable cost of several more dollars each year. If the husband or the midwife refuses, we will make the boy's need of a family known to the public. Many barren women will be glad enough to relieve us of this unwarranted dilemma."

She laid a hand over his. "Thank you, dearest husband. I will speak with the woman this morning, as you will convince her husband. She has a good heart; she will be a good mother to the boy."

"For ten years, or thereabouts, depending on his

physical development." Abercorn cautioned with a stern finger." That's my condition. Until he attains a suitable age, not younger than ten, to repay what he owes, when he will toil in the fields with the others to honour as well what remains of his father's indebtedness to me and to you. Billows by cowardly design reneged on our agreement; he ran from his obligation to work this land, in that way paying off the debt of their lodging, their daily sustenance, the care of their ailments such as his wife's, the boy's basic schooling, and a year-end bonus for work diligently performed." He slammed the table with a clenched fist. "That twenty dollars Billows will never feel the weight of in his pockets. Were he before me this very moment, and in my present mood, I would rightfully deduct the Italian's entire lost day from his amount. As for the boy, my dearest Lily, he will have a home. Simply not our home, which I cannot pretend to regret despite your current deep despair and disappointment." He went to her, kneeling. "You will have your own child, dear Lily. You will. You must trust in me to make things right."

Jed was put into the care of the agreeable young Italian woman who had brought him into the world for an additional five dollars added to her husband's year-end for his inconvenience, and one year later Mistress Abercorn proved the field hands and their women wrong about her husband's mechanics when she did give birth to a girl with pinkish blonde curls and a pinkish hue to her snow-white skin.

Being a product of his own birth, upbringing and social class, Abercorn had believed that Jed Billows would naturally develop into the likeness of his father and that one day, if he were not to abscond as well, he would repay the debt and earn his future keep with others of his kind in the fields. Or, were he to demonstrate sufficient wit, which Abercorn could not for a moment envision, possibly become a privileged overseer. He and his wife both very much astonished when Jed began showing an intelligence rarely exhibited in those of a lesser lineage, Mistress Abercorn at last convincing her husband of the wisdom of bringing the boy into their home in order that he would one day be of much greater benefit to them and, in the meanwhile, a companion for their daughter.

By age ten he was good with his numbers and letters, one year ahead of Rosemary in his class to whom he would read Alice in Wonderland and other stories when his studies and chores were finished, each day carrying her books home from school, which his step-sister Sarah made clear was very silly of him.

"The master's daughter is prissy, Jed. She isn't very nice and thinks too much of herself."

"Rosemary is a lady, Sarah, and you should not be rude to her."

"She is not a lady. She's a girl and I am not rude. She is, and I'm a year older. So why won't you ever carry my books home from school? Don't you think I would like that, to think that you care about me too? You used to care about me, Jed."

She stopped.

"What? What now? Are you going to cry like a girl?"

"I don't understand why you don't love me anymore since they made you leave us."

He made a face. "You're my sister, Sarah. Carry your own books. Boys don't carry their sisters' books."

She sighed. She did want to cry. Yet she wouldn't, because she knew he would tell Rosemary and they would laugh at her. "It's because you live in the house now, with her. Because I'm not as pretty with stupid blonde hair and stupid ribbons and stupid stockings." She was suddenly angry, punching him, her mysterious dark eyes moist and sad. "Don't blame me, Jed, because I don't have pretty dresses to wear. Blame him, the master. Do you think I like dressing this way, like a boy? Well I don't. So there. It's because of him."

He tugged at her pigtails, telling her to stop being a nuisance and to go straight home, unaware that since her father's death in the fields, his lungs filled with black dust from having laboured for his passage to America in the boiler room of the SS Majestic with hopes of a better life for him and his new wife, Abercorn had reduced her mother's annual stipend by half. But Sarah never stopped loving her brother, missing him each night that he slept in Rosemary's house and not in the simple cot beside hers when they once would have whispered incessantly until one followed the other into the bliss of childish dreams.

She missed her brother terribly throughout those middle years, her heart aching to see him with her, with Miss Rosemary. Then her schooling came to an end. She was an ordinary and unskilled girl, sufficiently educated to work in the fields and begin repaying her debt alongside her mother, each year evolving into a more exotic, compelling and desirable young woman to the one who increasingly thought himself a fool. Until one day he fell onto his knees to beg her forgiveness for his childishness years earlier and to thank her for being everything in the world to him.

Meanwhile Rosemary continued believing in her heart that Jeddore was the most wonderful of men, more affectionate towards him in her fantasies and dreams with each passing year. She would often sit in her window or on the veranda sipping lemonade to watch him toiling in the fields near the house, many days without his shirt, when she would go to him with a full jug and a glass on a tray that he would thank her for with a kiss on her cheek.

She adored Jeddore, entirely and deeply in love with him, secretly expecting she would marry him very soon. Even her father liked him very much. None of the sons of her parents' society were as strong or as handsome. None could ride a horse as well or make her feel like a woman when he was with her. Yet, as he was becoming eighteen that late spring, his body and his character already those of a man, her man, those special moments were increasingly fewer and she knew very well who was to blame: his green-skinned half-sister who was constantly talking with him, or walking with him, or bringing him water and sandwiches that she would eat with him.

She hated Sarah very much. Rosemary was petite and attractive to the countless young men vying for her and her father's attentions. She was graceful, slim and straight, with the slightest definition at her hips. She was delicate, her breasts girlishly small yet entirely noticeable even when concealed from anyone's true appreciation of them behind the long dresses she would button to her neck. Her hair was long, forever tied in a ponytail with pink ribbons. Her rosy white skin of her earlier years was splashed with freckles, her blue eyes accented with long and pale lashes, her lips thin and pink, and her nose appeared as though someone had lost their thumb in the middle of her face. She was her papa's little girl and, for that, she hated Sarah the most.

Sarah was tall and dark and exotic. Her unblemished skin tinted a light Mediterranean olive colour. She had a natural beauty with cherry-black eyes, her lustrous hair, always full and alive in the wind, was the colour of pitch. Her breasts were firm and full, her body curvaceous and not hidden from sight in skirts that came to her knees and shirts that left no doubt she was a woman.

One frightfully hot summer day, not finding the girl anywhere she searched, anxious to cause Sarah and her mother trouble, Rosemary told her mother the girl must certainly be shirking her duties, likely sleeping somewhere under a tree to avoid the hot sun. Though really she wanted to find Jeddore who was not anywhere to be found in the fields or in the stables. She was entirely frustrated. He was always happy to see her coming with her tray since he worked harder than any other and she wanted terribly to sit with him in the shade and sip her lemonade with him, remembering as she dreamily stirred the icy yellow sweetness that her Jeddore had a favourite spot to be alone atop a grassy knoll.

Rosemary screeched gleefully to her mother that she was leaving and went in a hurry to find her heart's love, humming and singing, her cheeks flushed with excitement, jerking to a stop the instant Jed Billows utterly and cruelly crushed her heart. She screamed, hurling her tray onto the grass, believing she would instantly die where she stood gaping. He was lying atop Sarah, the girl the same age as he who, until he was ten, he had loved and teased affectionately as a sister, coming to love her more ardently the longer they lived apart.

The girl's skirt and her shirt and her shoes were in a careless heap beside his. Her hands were scratching and digging into his glistening back and bare buttocks, her feet spread wide apart. They were kissing and squirming and making the most terrible noises, Jed's hands and boots braced on the grass, his arms taut, his entire body pounding relentlessly against Sarah's.

141

Jed's and Sarah's bodies were instantly flung apart by the invisible shockwave without any means to cover themselves, Rosemary frozen in time where she stood gaping, her breathing paralyzed. She had never in her life seen a naked woman, or thought to imagine one, let alone one so vulgarly spread out on the ground, propped on her elbows and smiling. And that she was seeing Jeddore completely exposed horrified her. She felt herself choking, her legs threatening to fail her. Never in the most heated of her dreams had she dared to imagine his private parts so alarmingly engorged or that he would for a moment think to violate her as brutally as he was fornicating with her. With his sister!

"Jeddore, with your sister! How could you!"

She wanted to die, twisting from the sight of them, fleeing from them as quickly as her feet could carry her to her mother, sobbing inconsolably. Screaming as she ran how she hated him, that she wanted him sent far away. She never wanted to see him, not ever again.

Jed Billows stood, watching her grow smaller in the distance. He figured ten or fifteen minutes before Hell's gates would swing open. He helped Sarah to her feet, kissing her, holding her close.

"I think you enjoyed that, you little black-eyed vixen."

"That her precious little boyfriend was making love to me, here, with that? Yes, my darling." She giggled. "We did nothing wrong. We need no one's permission to love each other. And it's not as though she's never seen a stallion's cock before. If she's afraid of it, I'm not."

"Still, don't be too quick to laugh. She's clever in manipulating her father and your stallion, I think, is about to be gelded." He opened his arms. "Get dressed, my love."

"As though her father would ever agree to you as her

142

husband. And how can she at her age believe I'm your sister?" Sarah brushed their sweat from her belly and her thighs with caressing strokes. "Next time the snooty bitch looks down at me she'll have this of me to remember and won't be as quick to believe she's better than me."

"You did teach her a lesson she'll remember. But do you intend to leave her father with the same fine impression of you, or will you get dressed?" He twirled her a tight circle, grinning mischievously. "We'll meet him halfway and firmly stand our ground. Anyway, the very worst I can foresee is that I'll be forced to marry you instead of her. Seems to me I'm properly buggered either way, Sarah."

She punched him hard, pushing him away, reaching for her shirt. He had already promised when and where they would marry: On his next birthday, May 31, 1889 in New York City.

Chapter Nine
Jed, Sarah & Walt Guntrie

Master Abercorn agreed with Rosemary in a violent rage, furious that his innocent daughter would be a witness to such a horrific display of debauchery, prepared to do whatever he must to defend his daughter's purity and virtue, leaving his wife to soothe the girl's extreme sorrow.

He came to Jed and Sarah galloping on horseback, reining in the horse too melodramatically, choosing not to dismount in order that he would maintain a superior advantage over the boy.

The two were holding hands. "Good afternoon, Master Abercorn." Sarah said nothing. "I have scarcely anything to add to Rosemary's story except to say that we are in love, Sarah and I, for what it matters to anyone. In addition to which, what your daughter came upon by unfortunate happenstance should be of concern to no one."

"Love be damned, Billows! You impudent pup. I would be completely within my rights to dismount and whip you severely for your despicable actions. How dare you, after all I have done to improve you?"

"Come down from your horse, Master Abercorn, if you believe yourself that capable," Sarah challenged in a calm voice. "I for one believe you would be very sorry. Jed is bigger than you, younger and stronger."

"You would do well to shut your mouth, girl. You are in more trouble than I care to explain for your debauched ways, daring to show all of yourself to my innocent Rosemary without the least shame or inhibition."

"And you, Master Abercorn, should be careful of your words. We are not your slaves from before the war. We're free to do as we wish. I lay on your grass with Sarah this afternoon doing no harm to anyone, not in your bed, and not with your daughter. This is not your business."

"Not another word, boy. You are your father's son after all. Take my word. The man was no good, as bad as they come. My one consolation that pleases me greatly is that you have disclosed your true nature to me on the very day I intended for you to learn of a much brighter future, a much brighter future indeed. However, since this is how you choose to repay me for all I have done, I will not now send you to college at summer's end so that you might one day with hard work become a learned and respected gentleman of means, with my Rosemary one day as your wife. Instead you may consider yourself disowned and unwanted."

Jed snorted, his lips forming a wide grin. He put an arm around Sarah's waist, pulling her closer. "And how exactly will you do that, Abercorn, since I was never your property to begin with? You think too highly of yourselves, you and your daughter whom I never intended as my wife. That was her girlish fantasy, never mine."

"And my great folly to believe in hers and Mistress Abercorn's fond impressions of you, that you could possibly be better than the common boy I see here, which I correct now with equal pleasure." He leaned onto the saddle's horn for superior affect. "This very afternoon you are released from my service, free from your debt to find your way as a pauper into Hell with all other creatures of your dark ilk. This I do with the greatest joy for my daughter."

"In which case I will take Sarah with me, seven months earlier than planned. This I do for her."

"The devil you will. She's with me for seven more years, and that many months. Longer if your fornication produces a bastard for me to feed. That's what I agreed with her dead father. That's the law, legal and binding. Unless she has in her indecent mind to repay the debt in advance of that occasion by lifting her skirt as often as she may throughout each day henceforth in the fields."

Abercorn's arm about tore from its socket. He landed on the ground hard on his knees in a heartbeat, his shirt crumpled into Jed's fist, Jed's other fist crashing into his jaw with two solid blows as Sarah stood stunned and weeping.

"There won't be any bastard." Jed reached into a pocket, tossing the shapeless rubber by Abercorn's feet.

Abercorn gathered his wits, reaching for a stirrup, standing unsteadily, dusting himself while forcing a smirk. "If you're that keen to show me what you shoved into her, boy, why not yank up her skirt and show me the hole she gave you to plug? And the rest of her for that matter, since she seems not to mind what anyone sees of her."

Sarah reached out quickly, grabbing Jed's arm. "He's not worth your trouble, Jed."

"You're done, boy. Get yourself gone this instant. You'll wait at the gate for my manservant to bring your few things. Your week's pay is mine for the damage you've caused to my britches. As for her, I'll make her wicked inclinations known to her mother, to insist on the thrashing she properly deserves. And to all the others, to make certain she won't soon open her legs again to any of their hard-working husbands or gullible sons. You have as much time with her as it takes to stand at the gate for your bag. Not a minute more." He glared at Sarah, sneering. "He stands there alone. You will go to your home where you will wait for your mother and not dare to defy me. Nor will you for a moment think to run with him, not unless your dear mother should spend her final day bent over in the fields on your account."

"You'll see me again soon, Abercorn. When I come to buy her debt and her mother's. Treat her badly in the least way and I will not just bash in your face. You have my word."

They left him, holding hands, Sarah crying and kissing Jed as often as she could as they walked, Jed telling her to be ready an hour after dark and where they should meet.

Jed Billows left the plantation several minutes later, Abercorn watching from afar to make certain he did, Jed stopping as the plantation became a mere speck in the distance. Near ten in the evening Jed returned to the vast property in the moonlight to sit with Sarah who listened dolefully, nodding her head without speaking. He believed he had never seen her as lovely. The years would pass quickly, he promised, with such fond and vivid memories and their dreams to sustain them.

Her mother, shocked and dismayed by what she was hearing, did promise Abercorn she would appropriately discipline her daughter as he suggested for the wickedness of Sarah's shameless promiscuity, her lack of remorse and disrespect of him. The woman apologized profusely with tears in her eyes, crossing herself, kissing the cross that hung from her neck and begging Jesus to forgive the corrupt girl.

Instead, when he left them, she smiled, hugging her

daughter to comfort and console her, wiping the girl's tears. Seven years would pass quickly, she told Sarah. And if Jed was the good and decent man she believed him to be, he would love her daughter again under the stars before leaving her for as long as he must…the very way her dear husband once loved her one dark evening after being torn apart, leaving her alone for years that passed quickly, returning for her again in the dark and bringing her to America.

She patted her daughter's cheek, taking her by the hand into her small room. Sarah would be as pretty as possible for her last night with Jed.

*

May 31, 1895 was the midway point of a gilded era, a decade filled with merriment, gaiety and expectations for those who had suffered for so long, a decade that Jed Billows, twenty-five that very day, would give to Sarah as part of his first gift of elegant new clothes, a real home with doors, a bath and a gate wherever she wished to live, and him.

Seven years had passed. Spiting Abercorn, Jed had decided against Hell as a destination, instead travelling to New York where he did live as a pauper while saving enough money to buy what would remain of Sarah's debt at the earliest possible date. He found employment at the dockyard working nights, soon after proving his worth to a mentor who by chance took notice of him as he was begging a Clerk of Admissions at the university to make an exception in his case. Assuring the man he was smarter than most and should not be judged by the poor condition of his wardrobe. The man was a kindly professor who recognized in Jed something worthwhile, undertaking Jed's tutelage, making him ready for the arduous years of difficult work and study that lay ahead. When the day at long last arrived that he would return to Charleston, bringing Sarah and her mother with him into a much improved life, he was an astute young man of letters, impeccably dressed with a strong back, a stevedore's fists made hard as steel, and a memo of credit from his bank.

Arriving at the plantation on the back of the steed he had purchased a few days earlier in Charleston, where he outfitted himself with a new suit and shoes for the wedding and rented two rooms that Sarah's mother would share, he went directly to Sarah's humble cabin, skirting the mansion without much worry. However this was no occasion for a fashionable suit and laced shoes. Sarah had always called him her daring and bold hero, and that's what she would see: Jed Billows decked out in polished black boots, black cowhide britches, a billowy black shirt and a Drifter Stetson that cost him a full day's wage pulled at an angle over his brow, sitting high in the saddle with a gleaming Smith & Wesson showing from the black and well-oiled holster at his hip.

He called out her name through the open door, his breathing rapid, his skin moist and not from the heat of the day. After so many years apart he had no idea what he should expect beyond what he had never stopped feeling in his heart.

Throughout the entire week while in his private berth onboard the train, and in his room at the guesthouse, he practiced the first words he would utter. Until the very instant, with his boots firmly in his stirrups, his one hand resting on his thigh, the other clutching a diamond ring nestled in a silk lined velvet box, his free hand instinctively gripped the revolver.

The man at the door was Walt Guntrie, Abercorn's

worst field boss, a heartless man Jed remembered as dim-witted, malicious and mean-spirited.

"What's yer business here, sir? And what's the purpose of yer gun bein' so handy?"

"Sir? Now that's a switch, a word I never thought to hear for your foul mouth, Guntrie." Jed chuckled, admiring the revolver. "The thing has only one purpose I'm aware of, not that I have need of a gun for the likes of you, Guntrie. I believe leather gloves would be a more appropriate weapon against you. If not the best protection against you." The gun remained in his hand.

"We're acquainted, you and me? Are ya here causin' trouble?"

"We are acquainted, Guntrie. We are, from what I consider an agreeable distance since you appear unchanged in your low opinion of soap and water. My name is Jed Billows. And my business here is not your affair. Now, why are you in Sarah's cabin?"

Guntrie's dull eyes opened wide, stepping closer as though he did not believe what he was seeing. "Billows. Well, I'll be buggered. Yer not dead after all. More's the pity. The sharpest nail prickin' at the prunes in my rear, that's what ya were. Worse than horseshit on my boots, come to think. State yer business or bugger off. Ya hear?"

"Don't be as stupid as you appear. Where is Sarah, in what field is she working?"

Guntrie retreated a few steps to the door, crossing his arms, setting his boots wide apart, bracing himself. He was suddenly afraid. "She ain't to be found in any field, Billows. She's laid deep under it, buried less'n a year ago, not a week after her ma quit her own breathin'."

Jed stopped breathing, his heart stopped its beating, his mind too frantically racing to other times and places, to their love and his promises, to make sense of what Guntrie was saying. One part of him choosing not to believe the impossible words, the other guiding his thumb and finger to the revolver's hammer and trigger. The hammer's first and second clicks jolting him into the present where Guntrie stood grim-faced. Neither man was blinking.

"Sarah's dead? Is that what you're daring to tell me, Guntrie?"

"All of it Abercorn's doin'. I swears to God Almighty Hisself."

"Abercorn? Abercorn killed her?"

"As much as if he put a bullet in her head hisself."

"Which I take to mean that you did."

"No. Not me. I swears to God I didn't. It was Abercorn's doin', pure'n simple. Her bein' dead is on him."

"How did she die, Guntrie? And if you think to invent a story in that dimly lit head of yours, I'll make a hole in it to brighten your day." He waved the gun. "In detail, if you please. I need to know the full extent of why I'm killing a man...or two."

Guntrie was dripping new sweat into his already soaked singlet. "What with her ol' lady dead and buried, Abercorn figured the girl's debt was more'n she was worth, bein' he needed new bodies to work the fields. That's when he come here one night, plannin' on makin' sure she be good fer the debt. He stayed from dusk to dawn stickin' her good'n hard as best he could and as often. That's what he boasted. Suppose he was makin' the best of his time, makin' sure the seed would take right quick. Anyhow, next mornin', what I seen of her was all beat up and sorrowful. The girl was broke-down. Abercorn farin' no better, his face all scratched, tore at and bruised."

Jed sat straight, his body numb. "He raped her?"

"He's the master. He does what he pleases."

"Tell me the rest, how she came to die."

"Less'n a few days later. With the ol' lady dead he needed room fer the folks comin' in. He took my shack, givin' me this place and the girl to boot, on condition I took on whatever come from their evenin'. That's how come I know he stuck her so good, told me hisself she was worthwhile my movin' in. So I done just that. Just seems she had no inklin' I was comin'." He put up his hands as though believing he might somehow stop a bullet. "Billows, I swears. I didn't mean her no harm, thinkin' to speak my mind since we be livin' so close fer a good while. I went into her room, thinkin' to make my peace, not expectin' she be pissin' in her pot. Jumped higher'n jackrabbit. Prettiest thing I ever seen. Made me stiff as a gun barrel, me makin' the suggestion she give me a ride since we be livin' so close, bein' she was right then and there partway ready to take me full and hard. She was mine fair'n square for the keepin', Billows, from the master hisself. I was at my rights to take her and I know'd fer certain ya was dead."

Jed put the ring into his shirt pocket, taking the reins, not certain how the horse would react to a gunshot. "You raped the poor girl too, Guntrie?"

"No, I swears to God. She run out, Billows, quicker'n hellbent, headed straightway to the pantry, screamin' yer name loud as can be, like she was callin' ya for dinner, her nightshirt refusin' to fall straight. Seein' her bare backside made me a mite dazzled, Billows. I had no inklin' of what she was thinkin'." He inhaled and blew out a deep breath, cupping his stubble-spotted face in gruff hands. "The girl stabbed herself hard in the chest, Billows. Took the blade and run herself hard into the wall. Damn thing came out her back. Craziest awful thing I ever seen. Dead on her feet. Smilin' with 'em black eyes wide open."

"Excellent idea, Guntrie." Jed Billows would not weep for her, not then. Weeping would mar his thinking. Instead he shot Guntrie's left foot, spinning him against the wall in a hideous dance of flailing arms and legs. "Not much like a jackrabbit, Guntrie, but good enough I'll warrant." Another shot followed, to Guntrie's gut, knocking his legs from under him, crashing him onto the wooden floor.

"Stay where you are, Guntrie. We're not finished, you and I. First I have similar business with your master."

Guntrie gaped at the wound, unblinking, planting his hands on the floor as if he were afraid to touch his exposed bowels. "Bugger yerself, Billows, for what ya done." He tried laughing, coughing blood. He needed to die. "Truth be told, makin' my peace here with the Lord, took her twice on the floor while she still was nice'n warm. Her starin' at me with them big wide-open black eyes, her mouth wide open like she was havin' a good ol' time and screamin' her thanks."

"I suppose Abercorn can wait a moment longer. However, I need you, Guntrie, to appreciate the torment of Sarah's last days. For which reason I will not put one into your head or your eye. I require you to take a while longer. And have no worry, Guntrie. The piss I see drenching your britches will dry before anyone sees you. Or cares to touch you, anyway." Jed's next two shots shattered Guntrie's knees, staying with him a few minutes longer as though watching for Sarah to see through his eyes as he dislodged the spent casings from the barrel and reloaded.

Then Jed was gone, galloping toward the mansion, Guntrie writhing all too slowly into Hell like the repugnant creature that he was.

Very few minutes later Jed reined his horse to a canter as he neared Abercorn's mansion. Abercorn was sitting alone on the veranda with a refreshment and notebook in his hands. He put aside the drink and whatever he was reading, standing guardedly to greet the stranger.

"Good day to you, sir. Are you perchance lost? You seem to have entered my lands elsewhere than the front gate."

Jed let go the reins, relaxing. "I am not lost. Very much the contrary. I am here to see you Abercorn, which was my second and not my first purpose."

Abercorn took a long step closer. "Am I to believe that we have previously been introduced, you and I? From where I stand you are not remotely familiar to me, sir. Neither your person nor your insolent manner."

"I expect you should, and that I am very familiar to you. Until seven years ago from this very day when you wished to make me a gentleman and, upon my eventual return, a devoted husband to your most precious Rosemary. Those were your words before I dragged you from your mount and made alterations to your britches and puffed-up demeanor."

He tipped his hat to Abercorn, not intending any deference.

"Jed Billows!" Abercorn stumbled backwards. "What in damnation are you doing here? Leave here this instant."

"Guntrie asked the same question of me. You can imagine my intense curiosity at seeing him very much at home in Sarah's cabin. And now it appears we have urgent business, you and I, of a nature I was not for a moment anticipating." Jed sat straight with his hands at his hips, his face devoid of emotion, his eyes dark and foreboding. "I came here for Sarah, as I promised I would to you and to

154

her, having transformed myself into a different and improved person as you can well see. To my dismay discovering a mere fifteen minutes ago how truly different I have become." He rested a hand on the revolver. "I came to free Sarah, to pay you her seven remaining months and to marry her this coming weekend. Instead I have killed a man, as I am about to kill you. You must remember, Abercorn, my other promise to you should you mistreat Sarah."

"I did nothing to her. She killed herself, Billows. She wasn't right in the head. She never was, chasing like a harlot after you, a boy as close to her as any natural brother. That's what she was. And you were no better."

"You raped her. Often, and not for your personal greed. You violated her fully aware my hour was drawing near. You wanted my life entirely ruined by seeing Sarah as a mother by your sick deed or Guntrie's, who should by now be discussing terms with the devil. You should have realized I would be here killing him and you anyway." He drew the gun. "For that one vicious night, Abercorn, you have killed three persons. You included."

"You would not dare to kill me this way, with no gun in my hand to make things even between us. Or are you as much the indecent lout that you were when I sent you away?"

Jed smiled for the first time. "Yes, I am. For which reason, well beyond my control and by virtue of my coarse lineage, when you are dead, I will very much enjoy inflicting upon your daughter and upon your wife what you did to Sarah."

Abercorn's body lurched forward, stopped by a bullet in his leg. He faltered, crying out. "Wife! Rosemary! Run quickly to the fields! Your lives are in the greatest peril!"

"I cannot imagine, nor will I ever imagine, Abercorn, the terror in Sarah's mind the night you ravaged her kind soul and her young body. For that alone I would kill you a dozen times more, were I able. This, instead, is the one thing I can do for her at this late hour, for the terror she frantically drove from her heart with the blade, and for which reason Guntrie waits for you in Hell." He fired a shot into Abercorn's groin, waiting, pleased with the theatrical aftermath.

Abercorn's scream stuck in his throat. His eyes bulged, the impact of his body slamming into a wall hurling him onto the floorboards, copious blood spirting from the part of him most injured staining his britches and boots, his upper parts splattered from the force of the rupture. He could barely catch his breath. "You will hang for this, Billows," he cried.

"Not the same feeling, Abercorn, from what I perceive. You seem not the least bit aroused."

"By God my wife will see you hung for my murder."

Jed Billows leaned forward. "Not when I'm done with her, Abercorn." He fired a shot into Abercorn's other leg, sitting patiently. "Since you for no reason attacked Sarah not for the sake of a cot, but for the destruction of me as a man, drag yourself up Abercorn. Look around. No one is rushing to interfere with your deserved passing. No one cares. I suppose no one hurried to Sarah's door either, when she was screaming as you beat her. We're done here, you and I. Do you remember those words? I truly regret that I cannot do more for Sarah, that I do not have the luxury of the long hours you spent killing Sarah's sweet soul. However I can, for her, remove the hands that beat her and mauled her so savagely. That I can do while you still live." He fired twice more, mangling one bloodied hand, removing the other at the wrist.

Jed committed the scene to memory guiding his horse to the gate, wishing Abercorn a few moments longer, wanting his wife to forever share the same spectacle that, for her, would be a lifetime of deserved nightmares. And for Rosemary, of course, without whom all would be well.

Not a hundred feet from the veranda a shrill voice howled his name. An instant later came a gunshot, muted, barely audible, Jeddore Billows, an accomplished young scholar, slumping forward with no particular opinion regarding his murder. He had lived a good life, his last day on earth making his life meaningful. He loved Sarah, and she loved him. A thin smile emerged on his lips as a strange warmth and euphoria consumed him at seeing Sarah come closer as though floating on air. She was reaching out to him. His smile widened, taking her hand, content that he kept his promise to Abercorn who likely was not feeling as much peace and contentment as he.

Reining his horse into a tight turn, his one hand held high in the air, grasping, he saw the two women running as fast as their skirts would allow towards him. He felt no ill-will towards the widow Abercorn, Rosemary was the one who deserved a special place in Hell with her papa and Guntrie. He had lied to Abercorn, needing to make his dying more painful; he had no intention of harming the wife. Or her, the root of all the evil that had come to pass, the one running at him with a long gun gripped in her hands, her eyes wet and glaring, wildly screaming his name.

He would be damned for all eternity if he did not shoot first, for Sarah. He sat as straight as he could manage, slipping his hand from hers. Taking aim, both hands steady, his eyes were bright and his voice clear. Squeezing the trigger he spoke his last audible words of love to Sarah. They would forever be together.

Rosemary died that instant, the bullet snapping back her head, her feet flying high into the air from under her, her body twisting, crashing in a heap onto the dirt path. Widow Abercorn wailed loudly, dropping her gun. She fell to her knees, cradling her daughter, crying copious tears.

When her mind at last cleared, barely able to raise herself, using the long gun as a crutch, she struggled closer and spit at the earth where Jeddore Billows lay serenely at rest.

Chapter Ten
Marcus Simms & Rosemary Sandra

May 31, 1994 was a truly magnificent day, a marvellous and momentous day. Marcus Simms, midway into his twenty-fifth year, was marrying the love of his life, notwithstanding the black sky or the avalanching dark grey clouds, or the annoying rounds of thunder still ringing in his ears as he listened to the preacher's monotonous words that, by then, he had committed to memory. Or the malicious winds that minutes earlier threated to rip the umbrella from his hands as he somehow managed to successfully bound across an asphalt swamp of deep puddles, except for the last and the deepest that had drowned his patent leather slippers and socks and splashed unclean rainwater halfway up the pants of his thousand-dollar suit.

The day was indeed magnificent and beautiful, for her, because she was.

She was Rosemary Sandra Rothstone, mere weeks into her twenty-second year, nervous and exhilarated that the most glorious day of her entire existence had arrived. What did she care about a little rain? She was a stunning bride, despite her parents' disapproval of her white satin bustier and bolero, her short silk skirt and stilettos and, in particular, her mother's near fainting spell upon seeing that her daughter was not wearing stockings. She was her own woman and mere minutes from becoming a wife.

Marcus was a post-graduate student working in Communications as an Account Executive with an after-tax income well above the average for someone his age, which he viewed as a stepping stone. He wanted more. He was ambitious. He wanted a career. He wanted to be his own man and take her along for the ride.

Rosemary Sandra graduated the previous year with a Bachelor of Arts after her preppy secondary years in private schools, working as an unpaid intern at a fashion magazine owned by a Rothstone friend. She adored the theatre, museums, and concerts. She adored being seen. She adored him, Marcus, very certain that one day his dreams would naturally blend with hers of becoming a model. That was her destiny, not becoming a patron, or a curator, or a pianist wearing stuffy black gowns. That was her mother's world and a quarrel that quickly fermented into her second worst argument with her parents, the absolute worst concerning the man she was about to marry.

If not forgotten or forgiven, what mattered at the moment was that she was at the altar on her father's steady arm squeezing gently to calm his anxiety.

He patted her hand, mechanically, his mind otherwise occupied. The preacher's words didn't bloody well matter. Empty hyperbole from the male perspective, intended for the frailer female condition; for tearful mothers and envious sisters and eager daughters who never seemed to satiate their curious obsession for gathering to bear witness to others' scripted oaths of devotion and eternal love.

What in Christ's name was it with all womenfolk, he pondered while lamenting that at such a late hour he could not shake sense into her fanciful head? They perpetually asserted in superior tones that a man's brain resided in his pants from the earliest age; whereas theirs, from birth, devoid of the least logic, clearly kept their delicate hearts beating more than the flow of their heated blood. He loved his wife, he truly did, for he had diligently nurtured and tutored her for years. She was the beneficiary of his patience and loving attention, a benefit his daughter could not hope to long for. What was done was done. He could do no more than shut his mouth and forever hold his peace. She had a capricious mind and untamed will of her own that he had recently and rudely discovered to a much greater extent than he ever desired. Still, she had a warm and welcoming home whose doors would forever be open to her whenever the day would happen that the doomed marriage would fail.

She was born into a life of wealth and privilege, prestigious schooling and summer vacations spent travelling the world, the best restaurants and a credit card with no limit whose monthly statement he doubted she ever thought to review. He harboured no misgivings that his daughter was spoiled. She was spoiled, an indulgence he could well and should afford his only child. Her poor choice of a husband could not, however, and now by virtue of her reckless impetuosity she was cut off.

The marriage had as much chance of enduring as she would in a one-bedroom apartment with bus tickets in her purse since she could no longer enjoy the luxury of a Rothstone company vehicle or the credit card she had put into his open hand the evening before. She would forever be his daughter, and he cherished her, but he was stepping away from her, giving her to another. She was no longer his to care for, no longer his full responsibility; she was becoming another man's wife in spite of his worries, his pleas and his frequent remonstrations.

Roger Samuel Rothstone of the Charleston Rothstones, the Rothstone Bank and the Rothstone Assurance & Fidelity, was transferring his wife's constant and maternal concern for Rosemary Sandra to the Marcus Simms who categorically refused to call them mother and father, mom or dad. Adding fuel to the already inextinguishable fire, and their unwavering belief that he was very clearly excluding Rosemary Sandra from his selfish considerations, he adamantly refused their financial support as well as Roger Samuel's considered wisdom that Rothstone & Simms Consulting would without question be an excellent joint business venture with his backing and leadership.

They simply did not understand the irascible young man, his obstinacy giving rise to several heated debates and frustrations while at the family home for Sunday dinners which were becoming less frequent. Marcus wasn't into family traditions, he was marrying their daughter, not becoming an adopted son. He was an orphan; no big deal. He did not need another mommy and daddy. His own parents were still very much alive in his thoughts and his dreams.

Worse yet, which put an immediate end to Mrs. Rothstone's usual Sunday probe, neither did he intend adding branches to the Rothstone family tree or his own. He categorically did not want children, he told them very plainly. He saw no justifiable need, enumerating and substantiating a plethora of reasons for not adding to an already and inexcusable burgeoning population of unwanted and unnecessary kids merely for the sake of proving to the world that he did not shoot blanks.

In fact, whether he did or did not was irrelevant. Besides, how would he know, he queried them with a smirk, other than by Rosemary Sandra's continued childless condition since falling in love with him two years earlier? He had nothing to prove to anyone except her and, he continued to the horror of one future in-law and the ire of the other, thus far their daughter was very pleased with his manly aptitude in matters of the heart. As was he, completely, with her agile manifestations of love. They were unconditionally in love, and what they chose to do with that love was a personal and private matter and certainly no one else's concern. To which Rosemary Sandra smiled and patted his cheek, Mrs. RS excusing herself so that she might retire to her private study to die quietly of humiliation.

To his credit, and in deference to his future bride, he mentioned not a single word during this particular and short-lived topic of conversation that neither did Rosemary Sandra want children. The very thought terrified her. Her private resolution to him was that she had not maintained her exquisite body throughout her many years in order to ruin her achievement with blotches, jagged marks, and a torn vagina damaged beyond his future pleasure. Or worse, that she would never again wear her tiny bikinis because everyone would see that a surgeon's scalpel had made an incision that later festered into a terrible gash that left her terribly mutilated and repulsive.

She would never think to so thoughtlessly threaten their mutual and undying love.

*

One year later Southeast Consulting was a room with desk, a chair, a computer, and a young man with a dream working tirelessly day and night. Rosemary Sandra was an entry-level editor at the same fashion magazine editing ads that others had written and wearing designer clothes she was able to buy from clients at cost plus ten, their Sunday dinners with her mother and father diminishing to not much more than quarterly events.

Marcus was putting in sixteen-hour days, coming home to a sexy and adoring wife who never failed to greet him in baby dolls, or décolleté slips, or stilettos and panties. Nothing in their marriage had changed, nothing except their address: The home Rosemary Sandra could not live without and a mortgage that Marcus was fairly certain he could live without. Nevertheless he loved her, to the extent that, by means of a simple medical procedure, Rosemary Sandra would never again have to worry about her bikini line.

By 2000 Southeast Consultants was a suite located on the fifth floor of a downtown Charleston corporate complex, boasting three Account Executives, two Marketing Specialists, and a disarming young graduate from secretarial college whose name was Beverly Benton and who recognized at first glance that her boss' wife was a pampered little bitch. Rosemary Sandra, at the same fashion magazine, fuming over her debonair husband's most recent hire, was promoted from writing her own ads to editing full-length articles that others had written. Life was good. They had even taken their first vacation since their honeymoon: three gorgeous weeks in sunny Spain. Rosemary Sandra's favourite destination.

Life was treating them well, despite the increased frequency of his nights away and his occasional sullenness that Rosemary Sandra began noticing that year when he arrived home late the very day before Christmas. Making matters worse, for her, he began excluding himself from her parents' time-honoured New Year's Eve gala. Which she tried to understand. Southeast was growing steadily, each year more successful, as he had promised. As was she.

In fact Rosemary Sandra needed and wanted his frequent absences in order to accomplish her workload that increasingly included writing original copy.

Until Christmas Day a full decade earlier when he had come home late that very festive day to find her weeping by the unlit tree. Excuses about the weather and missed flights, his futile apologies, meant nothing; the subsequent hours spent with her parents a far worse punishment for Marcus than her tearful histrionics.

Roger Samuel, of course, demanded to know the matter. Marcus reminding him, as he did often, to butt out. Nevertheless he did for the briefest moment, managing the slightest glimmer of a smirk, consider that telling them the truth would certainly send the Rothstones into an irreversible tailspin at terminal velocity.

What was worse for a young woman in love, throughout the entire week that followed, as was becoming a year-end tradition, was that he hadn't once touched her or wanted her as would any healthy young man in love. Adding insult to injury, as if he had not sufficiently wounded her feelings, he left Rosemary Sandra early on the Sunday, the 30th, in order to arrive in Houston on the first of the New Year well-rested and prepared to sign with his largest client to-date. A contract which in fact he had negotiated and signed the previous week. Not the worst creative narrative he would ever invent for her. However, like all those that would follow in the years to come, requisite to his continued survival.

His response to her tears was detached, "What choice do I have, darling? None," he assured her, kissing her, holding her tightly, his mind elsewhere.

None whatsoever. Particularly since six days ago, dear Rosie, I rid the world of toxic waste. He was released two months ago at the end of a ten year minimum sentence, and he was gloating about it. He mercilessly killed an innocent and elderly woman in her home for the sake of what little she might have had when she happened to discover him. Ten years was not adequate retribution, not by any moral standard. What was, was his incredible expression as he literally struggled with his body, ripping the nails from his fingers as he tore at his flesh, whimpering, unable to cry out, pleading for some miracle that would turn four fleeting minutes into three, two or one. What I did not expect, what came to me as the greatest and most pleasant surprise, is that I did very well without the least remorse.

"They must be the unkindest people to expect that you should miss my parents' party and that I should not be with you on your birthday, sweetheart."

"My birthday, darling. Not yours. The first of January has never once in my entire life been important to me. Yours, however, is as important to me as the day I took you as my bride. I would never think to miss either of your most important occasions. As for New Year's, I do not see the point, and neither do you. A sad reminder of failed wishes and false hopes carried over from the previous year, when, for me, every day with you is new and exhilarating. Besides, darling, you hate those insufferable old-fogy parties."

"Which I must now endure alone. Thank you. Thank you very much, sweetheart." She sighed a deep breath. "Nevertheless, I do understand. I do."

"I hate leaving you." He stepped back, holding her hands, taking in every inch of her. "And your delicious body," which I cannot use for this single purpose. Because of him I need to find closure with another as pretty as you. I need a singular comfort and joy that I realized from the beginning you cannot bring to me. Nor should you, the sole and unselfish reason I have not touched you. The very reason I must find a suitable and willing companion for a single evening. "I do love you very much. I do," which forbids me using you, using your body to that end, which would forever ruin how I regard you each day.

"I know you do, which will make me all the more lonesome on your birthday. Thirty-eight, sweetheart. Promise me you won't miss anymore with me. You may not have many more at this rate."

His smile was warm. "I do promise you, darling, to the best of my current abilities and the compliance I owe to my future responsibilities," that she and others to come will be nothing more to me than exotic vehicles rented by me for the sole purpose of freeing my mind of the most terrible dreams. Because I *will* have more dreams. I must. I have come to realize my true work is not finished. Killing him was easy, as were the others. I felt myself infused with no regret whatsoever as he expired before my eyes. This is something I can do, for which I can never offer you my sincerest remorse.

She wiped her eyes. "Then kiss me and get out of here while I'm still…compliant, and stay here by myself to call you the most horrible names while I'm dressing to dance with old fogies at the party."

He did, stealing her breath before leaving her to find closure in the bed and the arms of a young woman he would force from his memory within hours because he would require others in his future who would willingly comfort him and bring him the joy of closure. Marcus no less aware that his darling Rosie would one day too soon, and by his doing, become disenchanted with him, and deceitful, if she hadn't already.

A belief or fear that proved real, her tears less convincing each year.
*

In fact that day arrived much later than he expected or wanted, arriving home January 02nd from his fifteenth closure, and yet another neglected New Year's, to a dinner table she had not set for his forty-sixth and belated birthday. So, yes, she most certainly had something going on the side.

Southeast Consulting was then located on the entire top floor of the same building, his staff having ballooned from six to twenty-four, their clientele growing more than twice that number, and Roger Samuel Rothstone had yet to be invited to lunch and a personal tour.

Rosemary Sandra, elevated to Chief Copywriter, was working longer hours than Marcus. Sunday dinners were a thing of the past, happily long gone from Marcus' perspective, Thanksgiving and Christmas remaining as the sole and compulsory familial events. A fact that did nothing to appease her father whose fervent expectation that his daughter would one day return to the family hearth had not diminished. Whereas Mrs. RS could not for the life of her comprehend why her headstrong daughter insisted on working such long and arduous hours for a company she had no stake in when all their friends' daughters were contentedly engaged in more praiseworthy charitable work and their social obligations which included raising devoted children.

"Darling, please do not exaggerate. Did I not explain to you very many years ago Rosie, that my birthday is absolutely *the* most insignificant day in my year? No different in my view from the scratches one would expect to see in any death row cell meant to count the days remaining in the unfortunate resident's destiny that he has no control over. In his favour, or hers, the final date comes as no surprise. Whereas we, much less fortunate, must hope for the best and expect the worst each year as our most terrible hour draws nearer."

She could not believe what she was hearing. "Wonderful, Marcus. Absolutely fucking fantastic." She never used his name, not unless she found herself in the severe grips of feminine discomfort which women everywhere believed should be shared with men everywhere as a generic and deserved penance, a curse in lieu of jabbing a pin into the eye of a voodoo doll or a husband. "Simply fucking wonderful. You're counting the days until I die."

"Of course I'm not. I'm counting the days since you first fulfilled my life. That is the most important day to me. Your birthday and our anniversary equally so, neither of which have I yet missed in twenty-three and twenty-one years, respectively. Or will I ever."

"You're right, sweetheart. Your precious little Beverly is exceptionally good at reminding you. Anyway, I bought you a watch, a Rolex. You need one that matches your wardrobe and reflects your success." She passed him the box. "Not that you deserve such a gift meant for a gentleman. You don't."

He beamed. "Darling, thank you." He tore at the wrapping. "Does it have a date function?"

"What! No!" She punched him. "Why, when you have absolutely no idea how to read a calendar? Besides, we're dying. Remember?"

He freed the stainless steel bracelet from the half-moon form. "Wow, darling. I love it." He strapped the Swiss piece to his wrist, waving his hand in a figure eight.

"You should. And you're buying me dinner. I made reservations and I won't be a cheap date."

"Nothing worthwhile ever is, darling." He was fixated on the watch. "Then dessert at home. I presume I have a cake to blow out."

"No, you do not have a cake to blow out. I was afraid of what I could have done with it. I hate the thought of wasting food, sweetheart, and what if I missed? Imagine the mess on the wall. The temptation was simply too great, Marcus."

He nodded, realizing he was in shit, not so much accepting defeat as regrouping. "Just as well. I'm not over the effects of your mother's delicious Christmas feast, darling."

She scrunched her face. "Don't push it. I am too angry with you to hear your bullshit." She went to the door, expecting him to follow, to help her with her coat. "And, Marcus, this is your last chance. The very last or I will begin thinking the absolute worst of you. I do love you, and I want to love you very much. Nevertheless, do not for a moment think I'm stupid about it. I am not my mother. You have as much chance of moulding me, or screwing around like my father with whores, as growing another cock after my lawyer cuts off the current little one."

"Well, darling, that's a weak threat at best. As a gentleman, I can assure you that I would bring about my own death before even thinking to intentionally hurt you."

"Be that as it may, and thank you, I will gladly give him the knife and watch as you wither in poverty." She put a fingertip to his lips. "Now take me to an expensive dinner and suck up to me throughout our entire evening. Do a good job and I might possibly forgive how terrible you are long enough for you to thank me properly for your extravagant gift."

Enough said. Know when to stop talking. Do not oversell. Do not talk yourself out of a job well-done. Know when to leave.

*

The sex was great later that evening. The sex was always great, Marcus never confusing his loving and the Rosemary Sandra he loved with his enablers. In the deepest recesses of his heart he wanted to reward the evil that men do on a more convenient schedule, but such an expectation was impossible. Thing is, Christmas *was* the most convenient. People were the most relaxed, the least observant and, it appeared, most paroles and releases happened in early fall allowing him ample opportunity to mount a proper campaign. What was he to do? Not to mention that New Year's was the best possible occasion to meet the women he required ,who, for whatever their particular reasons, were alone, lonely, and, if not desperate, hopeful of finding their ideal man.

Out of respect for Rosemary Sandra, however, he restricted his choice of companions to the most enchanting, the most refined. His belief being that, if you're going to be caught, be caught with the best. He never remained with them longer than one night and rarely part of a day when an early departure was made difficult or impossible by virtue of the woman's need to feel that she wasn't cheap, immoral, or a whore when they were, that screwing a complete stranger in her bed was not a bad thing. Marcus unwavering in his belief that, whether or not he was as much a convenience to them as they were to him, were they to understand the full dimension of their true purpose, they would forgive him.

However, the next January, arriving mid-afternoon on

171

the 01st from Denver, Rosemary Sandra was not at home to greet him. Nor was she answering her phone, nor did she the previous evening. Nor was she at her parents; neither was she the previous evening, which engendered a round of questioning he was not in any mood to undergo. He disconnected, went to the bar and poured a generous and celebratory Johnnie Walker Blue for his forty-seventh birthday.

Rosemary Sandra arrived home at ten that evening wearing a short and provocative dress that wasn't part of her wardrobe when he left her on the Monday. Her purse was a new Carolina Herrera, her long and lustrous raspberry blonde hair that he had always adored was cut short and swept to one side in some sort of a wispy, shaggy layer style. In a word, she was irresistible and, he harboured no doubt, exceedingly approachable.

"Sweetheart, you're home. How nice of you to drop by for your birthday," she said, her voice flat, standing her carry-on by the sofa.

"Denver was a great success, darling. Now come join me. Tell me about this elegant new look, and why you were not at your parents' last night. They're frantic, beside themselves." He nodded toward the suitcase. "And possibly why you're coming home from elsewhere with that."

"They are not frantic. They called me after you called them."

"And of course you answered."

"Of course I answered. Why wouldn't I?"

"You didn't take my call. You didn't think I would be terribly worried?"

"Why would I, *sweetheart*? You didn't take mine last night."

"I do apologize. That was rude and inconsiderate of me

given the evening. I believed you were at your parents' and in the best of care."

"I was in the best care, until I no longer cared and began enjoying myself."

"As you should. For my part, we were at dinner longer than expected. Then one thing led to another and I found myself trapped into a longer evening. When I was finally able to make my excuses I considered the hour too late to disturb you, thinking you would be asleep in bed after a demanding evening with RS and your mother. You gave me no reason to believe otherwise." He sipped his drink. "The dress is lovely, darling, very intoxicating. And your hair, very cute and sophisticated. May I suppose something new and exciting with which to ring in a new and wonderful year? And is there more for me to admire in that?"

"Something new and exciting for me and, yes, two outfits in that. One for yesterday and a gown much more intoxicating than this for the last night's party. That you won't see me in because it's festive formal wear." She tossed the purse onto the sofa, sauntering to the bar since he was making no effort. She poured two-fingers of straight Ultimat, raising her old-fashioned in a toast. "Happy forty-seventh, Marcus. I bought you a gift certificate."

Not good. Nothing about this was good. "But no cake, I see."

"I spent yesterday, last night and today with Wendy. We went shopping, then to a private gala hosted by another of her friends who invited us and arranged a suite for us at the same hotel where we spent today at the spa drinking Bloody Marys to forget that we're too soon into our forties."

"Wendy, the perpetual and self-winding bachelorette?"

"Yes, Marcus. Her. The Wendy with the body to die for. The one all the men drool over."

"So how was the party? Many guests?"

"Please do not be coy. Say what you mean, Marcus. Yes, many. Mostly couples, a few single men, a few single ladies, one single wife." She sipped her vodka. "That would be me." She gazed at the diamond on her finger. "We had a marvelous evening. We danced and we drank and, oh, yes, we each promised solemnly to attend next year's event." Her expression conveyed neither anger, nor frustration, not even disappointment. As though she didn't care. "And I do intend to keep the promise."

"Rosemary Sandra, I will do whatever I must to repair the damage. In fact, call Wendy tomorrow. Invite her and a friend to an evening of dinner and dancing. My treat. Please, let me do this."

"No. I won't. Right now Wendy holds you in the lowest possible esteem. It's a female thing."

"Rosie, what I do, everything I do, is for us. Everything." He leaned forward, clasping his hands for emphasis. Bad move. The body language thing. "Be patient with me. This year-end situation won't go on much longer. The firm is growing exponentially, to such an extent that I scarcely remember everyone's name, and very soon others will be doing this portion of my work for me. I promise you."

She crossed her legs and her arms. More importantly, to him, her crystal green eyes were scarcely blinking. He knew a lot about eyes.

"If you're interested, Marcus, you are invited. They are very nice people. I like them. Otherwise do not bother coming home on your next birthday or the day after. In fact do not ever come home because I will not be here. Not for you, not for us. If you're not with me at that party next year," she sipped her drink, twice, "well, then, you should just go fuck off." She flicked her diamond with her thumb. "Because, really, without this bauble on my finger last night, that used to mean something pretty special, I very much doubt I would be sitting here with you right now. So I guess early forties isn't that bad after all." She leaned forward, not uncrossing her legs or arms. "Do we understand each other, *sweetheart*?"

Chapter Eleven
Christmas Day

Marcus Simms was caught between a rock, which was the realization that his lifelong obsession with Rosemary Sandra was increasingly transmuting into a quiet and contemptuous familiarity, her once feverish love for him clearly waning, and a hard place that was his sixteen-year obsession with injecting lethal pentobarbital into the bodies of what his research indicated were the worst of humankind. Admittedly, a hard habit to kick.

Unlike Rosemary Sandra, he was born into a normal, middle-class family, attending normal schools with normal friends until his family was broken asunder at the moment of the fatal car crash that left eighteen-year-old Marcus Simms alone in the world. After which he attended normal schools and worked his way through university with additional help from his parents' life insurance policies. He was self-made. He owed nothing to anyone, including Roger Samuel, the obtrusive father-in-law for whom he had not the slightest respect. Nor was Mrs. RS held in any higher regard. He had no relatives he could clearly remember, since none were named in his parents' wills, he supposed, and understandably, given the human condition, none had seen fit to visit with and console an eighteen-year-old orphan at the funeral home. A social commentary

176

to which he attached no particular significance then or now, for, much like the father and mother he could scarcely recall, he preferred being alone. Friends were an effort, a social obligation that began with Rosemary Sandra. Until which time he was very much a loner with little in his past to dwell on.

He believed in working hard and, regardless of the familial rebuke, once believed that people were fundamentally decent and good. A belief that, through the initial years of Southeast Consulting, allowed him to hire those he felt good with based on a few simple questions and a handshake, now each recruit acquiesced in writing to criminal and personal background checks because he perforce came to discover a notable flaw in his philosophy: He was entirely and unconscionably dead wrong.

Since the inception of his personal crusade sixteen years earlier, he had discovered very much the inverse. He came to understand indisputably that most people, those he passed on streets or those he saw in restaurants or sitting with him in first-class, those he observed at the ocean or in parks having picnics with their children, were intrinsically capable of wrongdoing. That given the least opportunity most of them would commit or did commit the illegal, the morally wrong, the bad or indifferent. That was the true essence of mankind he had come to recognize. Putting any 100 of them randomly in a room would, without question, produce an ex-con, a killer or thief; a shoplifter and those too afraid to steal; cheating wives and cheating husbands; child molesters, deviant clerics, teachers and trainers; men who mistreat women, women who mistreat children; those who know and don't tell; those who leave their trash for others or jump red lights at three AM because no one is watching. All that and worse is the human condition.

Neither was he remotely blind to his particular evolution. As familiar as he was with the minds of deviants and criminals, he understood the true Marcus Simms equally well. He harboured no self-aggrandizing illusions, other than he had not yet failed. Nor did anyone appear to care. Not the cops, not the press. Not anyone, excepting those who might thank him from the confines of cold graves or from the less tormented minds of those left behind.

Either way, the damage he caused in Rosemary Sandra's mind was never repaired. She went to bed without him, without any semblance of cutesy forgiveness and subsequent heated passion that she allowed him all those earlier years.

Marcus slept on the sofa in his home office, when he eventually drifted into oblivion, a decanter of JW Blue too readily within reach. He spent what remained of the night and into the early hours not so much imagining the future, for he saw the future in detail, which he failed to remember one year later when he arrived home again on Christmas Day.

*

Throughout the spring and summer they were civil towards each other, comfortable together. They increasingly discovered new restaurants for dinner the nights he was at home, talking of vacations that would serve as distractions and not at all as romantic escapades, her job and his, all in the company of strangers. They no longer held hands, or played footsy or even more daring intimacies in dark corners under a table setting that they, previously, long ago, would have rushed home to conclude. Or bought each other small gifts for no particular occasion. Those whimsically capricious days were a bygone era, faded memories.

In particular, and for good reason, Rosemary Sandra

made no other mention of the year-end gala with Wendy that was suddenly upon them. More notably, to her, neither had he. Nor had he bought a new tux, or rented a limo, or made reservations at the hotel. Whereas she did, for herself. A suite adjoining Wendy's that she would likely not pay for, and for him a room across town in a four-star, clearly intended as a statement, where she had transferred the bulk of his wardrobe.

That he was not at home Christmas Eve told her what she needed to do. She didn't care about reasons sheepishly texted from some executive airport lounge while he sat sipping expensive scotch and she was home alone working herself into a state, wondering why she had not slept with Dominic Drake on their third date when she very much wanted to.

She was forty-four and wasting her life with him. Her second order of business was to call Wendy who already had a date for the gala, to confirm.

Yes, Dominic was still very eager to escort her, Wendy scolded. What was she waiting for? He hadn't stopped phoning Wendy to talk and carry on about the ultra-fantastic Rosemary Sandra since their recent first, second and third dinners together in as many weeks. What did she know? What wasn't she telling him? Would Rosemary Sandra attend with him, wouldn't she?

"Rosie...hello? Something I'm missing here?" Then more uncertainty. Then: "No, Miss Rosie Rothstone, I will not call him for you. No way. Do your own dirty work. The man's pathetic about you. He's dying. So either kill him outright or do something to resuscitate him. Anyway, bye-bye, sweetheart. Love and kisses, and you make damn sure you call me back."

Wendy disconnected. She desperately needed a drink.

Girlfriends, especially attractive girlfriends, were such a huge pain in the ass.

Moments later so did Rosemary Sandra require a drink, a double as she saved her fourth date with Dominic Drake to her personal calendar, a schoolgirl prelude to the next sixty minutes. A new beginning after twenty-one years and her favourite girlfriend could wait.

*

Marcus Simms arrived home early Christmas morning, very early and very exhausted, prepared in his mind and his body for the absolute worst marital shitstorm. He had crossed the line. He had gone too far, not certain what he should expect: a stab wound somewhere on his person, a missing appendage, or a colourful tirade of unladylike expletives. Until he saw the note stuck between the door and its frame, choosing at first to ignore the temptation. She was giving him fair warning, in writing. He understood. He did. He was in dirty water to his neck and sinking deeper. He reached for his cell, scripting sweet words in his mind that he would convey with his most charming voice. Or not. No. Not smart. He returned the phone to his pocket.

Putting his ear to the door he heard no sound whatsoever, not the faintest. No music, no carols. Complete silence. And from the window he saw the Christmas tree, his tree, standing unlit and abandoned with not a single colourfully wrapped box on the floor. He crossed his arms against the ledge and dropped his head. He wasn't in dirty water to his neck. No. He was upside down in the wettest shit possible and he was drowning.

Again at the door he tried the lock in vain, giving up with a string of unseemly curses before realizing as he reached for the envelope that he must certainly be entertaining a few of their self-righteous Baptist neighbours. Or so they pretended. Screw them. He was first and foremost a Southern gentleman in the heart of upscale and gracious Charleston, South Carolina where decorum and discretion continued ranking highly in an otherwise rude world and he would most convincingly act the part expected of him. Whatever she had written, whatever scathing words she had chosen with which to punish and rebuke him, to make him feel worse than he did, he would not yell or scream or attempt to dislocate his shoulder against the solid oak door for the benefit of others.

Instead, for whomever, he lit a cigarette, leaned against the frame with his legs crossed at the ankles, and read the preface to his forthcoming obituary.
*

December 23rd,

Happy Birthday, Marcus, a week early and not a day late for once.

This is your gift from me, a new lock and entry code. Your newest and temporary address, until you find a more suitable home, is at the Marion on King. You are reserved for one month, paid in full for a week in advance on your account. I trust you approve of my choice. I also took the liberty of transferring the better part of your wardrobe to the hotel. The concierge was extremely gracious in assisting me. As for your summer collection, your lawyer may contact mine at his earliest convenience once you are settled more permanently. His information is on the desk in your new accommodations.

For the next week or longer I shall be staying with Wendy who, I remind you, lives in a building with a doorman and security personnel. She will not pick-up to you, or speak with you. Nor will my secretary. I have also changed my personal number. So please do not cause either of us undue awkward moments. This is either a fait accompli or a remedy in progress. I have no idea. This is on you, Marcus, from whom I justly deserve a lengthy respite.

My parents are aware, obviously, immeasurably pleased as you can imagine. Consider yourself forewarned.

In closing, as New Year's approaches, neither of us should feel constrained by any marital obligation. I intend this separation to be of long duration and, at its conclusion, decisive. You should not anticipate any sort of reconciliation, wishful dinners or recognition from me throughout the coming year. I require that reasonable interval for what my attorney calls 'discovery'.

I suggest we meet here on the first of next year for cocktails at four. Please do not expect a gift.

Should you disagree, you are at liberty to file against me when the mood suits you. I will not contest. Neither will I shrink from what is rightfully mine.

Happy New Year, Marcus,

Rosemary Sandra

*

Discovery? Did she really think so? Really? If she could for a mere instant conceive of what she could possibly discover of him, her brain would implode. She had no idea, and apparently no intimate familiarity with understatement. He wasn't angry, he wasn't upset. How could he be?

On the one hand he was an astute businessman who did or could still love his wife very much, which she was making somewhat challenging. That was on her, and running into someone else's arms, shutting him out to prove to herself that she was still a marketable female, was not for him to resolve. On the other he was an accomplished assassin who occasionally required external sources of physical and emotional release that were beyond his wife's ability to accommodate. That was business, not love; that he did for her.

She had made very clear that she intended to make herself available to men, to put herself out there. If she had not already bitten into the bitter-sweet fruit of adultery. Why not? Fair was fair. He coughed a laugh. Where had he heard that line before?

He was her first, or so he once chose to believe in part. Still, no man alive could ever rely completely on that possible or shallow truth. However, allowing that she was, or could be, she most assuredly had some catching up to do. He was somewhat ahead of her in the ratings, whatever his reasons or hers. That she would give her body to one or many didn't matter, not pragmatically, and not to him. Not as long as she realized that one would contaminate the female mind with heated promises and fantasies, as would the many others willingly and without ardour pollute her body for the sake of recapturing the urgency of her youth.

Truth be told, he didn't really care. Bodies, male or female, his or hers, were rental vehicles at best and never the property of the driver. So she got the itch ten or fifteen years later than any husband might expect. Good for her. He would give her the year and the next day engage a broker to locate a suitable pied-à-terre by month's end.

He had booked an early flight to Detroit for the following Monday, the 30th, expecting to give Rosemary Sandra his company for the week. Now he wouldn't. He had no need, nor did she. She had given him the proverbial finger instead. He would fly in the next day, after the broker. He would give himself a week to find a suitable companion for New Year's and his birthday, when and where he would evict her and Walter Guntrie from his mind amidst his comfort and joy.

183

Chapter Twelve
Marcus Simms & Patricia-Louise

Sitting on his favourite barstool at Frankie's, his favourite since the previous evening, he pondered how the next day would evolve. Who would be with him to celebrate his forty-sixth birthday? Whoever she was, wherever she was at the moment, no different from the many others, she would be his most cherished birthday gift.

He wondered why Northern cities had higher crime rates than cities in the South. Culture was certainly the primary distinction. No one would question the South being the nation's stronghold of charm, gentility, laid-back decorum and politesse in an increasingly ill-mannered era of indifference. Conversely, nor could any reasonably thoughtful person possibly refute how the North's dark winters and frigid bitterness reflected the icy personalities and chary temperaments of its time-sensitive and harried inhabitants. They were a different and unenviable breed, constantly rushing, never arriving. Which, for Marcus Simms, was a good thing.

Possibly the weather, possibly their Southern Belles who were decidedly more feminine and ladylike, definitely more alluring than their northern facsimiles whose menfolk appeared not to mind their women parading in public wearing flimsy muumuus the size of small tents. Worse, how often had he wondered whether what he was seeing was a male or a female? Not that he cared. The question was rhetorical, because if one had to ask...In any event, those women never being attracted to him was clearly a non-issue. Still, the flow of attractive women in Detroit was a mere trickle compared to the South's natural and uncontained resource.

Detroit was a get-in-get-out city devoid of glamour and sophistication. What was sensual in other metropolises like Miami, Charleston and New Orleans, here was too often tactless and lewd. As a people they lacked finesse and the sensitivity of diplomacy. Their idea of sophistication was women flaunting their overweight or shapeless bodies in skirts too short and blouses too tight. The men no better, proudly sporting shorts and sweats as though making a statement, as though someone should ask them 'who' they were wearing when they were wearing shit.

The real wonder was why any woman, especially the rare good-looking ones, would choose being alone on New Year's Eve: The last day of the midway point in his life, since his fervent wish was to endure into nineties. Who was Rosemary Sandra with, he wondered? Not her parents, not with someone new. Old man Rothstone would hemorrhage. Or were men becoming redundant, no longer needed for their specific service when a syringe in a lab would do the same job equally well? Could be she was with wet and wonderful Wendy, inherently dripping with sensuality. What would that be like for a night? Incredibly hot, he knew, letting his mind drift. The idea of getting her naked was intriguing, picturing her naked a matter of recollection and not fanciful dreams, since whenever summer temperatures would soar she and her Rio cut bikini would be first into the pool with Rosemary Sandra for a late-night dip.

She was a quintessential tease, forever tugging the wet bottom from her ass, then up, down, sideways, adjusting the side-ties for no apparent reason, always adjusting her top when she could as easily jump in naked and keep the Rio dry. Wasting her energies when she wouldn't hesitate to cut off his balls. Or was that the ploy? Get him naked and cut off his balls. Women were tribal, piss off one, piss off the tribe and Rosemary Sandra was pissed. She had been for a while, letting things fester.

He coughed a laugh, bringing the snifter to his lips. Or could be she was being a tease for Rosemary Sandra, which wouldn't surprise or disappoint him. She was at the house often enough when he was out of town, which gave him pause to wonder whether the heat index was registering hotter inside the house than out. They were night and day, opposites attracting: The haughty and the hottie. Strange bedfellows, not to say he wouldn't rent the video.

Wendy was a once-in-a-while passing thought, Detroit wasn't. Detroit was difficult. He did not like the place, often flying in and out the same day. This visit, however, was different. His meeting the previous week with Guntrie was the first of its kind for him in Detroit, his darker side wishing he had remained in town throughout the week to reconnoitre the best night spots, the best source of applicable women. The ghost of this Christmas past was the most insidious to-date, Beverly Benton going as far as to ask him why he even bothered.

Frankie's was subdued and high-end, highly recommended the by concierge at his hotel. Valet parking, not a bus stop. Sophisticated, not a pick-up joint. Suits and ties, not tee-shirts and caps. Silk dresses with a guarantee of more silk later that evening, not jeans and washed-out cotton. Sophistication. He didn't need or want the imprints of rings on slender fingers. He didn't need or want someone who was coming in hoping to meet him, or someone pissed with her boyfriend; he didn't need someone's husband walking in on them.

The banquettes lining two walls were occupied. Some were finishing their drinks, office workers going home early, mostly average women experimenting with the good life. Nicely dressed, not fashionable. Others were beginning their drinks, mostly men, mid-thirties, sitting in pairs and, judging by their grimaces and nodding heads, planning a decisive advance into greener pastures that would end in defeat when cheaper booze elsewhere and women better suited to cheaper booze would have levelled the playing field. They were out of their element.

The rest were checking their watches, playing table piano, staring at the entrance and waiting. The scattered low-rise lounge seating, set in twos, was the domain of men. Single or in pairs didn't matter. Well-dressed or not didn't matter. Any lone and attractive female daring to venture into their space would become a target, tantamount to walking through the doors in her silky lingerie.

Frankie's was a classy restaurant-bar, the restaurant fully booked for the evening since early November. Fortunately for Marcus the maître'd had agreed with his proposal the previous evening that such an elegant establishment warranted an additional table, in a corner, Marcus feeling compelled to acknowledge the man's amenability with two crisp 100-dollar bills.

His watch showed 6:30. He had no preconceived notions. He never did. After all, what was a birthday gift if not a complete and wonderful surprise?

The bar itself had one other guy sitting at the far end,

thinking, dreaming, regretting his life. Whatever he was doing he was not happy. He was at the wrong end of fiftyish and chubby, his windblown hair detracting from his otherwise neat appearance. Not into detail. He was a whisky drinker on his second since Marcus had come in fifteen minutes earlier, signalling for another. Maybe his wife had died, or left him, mournful over one or celebrating the other at twelve bucks a pop plus tip and tax. Or perhaps he was formulating how best to tell her he was out of a job while spending money he no longer had. Whatever the situation, he was doing Marcus a supreme service. Between them was an empty space dotted with eighteen high-back stools, no less dangerous to a woman alone than the man-space.

She came in at 6:50, pretty much when he expected her, and not much in the lounge's demographics had changed. She wasn't drop-dead gorgeous or primped for the kill beyond the norm for the festive evening. She was lovely, gliding as much as walking into the lounge. Not smiling, not sad either; her eyes bright and sparkling. She was okay with being alone, Marcus hoping that she was, eager to unwrap his gift.

She scanned the booths, glancing past the men staring at her, assessing her, stripping her naked, calculating their chances, wondering how much more their evening would cost and how the evening would end. Carnal ROI, the ever-important male-female return on investment. She scanned the bar, seeing the unemployed jilted husband cum widower, the empty space and Marcus. Sort of a no-brainer. She was alone. No gentleman worthy of the designation would ever allow such a lovely woman to enter a lounge unescorted.

He put her at thirty-three, four, his height in heels, 5'9"

without. She was confident without being obnoxious, successful without being self-important. She was all red. Everything about her was red. Her hair, a natural deep-cerise, swept to one side in long, wide curls; her earrings and pendant, a deep ruby, simple and exquisite; her lip-gloss, a shimmering crimson; her silk and satin cocktail dress, nicely short and flared in a muted claret, a stunning complement to her patent leather pumps and satin clutch. A simple silk scarf, a deeper tone than her dress, loosely adorned her shoulders.

She would not take a middle stool: Too 'Buy me a drink' obvious to any of the hopefuls in the man-space. Nor would she sit beside him for the same reason; he guessed more like three, possibly four stools away. Close enough to appear mildly suggestive, distant enough to maintain a barrier, Marcus remaining undaunted as she laid her clutch on the bar at the fifth stool.

The stylish swivel seats and backs were soft leather atop heavy stainless-steel bases, clumsy for anyone to move. Near impossible for a lady in a cocktail dress. Not acknowledging her would be absurd, ill-mannered in the extreme and the rightful cause of her immediate disdain for him.

She saw him slide from his stool, coming towards her with no particular expression she could determine. He was not going to buy her a drink, that wasn't the look; he was not going to sit beside her or hit on her. She stepped aside.

"If I may, miss, these things are incredibly awkward." He repositioned the stool effortlessly into a more accessible position.

"Thank you, sir. You're very kind."

Marcus casually extended a hand. "May I be of further service, they are somewhat precarious for first-timers."

She accepted his hand, stepping onto the brass bar bolted to the floor, gripping the edge of the bar for balance. "Thank you again."

He tilted his head, allowing a thin smile before returning to his seat.

The bargirl let her do whatever women do in their purses whenever they take a seat, Marcus correctly assuming the oohing and aahing phase would come next. Ooh, I adore your dress. Ooh, your purse. Ooh, I love your earrings. Ooh, ooh, taking the woman's order for a Johnnie Walker Black, chilled. Stepping in front of Marcus she noted another JW Blue with a curious smirk.

Her purse was an instrument, a distraction, something to play with while debating whether to look his way, to smile at him, to say something unrelated to the weather, until she had a drink to stare into. Whereas Marcus already had a drink.

"Thank you," she told the bargirl.

"Thank you, miss," he said a moment later, putting aside his swizzle stick.

One, two, three...fifty-nine, sixty. She glanced his way. "Johnnie Walker Blue, nice." She waited, sipping her Black.

He was genuinely surprised, taking a moment before realizing she was talking to him. "Oh, I'm terribly sorry, miss. Excuse my rudeness. I was somewhere else for a moment." He raised his snifter, swirling the liquid. "A rare treat. I don't get out very often, a sad casualty of the 'all work and no play' syndrome. When I do manage the occasional escape, I do my utmost to make the evening memorable."

She was happy, relieved. Her eyes were happy, the ice was broken and she hadn't fallen through.

191

"I didn't mean to interrupt you, my name's Patricia-Louise. Thank you again for helping me."

"My greatest pleasure, Miss Patricia-Louise. What a truly alluring name. I'm very pleased to make your acquaintance. My name is Marcus Simms."

"By 'Miss', and your charming accent, should I presume somewhere in the Carolinas?"

"Charleston, though not for several years. I live here, the Grosse Pointe Shores area. The accent, for some inexplicable reason, refuses to leave me."

"Waiting for friends?"

He shook his head 'no'. "Waiting for my table. I'm reserved for eight. And you, if I may enquire?" *And what exactly are you wearing under your dress, Patricia-Louise?*

Any chance you're dining alone? "New in town. Very new. A job transfer, sort of a new beginning. Temporarily I'm in Woodhaven. It's a bit of a commute and, not being sure about Michigan weather, I booked a suite for a few days across the street. Sort of a one-girl spa and shopping weekend." *Because no one asked me out.*

"I can't imagine you left them much to do beyond pampering you." *I really must undress you, Patricia-Louise, and make love to you.*

She smiled. "I absolutely loathe office parties any night of the year, especially New Year's." She palmed her thighs. "Anyway, it's been hectic. I wanted some down time, I spent a fortune on this outfit and had no intention of spending New Year's unpacking boxes, sitting alone, or in a hotel suite eating take-out pizza or room-service." She grimaced. "I hate hotel food."

Nor will you. "There's none worse, absolutely unworthy of a discerning palate."

"I had a late lunch."

"By yourself, which is a deplorable state of affairs."

She giggled. "I'm dealing with it."

"But Patricia-Louise, no husband, no attachment? One must assume you work and live amongst the most insentient of men, all of them lifeless in mind and body."

Okay, this is about when you should be asking me to sit closer. "Nobody. Not yet and no hurry. I'm a financial analyst surrounded by stuffed shirts and balding men, suck-ups, geeks, and bitchy women. Not a prime hunting ground, and I don't do the club thing. Too many freaks, and I don't want a man who loves God more than he'll love me." Please don't be a freak.

"Hmm," he paused, pursing his lips, furrowing his brow, "which makes me hesitant to suggest that we close this wide gap between us before some thoughtless individual comes to separate me from an enviably beautiful woman." A very delectable woman.

She chuckled, the sound soft and musical. "Perhaps I should transfer to Charleston. I can see that working."

She reached for her clutch, sliding from her stool as Marcus stepped from his extending his hand. Discreetly admiring her body was expected; not doing so, appearing too courteous, would make her question his ulterior motives. He helped her onto her seat, not releasing his gentle grip until she was settled, every set of eyes in the man-space conveying the same message.

He signalled the bargirl.

"I would say your ensemble is stunning, Patricia-Louise. The truth is, you are stunning in it. Absolutely ravishing." He grinned. "I cannot for a moment picture you in spectacles punching numbers into an adding machine."

"You mean with my hair in a bun and a pencil tucked into my ear? That's right, you can't." The bargirl came with her tray. She was happy for them, for Patricia-Louise. A girl thing, a tribal thing. Patricia-Louise raised her old-fashioned. "So Marcus, what should we toast, a new and wonderful year, more money," she paused, sipping, "a life?" Or maybe a pleasant evening together, two strangers crying over a crappy year? I'll buy the wine, the really good stuff.

No, to my birthday. "To a lovely lady in red agreeing to join me for dinner. I cannot possibly consider leaving you here alone and vulnerable. The thought is too repugnant and painful. My meal and my evening would be completely ruined."

"We can't have that, can we?" She glanced at her pink gold Cartier: 7:30. "That would be nice, Marcus. Thank you. On the condition we split the bill. I'll do the wine. That's my thing."

"That condition is unworkable in the extreme. I would be viewed as a cheapskate by everyone, and rightfully so." He pondered the dilemma a moment or two, beaming. His solution was brilliant. "I believe a more feasible strategy would be for you to invite me to a luncheon tomorrow, if you agree, and with the pre-condition that I give you no cause to change your mind this evening."

They shook hands.

*

Walter Guntrie was sentenced in 1986 at age twenty to a minimum of twenty-five years without parole for the double murder in Boston of a newlywed couple, their home-invasion, and the rape of the twenty-seven-year-old woman. He was a druggie, probably still was, looking for easy cash or things that others would buy or fence for pennies on the dollar.

He had a gun, a big one, a .357; the husband, twenty-eight, had an attractive young wife and he died standing in Guntrie's way. When he was finished with the girl, he killed her, looted the home at his leisure and left. He was apprehended the next day. He already had an arm-long record, sticking around too long after the killings, rummaging through drawers, closets, clothes and the car. All with his hands bare, drinking beer with his hands bare from bottles he'd left in every room before hurrying in their car to use their ATM cards to the fullest at *his* bank where he usually went on the first of each month to cash his government cheque.

He served twenty-nine, released in late September. Not for good-behavior, rather for lack of space. The nation was suffering from lack of proper housing for the worst criminals because too many of their white-collar counterparts were doing easy time and taking up needed space instead of forfeiting their homes, yachts, cars, investments and bank accounts. Those were the smart guys, the big guys, most of them fully functioning while incarcerated. The likes of Guntrie were not. They were, are, always will be the worst of society. Unrepentant. Underserving of second chances.

He currently worked in a 24/7 fast-food corner diner for minimum wage, spending his afternoons and day off panhandling in the downtown core, Marcus suspected, to improve his standard of living.

His shift was 10:00 PM to six AM, probably for an extra few bills in his pay envelope each week to offset the mind-numbing boredom of feeding hookers, addicts, cops, and various other bottom-feeders. His fridge was bare. Something about ex-cons that they couldn't or wouldn't cook meals. He had coffee and powdered milk, cheap

195

whisky and cheaper gin. Not a single slice of bread, or a dollop of butter because on his day off he ordered-in or brought home take-out.

He wasn't fancy when he wasn't flipping burgers, not the Beau Brummel of post-prison fashion: Two pairs of baggy blue jeans, scuffed work boots, soiled tee-shirts and two well-worn jean jackets in prison grey that he had saved on by unstitching his inmate tag to create a new look.

He had a clock radio because cons need direction, told when to stand-up, lie-down, eat and take a shower. Like the military until, eventually, that part of the brain withers into disuse causing untold and invisible traumas. He had a calendar, twelve young, coquettish and naked girls all frequently visited ahead of their due date. And a switchblade under his pillow to ensure he would be alive to hear the clock's piercing shrill. Old habits die hard, as would Walter Guntrie. However the timing was not ideal.

Guntrie lived in a spartan one-room flat reminiscent of his cell that took 'minimalist' to a whole new level, that he could walk into any time after seven. To that extent he wasn't predictable. Not that Marcus Simms was fraught with worry. He wasn't. He was more concerned about the weather. Guntrie was no threat, even if he did have the switchblade within reach. He was shorter than Marcus by a few inches, with an average build he hadn't worked on with any remarkable intensity over the years. Whereas, with fourteen previous encounters, Marcus was adept at this sort of confrontation. He knew what to anticipate, how to react. Guntrie didn't carry a gun; Marcus did, with a dart that would immobilize any man in a breath or two.

For that reason Marcus decided on a different tactic. The scribbling on Guntrie's calendar showed that he wasn't working Christmas Eve night. Instead he was pulling double shifts on the 25th and 26th. More money, better living. More importantly he had no food in his apartment. At some point he would bring food in or call out for something, Marcus hoping for the latter with a firm back-up plan if need be. Either way, Marcus was ready in his jeans that he had slept in for affect, boots that he had let soak overnight in saltwater, a wrinkled hoodie and gloves that he had soaked and twisted and let dry out of shape. He had two days' growth of beard that he darkened with a drugstore colorant and hadn't washed his hair in as many days. He looked the part. He was satisfied with himself, if not with the weather.

Were a single negative to exist within the framework of a Southern gentleman's repertoire of capabilities, it would be his unequivocal inability to manoeuvre any vehicle in the midst of a shitstorm of snow. The day was furious with high winds whirling snow, sleet and ice pellets in every direction. For which reason Marcus would not drive. He exited his hotel through the garage after storing his cashmere coat in the trunk of his rental, allowing himself extra time. A block later he hailed a cab, straightaway tipping the guy a hundred to curtail needless debate.

He would not risk arriving late, or not arriving at all. Or worse, not departing on schedule from his meeting. Hope for the best, plan for the worst. He had verified several times over the past few days that many entry doors of the tenements opposite Guntrie's were left unlocked. Why bother, he mused, when most of the tenants in them were the ones doing the stealing? And that's where he stood waiting, his view unobstructed. No one choosing to bother or question him.

Guntrie came running to his apartment steps at nine-thirty, slipping and sliding with empty hands. Traffic was a mess. That was a good thing. The bad, which came with a possible blessing, was that Marcus would have to wait for Guntrie's hunger pangs to set in. The blessing was that Guntrie had two nearly-full bottles and he was a reliable drunk.

The delivery boy came at three, the fifth or sixth kid since noon. Marcus greeting each one, disappointed. Until then. With this one he was good to go, bolting across the street waving his arms. Good timing, he told the kid, just getting stuff from the car.

"You're here for Guntrie, kid? Right? Apartment 212?"

"You him?"

"Yeah, I'm him? What's the damage?"

"Twenty even, plus tip. Took a fuckin' hour gettin' here, man. Know what I mean?"

"How about an even fifty, because you're a nice kid." Marcus passed him the bill, leaning in, towering over the kid. "Ever talk to me like that again, I'll smash your fucking nose into your empty head."

The fifty trumped teenage bullshit bravado. The kid left, Marcus watching as he drove off, snorting when the kid flipped him the bird. A future inmate, guaranteed. Attitude like that never transmuted into decency and respect. When the kid disappeared Marcus climbed the outer steps avoiding the rusted wrought iron railings.

Despite the ruined condition of his new gloves Marcus was not touching the buzzer panel for fear of electrocuting himself. Who would when the door was open? He climbed the stairs matter-of-factly, as he would from the basement to the main level of his luxury home the blonde bitch was threatening to close on him. So who was sleeping in his frigging bed when he was gone, if not Wendy? What kind of man would do that and not sleep with one eye open?

Two-twelve was midway down the dark hallway, two bare bulbs and narrow frosted windows at each end lighting his way.

He knocked twice. "Pizza. Pizza delivery for Guntrie."

The door opened wide. "Fuckin' about time. How much?"

"Twenty even, plus tip. Took a fuckin' hour gettin' here, man. Know what I mean?"

Guntrie grabbed the pizza, dropping it onto the floor, digging into unwashed jeans for a loose wad of crumpled bills, counting out a ten and two fives with hands that looked as though he'd been flipping his burgers without a spatula. "Twenty."

"What, no tip? Seriously?"

Guntrie waved the money. "Fuck your tip."

Marcus shrugged, bypassing the bills, ramming a gloved fist hard into Guntrie's nose, stepping into the familiar room with the gun drawn. He closed the door, three months of anticipation and planning coming to an end.

"Mr. Guntrie, please do not get up. Crawl as you are to the far wall."

Guntrie didn't seem worried. "What is this bullshit?"

"Retribution on behalf of four grieving parents." The furrowed brow caused him to think for a moment. "I do apologize. We take too many things for granted, we of a more civilized society. That means payback, getting justice, Guntrie. You know, for you killing their children."

"Get real. That was thirty-years ago, if they ain't all dead and buried they're damn close to it."

"Twenty-nine years, three months and counting, and not anywhere near as close to being buried as you are. Though I presume they'll incinerate you. In fact, all four are very much alive and lucid enough to rejoice at the forthcoming news of your deserved and creative passing." He snickered. "So let's forget the counting part, shall we? You're cooked, as it were."

"I'm rehabilitated. I'm doin' fine, got a job. I got prospects."

"No, you've got shit. You're a drunk flipping burgers for whores and pimps. You're pissed before most people eat breakfast, you spend your free time sitting on sidewalks begging for pennies and ogling women who are far and away too good to fuck in even the best of your sick daytime illusions and sordid dreams. It's simply a question of when, Guntrie. When does Walter Guntrie finally get so bored, so frustrated with fantasizing over enticing and innocent women light years beyond his paygrade that he follows one, or two, or three home, or to a car, or into an alley to rape and kill them?" He put up a hand. "The question was rhetorical. No need to reply. The answer, Guntrie, simpler yet: Never."

Guntrie clambered to his feet, eyeing the gun. "That real?"

"For the initial purpose, yes. A strong sedative, very real, very effective. More on that in a moment."

"You a vigilante or somethin', a dirty cop? The parents, they pay you to come here?"

"Vigilante, I suppose, however much I dislike the term. And no, my being here is a gratuitous mission of mercy on their behalf."

"Huh?"

"This is a freebie."

"That ain't me anymore. They added four fuckin' years. Four. Thirty years, that ain't easy time, not for a kid. And I got the scars to prove it."

"Scars I would prefer not to see. More to the point, an extra year for each parent when you should have been executed. Hardly a penalty proportionate to the crimes. You Northern folk, you get away with a bit up here. In the South we do not take kindly to anyone raping and killing our women."

"I was twenty, with shit for brains. I thought they was out, gone somewhere. I shot him kneejerk, not thinkin'. Then she was screamin', stampin' her feet, damn near naked, I dunno. Shit, I was twenty, from the wrong side. Seein' her that way. Shit, I couldn't help myself."

"Your thirty years were not as long as those eternal minutes of torment for little Diane, pinned to the floor beside her dead husband. Her name was Diane."

"Says you. Got any idea what it's like in prison at twenty for rape?"

"I miss your point entirely." Marcus Simms shrugged, discharging the gun, the CO_2 cartridge launching the slim missile, hurtling the one-inch needle into Guntrie's chest, knocking him into the wall.

Guntrie stared down, scared. "Fuck, no," he whimpered. "Please." A second or two later he collapsed to his knees, then onto his side.

"I imagine Diane begged for her life as well, crying, whimpering. Did she see you aim, did she see you pull the trigger?" Guntrie didn't answer, he was moaning. "Listen up, Guntrie, here's the thing." Marcus buried the gun inside his hoodie, reaching for the syringe, pressing lightly on the plunger. A minute amount of the mixture squirted into the air. "You've got a minute or two before this happens next, Guntrie. I like to walk my people through the process. Fair is fair. I'm sure little Diane realized you would put a bullet into her forehead when you finished terrorizing her.

Personally, knowing that, I believe I would more quickly die from the humiliation of soiling myself. Pentobarbital. Some states use this for executions, or did until the Dutch got queasy. Curious, really. They allow assisted suicide, just not the deserved disposal of human waste." He went to the inert Guntrie, kneeling. "Did I mention acid, and lots of it? A shitload. No? Well, here's the thing. The sedative is intended to, shall we say, cripple you. Not spare you. Imagine yourself skinned and tossed into a blazing furnace, that's what you are about to experience internally." He paused, Guntrie was crying, his speech badly slurred. "Excuse me? What? Are you trying to say inhumane? Is that it? No. Inhumane was staying in their home and drinking beer as if nothing had happened. Your neighbours, unfortunately, are another matter. Collateral damage, I'm afraid. They won't hear you scream because you cannot scream. You're too confused, your mind too chaotic. However, when they sometime tomorrow begin searching for the source of the intense stench, which will be you, since I will leave your door unlocked, they will literally scream bloody murder. They will find you with your bulging eyes threatening to explode from their sockets and more shit in your jeans than a California mudslide. They'll see your head swimming in more puke than you produced in the first five years on your knees in prison, your mouth frozen open and stuffed with whatever your corpse will not soon cough out. And blood, lots of blood." He tugged at the dart, sliding the needle into Guntrie's neck, standing. "If you thought thirty years was long, that was a ride in the park. Merry Christmas from Diane and her husband."

He snorted at seeing the first flecks of spittle, the rest was déjà vu. He stepped out into the hall, closing the unlocked door, his day was done, feeling no remorse for

Guntrie or the neighbours. None of whom, he supposed, were any better or worse than Walter Guntrie.

Disembarking the cab, he buried the gun, dart and syringe separately miles from the scene in drains as he scurried frantically to the hotel's underground parking to escape the raging blizzard. He needed desperately to feel warm again and to rest his tormented feet. He wanted to savour a single Blue, to shower in hot water and dress for a peaceful dinner like the civilized Southern gentleman he was.

The city's restaurants would be near empty, closing early, the serving staff depending on him to make their evening worthwhile. Star for star restaurant cuisine was never as palatable, the concierge's considered recommendation for his evening a short five-minute cab ride.

Marcus thanked the man, tilting his head, touching the brim of his fedora out of deference. He would walk. He could use the exercise. The earlier poor weather had abated and a pleasant stroll on a chilly but calm evening along an avenue accessorized with graffiti-painted trashcans would do wonders to clear his head of Rosemary Sandra, her mystery man who Marcus believed was very real, and to free his hands of his daytime wardrobe.
*

Marcus Simms remained fully awake after Patricia-Louise slid from atop his body to nestle into his arm and chest near four-thirty in the morning, purring softly, serenely unaware she had adeptly brought him comfort and the joy of closure, unaware she had left him with a single imperative as his thoughts began drifting. He had much to ponder, to comprehend.

He couldn't sleep, thankful. He didn't want to sleep. He

wanted more of her; he wanted to watch her, to study and to memorize her, to stroke her dark red hair and pretend all was well with him, with the world. They had shared smiles and laughter and tenderness for too few hours, fleeting moments he would within hours perforce chase from his mind. How effortlessly he could manoeuvre her into position, knowing he couldn't or wouldn't dare.

Patricia-Louise was indeed all dressed in red, right down to her bright red satin high-rise flounced panties with silk trim and her garters, which he gallantly aided and abetted in the precise and unhurried removal thereof. More importantly, which came as no surprise, she was very good in bed. Not mind-blowing wow good or insatiable, though definitely memorable until he would walk out on her and almost immediately forget her. She was an attentive lover, intense and meticulous as though directing a sensual ballet to the accompaniment of muted sighs, squeals and breathless gasps.

He believed he would miss her, particularly since he hadn't at any time since leaving Charleston thought to regret Rosemary Sandra's sudden and unexpected disinclination towards conjugal pleasantries. Perhaps he had been too busy of late to allot her the undue consideration she believed she deserved.

She ran hot and cold, an irreversible condition since their first encounter: One day sweet and charming, the next snobbish and condescending in a manner particular to Southern females whose daddies were wealthy and arrogant familial demigods. Daddy forever the most important figure in her life, the one he was meant to emulate. Like that would happen in his current lifetime, leaving Marcus no less vulnerable than any other male of species, never knowing when her red-hot blade would sear off his balls for no explicable reason.

If she was screwing around, good for her. She would have her interlude, take ephemeral pleasure in her lustful intrigues and come back to him. Or not. That would be her choice. He would not disgrace himself by piteously manipulating her misguided heart.

With Lady Fifteen nestled beside him, warm from their heated and urgent facsimile of ardent amour, who was he to cast the first stone? Irrespective of which, at his firm insistence, Rosemary Sandra would soon declare herself fit and reasonable to live with. As he would maintain his conviction to rid the world of vermin in a more pleasant season. If not for her, for himself. What would truly have mattered if he had kept Guntrie waiting until spring? Unless, in the meantime, he were to carelessly leave the world too quietly and too painlessly after his, Marcus', unspoken vow to the families.

Furthermore, what was her real problem? What was wrong with him coming home Christmas Eve, or missing New Year's, or missing *his* birthday? Not hers. He loathed the predictability of New Year's stupidities at the Rothstone's: the kissing, the hugging, the handshakes, dancing with strangers to music written before he was born, the toasting, blue-haired ladies believing they could shriek a single note without shattering a crystal goblet. Each year another of them MIA due to the past year, the one they twelve months earlier had rung in with exuberance and merriment, taking a terminally bad turn, the year's second best reminder that everyone in the room, him included, was closer to a silk-lined box than the cradle. At least they got to forget one occasion before the other crept in unwanted. He couldn't. One would forever follow the part of him that was Marcus Simms within a single second into the other, neither old man Rothstone nor his wife ever thinking to wish him happy birthday during the earlier years.

That wasn't the problem. She was. Rosemary Sandra was. Medical science was beginning to pay serious attention to patients with PTSD, those with adequate insurance plans anyway, those who should never have enlisted in the first place into whatever gun-toting career choice could require discharging a weapon at a human target or one day, any day, being that human target. Their apparently conscious choices made with supposedly clear, if not thoughtful and educated minds. Good for them, receiving disproportionate psychiatric care when the most in need of comfort and therapy were deliberately and pitilessly disregarded as needful: Husbands, constant victims of blood-chilling PMSD. Where was the support for countless victims of post-marital stress disorder, he wondered, those who lived in constant fear of castration and the female's need to draw blood?

Laying naked beside him, her leg crossed over his, he couldn't picture Patricia-Louise ever mutating into a Rosemary Sandra. She was too lovely, too warm and kind. Whereas Rosemary Sandra had become an argumentative and unreasonable bitch.

This one he had to escape from, quickly. Get out of Dodge while he could. Run. She was too tempting. Everything about her was captivating. The fact that he was in her room was somehow fanciful: A wonderful dream. Immediate flight was essential. If she happened to wake for any reason he would be swimming in that proverbial polluted creek. Sorely screwed. Defenceless and shot dead. How would he then ever manage a successful evacuation of self from her hotel room when she had, between orgasms, planned their day? He wouldn't. She would want more of him. They constantly wanted more of him, suffocating him, as if he was somehow ordained to make them complete. And how would he possibly refuse her, his body no less eager? He would not.

They would split a cab, she insisted, to his place where he would change into casual attire before driving her home to where she would light a fire and prepare a sumptuous dinner with a bottle or two of her finest twenty-dollar wines to celebrate his birthday: The single advantage he would gain from exterminating irredeemable criminals in the spring.

He would stay the night. He wanted to and he would, he made her believe. He would be her interim lover, giving her false hope of days or weeks, months or a real future with each other after coming together for a one-nighter in a posh restaurant-bar.

So, yes, he had to get the hell out before seeing her weep or sob and punch her pillows. She would loathe herself for being too naïve, too easy, too desperate for tenderness, too eager to provide a stranger access to her body, soon after converting her wasted energies into hatred, from then on regarding all men with disdain until one, the right one, would rekindle her heart's flame.

He drew back the duvet as best he could, easing her leg gently from his, her arm from his chest. His kissed her forehead and her cheek, cupping her shoulder, easing her onto her back.   He kissed her chin and her breasts still shimmering with silver body dust, that he had joked were still in their early twenties and extremely divine, lingering, pressing his hands into their warmth; he trailed kisses across her flat belly to where her body was the most pungent, not daring to arouse her beyond a protracted and deep breath while pressing his lips against the bitter-sweet moisture.

She hadn't stirred, hadn't moaned or twitched a single muscle. He eased from the bed adoring her, hating himself. If she could be that compelling in her sleep, what chance would he have were she to waken? She was testing his will, mocking his weakness. He inhaled deeply, pursing his lips. He was weak. So what? What the hell, all of her or nothing.

Kneeling by her side he kissed her face, her shoulders and her breasts, rolling her onto her front with affectionate murmurs. She was exquisite. He swept aside her damp hair, kissing the nape of her neck. He trailed more kisses to the small of her back, to the alluring mounds that were soft and warm to the careful pressure of his palms, his cheeks and his lips. He kissed one side of her then the other, inhaling deeply as he caressed one leg then the other, Patricia-Louise Valcourt too lost in the rapture of her heavenly dreams to wake at his final and expert touch.

Why had he lied about who he was? She was younger than Rosemary Sandra, thirty-four, more becoming inside and out, and not greatly enthralled with the weather, the city, or the populace of Detroit who she believed were largely unaffected by the miserable winter weather because one was as frigid as the other. What was he doing? Why wasn't he staying? Why wasn't he staying to love her instead of manipulating her for his closure? She was ideal. She was wonderful, warm and caring. In addition to which, with his newly intended springtime agenda, he would never give her cause to bitch or complain or sleep with other men.

If not now, when would he? When would the day come that he would stay, that he would return home to Charleston with whomever she might be and invite the forgotten Rosemary Sandra to the wedding?

He shook his head, rubbing his palms hard against his face. Never. He would forever worry and wonder, forever be suspicious. How could he possibly trust any one of them when they all so eagerly slide into their beds and a stranger's open arms with their legs invitingly parted?

He eased Patricia-Louise gently to one side, caressing and absorbing her, speaking to her in whispers, asking who else she might have brought to her bed if not him. Then onto her other side when he stood gazing at her for as long as he dared before dressing quickly and ensuring nothing of his remained in the room. Grabbing the fedora he despised and his coat he closed the door behind him, taking the stairway as a more private and expedient alternative to the elevator and lobby which posed too perilous a threat. At the parking level, he lit his last cigarette of the year.

Chapter Thirteen
Jed, Rosemary's Lustful Sin & Kirt Bradley

May 31, 1968 was Liberation Day for young Jed and
Rosemary, a day they worked hard to achieve three years
after graduating from college. They were twenty-four, each
other's eternal love and best friend.

Rosemary as a teenager was as delightful and charming
as she was defiant, an otherwise typical Southern Belle
with a heart as warm as the glow of a late-day sun and no
less radiant. Throughout high-school she was playful and
innocently coquettish, the antithesis of timid, forever
breaking other boys' hearts. But never Jed's. Throughout
her college years she evolved into an impossibly striking
and articulate young woman; she was arresting with pale
streaks of pinkish red in her long blonde tresses, piercing
green eyes and creamy-white skin. She wasn't very tall,
which she compensated for with breasts that perfectly
matched her slim build, breasts whose creamy smooth
pushed-up swells demanded the courtesy of one's attention
under her low-cut sweaters and unbuttoned blouses knotted
at her bare midriff. Her tush, many of their testosterone-
driven male friends agreed, amiably jealous of Jed for
getting there first, was premium-grade ass, gloriously
housed in miniskirts or cut-offs or whatever fashion
statement suited the occasion; the sum total of her body's

allures, an outstanding example of female design and symmetry.

The beach season was increasingly another matter as their freshman year brought new friends, newfound freedom away from her parents and the nucleus of a dream. Rosemary adored her days at the beach, insisting that she was a vibrant and healthy young woman, putting Jed in his place one day when she had had enough of side-glances and giggles. She was not an old lady. Don't like it, don't look. Or go fuck-off. That's what she said, not to Jed, to her girlfriends. She was not a heartless tease, she added evenly. Neither was she ruthless in debilitating the masculine mind, heedlessly wearing her imported strings and triangles. She never did anything heedlessly, and how could she possibly debilitate an already simple mind?

She knew exactly what she was wearing, as she did at the commencement of her long-awaited post-graduation summer. Her final summer of carefree abandon that she would embrace to the fullest, beginning the season in a daring thong, insouciantly stripping away her shorts to the raucous cheers of Jed's friends and the gaping mouths of her friends whose plainer bodies were draped in modest two-pieces accessorized with built-in skirts, panels, and secured in place with bum glue. Not her problem; the girls' palpable envy particularly apparent as Jed's lubricated hands began ensuring that her freshly exposed private flesh was properly protected from the sun's harmful rays.

She loved her body, she loved who she was and was becoming. She loved Jed. She had an ass, she told him. So what? Everyone had one, and what she did with hers was her private business. What was the big deal? He chuckled, squeezing. Her amazing ass was the big deal.

That was then, a segment in young lives when time-sensitive friendships dissolve, when graduates and dropouts follow their divergent paths towards success or failure.

She had long forgotten the girls from high-school. Most were contented stay-at-home moms at twenty-four or younger, their once eager steadies unhappily condemned to the best years of their lives in desperate marriages as an alternative to standing before a judge in a court of law and serving five of ten for good behavior before re-entering society with ruptured anuses and no possibility of prosperous lives thereafter. Most of her college girlfriends went the same way, too imprudently quick to avoid the humiliation of being the last one at the altar or in creating a perfect likeness of self as a loving mother. As their mothers were.

Jed's friends began excluding him at a rate consistent with their engagements and marriages, their fiancées and wives mistrustful of a bachelor's undue influence, particularly since Jed was still with Rosemary whose charms were not lost on their husbands whose minds had remained simple.

That was neither Jed's nor Rosemary's vision of an ideal life. Neither one had parents to impress or emulate. Jed's parents had died tragically early in his life, his guardian joining them a few surmountable weeks before his majority, leaving him a considerable inheritance. Conversely, Rosemary walked out on her tearful mother and angry father waving her degree after months of Sunday afternoon arguments. She would live *her* life, not relive theirs. If they so badly wanted or needed grandchildren, have another of their own. Good luck with that. She was moving in with Jed.

They were not interested in kids or marriage, neither institution a necessary, or necessarily reliable, expression of one's everlasting love; Jed making certain of one while allowing that Rosemary could possibly one day want to take his name. They had greater plans, dreams of a career nurtured over four collegiate years. They would one day open a fine restaurant where they would spend their afternoons and evenings working together before ending their day in a luxurious bed while gazing out over the moonlit ocean from an elegant beachfront home.

They no longer had real friends, shamelessly amused when occasionally encountering former college contemporaries burdened with two and three carriages, or when stepping out from their economical sedans and making excuses for what they were wearing. In fact neither Rosemary nor Jed had enough hours in their days to make new, high-maintenance friends. The marrieds were out, the singles still living with mommy and daddy single-mindedly interested in partying and having a good time, especially if one of them had Rosemary and a Shelby Mustang GT350.

They weren't interested. Dress for the job you want, Jed's professor told him. Clothes do not make the man, they define the man. And the woman, Jed told Rosemary as though she hadn't yet made her case. The two adamant that, for the time being, appearances were more important than their temporary reality. They had lived in a modest one-room apartment where no one was ever invited, saving every penny not spent on their gleaming new Mustang GT or their wardrobes that were current and fashionable for their days off, agreeing that using Jed's inheritance would be too easy and impulsive. Their single expertise in gastronomy to-date was dining out. They knew nothing about the mechanisms that would drive their success, wisely realizing that without proper apprenticing, however many years that would require, they would fail.

The professor's sage advice proved invaluable. For a full year they paid their dues working in a kitchen and waiting tables in a restaurant too rich for the palates of their forgotten friends, until their boss took notice, making Jed bartender out of necessity and practically doubling his Happy Hour clientele. A few weeks later Rosemary found herself behind the bar as well, making the establishment the poshest after-hours stomping ground for young executives. Three years of hard work, studying and learning everything they could about wines and spirits and gastronomy until the early spring of '68 when Jed and Rosemary felt ready and went to the bank.

May 31st they opened for business after weeks of exhausting sweat equity, dealing with contractors, designers and her parents, their ex-boss amongst the first to wish them success as he toasted them with a glass of his finest Pomery. The beachfront home would come later, as would the world-famous ocean view restaurant on Hilton Head Island where they would vacation for a week as soon as they made a profit. In the meantime they would make do in the three rooms over their newly opened wine bar, that was The Wine Bar, where, from their double bed, they had no view at all.

Rosemary's father was livid upon hearing of Jed's sacrificial operation and his daughter's constant refusal to confront her shame and return home. They were a laughing stock, their associates and neighbours ridiculing them behind their backs with insensitive barbs.

The notion of his daughter indecently living with a man in such poor conditions, a man who would never make her whole as a woman, was ludicrous. The entire purpose of marriage was family, her father declared through his wife. Rosemary replying through her mother that he should chill out. That was her entire point. She did not want family, she did not want some creepy little thing crawling inside her for nine minutes let alone nine months, which sort of obviated the need for marriage. No big deal, and certainly not worth a massive coronary or stroke. So let's all get real.

The summer and fall went quickly, The Wine Bar gaining in popularity each week, their single source of leisure an hour or two each weekday morning virtually alone. Then came Christmas, her favourite day of the year, then New Year's and his birthday. She was excited. She had prepared a special picnic-lunch for them and a special gift for desert. She could finally afford to buy him something nice. Her extra special gift was her bikini, she wasn't wearing one. No one ever went to the beach New Year's Day. Anyway, what if they did?

Not bothering to sit she stripped away her tank top and shorts, tossing them aside, laying on her side and patting the blanket, giggling at his drawn out "whoa" and 180 degree twirl.

He stood gazing at her, pensive. "Nice. Very nice," he said flatly.

"Gosh, sweetheart, don't get too excited." She frowned, pouting. "I mean, really." But, really, she understood when her man was troubled.

He sat beside her, stroking her hair.

"Sweetheart, don't be so glum. Last night was a tremendous success, we're at the beach on a gorgeous day headed into a gorgeous New Year…and happy birthday." She reached into the hamper for the little box. "Open it. Hurry."

Jed hated celebrating his birthday on the 01st that held no particular relevance for him, he hated the attention; he had ever since the night his parents hadn't made it home to celebrate his fifth after their last New Year's party, killed by a drunk driver. He tore at the ribbon and paper, raising the lid slowly, Rosemary assuming he was teasing her. He wasn't.

"Wow." A plain gold bracelet with 'Jed' engraved on the face. He read the inside script. "This is special, 'From me, January 01st, 1969', thanks Rosie."

She punched him. "Thanks Rosie? This is special? Wow? Like you're drinking glue and not our most expensive champagne?" She gulped her bubbly. "I'm lying here naked, Jed. That thing cost me a frigging fortune, and that's all I get? Well, fuck you sweetheart."

He chuckled, dressing his wrist. "I love it. I do. But this year, Rosie, won't be gorgeous in the least." He tugged the letter from his shirt pocket. "Seems our president wants me to stop serving wine. Apparently he needs me to kill a few Viet Cong this year instead." He sipped his champagne. "I report in seven days."

"What!" Rosemary dropped her fluted crystal, scrambling to her knees, her body shuddering from an immediate deep chill. "No! You can't. Tell them you're a conscientious objector. Tell them they'll ruin all our hard work."

"Neither of which is true, Rosie. Not that they would care. We'll get through this. Besides, you're the main attraction at the bar." He coughed a laugh. "I just do all the hard stuff."

She wasn't amused. "Shit, sweetheart, people don't work in a bar one day and go killing someone the next. Shit, Jed."

He wiped her eyes.

"No tears. Not here, not today. We knew this was coming, Rosie. It's my kick at the cat." He shrugged.

"Anyway, if it's a choice of me or the other guy, yeah, I'll do some serious killing. I'm not one for running. You know that." He ran a fingertip across the bracelet. "One year, I promise." He eased her gently backward. "Now let's do something about you being all naked."

A week later they kissed at the airport, Jed promising to write often and come home to her in twelve months intact.
*

He kept the first promise, his letters smudged more often than not, damp with his sweat or the jungle's high humidity; Rosemary's letters at first scented with her favourite fragrance. Then not, then fewer letters were his to read until none whatsoever came in the last several months of his second tour of duty. Which didn't matter, letters had a way of getting lost in war. She was safe. His letters to her were more important, each week telling her in creative ways that he was a better shot than the VC. Sergeant Billows had been gone two years less a month, his final letter telling her he was coming home and would do his best to stay alive four more weeks folded neatly in his pocket.

"Son, listen up. That is *the* worst precursor of bad luck," his captain had reprimanded him, "*the* absolute worst. You should damn well know better. Sending home a letter like that so near the end makes a soldier careless. Makes him believe his time's done, and too often a Cong bullet or bamboo spike makes that happen. You need to soldier-up and not make promises that are not yours to keep."

Those weeks were interminable, the flights home to Charleston seemingly endless. He was not the same man stepping from the taxi that Monday night, not after two years in the jungle. When he left her he was young and fit from swimming in a clear blue ocean and his annual gym

217

membership. Now he appeared older than his two missed birthdays. His skin was several shades darker, his body rippled and lean from trudging through dense forests with a fifty-pound backpack, or traversing swirling brown rivers in filthy water with his rifle held high, day or night, often submerging entirely either by accident or for as long as his lungs held out before the kill shot.

She would not recognize him, he scarcely recognized himself. His thick, wavy hair she would have remembered was gone. What remained was a sunburnt scalp. His eyes were no longer a dark liquid brown, they were sad and dull. The light had gone out from them, the skin around them creased from squinting so many times into his rifle sight before squeezing the trigger. Worst of all, he had lost his humanity.

She wasn't expecting him. The letter was never sent. She was in The Wine Bar, he saw through the window, as pretty and seductive as ever. The man standing with her was a complete stranger, something they had agreed on. Managing the bar on her own would have been impossibly demanding, though after her first letter she made no further mention of him, writing instead of how well the business was doing. What he was seeing, however, he was not expecting. Not a single barstool, banquette or table was empty on a Monday night.

He went to the side door, trying the key and stepping inside, pausing a moment to relive the times he'd hauled her up the stairs over his shoulder, ignoring her squeals and giggles. In their little living room nothing had changed. When would she have had the time? In the bathroom nothing had changed, even his towel was hanging on the rack. He grinned. She might not recognize him at first, but sure as hell she would be leaving the bar early and going in late the next day. Or perhaps Wednesday.

She wouldn't be angry. He had explained the reason for his second tour in countless letters. A few weeks prior to his discharge half his platoon was wiped out in a firefight: an entire squad, fifteen buddies dead in as many minutes. Those who didn't die re-enlisted. They had a new mission: Get even. And they did, locating and taking out that particular and entire VC village. That was a defining moment. The remaining squad became the battalion's best, all fifteen surviving the second tour.

He threw his gunny sack through the bedroom doorway, anxious for a shower, anxious for clean civilian socks, his linen slacks and cashmere sweater: Simple luxuries he had nearly forgotten.

At the bed he stood staring curiously at her night table. His photograph was missing, replaced by a short stack of hospitality magazines. He scanned the room. The sweater on the clothes horse wasn't familiar; he would never think to wear argyle. The shoes were laced, and not his. At his closet a full array of men's clothes were neatly hung. Again, not his. Five cardboard boxes were stacked in the corner. He tugged open the top box, inadvertently groaning at seeing his springtime fashions, mechanically prying open the other four, his dazed mind racing freely between the past, the present, and all those missed letters.

His entire wardrobe was neatly folded by season, his footwear in the bottommost box topped with his photograph. He went to his highboy, nothing inside was his. He went through her dresser and closet. Nothing had changed. He returned to the bathroom where in the medicine cabinet he saw a straight-edge and shaving cream, a roll-on and cologne that weren't his. In hers all that had changed was the dispenser of mandatory morning pills

219

requisite to maintaining a childless state.

He went to their small office desk in a corner of the living room, searching the drawers, her side, his side, dropping into the chair to read the document dated May 31, 1970 that joined Rosemary in holy matrimony to one Kirt Bradley. Not eighteen months after she had made feverish love with him at the beach, smothering him with heated kisses, weeping warm tears onto his face. Who the hell was Bradley and how many months before that had they spent fucking in his bed while he was doing all he could to stay alive for her? Almost worse, he found not a single letter he'd written.

He snorted. Yeah, he could understand not receiving letters, his mind kicking into survival mode, cautious curiosity restraining him. One thing to check: the strongbox at the bottom of the highboy, his highboy. This time he snorted a tad more derisively. What was the point of locking a strongbox and keeping the key in the lock, particularly when concealing a loaded .38 revolver? Not the wickedest gun he'd seen recently, though definitely adequate at close range. Now get out!

If he had learned anything in the army he knew when to retreat, to regroup, never to rush into an unknown situation. He retreated, leaving the place undisturbed. He didn't need or want his old clothes. At the street he flagged a cab, soon after booking a motel room at the far end of town for a week and paying cash. He needed space, he needed time. Staying anywhere better would possibly or very likely cause him to cross paths with any number of curious acquaintances he didn't want to encounter because he wouldn't have answers that would make sense. Anyway, nothing would change in seven days that hadn't already. Most of all he needed a serious drink.

The next day he went shopping for a few ensembles of snugger-fitting casual attire and boots that would complement his trimmer post-war physique without making him conspicuous. Later in the afternoon he stripped the contents of his gunny sack of his ID and dropped the bag with his dress uniform into a mission box. He was done with saluting, his clothes sticking to his body like a thick scab, slop for food, sleeping on soggy ground and using his helmet for a pillow.

Wednesday he drove to Savannah to speak with his bank manager long-distance, telling the telling the man who had no reason to doubt his client that he was calling from the West Coast.

"The Wine Bar is indeed doing well, Mr. Billows, "the man said, "I suppose."

"Excuse me? What do you mean, 'I suppose'?"

"Well, last May Miss Rosemary transferred your business account to another institution using the power of attorney signed by you. Business we sorely regret losing, I must say. We were very pleased to have such a progressive young couple as clients."

"I never signed a power of attorney. Nor would I ever. The bar is owned by me, in my name alone, in the event things don't work out. Are you saying there's no balance?"

"Not a penny. The account is closed."

"Do you recall how much she transferred?"

"Close to half a million."

"What?" His heart was throbbing. "Five hundred thou, in sixteen months?"

"Which I assume is considerably more now. As I said, we were extremely sorry to lose you."

"You haven't. And my personal accounts?"

The man had already snapped his fingers, he had the

information at hand. "Your chequing account is flat, the government deposits withdrawn monthly by Miss Rosemary by means of your pre-signed cheques. As for your portfolio, currently with interest your balance stands at close to 2.3 million. No negative transaction in two years."

Nah. What's half a mil? "Good. Make sure it stays that way. I'll be in to see you next week with Rosemary."

The bank manager cleared his throat. "Mr. Billows, does the transfer and monthly withdrawals constitute a difficult predicament between you and this bank?"

"They do not."

Jed disconnected, amazingly not slamming the receiver into its cradle. He went for a late lunch on River Street, doing his best to make sense of Rosemary being married, of her stealing eight months of his army pay since marrying Bradley. Not to mention the half- million that previously was equally his and hers to share. Not now. Not a chance. He put in three-quarters, he would take out three-quarters or kill the two-faced bitch in the process. Fair was fair. Yeah, right. That rang a bell.

He drove home seething to spend a sleepless night. Making any sense of the last forty-eight hours was impossible. What had he ever done to her except adore her and love her, other than reenlisting with his squad to help bring meaning to those who died? Nothing.

Thursday he went to the beach for a few hours of jogging and calisthenics, formulating. Another lesson he had learned in Nam, in the army: Do not take shit. Someone kicks your balls, boy, you fucking well cut theirs off. Do things right. Do things once. And Rosemary had kicked him in the balls, big time. Now he would cut hers off. He had the advantage; like the Cong in the village, she

222

wasn't expecting him. Not the man he'd become, not the hard-ass, jaded mother-fucker with attitude.

Rosemary in a previous, long-ago life had two steadfast quirks. Without fail she would spend two hours Friday afternoons at the gym working up a sweat, and with greater dependability two hours every Saturday afternoon at her salon to ensure her undiminished allure for the more lucrative nighttime weekend crowd. In addition to which, she had metamorphosed into a capable criminal. What would daddy say about that, he wondered?

He felt better about himself, he did. He was resolute, dropping onto the sand. Reaching for a cold beer his bracelet glistened in the sun. He hadn't thought about the bracelet or their last day at the beach since Monday evening. Standing again, undoing the clasp, 'From me, January 01st, 1969' went whirling into the ocean's blue water.

Chapter Fourteen
Jed & Kirt Bradley

Prior to the president's personal invitation to Jed to tour Vietnam, Jed was an anomaly. He could easily have been the all-American golden-haired boy gifted with inherent intelligence, natural abilities and charm. Arrogant and self-centred. He chose another path, not entirely without help, guided by his aunt.

His parents before their deaths were professional and well-to-do, as was his loving aunt who then became his legal guardian. Soon after he was born, as mothers are wont to do, his mother exacted a promise from her sister to take charge of her son in the event of a tragedy she may have foreseen.

His aunt used not a cent of his inheritance towards his upbringing. Instead she invested wisely on his behalf and, when she too soon passed away weeks prior to the commencement of his college years, Jed only then discovered she had bequeathed her entire estate to him as well. The kid was set with his feet firmly planted on the ground. He had a strategy, a good one, determined that his family's money would not contribute to his initial success. Engrained in his thinking was his aunt's firm belief that, if he could not succeed without such a solid financial crutch, his plan would prove hopelessly flawed.

Which was not the case. His single flaw, very recently apparent to him, was his choice of partner.

The second Friday in January was a balmy sixty-one degrees, the pale-blue sky lightly accented with wispy white clouds, the light breeze scarcely enough to tease a man's eye with delicate silk hems flouncing around shapely thighs.

The pre-rush-hour traffic was flowing smoothly, The Wine Bar catering to the few clients extending their luncheons or weekends. Jed no longer felt right decked out in linen trousers and penny loafers. Not after Nam, not after his unspeakable discovery that incredibly had not debilitated him. He stepped into the bar in oxblood dress boots, oxblood leather pants and a burgundy silk shirt with its sleeves rolled midway to his elbows. The fashion was ideal for January in Charleston, albeit considerably different from the woolen suits, silk ties and French cuffs occupying the remotest corners.

"Afternoon," the man behind the bar started as Jed slid onto the stool. "Welcome, stranger. Can't say I recall seeing you in here before. Tourist? Business?"

Yeah, my business. "Vacation. Been gone too long in the Northwest where they believe a perfect day is when it's not pissing buckets." He chuckled. "Go figure. I'm staying with family at Hilton Head for a while, taking some beach time." He scanned the bar. "Nice place. Been here long?"

"Three years, give or take. Started this place with my wife. If you stay awhile longer you'll meet her." He put out his hand. "The name's Bradley, Kirt Bradley. My wife's Rosemary."

Bradley was taller than Jed, early thirties and not a problem. Seems Rosie was into older men. He was Dockers and button-down blue denim, Jed thinking the guy was likely standing in tasseled loafers and Argyle socks. Pure South with a drawl worked on to achieve positive results with the ladies. He was smiling, the kind of smile that disappears when he does. He was tanned just so, not too dark, not too light, his skin too smooth, his teeth too white, his eyes too blue, the kind of blue he would pinch out at night.

Jed reached out, not surprised. No grip, no pressure, like he was shaking the hand of a blow-up doll. "Marcus Simms, pleased to meet you. Unfortunately, noticing your place, I thought to come in for a quick hit. Curious. I'm glad I did. Family's good, know what I mean? But nothing beats alone time. A man has to have space. Guess now I'll have to come back to meet your lady. I've got another few days."

"Make sure you do. What's your pleasure?"

Killing you, asshole. "JW Black if you've got it. Red will do if you don't."

"We do." Bradley twisted from the hip, reaching. "You a one-finger man, or two?"

"Two. No ice." He waited until Bradley replaced the bottle in its nook. "Must be nice, having a place like this."

"Yeah, well, it's hard at first. Painfully long days, worrisome sleepless nights. You know, the bank and all. Thing is, you want something badly enough, you do what needs to be done. Takes time is all. Knock on wood, and a good woman. Couldn't have done any of this without her, if I'm being honest."

Yeah, or without me, asshole. "She sounds like a very special lady. Not too many of them up for grabs these days."

"She is, and now I sleep like a baby. We both do. Just takes time. That's the key."

"Been married long?" He sipped the Black. "I'm asking because that's the real reason I'm here, thinking things through. Do I ask her, give her what I know she wants, or does she give me the finger? That sort of thing."

Bradley poured a jigger of rum for himself. "Well, Marcus, from where I stand marriage is like jumping from a plane. You're good to go if you're all suited up and ready. If you're not, well, it's gets real messy real fast. You know what they say…when in doubt, get the hell out."

You have no idea how messy. "A sage perspective, Kirt. Guess what I really need is some balance."

"Well, Saturdays here will give you plenty of that. Won't be any shortage of balance. That I guarantee."

"Saturday, hmmm," he was thinking. "I could see that working. When's a good time and what's the demographic?"

"Young professionals who prefer Bordeaux to beer, which we don't serve. For a hook-up I would say the earlier the better. The single girls come in early, and never alone. Sort of like a security detail. It's pretty much divide and conquer, though I don't see that you'll have much of a problem. For easy talk, maybe somewhere near ten with no need to make a quick choice. Last call's at midnight, lights out at one. We have a quality-based clientele, not quantity. It's a popular place. You won't be sorry."

You will be. "Any code?"

"As the man says, dress for success."

You got that right. "Thanks, Kirt." Jed smiled, checking his watch, downing his Black. "I have to say, I'm feeling sorry I didn't find out about this place earlier on. Probably wouldn't have spent as much time thinking about my girl. I like it, very much. There's a homey feeling, something a man could imagine having for himself. In a dream anyway.

227

You and your wife have created something very special here." He sighed, standing. "Like you said, do what has to be done. I'll definitely be here tomorrow, if family doesn't get in the way. That's a promise." He put a ten on the counter, grinning. "Keep the change. I'm thinking tomorrow is exactly what I need to get her out of my mind." And you. "Thanks. Guess we'll see each other then, and," he feigned a momentary blank, "Rosemary, of course."

He left without drawing undue attention to himself, fully aware the small contingent of female clients in the bar was checking him out, comparing him with theirs. That's what females do, no matter the species. Ceaselessly on the hunt for a better stud, never content, forever choosing the challenging winner.

Jed went to his motel room. He wasn't sticking around to see her sauntering in to The Wine Bar, half-believing he would cross the street and throttle the bitch on the spot. Two years and counting without a woman. Living two frigging years like a monk. He had given up *not* thinking of her as an absolute conniving bitch. She was one, the supreme priestess of all bitches. Two years, when other guys were getting seriously laid in Laos, Phnom Penh and Da Nang while he sat huddled in his lean-to writing frigging love letters to a slut. Yeah, she was *the* most absolute and complete bitch.

That evening he slept soundly. He always did. No one surviving even one tour in active Vietnam combat had any reason not to. Sleep through that, sleep through anything. Humans were adaptable, especially US Army Nam vets. Yeah, guys like him. He put Rosemary out of his mind. Kill enough men and, know what? Your thinking changes a tad. If you didn't shit yourself the first time out, managing to get yourself shot-up or killed, you learned real fast not to give a good shit. Killing meant living, and Jed no longer gave a good shit.

Somehow he knew he would meet someone better soon enough who would come to love and comfort him for who he was. Whoever she might be, he would dream of her, did dream of her.

Waking early Saturday, the day reminded him of Kirt Bradley's eight-month wife: an all-out bitch. The sky was black throughout the entire day, the furious wind hurling rain droplets like missiles against the faces of occasional pedestrians whose coattails frantically whipped at their legs, whose hats were a frozen and tenuous hand away from soaring into the maelstrom. Teenage girls trying to appear groovy, running from store to store, were soaked through, uncaring, their faces grotesquely streaked.

Jed Billows was not soaked through. No. He was savouring his second expresso and, halfway through his pecan Danish, peering across the street to The Wine Bar. Waiting, waiting. He understood her like a book he had read too many times, knowing the outcome without seeing the words.

She arrived at 5:00 sharp, her newly re-coiffed pinky blonde do wrapped tightly in a kerchief, stepping through the doorway to her upstairs apartment. He went to the motel for a nap, setting the alarm for eight when he showered and dressed in sneakers and jeans, a tee-shirt and jean jacket: A disposable wardrobe. At nine he hailed a cab a block from the motel and went for a peaceful meal at a diner where no one took notice of him. At eleven, in his room, he began his preparations repeating each phase of the mission over and over again in his mind.

He was conditioned, steady. He didn't need a drink,

didn't want one. First and foremost he needed to be alert, he wanted to enjoy his evening.

His first weapon was stealth, making no sound as he walked, no sound as he breathed. His back-up would be his throwing knife, if for any reason he messed-up. After two years the sleek stainless steel blade was an extension of his hand and arm. The guys in his squad had little else to do when not killing the VC other than to practice killing them when rifles and pistols were not a good choice. Poker was primarily a payday diversion, considering that IOUs were not really practical in a war and reading was difficult at best. Pocket books never survived the heat and humidity past the second or third chapters. So they practiced.

He never missed a real or imaginary target at thirty feet. At twenty he would bury the blade to its hilt in flesh and bone and hear the impact. When hitting a paper VC nailed to a tree he would hear the high-pitch reverberation of a tuning fork. However, at three in the morning, in the middle of a deserted bar district, he doubted the quieter blade would become his weapon of choice.

He arrived across from The Wine Bar at 12:45 AM. The rain and the thunder had abated hours earlier. Surprisingly, standing in the dark peering through the panes of his ruined dream at men and women who were once his clients was easy. He felt nothing, unless utter emptiness was something. They were faceless, no longer important to him. She was no longer important to him. Unyielding memories of *their* Saturday nights, *their* impromptu dancing behind the bar, *their* romantic mornings at the beach were now so shadowed by foreign yet deep hatred and disgust as to be unreal and meaningless hallucinations.

At 12:59 the lights flickered, the doors opened and patrons began filing onto the sidewalk. Jed disappeared into a recessed doorway, not particularly concerned that anyone would recognize him. He doubted Rosemary would. At 1:15 three young waitresses Jed remembered walked out together chattering. Five minutes later the lights went out, Bradley and his wife exiting The Wine Bar and disappearing into their private entrance, Jed suddenly realizing with a chuckle that he was the one to argue against an interior entrance to their apartment.

The rest of her evening he knew by heart. She would undress and sit naked at her vanity, pampering her body, teasing him. Then she would put on something silky and take him to bed where she would transmute from a sophisticated Southern Belle into a sultry Southern tramp. Unless Bradley was somehow deficient, which he doubted. He knew her too well; she would never let anything near her that wasn't first predetermined as a good fit.

He had time. She never lasted past two. He strolled an entire mile, retracing his steps, killing sixty minutes. The upstairs windows were predictably dark. Forty minutes later he crossed the street.

The key went into the barrel noiselessly. Standing inside he let his eyes adjust to the darkness as he worked, silently reciting his revised letter to Rosemary dated five weeks earlier, adequately steamed and smudged.
*

December 14, '70
My dearest, darling Rosie,
Merry Christmas. Happy New Year.
I'm coming home, albeit a little worse for wear. I'm looking a little beat-up, Rosie, with maybe a bit less hair. I have none. The war's taken a toll. Nothing a week between here and there won't take care of. Besides, I'll need the time to myself to buy a new suit and a ring. I've had my fill

of army fatigues, wet boots and steel helmets.

My war is over. I'm done. I paid my dues, staying longer than promised to do what was right for my squad. That was the right thing to do and I'm glad you forgive me.

I'm glad because all this killing's made me think of life's fragility. We're getting married, you and me, taking that vacation at Hilton's Head. That's my Christmas gift to you, the very last Christmas I will ever miss.

I can't wait. But I need that week not to scare you, Rosie. You make sure to have a glass of our finest Pouilly-Fuissé waiting for me, for us. Jan. 18, Rosie, that's when I'm coming home.

Your ardent lover, Jed.

PS: My captain jut gave me the height of hell for thinking to send you this letter. He said I was too close to the end to screw-up, when what I want is for you to be close.

What the hell! I'm coming home.

Jed.

Chapter Fifteen
Jed, Mr. & Mrs. Bradley & Alysyn Dunn

The real letter was gone, flushed and forgotten. It was much longer, each word written with the wrong emotion. This one would suffice, believable enough to anyone reading it. He climbed the stairs, leaving his shoulder bag at the door, the knife held ready in his right gloved hand, a soaked facecloth in the other.

At the top he eased through the second doorway, padding slowly into the bedroom. She seldom stirred in her sleep, never tossed or turned, too worn out from loving him. Hopefully, he mused, some things never changed. Though somehow he couldn't picture her playing giddy-up horsey with strait-laced Bradley.

Seeing her in lying in bed with Bradley was surreal. By her side, he stood for a few moments taking her in. She was undoubtedly attractive, if no longer heart-stirring. Not his heart. He felt nothing, not sorrow nor jealousy. Drawing back her cover, her silk slip bunched under her breasts, he slid his arms under her, pressing into the mattress not to disturb her, not remotely aroused by her nudity. He felt nothing, when before Nam he would have teased and titillated her awake. Carrying her into the living room, feeling the weight of her soft flesh, smelling her sweet scent, he struggled to refrain from a fit of laughter. In the

233

middle of the room he eased her body into alignment with his, not in the least tempted to kiss her or whisper her name.

Instead he abruptly jostled her, twisting her violently to startle and terrify her. He was at his point of no return. In the same instant, praying the information on the bottle's label was accurate, he clamped the facecloth drenched in ether firmly across her mouth and nose. Satisfaction guaranteed. Rosemary was out cold in under a minute, her kicking and flailing diminishing rapidly, her grunts and groans ceasing almost immediately. She was in a better place where he let her free fall into a sprawled heap of tanned flesh and silk.

In the bedroom, he went directly to the highboy reaching for the strongbox with a gloved hand. Removing the gun, he laid the box on the floor where he would remember it, freeing the weapon from its holster that he concealed in a dresser drawer under a jumbled palette of silk and satin panties. He checked the gun's cylinder. Good. Full.

He went into the kitchen for a glass of water, then to Rosemary. Kneeling beside her, raising her, he dropped a roofie into her mouth, helping her to drink, massaging her throat to help her swallow. Returning the glass, he swept her into his arms effortlessly and carried her into the bedroom where again he let her fall freely to the floor before flipping the light switch and kicking the edge of the bed.

"Kirt! Wake up, big guy. We've got some overdue business here and I'm running short on time." He kicked the bed twice more. "I need you to cooperate here, Kirt. Get the fuck up."

Bradley jerked, disoriented, snapping his head towards

his wife's empty pillow, twisting. "What the fuck!" He shook his head. "Simms? Is that you?" He saw his wife and the knife. "Jesus Christ!"

"No, not Jesus Christ. Jed Billows, the real owner of the bar you didn't start with your whore of a wife three years ago. And you're in my bed."

Bradley rubbed his face hard. "Billows! Holy shit." The shock was real.

"Yeah, pretty much. A whole whack of it, coming at you. Now get out of my bed."

"My bed. Yours went out in the trash, pretty much like you. This isn't your place anymore." He stared at his wife sprawled at Jed's feet. "Christ, Billows, show some decency and cover her. Is she okay?"

"I'd say that's pretty much subjective, Kirt. Let's say she's doing a shitload better than you for the moment." He glanced at Rosemary, taking a deep breath for affect, smirking "You know, she was always obsessively fascinated with her ass. Everyone was, but you know that. I don't think she would mind me having a few last peeks. Nice chemise, I must say. You buy her that?"

"Screw you."

He shrugged. "I need you to stand."

"We thought you were still in Nam."

"Don't say Nam. We get to say Nam, not you."

Bradley snickered, beginning to laugh. "Thanks for dropping by, again. You've had your fun. Whatever you did with her, good for you. I'll get over it. Now get out. We're married. There's nothing you can do about that. And the bar, good luck with that. She's one smart woman, Billows. Jed who?"

"Not smart enough. Not by a longshot. Stand up, by the bed." Jed went to the bed, dropping the letter. "Read it."

"Maybe not."

"Maybe so." He brought the gun into view. "Read it."

Bradley kicked the bedcover from his legs, Jed particularly pleased to see the pyjama bottoms. Bradley crumpled the paper contemptuously in his hands, tossing the ball onto the bed.

"So what?"

"Well Kirt, she got that a week ago, maybe sooner. She made you aware of it tonight. She had no choice, terrified of what you would do or say. I was coming home on Monday to marry her. She lied to you about me, about downstairs, about me being the sole owner of the place. Got to say though, you're pretty good at spewing bullshit yourself. Anyway, the two of you argued uncontrollably from closing until," he checked his watch, "three-thirty. Or thereabouts. Until in a fit of jealous rage, after all you've done for her, you beat her savagely for her lies and deception. You tore away her slip, slapping her viciously, throwing her to the floor. She was hysterical, terrified for her life. She was frantic, out of her mind with fright. That's when she remembered the gun, this one. Mine. Her one chance to survive her horrific nightmare. That's when she killed you in self-defence."

"What!" Jed's final words took a while sinking in, his unblinking eyes and vanishing smile driving home the reality. Bradley convulsed in some sort of impromptu and grotesque dance, reaching outward. "No!"

"Oh yeah, you're pretty dead. Till death do we part, etcetera. She just killed you for kicking the shit out of her. That's a preview. Do what needs to be done. That sound familiar, big guy?"

Jed dropped in a flash onto his side by Rosemary, squeezing the trigger, slamming Bradley into the wall

236

where he stayed staring dumbly at his chest, then to Billows who could not believe the guy was blubbering. Of all the men he killed, that was a first.

"Yeah, I know. It truly sucks." Jed fired again, Bradley stumbling forward, teetering a few seconds before falling face down onto the bed.

Jed placed the strongbox back in the highboy, with the lid closed and the key turned in the lock. He knelt beside her. The ether was wearing off as the roofie was taking effect. Precisely what he wanted. She would not remember a single moment, regaining consciousness in a few hours and feeling like shit, blaming her dead husband's beating. Stunned by fear, not knowing what to do, her entire world insanely shattered, she would call the police.

He lifted her, with his hands bare, keeping her feet from dragging on the floor, hugging her closely, dishevelling her hair. Bringing her to the bed where he held her unsteadily at arm's length by her throat, he slapped her face twice, brutally, wincing from the stinging sensation in his palm before making a fist and punching her stomach so hard that she coughed violently and opened her eyes.

With a single downward thrust he ripped her chemise from its thin straps, bruising her shoulders, shredding the silk and baring her breasts. He swept her around, guiding her forward, releasing her, her momentum crashing her clumsily onto the floor by the highboy. By the bed, his fingertips once again protected in leather, he ripped a lamp from its wall plug and hurled it to within inches of her face, shrugging.

His evening was coming to an end. Given the possibility she might oversleep, found as she was before waking, he positioned her onto her side as she would have scrambling for the gun that he fixed firmly in her hand

237

while lying beside her, judging the best angle, helping her discharge a round into the wall near the bed by her dead husband.

Know when to leave, which he did, after taking a leisurely moment to ensure that the first cops to arrive on the scene would enjoy the best she had to offer. His final gift to her, male adoration, apart from which he had done all he could to make her a victim.

He snorted, glancing without the slightest emotion from husband to wife. What he was seeing at his feet was how he would remember her, at least for a short while until finding someone decent and pure to love.

At the bottom of the stairs he accounted for the knife, the bottle and the facecloth. He stripped from his jeans, standing on them to tug at his sneakers and socks, to strip off the jacket and tee-shirt and dress in something more becoming of a gentleman returning home from an agreeable evening at the theatre.

Closing the door behind him, he added his gloves to the mix, emptying the shoulder bag into sewers and bins as soon as he strolled beyond the five-block radius he expected of the next day's police investigation.
*

Late Monday afternoon the limousine pulled up in front of The Wine Bar. Jeddore Billows stepped out cautiously at seeing the sidewalk cordoned off with yellow police tape and the morbid audience of onlookers. He was dressed for the special occasion in a dark blue suit, crisp shirt and dark red tie. In one hand he had a dozen red carnations, Rosie's favourite, in the other a tiny blue velvet box.

The chauffeur asked whether he should wait, Jed replying that, yes, he should.

Two patrol cars were parked nose to nose. On another, a

black sedan, a woman was leaning on the hood writing notes. Seeing Jeddore, she stopped.

"Can I help you, mister?" she called out, not impressed with his ride.

"Well, I suppose you can. I happen to own this place. What's going on?"

The lady cop strode towards him, no different from army women. Pure attitude. She was important to herself in her beige off-the-rack pantsuit and brown pumps she bought at the Shoe Barn. He could tell. The Glock and silver shield on her faux-leather belt told the rest of her story. She hadn't made the grade; she was plain clothes hoping to one day solve the ideal murder that would give her full detective status. He wondered how she would look glistening in a one-piece high-rise thong at the beach with a different attitude, like a smile. Pretty good, very good. Women with attitude and guns: A crazy mix to begin with and obnoxiously proud of being part of an elite T&A sorority.

"We've been expecting you."

His worry was obvious. "How's that? Has something happened to Rosemary? Was there a robbery? Is she hurt?"

She held out a hand. "First, let's see some ID."

He obliged, placing the flowers and ring box on the limo's hood. "The name won't change, lady, the longer you stare at it. What the hell's happened here? Where's Rosemary?"

"Rosemary Bradley was arrested yesterday for the first-degree shooting death of her husband. We got the call when her staff found the place closed. We found her huddled in a corner still holding the weapon. Claims she can't remember what happened."

He paled. "Rosemary? What! No! That's impossible."

He pointed at the flowers. "Those are for her, for Rosie, and the ring. We're getting married. I got home from Nam a week ago. She knew I was coming. She was expecting me."

"We read your letter. Apparently Bradley did too and things got nasty. Mrs. Bradley had a few secrets, it seems."

"This is insane, officer, completely impossible. Can I see her? Can I at least talk with her?"

"No, you cannot. Not unless you're a lawyer. Anyway, why would you want to? She played you, and she played him. She even insists she's never seen the letter. If I were you, I would get my own lawyer, Mr. Billows. She's also claiming sole ownership of this place."

He slumped against the limo, cupping his face. "I should have come home right away. What happens now?"

"Interrogation, half-truths, lies, lawyers, a court date several months from now with twelve jurors who may or may not believe her."

"And the bar? We have employees, we have customers."

"The place stays closed for a few days. You'll get the key when we get proof it's yours. If I were you in the meantime I would forget the 'we'. I would find another bar and get royally totalled. You will not be needing that ring. Not for her. The best she'll get is life. We found the gun's holster in her dresser. The gun box was locked and empty. Not very good planning. She was expecting something to happen, Mr. Billows. And it did."

"Officer, you said the best. What could be worse than life?"

"Making a choice between lethal injection and electrocution. This is South Carolina, Mr. Billows."

The silence between them was awkward. Jed was

devastated, his face drawn. Staring at the ground he crossed his arms in a tight hug as if he were searching for any means possible to save Rosie. "I'm not standing here in someone else's nightmare, am I?"

"Her nightmare, Mr. Billows, not yours."

"Are you married, officer, got a boyfriend?"

Her brow furrowed. "No."

He snorted. "Shame on him. His loss whoever he is." He twisted, reaching for the carnations. Forcing a smile he handed them to the cop, closing a fist around the ring box and stepping a few paces to the rear door. "We'll be in touch, I suppose?" She nodded. "I'll be at the Hilton." He opened the door, pausing. "As soon as I'm done with those drinks you suggested."

She was smiling, probably remembering she was a woman. Good. Jed was smiling as well, if only she could see how widely.

He lied, in part, about the drinks. First things first. Priorities. The limo waited while he checked-out from the motel, driving him to the Hilton where he booked a suite and called his bank manager to set up a next-day meeting with his lawyer at Rosemary Bradley's bank.

*

After dinner Jed hailed a cab, the doorman at the exclusive Gentleman's Wish opening the door with one hand, accepting his five-dollar tip with the other. Jed was no stranger to the place, simply forgotten. The strip club was topnotch. Proper attire required. No jeans. No leather. 21 Plus and no trouble.

Inside, a twenty changed hands ensuring Jed of a private corner with a clear view of the dancers on their platforms and at private tables where he could assess them, visualize them, determine their intrinsic value.

He ordered a Black, neat, and sat back, politely refusing the first parade of young ladies eager to tantalize him on a stool for three minutes. They were all top notch, their bodies alluring and lithe, dancing and stripping for five bucks a song, the thrill or the adoration, all gifted in the art of sexual fantasy or frustration; not one of them meeting his criteria.

He was waiting for *her*, the special one, to first see her perform. He was patient, the club boasting more girls than a university dorm, Jed lingering on his second Black when she chanced to see his smile from under the rainbow of spotlights.

She strode to his table without the slightest unease. "Hi there, I'm Alysyn. I saw you watching me. Are you waiting for your wife or a girlfriend? You seem kind of lonely here."

"No, Miss Alysyn," he replied, "I believe, seeing your performance, that I am waiting for you. Please join me."

"Sure, I'll dance for you. Five dollars, up front."

"In a few minutes, and more than five. In the meantime, please sit with me, Alysyn. I have a short-term and very interesting proposition for you. If you're interested, if you're able."

She sat. "We've got lots of big guys here, mister. Don't get freaky on me and do not ruin my night."

He ordered her a soda, another Black. "My name is Marcus Simms and, I promise, in a month or two I will not look half as scary as I do. I'm a nice guy who's home from Nam. I'm twenty-seven and college-educated. I recently discovered my girlfriend went and got herself married which pretty much put a stick in my spokes. I need a companion for, oh, a year give or take. You Alysyn, if you're willing. For which you will receive a generous

242

lump-sum payment and full expenses for whatever you require. A wardrobe, spas, that sort of thing. Whatever you need, all expenses paid." He exchanged glasses with the near-naked waitress, paying her due respect. "There's more, but I would prefer hearing about you."

"You want me to live with you?" He nodded. "That is really, really creepy. You don't even know me."

"I know what I see. What I want is for you to consider spending a year with me before we meet, the two of us together, with my lawyer to draw up a binding contract." He waited. "Sometime within the coming year I expect my life to end, regrettably. What I want is to relish each remaining minute with you, for which I will pay you one hundred grand, tax free, held in escrow for the year. That's the deal. I assume you're not a virgin, Alysyn?"

She ignored the question. "You're serious, a hundred grand?"

He nodded, passing her ten fifty-dollar bills, tenfold the going rate for a stripper. "That's for the next ten dances. Nine for you, one for the boss. Yes, I am very serious."

"Why me? I've never seen you before."

"That's fair. Simply put, you're young, I'm young, and I believe we're a good fit. You're very attractive and I like what I see of your body. Albeit nowhere near as striking as you soon will be. I have neither the desire nor the latitude to waste on Southern romantic BS or courtship, or flowers, or dinners before luring you naked into my bed. Or being screwed over twice in one year by any woman. Hence the contract, all or nothing. The flowers will come, and the romance. That I promise you. Nor do I believe you will be disappointed."

Again he waited, sipping his Black.

She leaned forward, drawing soda through a straw into

243

her dry mouth. "I'm twenty-two, a graduate in psychology, working here to finish paying off what's left of my student loan." She stopped abruptly, sneering at his undisguised amazement. "That's right, I'm smart. This is my fourth year here. I'm practically debt free. The ones who aren't, the girls, think I'm a cheap slut. The guys, the ones who couldn't get through the doors to see me naked and jerk-off in their parents' home, called me a whore. They still can't afford to drink here and still live with mommy and daddy. Is that okay with you? And, no, I am not a virgin." She sipped her soda. "Three, if you're wondering, times three boring minutes." She glanced around. "It's a miracle working with these absolute dolls that I'm not a freaking lesbian."

He chuckled. "A smart lesbian. And who could blame you? Nor would I for a moment consider incorporating such an unkind restriction into our agreement."

"Sorry, you hit a sore spot. I saw what you were thinking."

"A lapse in good manners for which I sincerely apologize. What of your parents, Alysyn?"

"I left home at eighteen. They never wanted me and I didn't need them. Not working here." She sipped more soda. "What are you dying of? Not AIDS or anything like that? Your dying doesn't mean I have to."

"Suffice it to say, for the time being, a broken heart."

"Listen, Marcus, I have to start dancing for you or I'll get in trouble. In here talking is dancing and we're at number four. Besides, if this is not a sick joke, you won't be able to say you didn't see the goods close-up and personal. And please do not touch me. Signing a contract is difficult with a broken arm."

"Or you quit and we'll go for drinks somewhere else."

Alysyn tucked the bills into her change purse, stepping onto her stool, gyrating and swaying smoothly to a new song. By the seventh she was naked, her camisole and thong lying on the table. He was pleased with his choice. Everyone was pleased with his choice, disappointed when she stopped for a breather.

From then on he wanted her privately, he told her, asking that she slip into her tiny pieces of clothing. The masses had seen enough of her. He ordered another soda and a Black. Three songs remained.

"Ask me anything you wish, Alysyn. I will answer every question as truthfully as I can."

"Never mind. Instead you can invite me for that drink before it's too late for dinner. I've already decided, I think. After you leave I'll beg off, not feeling well. This job isn't as easy as it seems. Then we'll talk for real, over a nice meal. I need to make sure you're not an orangutan in a suit. Then I go home and you go home. Say all the right things and tomorrow I want to see where and how you live. I haven't spent four years here to get caught up with a sweet-talking loser, or worse. Then we'll visit your lawyer, when and where I will get a contract and ten of the hundred in cash up front. You will also prove to me that you're clean where it counts, without the expectation of anything more. Then I quit this place, not before."

"Is that all?"

"Yes."

"Good. Ever been to South Beach?"

Jed was ecstatic, Alysyn no less jubilant the next day when she cleared out her locker at the club after depositing ten grand into her account. They would remain in Charleston for a few months. Marcus, she discovered, had some personal business to finalize first. After which they

would leave for Miami and never look back."
*

Within the week Rosemary's transaction was reversed into his personal account to the tune of not far from a million, Jed regained ownership of the bar that he immediately put up for sale and Mrs. Bradley was remanded into custody to await her criminal trial for first-degree murder.

The bar sold quickly below fair market value to his staff of three young women and their parents. They were good kids, eager; he wanted to help them out and he didn't need the money. He gave his clothes to the mission, her worldly goods and Bradley's to the garbage bin. Whatever the girls would later do with the place was not his business, Jed moving in February from the five-star to a beachfront condo leased by the month where he stayed until the trial was over. He never returned to The Wine Bar.

The trial began May 31st. Two months later the jury of eight women and four men quickly regarded the letter as sufficient provocation on Kirt Bradley's part to become incensed, finding differently regarding the extent of Rosemary Bradley's actions. She clearly anticipated her husband's violent reaction. Afraid for her life or not, she acted with criminal intent. She was planning in anticipation of the worst, the locked box in the highboy and the holster concealed in her underwear drawer difficult for the jury to discount. Given the violence that erupted she would not have had the luxury of time or the presence of mind, they contended. She was indeed fully cognizant of the evening's potentially fatal consequence because she had in fact devised the outcome.

Jed Billows was called to testify as a character witness with little to add when asked to elaborate. He never met Kirt Bradley, never heard of him other than the news of his hire. Either way, the man should have walked away. A cheating woman isn't worth dying for. Yes, he told the court, staring directly at her parents, she was very much a high-school tease and college flirt, constantly wanting her way and constantly getting her way. Which wasn't entirely her fault alone, more a question of proper upbringing. Or the lack thereof, he supposed.

Cross examined and dismissed, he stepped from the stand adding innocently, "I simply cannot comprehend for the life of me that anyone could so easily kill another human being." Like forty-two VCs, the ones I counted.

Gulping air and sobbing as the verdict was read days later, Rosemary Bradley was sentenced to twenty-five years before any possibility of parole, the jury recommending her natural life.

Taken immediately from the courtroom, her face entirely drenched with tears, her green eyes strained and blurred, his contempt shone through like a macabre beacon, his smirk a silent and private confession leaving Rosemary Bradley with no doubt whatsoever who could.

*

As Rosemary Bradley was being transferred without any delay to the state's maximum security prison, Jed Billows was driving home to Alysyn. He was finished with Charleston. They were moving at long last to Miami. To do what, and until when, he didn't yet know. With a few million in his portfolio and a woman who had quickly and amazingly transformed from the inspiration of neglected men's dreams into a sophisticated lady, he was in no particular hurry. They arrived August 01st.

She had never visited South Beach, too busy studying and working, and after six months with Marcus she had forgotten she ever worked as a naked and squirming mannequin for inebriated and salivating men.

Each day they visited another condo that was nicer, higher, more expensive and more exclusive until Jed felt at home in one on the eighteenth floor that had every amenity he could imagine including her, formalizing the sale as she went shopping on his dime for a new and elegant outfit to wear that evening at dinner. He couldn't put her from his mind even when they were together. How could he when what was happening was too special. Days and nights were never long enough. She was magnificent.

Christmas Eve, with Rosemary successfully driven irreversibly from his mind, they were sharing a chaise-longue on South Beach celebrating her "yes, Marcus, I will" and her diamond ring with an ice-cold bottle of Moët & Chandon. Yes she would marry him. They had fallen deeply in love as Jed knew they would, from their very first night sleeping together after meeting with the lawyer and every night since.

The flowers did come to her as he had promised, frequently. He was a hopeless romantic and affectionate, doting over her constantly. To Jed she was a dream come true, a precious reality after two agonizing years of war and sterile loneliness; to Alysyn he was her savior who came to her years before she may have begged for one had she ever become trapped.

New Year's Eve they were on the nineteenth floor, alone in the rooftop spa under a Plexiglas ceiling, swimming and frolicking naked in heated water under the stars. He adored her, adored her body and her mind.

"What's wrong, darling? It's New Year's. We're going to have a wonderful dinner, come home to make love, and tomorrow we'll be married by the captain as we sail towards an enchanting honeymoon." She pouted, floating weightlessly in his arms. "You haven't changed your mind, have you?"

"No. Never. Tomorrow cannot come soon enough. I need tonight to be over. I never did like New Year's. Never understood the point of it all."

She pressed her lips to his. "The first with me, darling. Can you believe a year has passed, that I am actually teaching? What would they say about me now?"

Such was the problem. Despite the lawyer's cheque she received that morning honouring the balance of their initial arrangement, she had forgotten his most important words spoken one year earlier. He spun her in a tight circle, swirling the water, carrying her from the pool to the sauna where they had left their towels and robes.

"What does it matter, sweet thing? You're better than them. Anyway, how will they know unless you show them? They won't. So show them and luxuriate in the moment. Attend the next class reunion in your Jag and Armani. Teach them a lasting lesson. You are a teacher after all. You should, sweet thing, with me as your escort unless I'm elsewhere engaged. Not that you require an escort. You should. You'll blow them away, as you do me." She reached out, swinging open the door. "I adore everything about you, everything I see." He stepped onto the lowest cedar bench, holding her more tightly, aligning her into position, sitting on the highest and framing his legs with hers, the fresh droplets of pool water clinging to her body mingling enticingly with glistening beads of sweat.

He kissed her and cupped her breasts, sliding easily into her, securing her in place with intent fingers kneading the soft and firm flesh of her perfect bum, letting her take control. She was an accomplished and unquenchable lover, had become one, her energy endlessly outlasting his, her triple teenage three-minute and impulsive bump and grinds long-forgotten.

When at last she showed him mercy, collapsing against him, they remained as they were until the duet of heavy breathing abated and she dismounted, laying back.

Jed reached for his towel, Alysyn didn't. They had been caught off-guard once before when he instinctively reached for his fleecy modesty curtain. Alysyn, on the other hand, enjoyed an acquired comfort zone. Impishly unaffected, she remained propped on her forearms wondering what his problem was. Better to shock or entice, darling, she told him, smiling at the couple, than to appear foolish and clumsy trying to hide what they would imagine of her anyway. Possibly not recreating the unknown to her best advantage. Now they didn't have to, she added, asking them whether she was right or wrong.

She was right, they agreed with smiles, the man complimenting Jed on his good taste and good fortune while tugging at his own lady's towel, the woman unabashedly telling Alysyn as she stretched out that she was awesome.

"We should go, sweet thing. We have reservations."

"No, darling. We should stay home," she argued in a whisper, "order a pizza and get drunk with champagne after we pack."

"And miss the boat. Not a good idea. Get up, Mrs. Simms." He stood, taking her hand. "Besides, I want to watch you dress…before I undress you." He stepped onto the slatted floor. "You are enchanting. Promise me you will never change, that you will choose a man to marry who loves you as much as I do now. Promise me."

Alysyn stood, rolling her eyes. "I think I did promise you, darling. Ooh, I think you'll have to carry me."

He held open her robe. Then he cursed. "In all this wedding and honeymoon excitement I completely forgot. I have papers downstairs for you to sign, making you my sole beneficiary. My lawyer, being the stuffy stickler that he is, insisted that he call you tomorrow to confirm. Before we leave. In case I fall overboard on the cruise, I suppose."

"A day before my wedding I'm already a wealthy widow? How nice, darling. Thank you."

He coughed a laugh. "Very wealthy, laugh-in-their-faces-at-the-reunion-wealthy."

She put a finger to his lips, shushing him, walking out.

New Year's Eve came and went, dinner giving way to dancing, dancing surrendering to quiet whispers of dreams and desires. The restaurant was less than a mile from the condo on the usually busy Lincoln Road Mall. The evening was balmy and Alysyn wanted to stroll home hand in hand like young lovers. She was twelve hours from becoming his wife and, apparently, he had not yet heard sufficient details of her coming day.

The man coming towards them was non-descript: thirty to fifty in baggy jeans and sneakers, a ponytail and beard, a baseball jacket and mirrored sunglasses at 1:00AM. Jed paid him little attention, as a precaution slipping a hand into his tuxedo to finger the stainless steel handle of his favourite blade. Then he saw the gun, the one aimed at Alysyn.

"That hand of yours, mister, it better be reachin' for some cash in that fancy suit. Lots of cash."

He didn't look around. He knew help was nowhere near, his ears still attuned to the sounds of footsteps that were not his. He didn't need help. "Here's the thing, I've got a few hundred. I'll put it on that bench and we go our separate ways. No drama, no grief. No one gets hurt."

"Don't think so. I'm thinkin' you'll toss me your wallet, the bitch's purse, your shoes, and then you fuck off out of here." The man cocked the gun's hammer.

"Deal, but no wallet. Money clip. Same for the lady. Sorry. "Jed tossed the clip thick with bills, reaching into Alysyn's purse and tossing hers to within an inch or two of his.

"Alright!" The mugger was thrilled, stooping. "And the bitch's ring."

Jed stepped in front of her. "Sorry, we can't help you with that one. I'll give you her bracelet instead. Rubies and diamonds, worth three grand. It's in my pocket and what she doesn't yet have she won't miss. Deal?"

The man nodded. Jed nodded. Reaching into his jacket, a millisecond later the throwing knife left his hand, striking its target, buried deep to the hilt; the bullet from the .45 crashed Jed into Alysyn, crashing them both onto the sidewalk.

She screamed his name, screeching for help. Worried and uncertain faces crammed behind restaurant and lounge frontages, entranced, witnessing the failed mugging like some gruesome theatre production, brave enough to gawk, cowardly enough not to help.

He was bleeding profusely, smiling. He would not embarrass himself or taint her memory of him.

She cradled his head into her lap, stroking his face. "Marcus, help is coming."

He gazed into her eyes, a trickle of blood dribbling from between his lips. "You are enchanting, Alysyn, you are. Never forget your promise to me. Never change. Be certain the man you marry will love you as much as I do. Promise me, sweet thing."

She was crying, warm tears splashing his face. "I

252

promise I will marry *you*. You are not leaving me. You are not allowed."

Sirens screeched in the distance. "Yes, I am. I must. I always do, sweet thing. Tonight I believed I might be wrong. I wanted to be wrong, for you, but I wasn't. I never am. This is what I must do."

"What?" She shook her head, she didn't understand "No!"

He raised a hand to her cheek. "Forgive my lie, sweet thing, which here and now hardly matters to either of us."

"What lie, Marcus? You would never lie to me."

He coughed. "Take his call in the morning, sweet thing. He has much to tell you. Then you go for me to the reunion. Blow them away. Do that for me."

"No. You stay here for *me*, Marcus. Do you hear me? They're coming. Do not be stupid about this. They're coming."

"There is no light, sweet thing. There is no light. Not for me."

Jed Billows died in Alysyn Dunn's arms, a thin smile on his closed lips. He died quietly, closing his eyes. He knew how to die, strangely feeling the warmth of her hands until other hands gently pulled her away.

253

Chapter Sixteen
Marcus Simms & Evita

The entire year was a success first and foremost due to
Southeast Consulting's dynamic foray into the Southwest.
That was business. His personal triumph however was a
glorious sun and sea vacation without Rosemary Sandra,
his first that wasn't excruciatingly endured in museums or
churches or peering through wrought iron fences at palaces
or touring dilapidated castles to help impoverished earls
and dukes pay their taxes.

She hadn't once in her life cared to embrace the charms
of South Beach, this despite her single-minded summertime
ambition of her youthful fun years of wearing the smallest
possible bikini at the beach. Unless where other women
were topless or backless or both. The Caribbean? No way.
If Miami was lewd and distasteful, the islands were an
archipelago of exhibitionistic debaucheries. Which is where
he went, as a social experiment, to debauch, to test whether
or not she was correct. Or a stuck-up prissy bitch whose tits
and ass had forgotten or resented their better days.

The latter of which he naturally predetermined and later
confirmed with an open mind after three weeks of keen
observation on three islands with three single women in
exclusive clubs who were conducting tests of their own: To
prove whether, at the desperate end of thirty, their bodies

enticingly bared at the beach and scantily clad in provocative eveningwear, they were still a marketable commodity.

He left them with kisses and hugs, fully aware each would soon forget him, their private spaces rented out to the next short-term occupant deemed suitable for the very low cost of his preferred company and the visible proof to all others of their marketability. After which they would return home rejuvenated, after divorces or break-ups or extended dry spells feeling viable and good about themselves. As he did, perfectly acclimated to living without her.

That was in September, the women forgotten, his tan less deep, Marcus thinking he should perform a similar experiment in the spring. He found the subsequent weeks long, filling his daytime hours with work, his nighttime hours with Kirt Bradley until the previous week when the man died unexpectedly in Miami of an in-home execution. Since then Marcus felt sullenly agitated. He always did at year's end, but this week was particularly difficult.

Naturally he knew the source of his malaise, fuming as he sat on his Miami luxury terrace waiting for his in-room breakfast. Not Bradley, not by a longshot. Bradley was gratifying, one of his best. She wasn't. Her. The queen of all bitches who had left a detailed message with his secretary Beverly practically dictating that he appear before her on the first of the year, Her Imperious Majesty, to discuss his reformation and the discontinuance of their current state of affairs either by submission or decree.

Delivered verbatim by Beverly with theatrical flair the day before he left for Miami, Marcus erupted into hoarse laughter, asking the young woman what the hell that meant. Beverly had a sense of humour. She said, "You are royally screwed, sire," while pouring him a two-fingered Blue and curtsying respectfully before leaving his office.

He didn't care about the day, he never did. In fact he cared very little about her, if at all. He had been in Miami since the 17th, the commencement of the worst week of any year to travel, experienced flyers set upon by wailing babies, dumb-ass teenagers devoid of respect believing their pillows were cleaner than coach, someone's grandma and grandpa thinking a free cookie and apple in a bag was absolutely wonderful. When what was truly wonderful was an over-priced seat in first-class.

The hardest part throughout the week was keeping his distance from stunning and near-naked sexual predators, even telling one delectable and disappointed hopeful in a to-die-for suspender thong that he was gay. He could not risk complicating his last day. He needed the week alone for mandatory withdrawal from the physical and cerebral high of killing, from luxuriating in having made the world a better place.

He noticed her during his first morning walk, and every morning after, biding his time. He didn't need her with so many to choose from, he wanted her. She was alluring, sitting on her beach bed reading, facing the ocean. Not staring was difficult, not wondering about her was impossible, gazing at her each afternoon from his terrace through the 500mm lens of his Nikon, discovering that what he first believed was a radiant tan was actually the radiant complexion of a beautiful Latina.

He put her at mid-thirties, each morning and afternoon walking imperceptibly closer to her bed, until the previous day when he sat reading on the bed beside hers that he booked for two days. With the precision of a Swiss timepiece she left at 5:00 each afternoon, forty minutes before sunset, making the most of her day, returning each morning near 9:00.

Each day she wore a different sundress, each day a different set of triangles. He never noticed a cellphone or tablet. She read real books, thick books with hard covers. Which in itself spoke volumes. She was smart. She waded into the ocean once each hour for five minutes, dunking her body several times, occasionally her hands disappearing, adjusting her bikini which he assumed served the dual purpose of rinsing the tiny fabric. She ordered lunch that came to her each day at one, her first tall cocktail at three, her second at four.

Marcus checked his Rolex: 2:50. He stood, shrugging into a gauze shirt, meandering idly to the hotel's poolside bar, advising the waiter with a ten not to bother. Precisely at three he bowed slightly forward under the woman's canopy, extending the tray.

"Buenos días, señorita." She glanced at him, leisurely, deliberately, not the least taken aback. "Please excuse the interruption. The bargirl assured me you would like a Michelada and I could think of no better way to introduce myself. Also, those three words are the sad extent of my deplorable Spanish vocabulary. I am truly hoping your English will allow me to continue talking with you"

She wasn't hesitating. No. She was making him wait. "You are very thoughtful and gracious, señor. Gracias." She removed her glass from the tray. "By your accent I would not expect you to speak my language. Not many here do. Atlanta, perhaps? Or Savannah?"

"Worse, I'm afraid. Mobile. Here for a year-end reprieve from the other fifty-one weeks, to help mitigate the effects of an incurable workaholic disorder." He extended his free hand. I'm Marcus Simms, guilty of waiting too long to meet you. I was uncertain of the protocol set in place for approaching an irresistible lady on a beach."

No reaction. She was accustomed to men's flirtations. "Mobile. How terrible for you." Then a glimmer of a smile. "I am Evita Mendez." She watched him lay the tray on his table, sitting on the edge of his bed. "He who hesitates is most often lost, Marcus. Yesterday must have been difficult for you, and possibly your days spent strolling by the water. Do I appear that dangerous to a man as gallant and charming as you?"

He beamed. "I admit, extremely difficult." He gazed towards the blue horizon. "As with delicate creatures of the sea, the most exotic are the most dangerous to touch. However, having conquered my fear I should not waste what remains of today, or this evening. Please have dinner with me, Evita." He held out his left hand. "No ring, no girlfriend, and I have references." He waited. "Unless you have plans with friends, or family, or with a man more fortunate than I who waits to escort you into a new year that I trust will be as exquisite as you."

She sipped her cocktail. "No such man exists, my family is in Mexico where I vacation in the summer, and my friends are nine-to-five at a research facility. They are very nice, also extremely white and deathly boring. No offense, Marcus."

He chuckled. "None taken."

"I tell them I am going to Mexico each year at Christmas, which you see is not true. I come here for ten days to pamper myself at the spa and enjoy the sun. Most days I do not see the sun until it is almost lost in the ocean."

"In which case I will definitely put Miami on my next year's Christmas wish list." Because I definitely want to unwrap you. "Or come here more frequently on business."

She ignored the implication. "I will return home on Sunday when all this New Year's hype is forgotten. And you, Marcus?"

"Sunday as well. Suddenly too quickly." He tasted his Michelada, nodding his approval. "You're not a fan, of New Year's and parties?"

"Celebrating the countdown of our lives, each New Year closing with more haste. No, I am not. I prefer not to regard my life in such a way."

He sighed. "Must I sadly assume we are not celebrating together this evening with champagne and dancing?"

"Celebrating? No we are not." She put her drink onto her table. "I would accept your kind invitation to join you at dinner, Marcus, however I would spoil your entire evening and feel terrible. Perhaps tomorrow, if you are free."

"You will spoil my entire evening by not joining me, Evita, not to mention the utter destruction of my ego. May I suggest a compromise, possibly a quiet dinner and digestif somewhere of your choosing, somewhere quaint? Quaint and quiet."

"Un degestivo, sí," her smile widened, "In this case I do accept. Thank you."

"I did bring a tux, though. Would you mind?"

"Of course not. I will dress accordingly. Thank you for telling me."

He raised his glass, she raised hers. "To our evening…and confronting groundless fears."

"Yes, to very brave gentlemen. I assume we will also be close neighbours here at the beach until Sunday, Marcus?"

"Definitely, unless I annoy you this evening."

"Then you must not, Marcus. Latinas are not pleasant

259

when we are angry." She swung her feet onto the sand, standing, glancing at her watch, allowing him fleeting moments to admire her body since he had very little to imagine and had demonstrated reasonable restraint in not ogling her as they spoke. He was a man after all, and she was Latina. "I was not expecting your invitation, although I did suspect you wanted very much to meet me. We should go for a walk to talk and to dip into the ocean, to know each other better before dinner and another cocktail here while not sitting so far apart as strangers."

They strolled and dipped until four. She was interesting, a government lab rat who did not have to tell him she did an hour in the gym each day. He couldn't wait to spend his evening with her, to touch her and to please her. The afternoon was progressing well, the last hour spent propped against the pillows of her bed completely excruciating, Marcus cursing himself for wasting the morning, Evita as comfortable with him as she would be with a close friend.

On the hour the waiter came to her bed, taking the dual order, noting Marcus' room number.
Evita wasn't a guest, she had rented a ranch-style villa with a pool which she pointed out as they walked, where she ended her days privately to even her tan, which was decidedly too much information for a desperate man. At five she invited him to a freshwater dip, leaving him alone seemed somewhat silly given their dinner plans.

First she called her favourite Cuban restaurant in Little Havana, preparing a final afternoon cocktail which they sipped while drifting in inflatable chairs, sometimes colliding, sometimes drifting apart. She kicked him out at six, and would expect him at eight.

This one would be difficult, he realized, leaving from the beach entrance, the sand cooling under his feet. They would not be awake until three or four in the morning testing each other's carnal endurance. She was a seductress, she would demand a tantalizing prelude to sex. She would undress for him, not teasingly, deliberately. She would want to see and feel his palpable desire when seeing all of her. She would want him in his straightbacks until ready herself to push them free of his feet. The sex would be urgent, not frantic; deliberate and unhurried, each caress engineered and executed for specific individual needs and mutually cataclysmic climaxes.

He was eager.

*

Kirt Bradley was sentenced in 1995 at age fourteen to four years in juvenile detention until his majority when he was transferred to a California state prison for a term of sixteen years for the murder of his teacher, eight classmates, and the wounding of seven others. He was released in October, ending up in Miami as a dishwasher after no one wanted him in several other cities including his parents.

Well before his teen years he was an outcast, dark and morose, gradually sculpting his persona until that's who he became. Easier than trying to fit in and being rejected or ridiculed. He wasn't particularly good-looking, never popular. He had no friends, never thinking to search inward for answers that would prove him wrong, forever blaming others, his invisible loathing festering until a rainy, dark and dismal day in early June he went to school without his lunch or books in his knapsack.

He wasn't a rich kid from a wealthy home. His parents were average, struggling to stay afloat, his father never certain of his job, his mother helping to make ends meet by working part-time at coffee shops and pizza parlours. Parents who fed him and clothed him, who gave him a bed in a modest home and not much else, believing they were doing the best they could afford. Parents who should never have conceived of having a child, the same parents who sat stunned when hearing their kid went coolly to the front of his class to take aim at his teacher and the closest of a classroom filled with terrified and screaming students.

Minutes later he was found sitting calmly in the pouring rain on the doorsteps of his home. Amidst sirens, flashing lights and curious eyes peering from behind windows, he calmly raised his hands and lay flat on the walkway with his face down and his arms spread wide.

Kirt Bradley, thirty-five, arrived in Miami a few weeks earlier landing his dream job in a stand-up fast-food diner on the wrong side of town. For an entire week Marcus dropped in each night but one for dessert and coffee, leaving shortly before the 11:00 PM closing, arriving at the ex-con's low-rent apartment building half an hour ahead of him to set a schedule. 11:40, consistently. Except on Christmas Eve when they would close at 6:00, Marcus correctly expecting him at 6:40. On the off night he made his way inside with his German pick set, hoping for the best and prepared to plan for the worst.

The place was nothing special, not for 499.00 a month. The two rooms were sparsely decorated, Marcus questioning his choice of words, thinking that on Christmas Eve he would come equipped with a scented hanky. One room had a bed, a clock, a half-empty gin bottle on a liquor store box reinforced with packaging tape, and a smudge-stained radio on the floor. The other room boasted a second cardboard box by the side of a worn recliner, a third box under a 70's pink television, and two appliances in the corner that resembled a two-burner stove and a fridge that was as empty as the closet except for a few six-packs.

Living the good life. The bathroom belonged in a Somali bus terminal.

The man himself was comical. He stood a straight 5'5" in black sneakers with a stubble-carpeted head, shorter when he waddled hunched over in his black oversized raincoat on picture-perfect nights with his black tuque pulled to where his thick eyebrows converged with a crooked nose, his hands stuffed into his pockets. His curious gait and crooked nose likely the results of his early years as a prison hand-me-down if not a favourite.

He had no strength, no tone. His arms were weak, his chest concaved, Marcus assuming he had no teeth since he had discovered a large tube of No-Name denture adhesive on the bathroom cabinet but no toothbrush. Killing him would be a crime of goodwill, doing the gnome a favour as much as the society he no longer deserved. He didn't deserve to live; he probably didn't want to, in spite of which he would sure as hell change his mind in the first fifteen seconds.

On the 24th Marcus arrived with two hours to spare, first knocking several times and waiting in the event Bradley had either lost his job or had no dishes to wash. The afternoon was warm and bright, the evening promising a clear sky and gentle breezes, ideal for a stroll along the boardwalk before dinner.

At 6:00 he stood inside the bedroom, opening the blinds for added light. Bradly walked in forty minutes later, flicking a light switch. A moment later Marcus heard the fridge door slam shut, the tab ripping from a full beer followed by a drawn out belch. Enter Marcus Simms.

"Hello there, Bradley."

Bradley blew foamy beer from his nose and mouth, his jaws and deep-set eyes locked wide open in fright. "Who are you?"

"My name hardly matters. What does matter is your future, Bradley. You don't have one."

Bradley spun around for no reason. "You a cop?"

"No, and I'm alone. Here to make things right for a young woman, eight young girls and seven boys. And please do not tell me you've done your time and that you're a better person. That is so very trite. Why do all ex-cons say that?"

They stood apart like David and Goliath. Bradley seemed to shrink, dropping his beer and burying his hands into his armpits.

"I have. And I have my high-school."

"Wow. An ex-con with high-school in the twenty-first century. Goodie for you, Bradley." He snorted. "I believe what I propose is a far better option for you, more humane in the long run. Much quicker, if exceptionally more painful for too few minutes while you literally lose your mind. Like pulling a Band-Aid, get it over with and soon all the hurt goes away. At any rate, much better than living in this shithole for a lifetime. Of greater importance, those few minutes will bring tearful smiles to the faces of sixteen families because they *will* hear of this. I will make certain they do."

"This is crazy. I just want to start over. How do you even know about me?"

"You're part of a non-profit pastime. You killed nine people. You don't get to start over. How do you even do that, kill children?"

He brought the gun from inside his windbreaker.

"I'm sorry. I am. Please believe me."

"Take off that ridiculous outfit and look at your watch. I cannot do this while I'm pissing myself."

Bradley shrugged from the coat obediently, tugging at his tuque. "A quarter of seven. So?"

"Well you'll be dead at 6:50, in five minutes, wishing you were dead long before that. A veritable lifetime. But at least you've got a heads-up. Those kids didn't go to class thinking they would be gunned down. They didn't have the luxury of praying, or crying out to their parents. Or even messing themselves. You do. So feel free because when the cops find you they won't even notice your wet pants. They'll be too busy puking at a crime scene."

"They all laughed at me. Said things about me, called me names."

"They did not. Court documents contradict that. They simply did not like you. Not the same thing. You were simply too fucked-up for them, blaming them and not yourself."

"If anything, you should have killed your parents. They're the ones who did the worst harm, creating another low-income social misfit, a monster." Marcus stepped a few feet closer. "Unfortunately you were a minor. At eighteen they probably would have executed you and I wouldn't be standing here. I would be killing somebody else. It's what I do, my way of getting through Christmas. I really do not like Christmas."

"I know what I did was wrong. But what they did to me, the cons, I should have killed myself that day at school." He began weeping. "From the day I got out of juvie I had my ass stitched so many times I can't cough anymore without shitting myself. And my nose, smashed in because I puked on the guy's balls the first time. Yeah, I should have killed myself."

"I agree. Poor career planning on your part. But your coughing predicament, you really have no idea."

265

He didn't understand. "I can, you know…kill them, my parents. I can do that. I'd get twenty-five, maybe more. I can do that. You don't have to kill me. I can kill them instead. We can do this. And the cons, they don't bother me anymore. I'm not young enough."

"They're not my raison d'être in this life, I'm afraid. You are. In fact you're my sixteenth, shall we say, disposal. Ironic, don't you agree? You killed nine and severely wounded seven others, and here you are with me. Number sixteen." Marcus launched the dart from the gun. "The thing in your neck is a sedative to make my job easier." He pocketed the gun, retrieving the syringe from another. He removed the protective sleeve, deliberately aiming the needle close to the floor, squirting a thread of lethal liquid through the air for affect and to remove the slightest bubble that might detract from the event. "This isn't. This is pentobarbital, which I'm sure you're familiar with. But here's the crux of your current situation, I am not inherently a forgiving person. I do not believe in an eye for an eye; I believe in removing the head for an eye. Figuratively, of course. Accordingly this is a fifty-fifty blend. One part pento, one part sulphuric acid. For the kids. Enough pento to kill you in due course, sufficient H_2SO_4 to chemically dissolve much of you in the meantime…and thereafter. When they open you, if they choose to, it will be messy."

Bradley's eyes bulged at seeing the lacquered parquet flooring blister and fizz, lunging for the door a mere second before collapsing. Marcus Simms knelt by the inert body, Bradley's speech slurred and irrational. He was whimpering, leaking urine onto the floor.

Marcus inserted the needle into Bradley's forearm, pausing. "Goodbye, Bradley. My regards to your dark

master. Remember what I said, like pulling a Band-Aid."
He thumbed the plunger and stood. He didn't need to watch his work take effect. He knew what theatrics would ensue and how instantly. Instead he went to the bedroom for his new shoulder bag, retrieving a letter he wrote several days earlier in Atlanta before printing a single copy at a local stationary outlet. His first ever and final communiqué.

Dearest First Responders,

Deepest and sincere regrets for the unpleasant mess on the floor.

He had an adverse reaction to a complimentary cocktail of pentobarbital and H2SO4.

Sixteen families in California must hear of this in some detail, for their closures. They should understand to what extent he left this world tortured and bawling, his vomit stifling his screams.

Me,

XOXOXO

He dropped the letter onto the recliner, ignoring the high-pitched whines and violent spasms consistent with a justifiably violent death. Bradley was beyond salvation, the pento taking effect, his body already an empty shell, voided and humiliated in death, his gaunt mask a picture-perfect post-mortem depiction of his agony and terror for those who would first see him.

Marcus gathered his bag, accounting for each piece of his work kit, confident that Bradley required no further attention. He left, walking several blocks before hailing a cab free of his tools save the pick set. He disembarked on Collins Avenue, walking through the noisy lobby of the Seaforth Hotel to the men's room where he changed entirely into a fresh outfit.

267

Exiting through the beach entrance onto the boardwalk a few miles from his hotel he made use of a half-dozen trashcans before tossing the empty leather bag onto the sand.

*

His head snapped into the air as though gripped by a vicious hand, his heartbeat racing. Her soothing voice and warm hand resting between his shoulders were calming, the pressure of her fingertips gently kneading pleasantly arousing. He needed more time, an eternity of seconds to transition between his realities.

Why had he said such a terrible and cruel thing to Alysyn when his eyes were clearing, when he was regaining consciousness, returning to her? There *was* light for him, lots of it, shining brightly through her garden doors leading onto the pool deck. He wasn't killed! He remembered the pool, was remembering, his erratic breathing subsiding. He knew to remain still, to say nothing. Somehow he knew.

The weight of her body shifted beside him. "Marcus, it is me, Evita. I am sorry. I touched you while you were dreaming badly. This was wrong of me. I startled you."

"Evita?" he whispered.

"Sí. Soy yo, of course."

"I was dreaming. I'm sorry if I frightened you."

"Lo siento, Marcus. I wanted simply to say buenas días y ¡feliz cumpleaños! This is your special day."

The fear she had instantly ignited in his mind was ebbing, the familiar and sickening sensations of dread and uncertainty twisting his gut beginning to wane.

She was Evita. Evita, yes. Alysyn was gone and he was no longer Jeddore Billows. He wasn't, and Kirt Bradley was expunged from his mind without the slightest consequence.

She was watching him, studying him, wondering about him, about all the things he hadn't told her or what she hadn't told him. He could feel her breath against the perspiration glazing his back.

Oh, God. "Happy birthday. That's what you said?"

"Sí, the day you do not like. However this is my villa, my rules muchacho. I will prepare a special Mexican breakfast for you with mimosas."

The only thing special about the day is pissing off the supreme bitch. "Don't remind me."

"Expressos are ready for us at the pool when you are. Do not hurry. Your sleep was fitful. I should have known better than to alarm you. However the warm sun will do wonders for you. Come to me when you are ready. A robe is by your side."

"Did I tell you that you were absolutely stunningly enchanting last night?"

"Sí, you did, many times. Thank you. We were a lovely couple. Many people stared at us."

"At you, wondering why you were with me."

Evita stroked his hair, sliding smoothly from the bed. "Come to me when you are ready. We have two full days, Marcus. We should not waste them since I am no longer dangerous to you. I want to enjoy my short time with you. We will understand soon enough what else might happen between us, whether we were speaking of possible true love or fleeting love made real by warm breezes and warmer embraces. We will see."

She kissed his shoulder and cheek, padding onto the deck, her body cloaked enticingly in a muslin sarong. Marcus remained as he was, one side of his head buried into his pillow, recapturing the previous evening, striving to remember what he did and did not say. What he did remember was that he wanted to stay. He did.

Precision was a big thing with him. He arrived at eight, precisely, armed with a dozen long-stem red roses tied with a silk ribbon that his hotel concierge had somehow managed to beg, borrow or steal for him.

When Evita swung open the door he stepped back and gasped. At forty-three she was the oldest of his comforters, on paper. Seeing her, she wasn't. He could almost forget she was dressed. She was stunning. The slicked-back midnight brassy-coloured hair she'd fashioned into one of those Latina buns for the beach was gone, replaced by lustrous curls. Under the porch light her brownish-green eyes sparkled at seeing the flowers, her bronze lips moving in a concert of passionate expressions. She was pure female, her body screaming for attention in a patchwork leather cuirass dress that would drive everyone's attention to her legs, their imaginations wild.

Her sandals were open-toed, her toes and fingers lacquered in bronze. No nylons. No need.

"I'm breathless." He truly was. "I want to say something you haven't heard before. You are an incredible vision, Evita. I should have bought a Spanish dictionary. I must believe Latinos possess words more appropriate than divine and heavenly."

"Those will do nicely, Marcus. Thank you." She reached for the bouquet. "They are lovely, and you are very handsome in your tuxedo."

"How can I possibly be standing here and not be worried about your jealous husband or boyfriend challenging me to a duel?"

"Because my jealous husband has not yet asked me to marry him. Perhaps like you he is afraid of exotic sea

270

creatures." She inhaled the petals' fragrance. "Come in, Marcus, before you trip on your tongue and fall down."

"I'm staring, I know. Forgive me."

"We Latinas, we enjoy men staring nicely at us. Sin embargo, you can stare at me inside. I have poured you a Patrón Añejo, neat. It is a man's drink. Too many, however, and *you* will want to marry me."

"I do already."

She excused herself for not having a proper vase, filling a sangria jug with water. Then she went to him and kissed him. To ease the tension, she told him, and because she liked him. Which suited him just fine, he answered, pulling her closer. Because he liked her too.

They arrived in Little Havana by nine, holding hands, to a quaint bistro setting where the owner had set a special table in a secluded corner for her favourite customer, giving Marcus the female onceover and Evita a mischievous wink.

They began with another Patrón, lingering, Marcus allowing Evita to select the wine. The meal was sumptuous, the wine tasting as delicious as Evita looked. And he told her so. For dessert they shared a flan de arroz con leche and a Patrón XO Café talking in subdued tones as though they had known each other years longer than eight hours.

Leaving, Evita kissed and hugged her friend who then ignored Marcus' hand and hugged him tightly as well. She didn't want to walk on the beach, or the boardwalk. She wanted to spend what was left of the evening at her poolside with candles and soft Latino music and, "to be alone with you, Marcus." She giggled, the sound soft and sweet and sensuous. "If you are not afraid."

At the villa she kicked off her sandals, asking him to serve their nightcaps while she attended to the candles and CDs. At the pool under a starlit sky they talked endlessly,

271

sharing a loveseat, Evita cuddled into his arms when they weren't dancing and kissing, their bodies scarcely moving.

Midnight passed them by without champagne, regrets or false hopes for a better year.

"Marcus, will you stay with me? Will you come with me to the beach tomorrow and stay with me here in my villa until we leave together to go our separate ways?"

"I will, until I leave with you on Sunday eager to see you again and again." He kissed her. "I believe I do want to marry you. Unless I wake in a few hours to discover I'm dreaming."

Evita inhaled a deep breath. She believed him. She wiggled from his arms, patting his cheek, standing facing him. She unbuckled one leather clasp at her shoulder, tugging the slim zipper hidden by leather from under her arm to the hem, letting the Louis Vuitton creation crumple to the deck. Pleased with his reaction to her bare breasts, she plucked at the side ribbons of her thong, Marcus reaching out quickly to stop her, taking full control, sliding the silk and satin from her glistening lips to her knees when he tugged the ribbons apart, secreting them with a crooked grin into his shirt pocket. The fragrant scent of her arousal was infectious. She was breathtaking.

Marcus stood, running his palms along the entire length of her body, paying particular and respectful attention to each of her compelling curves, choosing to bypass the warmth of her visible moisture. She was a soft and sensual living statuette. He adored her. He truly did not want to leave her.

Naked, the captivating Evita twirled playfully and sauntered to the Ferro-concrete steps, stepping waist-deep into the heated water where she sat hugging her knees, waiting and watching.

Men didn't strip, she mused. They couldn't. Some things were impossible, like white guys believing they could dance. Yet he could dance, and sensually, never faltering. Most were at a serious disadvantage without the accoutrements of sexy garters and nylons, detailed bras and camisoles, teddies and silk panties. They were men, designed to be functional. They were clumsy, awkward. Yet he was not, Evita visibly surprised at how smoothly he was stripping for her into silk, into something not much smaller than what he wore at the beach and the pool. Something a Latino would wear, a young Latino, not the bunched-up cotton boxers of middle-aged Americans she was praying not to see. She was enjoying the show, thinking she could one day very soon come to love him, praying secretly that he wasn't the worst liar in the world. That he would come often to be with her after Sunday as he promised, that he would move some day from Mobile to Charleston where she could transfer to a sister lab. That's what she wanted. She had been alone for too long.

He came towards her in his straightbacks, telling her with a smirk that whatever happened next was for her to decide. No problema! She pulled them to his ankles, not at all disappointed, held out her hands and led him into deeper water where she clung to his neck, kissed him, and wrapped her legs loosely around his waist.

Much later in bed she was no less urgent. Now she was waiting for him on the deck, making him breakfast while Rosemary Sandra sat waiting for him in Charleston.

Throwing back the sheet he slipped into the robe and went to her with a better idea than a day at the beach. They made love and lingered over breakfast. They went to his hotel where he checked-out, Evita waiting in her car. They spent the afternoon in the pool, went for dinner and danced again under the stars.

Saturday they went to the beach, Evita wanted to be seen with him. They walked and talked, frolicked in the ocean and shared a bed. They began their cocktails at two o'clock and were in the pool before five where they remained until darkness when Marcus sat watching her grill steaks, wondering who he would kill next and where. He wondered about incensed Rosemary Sandra, whether he should divorce her since he hadn't seen her in a year, hadn't missed her, and when he did think of her the fondest memories seemed more fabricated than real.

Mostly he wondered about Evita, whether he would see her again or whether he should, which would require a fictional move to Charleston and then what? How would he explain being married or getting divorced? He didn't know. He needed time. He needed space. He wasn't expecting anymore of her than comfort and the joy of closure, which she was giving him in full measure in a blur of insatiable passion over three days and three nights.

Being with her was a fantasy, the thought of marrying her even more whimsical. Seeing her, the taste of her lingering on his lips, her scent fresh in his mind, made thoughts of deserting her impossible. A rare delicacy, once lost or forsaken impossible to recover, Marcus' mind silently at war with his body to see her as a number and not an incredibly exceptional woman who after three days wanted more of him in her life. Number sixteen. What would she think of that, or of sixteen Kirt Bradleys? No different from numbers one through fifteen. Winning numbers in a random draw.

He stood when she called his name, her candlelight dinner a prelude to another evening of rapturous romance owed to them after an eternity of deprivation. She didn't want the evening to end, or to fall asleep, which she did, curled into him, believing her body and mind depleted by their single-minded lovemaking, each one enduring for the other, Evita struggling not to close her eyes. Yet she was powerless, succumbing quickly in her weakened state to the few droplets of strong sedative in her wine.

He carried her to the bedroom, laying her on the récamier. He sat beside her, kissing and caressing her, arousing her in her sleep with a faint and tantalizing pressure. He had no reason to hurry, she was sound asleep.

He had an early flight, she knew that. Leaving her in the morning would be crueller by far, hurried as if he were running away. This way she would expect his call Sunday evening, sitting dreamily by the phone until days later she would understand he was not coming back.

He waited with her as long as he dared, afraid to dilute his resolve, afraid he might wake with her. She was too tempting and had done her best to sap his strength.

Pouring a final two-fingers of Patrón he stepped onto the deck and called for a taxi, giving himself thirty minutes. Padding through the villa, cleaning up after their evening, the dishevelled bed spoke volumes of their passion. Accounting for his clothing and accessories, he put her New Year's panties into her suitcase with other discarded thongs and bikinis. Leaving her was difficult enough, he didn't need or want painful reminders that abandoning her was a terrible mistake. Yet he had no choice.

When he was done he stood gazing at her until the tequila was finished. Kissing her lips for the last time, he left through the front door. A man with a suitcase on the beach at three-thirty in the morning would be difficult to explain to a curious cop. He stood in a dark corner at the gate, lighting his last cigarette of the year, flicking the butt onto street when the car's headlights broke his reverie.

Walking the last block to the hotel where he had left the rest of his clothes, he entered by the garage. In his room he poured a scotch, showered and fell into a deep sleep. When he woke he ordered room service. He dressed and called Rosemary Sandra, holding the cellphone from his ear, agreeing to see her the next day at the prescribed hour.

Checking out, he drove his rental to the airport and flew home relaxed in-first class to Charleston, his mind free of all worry and guilt.

Later that morning, when the owner of the villa arrived shortly after ten to return Evita Mendez' security deposit, he was at first startled and embarrassed to find her lying naked on the récamier. Seconds later he ran in a blind panic to his car and his phone, frantic. Police investigators later determined she had been dead seven hours.

Chapter Seventeen
Four Days Late

Marcus Simms arrived at his home at four, without wine or flowers. This was a business call which he had postponed of necessity. He was dressed for business, his pleasure index emitting a low value.

He pressed the bell pad once, waiting dispassionately for the gates of Hell to fling open and the glare in her green eyes to scorch the tan from his face. He hadn't seen her for an entire year, his expectations nil, mildly curious about how she would look, how she would react to him since he hadn't changed one iota.

Of course her expression would betray no real surprise. She would see him arrive, watch as he stepped from his car, and follow him from the driveway. She forever did that when expecting guests.

When the doors did open, the "What?" was caustic.

The stage was set. She had obviously spent the afternoon prepping and primping herself. Not a crease or a wrinkle. Nor the faintest glimmer of a smile, pissed with his non-reaction. A good beginning. He read her like a book. Once dressed for an in-house gathering, she would never think to sit until company arrived. Creases were verboten.

"Nothing. I'm simply at a loss as to how I should greet

you. Good afternoon? How are you? Happy New Year? It's been a while? Have any good sex lately?" He grinned.

She glanced at her watch. Something to do. "You're on time for once, Marcus. Thank you."

"You said for cocktails, Rosie. I trust by that you've replaced my favourite Johnnie Walker."

"I bought you a small one. I'm not expecting you to stay long." He stepped in. "You look well."

"I do. Thank you. I enjoyed a good year. As I see you did. New hair, new look. What's his name, something generic and safe, Sweetheart possibly?"

"He's Dominic Drake. Come into the parlour." His Blue was in an old-fashioned by what was once his seat. "Please sit, Marcus. I'm eager to hear about your year as I'm sure you're anxious to hear about mine." She proffered a hand. "May I take your jacket?"

"No. I'm good."

He was committed to seeing her through unblemished eyes, for who she had become. Who she once was didn't matter anymore. His first thought: She was no Evita, not even close. She was even more reserved than he remembered, dressed in heels, flared slacks with no panty line and a high-neck cable sweater that wasn't anywhere near tight enough to choke her.

"Ladies first." He sipped the Blue, not greatly impressed by the meagre amount. "I trust you've done nothing untoward to detract from your pure status, Rosie, other than screwing another man for a full year? How's that working with ma and pa Rothstone?"

"They're dealing with it, and please do not be vulgar. The year was an experiment. How else would we determine an outcome? Dominic has become a good friend. He's a good man, he's attentive and caring." She sipped her wine.

"What's more, I've been with him two consecutive New Year's."

"Touché, still about dates and daddy's party. I was in Miami for my birthday. Sorry about that." He scanned the room. Nothing had changed. "So is he the only one, the first one, or the best one to-date? You know as well as I do you're fussy about things like bodies and brains, Rosie. Did this guy take a while to find?"

"We dated a few times before you left. He made the grade. We felt good together, we still do. He wants to marry me. He proposed New Year's Eve."

"How romantic." Marcus glanced at her hands. "Did he get teary-eyed when you refused, or can't he afford a ring?"

"Don't be snide. He's very secure. I told him I wasn't sure, that I was meeting with you the next day. He knows you're here, and why. He understands."

He snorted. "Now that's the Rosie I remember. Forever teasing the boys. Wiggle your tanned ass, get them hard, and pull on your pants."

She glared. "I never did that."

"You always did that. Now old Dominique is wondering whether I'm here screwing you or we're both sitting here screwing him."

"That is so like you."

"And why are we sitting here, exactly?"

"To talk."

"For you to make a right or wrong choice."

"To see and hear if you've changed. Being here on your birthday would have told me a lot."

"I was in Miami celebrating."

"With a woman?"

"She convinced me to like New Year's. She wasn't easy to leave." His third sip emptied the glass. "So yes, I'm reformed. My year-end schedule is a thing of the past with no possible means of proving that to you at present." He waved his glass. "Seems I'm staying longer than you expected, Rosie."

Taking his glass her expression remained somewhere between curious and superior. Coming back a moment later with two-fingers of Blue in the crystal, she sat waiting.

"Your lease expires in a month."

He shook his head 'no'. "I renewed for another year. Anyway, it's a pied-a-terre for Southeast. Not a big problem. The problem is your Dominique. I wasn't as proactive as you. I wasn't active, period. Too busy earning a living to pay for this place. The woman in Miami was a birthday gift to myself, a reward for being good all year while you were humping Dominque in my bed."

"Not in my bed, in his bed. He has principles. Like I said, he understands."

"How often?"

"How often do you think? We've been together for a year. He wants to marry me."

"So where do we go from here? Do we make all sorts of promises to each other? Do we hug and kiss? Do we have hot and steamy sex? Because it seems to me, Rosie, you might not have fully grasped this situation."

"This *is* my situation, the reason you're here."

"A female perspective. Here's the male viewpoint. You've been screwing this guy hot and heavy for a year, being inventive and curious because you're new and he's new. Now here I am. I haven't seen you for twelve months, let alone naked with your pretty ass in the air, which puts me at a distinct disadvantage."

"You put yourself there."

"Is that it, I'm here to sleep with you, to measure up?

Or do we get the tape measure and do things right?" He raised an open palm. "How old is this guy, Rosie? What does he do apart from screwing unhappy and pampered wives?"

"He's thirty-eight, a high-school basketball coach."

Five dollars of exceptional scotch blew from Marcus' nose and mouth. He lost his breath, his dark complexion flushing to a deep purple with hysterical laughter, his eyes dripping tears onto the back of his hands. Uncertain whether to throw something or cry, Rosemary Sandra sat fuming with her hands in her lap waiting for his hurtful reaction to subside.

"Rosie, the age thing I understand. A younger man. Good for you, you are getting on after all. But let's get real. Divorce me and you lose big time. Southeast is fully mine, not yours. You get half this house, your car, your investments and your clothes. That's it. Not a dime from me or Southeast. Half the mortgage and the taxes on this place come close to forty grand a year. You make fifty pre-tax, he pulls in maybe forty. Getting a clearer picture now, Rosie? And remember, you're the one divorcing me. You're the one putting out for junior, not me."

Rosemary Sandra sank into her sofa. "Marcus, please be civil."

"Of course he wants to marry you. He sees this place, your Lexus, the Lady Rolex. Compared to what, a duplex, a Timex and a scooter? Really, who pays for dinner at the food court? Or do you order in?"

"You're wrong about him."

"I am not wrong. If he's that completely enamoured of you, why after a year of wondrous love is he permitting his possible future wife to spend the night with me, to commit all manner of lewd and lustful indecencies with me?" He chuckled. "His imagination must be wreaking havoc on him. Because that is precisely what I require. You see, right now you and I are tense. We're both aggressive, both defensive, which precludes a courteous conclusion irrespective of the final direction we choose. Otherwise what basis does either of us have to determine who and what we are to each other? You appreciate my quandary, Rosie, and yours. You have placed yourself in a very precarious position."

"We can go to dinner, Marcus. We can spend the evening talking this through if you promise you'll be reasonable."

"Excuse me. He gets off fucking you for an entire year, probably this morning as well with a specific purpose in mind, and *I* take you to dinner? How does that work exactly in your confused female mind?"

She drained her wine, frustrated. Marcus was exhausting her. "I don't know. I think sleeping together would be uncomfortable after such a long separation, for both of us."

"As I recall you weren't uncomfortable the first time you threw yourself on top of me. Am I right? Is that why you need a younger man, to recapture your youth?"

"We can't pretend the year didn't happen. It did."

"The year you insisted on when you were already a good fit with Dominique."

"We found each other by chance. I never went looking for another man. I would never."

"Then we divorce. Simple as that. You move into a duplex with the man you enjoy fucking, a man you don't love and I maintain status quo. You see, I have no adjustment to make. You did that for me a year ago. You're the one who has to adjust to Dominique the all-star, not just when you feel the need to get lubricated. Or else you would have said 'yes' to him."

Rosemary Sandra stood. She needed more wine and he wasn't offering. "You haven't told me about your year."

"In fact I did. Work, no play, no lady except for a very vivacious Latina." He snorted. "That's right, Rosie, a Mexican lady. A very hot Mexican lady who did not want me to leave. Yet here I am practically begging my wife to sleep with me." He finished his drink. "You didn't think this through, Rosie. Not by a long shot. I don't suppose he was much help, or your ever-faithful confidante. By the way, how is Wendy?"

She shrugged. "She likes Dominic. You, not very much. Not since last year."

"I always had a little thing for her."

"I know that. She does too."

"Great, now you tell me. Too bad she never stayed over. Could have been fun, the three of us."

"You should have acted on your male instincts. Who knows, you could have had a memory instead of wet dreams."

He put down his empty glass. "At least that would have been honest. What you did was not."

"Marcus, are we going to dinner, or not? I cannot do this anymore. You're wearing me down."

"Yes, if I'm spending the night? No, if I'm not. What's the point? Or don't you remember your letter from a year ago? Or your call to my secretary, Beverly?"

"You don't care?"

"A trite and gender-specific question and the answer is yes, I do. That said, I do have to pit my carnal prowess against a basketball, hmmm, coach for your benefit. You have to feel the heat of that rekindled flame as much as I do, Rosie. In short, a full night of lovemaking or a few incomplete moments of mutually inept intimacy."

She leaned forward. "Do you want a refill?"

"No. I want to take you to dinner. I want to bring you home to our bed and put an end to this discord with renewed passion or a beginning to something permanently different with complete and mutual indifference. I'm good either way."

"You're indifferent, that's what you really mean."

"I'm pragmatic. You know that about me."

"I wasn't expecting this."

"Yes, you were. I gave you a year to play, Rosie, and I have changed. The question is: Did you enjoy too much playtime? That's for you to determine and you cannot do that over a dinner and a glass of wine. Naïve and wishful thinking. What *is* requisite at this juncture is purely physical, or else we would not be sitting here. At best you'll call the coach, thank him for a good ride and say goodbye. At worst, we will fail miserably and part company. If that can be considered worse. At which point you'll clean yourself up, disinfect yourself from your past, me, change the sheets and invite the new guy over to console you. Either way your coach is a winner."

Rosemary Sandra sat mutely staring at him, perplexed. He wasn't the same Marcus. He was reading every worrisome thought in her eyes. She was right, he mused. He was not yielding. Why would he? She had wrongly expected something much more acquiescent of him, finding herself floundering through her own custom-made dilemma. She didn't know what to do. He wasn't pleading for her forgiveness or begging to return home. He was reiterating her threat of divorce and the loss of all things she held dear.

"I don't know what to do."

"We'll go for dinner. No screaming, no female moodiness, or I walk and you're stuck with the bill." He stood. "I'll wait for you at the car."

"When did you cease being a gentleman?"

"When you ceased being a loving wife. The gentleman will re-emerge when the loving wife does."

At the car Marcus was seated behind the wheel. They drove to The Isle of Palms, to a restaurant with a view of the Atlantic. Marcus pulled out her chair, proving he wasn't an absolute boor, Rosemary Sandra acknowledging the fact.

They stayed two hours without any mention of analytical sex or threats of divorce, the ambiance was too intimate which did nothing to stimulate their moods. They spoke politely, visibly out of place. Not leaning into each other, not whispering, smiling or holding hands.
Asking for the bill, Marcus processed his card without speaking.

"Thank you for joining me, Rosemary Sandra. Your company was a welcomed change from my usual corporate dining obligations. Come, I'll drive you home."

"You win, Marcus. Your rules again. A full night of lovemaking or a few incomplete moments of mutually inept intimacy. That's what you said. That's what we'll do." She added, "With an open mind. No expectations, no regrets, no tears. Breakfast together in the morning or a divorce as soon as possible. I'll have to face Dominic tomorrow either way."

At their home they prefaced their lovemaking with nightcaps, sitting as close to one another as they dared without making the moment seem contrived. Until he stood, taking her hand. In the bedroom Rosemary Sandra sat on her settee, pulling away her sweater matter-of-factly, not speaking. She pushed her slacks to the floor, leaving them there. She unhooked her bra, shrugging it from her shoulders without the slightest flourish or fervour. She was nervous, walking in her matching silk thong to where Marcus was dragging back the covers.

He opened his arms to her, kissing unresponsive lips, holding her at arm's length, taking her in. She hadn't changed. Everything was tight and firm, her body rigid and cold, her eyes staring into his. Kneeling, he pulled her panties to her ankles, feeling the subtle shudder. She was not having a good time and he suddenly wondered why the hell he was there.

He laid her onto her back, Rosemary Sandra drawing the covers to her shoulders. Marcus pondering how many times Drake was at first required to fuck her in the dark before seeing the total package. He went to his side, speaking in a low tone about how he missed her, undressing as well as any man could without appearing clownish until slipping from his straightbacks to join her.

He kissed her lips, fondled and kissed her breasts, patiently inching her legs apart. He couldn't for a moment pretend all hurts were healed and forgotten, or that he could out of the blue reanimate her into the insatiable lover he remembered predating her decline. He reached under her, clasping a gentle hand to a firm cheek, squeezing, Rosemary Sandra complying reticently as though turning onto her side for a clinical rectal exam, not throwing a leg over him, or an arm, to facilitate the task at hand.

He adored the texture of her skin, her scent, the soft flesh of her breasts, and told her so. Requisite words, just words. Something to say and she thanked him. Bringing his moist fingers to his lips, tasting the tangy wetness, he inhaled, a low guttural moan defining his pleasure. Essential to the moment. Drawing away the sheet he shifted his weight to facilitate tasting the sour sweetness directly, Rosemary Sandra putting a preventative hand firmly to his shoulder. He understood, relenting. Too much too soon. Or was that Drake's private indulgence? Perhaps.

He went to pull her over him, female superior, thinking with a mental smirk that he would adapt the situation to her mood, beginning to believe he had made a mistake, that he would have more fun fucking Wendy in a freezer. No. She didn't want that either, which would mean having too much fun, deeper and dirtier sex, rocking and rolling, jerking herself into a frantic orgasm.

Instead he pushed her legs wide apart before she went into total lockdown. She was mutating pleasure into purpose. He needed to get in and get out, of her and the house, increasingly of the opinion that his being there was about using him as a catalyst to either put Drake in his place or get rid of him, not to rekindle the cold and grey ashes of a deliberately extinguished passion.

He slid into her easily, when he really wanted to smack her, working alone to raise her into position and feeling foolish; Rosemary Sandra's arms flat by her side, her head turned sideways. After the first few unproductive thrusts he began counting. Reaching 182 he withdrew from her with no more satisfaction or emotion than finishing at a urinal. He wasn't impressed. Worse, he didn't understand the game.

"Well that was disappointing freezer burn, expensive also. More in line with a pizza and beer, not a 200-dollar romantic setting. Money well-spent though, I suppose." He kicked his legs free, swinging his feet over the side of the bed, reaching for his straightbacks and slacks. "If I didn't know better I would believe Dominique the Coach has converted you into either a beer drinker or a lesbian."

"Or perhaps I was one already, Marcus, before you. Perhaps Dominic has the same fantasy as you. Perhaps now you're simply very boring. It happens you know, with age." She sneered. "I told you Wendy liked him."

He chortled without looking at her. "A double dribbler, good for him. However I'll keep that imagery from imposing on my sleep. My best regards to Dominique et al, if he doesn't throw you out from his duplex and keep your girlfriend to himself for doing this to him, for whatever reason you did. That is, if you tell him." He glanced at his watch. "You have the time to disinfect yourself and change the sheets unless that's another fantasy. In any event we're divorced, Rosemary Sandra. Do anything with or without your daddy to screw me over, with Southeast, or half this place, or anything else that is rightfully mine, and I will fuck you up one hell of a lot deeper and better than I did a few minutes ago. Do we understand each other, *sweetheart?*"

Chapter Eighteen
Jed, Daisy & Antoine Beauregard

May 31, 1945 was long in coming for young Jeddore Billows, four years long until V-E Day twenty-three days earlier. Four years spent killing Germans in France when he wasn't squatting in trenches that were never deep enough or hiding behind trees whose bark was being stripped by German bullets, praying not to soil his trousers because they were doing their best to kill him. He didn't keep count believing that if he did, he would one day after the war carry the burden of guilt for taking the lives of men merely to save his own. What he did know was that he missed many more each day than he hit.

Those were all too frequent moments each day when his thoughts drifted from Rosemary, since staying alive was critical to keeping his tearful promise whispered four years earlier at the train station to marry her. So enthralled was he with her that other men in his troop began refusing to share his lean-to which would entail insufferable hours of hearing about her.

May 31st began as the happiest day of his life. He was going home. His passage was booked. He was sailing that evening on the last troop transport to leave Calais. He would see her in two weeks if not sooner. He was elated, his heart bursting with the joy of anticipation.

Sitting on the window ledge of his modest room in the quaint gîte he watched as young French women waved at an endless parade of liberating soldiers leaving their country, hugging and kissing them, dancing with them in the street, the hems of their skirts playfully fluttering at their knees. He shouted to them and waved, they waved at him and blew kisses.

The sky was silver-blue, the sun was dazzling, a soft breeze rustling the curtains. Her letter had come to him late the day before, which he chose to read later because he'd been out drinking with the boys who were going home with him.

He had only written letters to her on rare furloughs when he would barter paper and a pencil for a pack of cigarettes, explaining to her that bullets whizzing around his head most days was somewhat of a distraction. Throughout his first year she had written fifty-two letters, most of them bound together with ribbons; the second and third years she wrote one each month, explaining she had found full-time employment in a munitions factory and was frightfully busy with the war effort. Throughout his last year she wrote one, the thin one he was holding in eager hands.

Peeling open the envelope he was excited, reading the few lines too quickly, shaking his head. He didn't understand. Reading again, he wailed past the window into the warm air, the young women waving and blowing more kisses at him.

He read the letter countless times until he passed out with her letter in one hand and an empty whisky bottle in the other. The letter ended with her deepest affections and was signed by one Mrs. Dominic Drake who explained as well that she had relocated with her husband from

Charleston to New Orleans.

His captain's lecture to the troop days earlier was simple: Be there. The ship will not wait.

The next morning Jed woke to more unbearable gaiety beneath his window. His temples pounded with a miserable headache, his eyes sore and red. He felt wretched. He was wretched, hugging his knees, his churning stomach cramped into tight knots. He forced his body and soul from the thin mattress, stumbling to the window, slamming it shut, the sweet aromas from the café-terrasse below making him feel worse. He was lost. Worse, he was abandoned. He had no reason to go home. No one was waiting for him. Yet he had little choice. He didn't speak a word of French and, even if he could, what would he do? How would he survive?

He stood at the window gazing at the pretty girls, his eyes stinging, woefully regretting he'd shot one too many Germans, the one who could then have spared him this cruellest of miseries. He had barely enough money in his pockets to remain a few nights longer in his room which he currently had no right to reside in, possibly enough to board a ship to Liverpool where he could hopefully arrange passage by working his way to the States.

He went to the owner of the gîte, explaining his predicament to the older lady who took pity on him. She fed him a hot breakfast and allowed him to bathe in her private apartment, telling him not to worry. The room was his for as long as he needed to find passage and he need not worry about money. Her husband, an affable fellow who disliked the stiff-lipped British as much as the Germans, agreed despite serious doubts. The best the young man could hope for was a merchant ship whose captain would likely be a better thief than a mariner.

291

Leaving his wife to fuss over her newest purpose in her life, he went out to share a glass of wine with his friends, chuckling at her raised eyebrow. He returned home not long after for his lunch, beaming, pleased with himself, pouring a glass of wine for each of them and telling Jed to pack his bag. He was going home, at least as far as Dover.

He had a friend with a sturdy boat who quickly agreed to help the young liberator cross la Manche to Dover from which point he could thumb his way to Liverpool. The crossing was twenty-two miles, one hour on a calm sea and the man was presently waiting at the docks.

The woman gave Jed a motherly hug and kissed his cheeks before filling his arms with ample food for that evening and the next day. Her husband went with Jed to the harbour, introducing his friend, leaving him with a firm grip, two bottles of wine for his journey and 100 francs. All he could afford

Jed could not believe his good fortune or that the thirty-foot open motorboat could possibly skim across the Channel in an hour, embracing the Frenchman tightly when he nosed his craft onto the English shoreline shy of an hour later. Not many minutes after his landing he found himself explaining his dilemma and the foamy wake of the vanishing French motorboat to a surly constable on a bicycle. Reluctantly satisfied after a lengthy ad hoc interrogation which included the soldier's sad tale of unrequited love and a thorough examination of his papers, the stern-faced official pointed Jed in the right direction admonishing him not to enlist the comfort of innocent English girls in the mending of his damaged heart.

His journey to Liverpool began June 01st, lasting ten days, his stomach and his army boots spared harsh punishment by the good graces of villagers and townsfolk along the way. They opened their doors, setting an extra place at their tables, giving him a bed or a barn to sleep in, and let him share their horse-drawn carts or their cars.

Arriving early Sunday evening, weary from walking the last ten miles and wanting to save his money for his passage, he found a park bench to sleep on. Soon after the resonating clang of a constable's nightstick crashing against the metal bench near his head propelled him gracelessly into the air and onto the ground.

"I'll have no vagrants slumming on my beat, boy. Get to your feet and be off or you'll be spending the night with thieves and drunkards and foul-smelling whores, the likes of which I'm certain you're not unfamiliar with."

"I'm not a vagrant. I'm here for one night, hoping tomorrow to find space onboard a ship to the States. I'm American. I'm a soldier."

The constable stood with his feet apart, slapping his stick into a cupped palm. "I see the uniform, boy. So you either think I'm daft or blind. Is that it, do you think I'm dippy?"

Jed scrambled to his feet. "No, sir. I do not. I believe you are an educated gentleman of enviable character, as am I. The name's Jeddore Billows. I do have money for a room, but I need every penny for my passage."

"There's no ship leaving here till midweek, which causes me to believe you're fairly buggered Master Billows. I won't have you scaring off decent folk by sleeping on my bench that many days and nights. What I mean to imply, if you're not entirely dimwitted, is that you don't have a pot to piss in. Which, in particular, is of considerable concern to me, boy."

"I can't walk all night and the inns will be full at this late hour."

"Yes, because their guests know better than to sleep in my park or to let a whore in my jail lace their willies with the clap."

"Then I guess I'll walk." Jed reached for his duffle bag, heaving the familiar weight onto his shoulder. "Is there a particular direction you would care to suggest, somewhere that isn't a considerable concern to you?"

"I suppose there is, boy." The constable pointed with his nightstick. "That way, crossing three streets until you see the sign where you'll get a proper bed and a breakfast. Better than any inn you'll find, at half the cost and a piss pot with a pull-chain to boot. Tell the old woman in charge the constable sent you."

Jed thanked the man. Several minutes later he came to the three-story Victorian boarding house. The plaque on door instructed him to walk in, where a middle-aged woman greeted him with a cheerful smile. He asked to speak with the older lady in charge, telling her of the constable and the bench. Amused, her cheeks glowing, she replied that her dear husband was very strict about the goings-on in his park.

"Your room is situated on the third floor, sir. You're across from the Beauregards from New Orleans. Somewhere in America, they tell me. He's an older gentleman set in his ways," the constable's wife told Jed, "the missus much younger by too many years, if you care to hear my opinion on the matter, and very fetching. A real eye-catcher she is, as you'll see for yourself in the morning. The mister must be well-heeled indeed to attract such a young and pretty one as she and keep her at home. Or impressively long in the leg," she added mischievously. "Not that it matters. The poor thing spends her days alone in her room or the parlour whilst he goes about his business. They're leaving on Wednesday, sailing to New York. In a stateroom, thank you very much."

"I must ask them the name of the ship, and go tomorrow to the docks to acquire a booking."

"Breakfast is at seven. They come down together. Hasn't taken her arm a single time, hasn't pulled out her seat either. It's a terrible way to treat a lovely young girl."

He grinned. "Perhaps I will."

"See that you do." She reached under her counter, giving Jed his towel. "The bath's situated at the end of the hall. Keep it clean and proper, Mr. Billows. And bolt the door. We wouldn't want the pretty young missus walking in on you and getting herself all excited and flustered. Would we now?"

"No, ma'am. We wouldn't. I can't think of anything more frightful to a young woman."

She shooed him to the stairs. She would make him a pork and lettuce sandwich, a hot cuppa and bring the tray to his room, which he was not to expect every night.

The next morning at breakfast the constable's wife introduced Jeddore Billows to Mr. and Mrs. Beauregard, Antoine and Daisy. The constable questioning Jed on his well-being and the comfort of his night's sleep, Jed replying that he slept well, questioning the constable with a smirk on the condition of his bench.

Jed placed Antoine at late fifties, Daisy at mid-twenties. He came to the table in a brown three-piece tweed and tan laced cap toe Oxfords. His hair was cut short, his eyes covered with thick-rimmed glasses. He greeted everyone at the table matter-of-factly by their family names, despite residing with them as a guest for a week, not impressed when Jed stood to pull out Miss Daisy's seat. Nor was he impressed with the open collar and rolled-up sleeves of

Jed's khaki shirt, his uniform in dire need of attention and certainly not befitting polite company.

The man was humourless and unsmiling. Wealthy or not, long in the leg or not, Daisy was married to a stuffy and stogy old man. He felt sorry for her.

Daisy was everything the constable's wife described, thanking the young soldier for his gallantry, speaking with him reservedly at first, unsure of him, while her husband and the constable, closer in age, engaged in conversation about efforts to recover from the war. The only effort of interest to Jed was his personal and private recovery, he told them. Because of him a few dozen German families no longer had husbands and fathers, which caused Antoine to clear his throat and adjust his glasses.

They were sailing Wednesday afternoon on the Queen Mary, Daisy replied to his enquiry, suggesting they should share a dining room table throughout the voyage. Her husband quickly reminding her in a proud tone that proper dress was required for each meal of the day on their privileged and restricted deck.

When Antoine stood Daisy rested her teacup in its saucer, wishing everyone a good day, Jed quick to stand behind her. He remained at the table speaking with the other guests and the constable, asking directions to the docks where he went mid-morning to secure his booking. He returned to his room an hour later, crestfallen. With the French francs and his thirty dollars he was short by close to a hundred pounds and the Queen Mary did not hire unskilled personnel to work for their passage.

He flopped backward onto his bed, despondent; he was a refugee in a foreign land, stranded. He would speak with the constable and the constable's wife when his mood lightened, they would know of someone nearby in search of a handyman. He went to them the moment he believed the constable would be finished his lunch.

Plenty of people were hiring, rebuilding the country, he told Jeddore. However Jed was in the country without proper authority. The best the constable and his wife could manage was free lodging with his meals for a short while and a few shillings each week if he was any good with a paintbrush. Hardly sufficient to carry him across the vast ocean, the older man cautioned.

Jed accepted, willing to begin his chores the following day. He had little choice, yet he was grateful, figuring if he survived the thousands of German bullets intended for him, he would survive this.

Early in the afternoon, certain everyone was gone from the house, Jed went to the lavatory for his first bath in eleven days. He filled the deep cast-iron tub three-quarters full until the water began to run cool. Sinking to his shoulders, his skin prickling with rejuvenating heat, thick steam engulfed him to bead his brow with salty sweat.

He remembered the French couple who selflessly helped him, and the motorboat captain; the rigid constable at the shore who was kinder than he pretended and the constable's bench in the park. And the letter. Eleven days that were altering his entire life because of a few heartlessly scribbled lines, signing the note that was scarcely a letter with her new name.

And who was this Dominic Drake? Where did he come from to cajole and mystify a young girl, possibly with power and money as Beauregard may have bamboozled Daisy? Or was she the one at fault, forever savouring the attention of boys and men of any age in awe of her green eyes, pink-yellow tresses and sweet smile. He didn't care a damn about either of them. Together they had conspired to ruin his life.

He sank in deeper to his chin, bracing his feet against the ancient and brassy-green faucet, wondering how long he could exist as an illegal alien before being arrested and incarcerated. Or should he organize his mind with thoughts of staying in England and evict her from his mind entirely?

Acclimated to the cacophonies of war he was immune to whispers and gentle noises, irritated when those near him failed to speak clearly, which wasn't the case when she breathed in a loud and startling gasp. Jed jerked wildly, splashing agitated water onto the floor. He disappeared instantly beneath the surface, his feet in the air, his arms instinctively flailing to save himself from drowning, his hands at last grasping the cast-iron rim, dragging himself to safety.

Mortified, Daisy's mind raced to do what was right. He'd seen her, the shock on her face. Hurrying out to hide in her room would cause her unbearable anguish, causing them immeasurable embarrassment the very next morning at breakfast. Whereas remaining as she was, she could confront the situation with as much poise as she could possibly muster, apologize to the young man and leave him to complete his bath with a modicum of dignity.

Then again, he was a comical sight. He was adequately submerged and his private parts were hidden from her view. He had no reason to feel ashamed. She faced the wall, gripped by a sudden and irrepressible fit of the giggles.

"Please forgive me, Mr. Billows. I had no I idea whatsoever that I would interrupt your bath. The door was unbolted. Please believe that I am thoroughly embarrassed."

Jed dragged himself into a more appropriate sitting

position, sputtering, shaking his head. Water sprayed everywhere, his thick brown hair a frenzied mess. "I am without question the one at fault, Miss Daisy. I falsely believed I was alone. After too many years on the battlefield and in tents, bolted doors don't mean very much to me. I am the careless and culpable party who must therefore beg your forgiveness, Miss Daisy." He chuckled, "In fact, truth be told, you have done much to brighten my day with your musical laughter. Am I that humorous a spectacle?"

"Yes, Mr. Billows, you are. But now I should repair to my room." She reached for the doorknob, hesitating. "Mr. Billows, please pardon my awfully rude curiosity. How did you fare at the docks? Will I see you during our voyage? I do hope so."

"Regretfully you will not. I'm here awhile longer, it would appear. I came up a bit short on the cost of my passage, for which reason the constable has kindly agreed to take me on as a handyman. However I will enjoy your delightful company to the fullest at breakfast tomorrow and the day after. Perhaps by then your giggles will have subsided and not arouse suspicions, Miss Daisy."

"I promise I will not." She twirled, facing him. "Please do call me Daisy, Mr. Billows. And if I may once more be rude, to what extent are you short on your fare?"

"Close to one hundred pounds."

Daisy displayed no surprise at the exorbitant amount. "For a lower deck, I presume."

He nodded, his expression pleasant. "No worse than four years on one side of a lean-to atop rough ground, Daisy."

"And for 200 more you will be on the same deck as me, Mr. Billows."

"Jeddore, please. Sadly, I believe I am as close to you now as I will ever be. I must say, however, that I am now eager for sleep and the indelicate dreams your impromptu visit will certainly provoke."

She crossed her arms, leaning against the door. "Jeddore, you will have your passage this week and you *will* be on the same deck as me. As you may have deduced the single commonality I share with my husband is that we are both still alive. His single kindness to me is affluence, the rest of my life is a collage of intolerably boring days, loneliness, and spontaneous chastisement for whatever reason suits his purpose at the moment. He is not a pleasant or devoted man, given to cruel outbursts whenever the upper hand is not his."

"That is painful for me to hear from such an appealing young woman, Daisy. You do not deserve such loathsome behavior. However I have never in my life taken charity. I do though thank you very much for your kind offer."

"Nor have I ever given charity. I am, in point of fact, forbidden. He believes men deserve what they work for, nothing else. He's blind to the sufferings and misfortunes of others."

He chuckled. "I'm in a bath talking with you. I would hardly call that suffering, Daisy, and my fortunes will improve very soon."

"Not by doing odd jobs. I propose that your work will be keeping me company while he plays cards with his brandy and tobacco." She glanced at her timepiece that was a pendant dangling from her neck. "The day is still young. Antoine never arrives here before six. He prefers brandy and cigars to me. Come to my door when you are dressed, Jeddore, and then you must take a taxi to the docks for appearances until we have you properly attired for your journey. When you return I will play the brazen harlot and enjoy a glass of sherry or wine with you in your room to plan our day together tomorrow. We have to present you as a gentleman, Jeddore, not show you off as an indigent warrior."

"The thought of having you in my room, Daisy, is the most pleasing my mind has created in a very long time. However, I daresay your husband's thoughts on the matter would be somewhat less pleasant."

"We sleep separately each night and you, a stranger, this morning made me feel special. When he arrives he will find us sitting appropriately in the parlour enjoying polite conversation."

Daisy Beauregard walked out, giving him privacy to stand and towel himself. At her door, dressed in the cleanest shirt he could pull from his bag, he accepted her gift, swearing he would reimburse the full amount as soon as possible. To which she explained the meaning of a gift.

Jed returned soon after with his passage secured and a bottle of sherry the clerk told him was the finest in his store. Walking into his room he was pleasantly surprised to see Daisy seated by the window.

She was radiant, somehow younger than an hour earlier. They spoke for another hour or more, sitting together at the window, sipping sherry. She was twenty-three, her husband fifty-eight. She was an uneducated orphan working as a waitress in a coffee shop when he first saw her. He came to the shop several times, finally making the most ludicrous proposal that she accepted after a prolonged and difficult period of reflection: He would take her from the slums of New Orleans and educate her, he would give her an elaborate wardrobe and generous allowance, a driver and wonderful holidays once his personal physician determined her purity. He would take her from the rags of a serving girl to the riches of the lady she would become. In return, she would be his priceless jewel that no one else could dream of possessing. She would spend her days at the pool in the latest fashions, dressing in elegant gowns for fine dinners amongst strangers twice her age, though never dancing, never skipping in the rain, never feeling the passionate touches and heated lips of a young and passionate lover.

She willingly sold her soul in return for a marriage that was her guarded prison, a prison where music and gaiety were forbidden, when the worst she had imagined was a man older than her dead father equitably demanding her youthful body on occasion, which never happened. Instead he derived the greatest pleasure from beating her, as other men might from tenderly embracing her, Daisy confiding she hadn't once encountered her husband unclothed. Escape was impossible, his grip deathly tight. Now all she wanted was to see him dead.

More importantly, she sighed, the next day she and Jeddore would spend the day shopping for men's suits and trousers, shirts and sweaters, shoes and ties. And he was not to say a single word that would spoil her day.

What he did say, refilling her glass, her cheeks rosy pink, was, "Daisy, can your life possibly be as atrocious as what I'm hearing? Can any man be that harsh and unpleasant to a girl as lovely as you?"

Daisy wiggled from where she sat beside him. She unbuttoned her dress unabashedly from the hem to her pendant, dropping it to the floor. Turning, she pushed her underpants past her buttocks, raising her slip to her shoulders.

"The yellowish marks on my back, Jeddore, are a month old. He made the red marks on my bum last night once seeing you with the constable's wife, defying me to acknowledge you." She dropped her slip, reaching under the silk to tug at her underpants, Jed leaping from his perch to stoop for her dress.

"Then he will harm you again this evening for what I did this morning?"

"No. When he goes for dinner I will feign feeling unwell. When he returns I will be asleep in my own bed. What I care about is tomorrow with you and your company throughout the entire voyage."

"If he does, Daisy, all you need do is scream out."

Chapter Nineteen
Jeddore & Daisy & the Queen Mary

At 5:00 PM Daisy left his room and went to her own; at 5:30 she was delighted to see him sitting in the parlour engaged in conversation with the constable's wife. He stood to greet her, asking about her day, Daisy replying that her day was absolutely magnificent. And yours, Mr. Billows?

"A magnificent day by yourself," the constable's wife added sympathetically, patting Daisy's knee. "How awful that you and Mr. Billows could not have become better acquainted here in the parlour. Each of you locked in your rooms all day but for Mr. Billows' hurried expedition in a taxi to the docks."

"An opportunity sorely missed, Mrs. Beauregard," Jed added.

"Indeed, Mr. Billows."

"You'll be surprised to discover, Mrs. Beauregard, that Mr. Billows has secured passage to New York. He's sailing with you this week."

"How wonderful for you, Mr. Billows."

"The purser was very agreeable, Mrs. Beauregard. He apologized profusely for this morning overstating the cost of the voyage, further apologizing by upgrading my ticket to a superior class. I was very fortunate. In fact, I would

304

wager that my day was as magnificent as yours." He went to the trolley. "May I offer you a sherry?"

"Yes, sir, you may. Thank you."

Precisely at six Antoine Beauregard stood in the doorway to the parlour, studying them, suggesting to his wife that she dress for dinner.

"Antoine, dearest, I feel unwell. Would you mind terribly dining alone this evening? I'm afraid I will embarrass you if I put any food whatsoever near my mouth or my nose."

He noticed the sherry. "Are you certain, my dear? Perhaps a brief rest before we go out would improve your unfortunate condition."

"The poor girl's been under the weather all day in your room," the constable's wife added. "My fault, I'm certain. I feel responsible for not properly frying my sausages this morning, coaxing her from your room for a small taste of sherry to calm her sick stomach. Mr. Billows kindly stopped in to offer his service were we to require medicaments from the apothecary."

"I would be pleased to join you for dinner, Mr. Beauregard." Jed proposed. "There's a place up the street serving steak and kidney pie for under a pound with a mug of ale in the price, if you can believe that."

"Thank you, Billows. Wine is more in keeping with my plans for dinner." He took a watch from his pocket. "Daisy, my dear, please feel better by later this evening. I shouldn't be very long. Nine at the latest." He eyed Jed, turned on his heels, and strode out.

Hearing the door close, the constable's wife held out her glass. "Mr. Billows, now that he's gone I believe Mrs. Beauregard and I quite fancy another sherry, if we may. After which the two of you will continue your magnificent days at supper with me and my hubby." She patted Daisy's knee once more. "Good for you, my dear. He's not at all the man this young one is."

Later that evening Daisy retired early to her room, Jed maintaining a vigil from an escritoire in the hallway where Beauregard, padding to the lavatory in his slippers and robe to prepare for bed, was surprised to see the young man with a book in his hands. When Beauregard returned to his room, neither man acknowledging the other, Jed remained on guard another hour.

The next morning the constable greeted each of his wife's guests with a handshake, Jed in particular before the Beauregards appeared. "I had a good feeling about you the other night, boy. Don't let that fancy voyage of yours go for naught. The girl's given you more than a wonderful gift. Make very certain that neither her money nor her enviable charms are wasted on you. The world is already excessively populated with blind fools. Or must I beat sense into your head with my nightstick?"

"No, sir. I believe your stick has already worked sufficiently well to enlighten me."

With their breakfasts concluded the guests excused themselves one by one, the constable's wife in due course cleared the table, Beauregard left to complete his last day of post-war commerce, and Daisy met Jed in the parlour without the shallow pretence of the previous day.

They took a taxi first to a barbershop where Daisy sat and giggled at seeing his face smothered in a steaming towel, cringing as the gleaming straight-edge scraped white foamy lather from his neck, then to a street lined with Liverpool's finest haberdasheries where they completed the morning outfitting Jed in several new summer suits, various accoutrements, a gold watch and steamer trunk At noon, newly attired, Jed took Daisy to lunch insisting that he pay in order that he maintain some semblance of manliness, secretly worried that he would require a lifetime to repay his debt to her.

After lunch they found a pristine and deserted park where they strolled and talked of their dreams and aspirations, of Antoine and Rosemary, Daisy taking his hand, now and again stopping to press her lips to his. She had a plan. She was in another world, hating when he tapped the face of his new watch at four o'clock when they returned to the various stores to gather their purchases.

At five Jed invited the constable's wife into the parlour for a glass of sherry, the older woman pleasantly astonished by his dashing appearance yet saddened by Daisy's dismay, insisting the young girl had no reason whatsoever to fret.

At six a frustrated Antoine Beauregard had no option but to accept her invitation to dinner with her husband and Mr. Billows. Her table was set and her stew was a delectable treat not to be missed. She would not hear any excuses.

Seeing Jed splendidly attired and handsomely groomed provoked an immediate and barely suppressed suspicion, his frustration transmuting into annoyance at hearing over dinner that Jed was not only sailing the next day aboard the Queen Mary but that he would be a close neighbour on the very same deck.

They remained at the table until near ten, Beauregard certain who financed the soldier's unforeseen windfall. Preparing for his sleep he found himself unreasonably infuriated at seeing Jed sitting once again at the escritoire reading the same book, scowling at the younger man's rudely expressed wish that nothing would disturb Mrs. Beauregard's peaceful night's sleep.

307

Nothing did by the time Jed went to his bed at midnight.

The next morning after breakfast Jed arranged his new wardrobe inside his trunk, bearing its weight effortlessly to the front door without need of assistance, throwing his uniform and full duffle bag with the letter into the bin in the alleyway. Antoine Beauregard began his day vexed at having to request the constable's assistance since he could manage neither Daisy's lighter trunk nor his own. The constable suggesting with a furtive and sly wink that perhaps the young Mr. Billows would kindly manage the young lady's.

On the street when the hackney cab arrived the constable shook hands with Mrs. Beauregard and the men; his wife hugged the now Daisy and Jeddore tightly, wishing them well as though the agitated man standing close by wasn't her husband, insisting on receiving news of their safe arrival in America. Stepping back she thanked Mr. Beauregard for his kind patronage and watched as her husband, Jed and the driver jammed the three trunks into the vehicle.

As they squeezed into the cab with one bench left to share and drove off, the constable's wife only then told her husband what she knew, afraid of what he might have done.

"You know me too well, woman. I would have forgotten that I'm a man of the law and snapped the bugger's neck, at least made a muck of his face. Instead he'll deserve whatever our young Jeddore dishes out. I have no doubt of that."

Not soon enough for the husband they arrived at the dock where they were processed and escorted to their elaborate accommodations within the hour.

Daisy was excited. She had never before sailed on a ship, leaving her husband to inspect the sleek vessel while he went to the gentleman's lounge for a brandy, a cigar, and the company of likewise refined gentlemen. Jed Billows remained in his quarters, marvelling, absorbing the luxury, pouring a generous Johnnie Walker Black he could never before afford. For Daisy he poured a sherry and waited for her to knock on his door, certain in mind and body that after the previous two days he could not possibly live without her. He didn't wait long, Daisy stepping into his room without caring to check behind her.

"I could never have imagined two days passing with such haste, Jeddore, or two such painfully long nights."

"We have six full days on the ocean together. Try to imagine that instead."

"But not six nights." She kissed him more ardently than in the park. "I spoke with the purser.
He was pleased to arrange our seating at breakfast and dinner. I explained we were very good friends."

"And how much does that add to my debt, Miss Daisy."

She smacked him. "Ten dollars."

He snickered. "He won't like that coincidence very much."

"I don't care what he likes. He'll like this even less." She unbuttoned her jacket, shrugging it from her shoulders and reaching for her sherry. "Jeddore, let's not make this awkward and don't pretend you don't want me. I'm not spending a week acting like you're my brother when you've already seen my bum. Besides I'm divorcing him, whether you run off at the end of the voyage or not. Either way, I will never regret sleeping with you." She unbuttoned her blouse, draping it over a chair, unzipping her straight skirt and pushing it to the floor before tugging her slip over her head. Jed stood paralyzed, he had never before seen a live woman in her unmentionables and stockings. "I believe, Mr. Billows, this is where you take off your shirt and your pants."

He did, along with his shoes, standing in his shorts, his singlet and socks held up with braces and feeling not nearly as striking as she.

"I feel at somewhat of a disadvantage."

"Don't." She sat in the chair unclasping one garter, then another, rolling the stocking to her foot. Undressing her other leg she unhooked her brassiere and stood quickly to push her underpants to her ankles. "This is the rest of me." He stood in a silent daze. "Okay, this is when you say something really nice, Jeddore."

"I know now why the Germans couldn't kill me, Daisy. They thoughtfully left that to you."

Her auburn hair was styled in loose curls, her breasts small and proud; her nipples were petite, the colour of caramel, her slender 5'6" frame bruised at her shoulders and thighs, her labia sparsely adorned with paler auburn curls. She went to sit on his bed, waiting.

"Must I instruct you in every detail, Jeddore?" she giggled.

The singlet came off with a tug, Jed proceeding to hop around the room tearing at his socks and braces. When he dropped his shorts she stopped laughing at the antics and smiled.

"You may have to tell me everything, Daisy. I've never done this before, wanting to save myself for someone whose name I can't remember at the moment."

"Yes, you do. My name is Daisy and yours is the first I've ever seen." She stared at his eager member. "Anyway, if you're not certain how to please a lady, I believe some part of you appears endowed with a superior knowledge."

He clambered onto the bed. Unsure of his durability

beyond his occasional self-indulgence, he wasted little time easing into her, Daisy seemingly like-minded, each of them straining to witness the once-in-a-lifetime primal event. Once at depth and firmly pinned together, they exchanged curious glances, their noses inches apart. Never considered questions raced through their minds, all of them answered instinctively within seconds. He first braced his weight on his arms and his shoulders, until she pulled him closer. Unhappy with their heads side by side and not seeing each other, they welded their lips together, Jed thinking to dig himself impossibly deeper, Daisy wanting the same, grinding her hips hard into his weight.

She wrapped her legs around his legs, his waist, her arms around his neck, his back and his buttocks which she seemed to relish the most. They rolled onto their sides, testing, caressing, the other side, testing and groping. She wanted the superior positon. She wanted her weight sitting on him, her legs framing his, both of them revelling in the freedom of their hands. Jed most of all. He was not doing well at slowing the pace, his or hers, taking care to avoid touching her bruises, positive he shouldn't ask whether he hurt her when she shuddered and shrieked and collapsed onto his chest, her arms and her legs spread wide apart like an angel in flight.

They remained as they were, locked in place, their bodies slick with sweat. Their chests were heaving, their hair matted against glistening brows.

"You were trying to kill me."

"If this was our first, I cannot wait till we've had a few more lessons." She giggled. "But for the moment how exactly do I climb off of you, Mr. Billows?"

He squirmed for an instant under her weight, testing. "Apparently you don't have to, not right away." He chortled, rolling her onto her back. "The wonderful thing hasn't once before been this considerate of my need or my feelings, Daisy. Not taking advantage of its generosity would be impolite, don't you think?"

She did, content and fully ready for her second lesson. When mutually depleted and satiated, soaked and glistening with each other's sweat, the two of them amazed at the sight of his retreat from her, Daisy swept her hair into a glossy headdress as he went to his trunk for a robe and to pass her the glass of sherry.

Understanding from his smirk that the robe was for him, she tugged the sheet to her breasts.

"How can I not love you after that, Jeddore? I believe that I do. I feel incredibly wonderful."

"You are incredibly wonderful."

"I cannot possibly be in his room tonight. Not after this, not after you."

"You must, Daisy, my darling, for the time being. Your wardrobe is there and your beds are separated by space and by me."

She helped the sheet fall to her lap. "He hasn't ever seen me this way, Jeddore. I believed at the beginning that was why he wanted me. Even when he beats me, he does so through my clothing."

"I'm glad he's never seen all of you. Not wanting to see you is another matter. He must certainly be concealing from everyone that he is in fact a homosexual. He does appear to enjoy the company of men and who in his right mind would not want to see you naked? The thought of not seeing you until tomorrow is horrible."

"You will. I'll come to you after our dinner, when he's in the gentlemen's lounge. I will. He never needs me on his arm or by his side after we've entered a room or been introduced. Even at the pool he ignores me completely."

"A homosexual and blind. Even the most zealous of them should acknowledge such rare beauty."

She palmed his cheek, swinging her feet onto the floor and padding into the bathroom. Jed followed, lured by a beckoning finger, his day fast becoming one of discovery. Never before had he even dreamed of washing a woman. Neither one noticing that Liverpool and England had disappeared from the horizon.

Dressed, with her hair blown dry, Daisy left his room and went to hers where she was alone to dress appropriately for dinner. She chose an elegant knee-length gown, a simple diamond necklace and low-heeled shoes. Satisfied that he would think she looked striking, she went for a stroll on the same deck where, passing a lounge, she was pleasantly surprised to see Jeddore Billows seated at a table with another young couple.

The two men stood to greet her, Jed insisting that she join them for cocktails before dinner. She graciously accepted, neither the man nor his wife thinking to presuppose that Daisy was travelling with her older husband. The women spoke of the newest and more daring post-war fashions that pushed the limits of decency, their families and children. Daisy had no family, and currently no suitor. Her parents were dead, since lies to strangers never mattered, hoping that one day she would marry a gentleman as handsome and debonair as Jeddore. The older man they might see her with on occasion was her uncle who insisted on acting as her chaperone throughout the voyage.

The men spoke of the war, the economy and two charming women in particular. The couple was going dancing after their dinner, imploring Jed and Daisy to join them. Daisy accepted without hesitation.

Finishing their cocktails the couples went separate ways. Jed and Daisy descended a stairway to two decks below where Antoine would not be caught dead. Less privileged passengers strolled arm in arm or gazed across the sea, the men dressed in tweed jackets and caps, the women in heavy wool coats, thick stockings and flat shoes, paying as little attention to the hoity-toity couple as Daisy and Jed paid to them.

They roamed the deck for an hour. Whereas Daisy was wishing time would stand still, Jed wanted the week to pass quickly, concerned she was taking too great a risk provoking her husband and wanting her beyond reach of the man's unpredictable moods as quickly as possible.

The first sitting was a seven o'clock. At 6:30 Daisy sent a steward to her stateroom with a note explaining that she would meet Antoine at their assigned table of eight. He arrived in a flustered state, Daisy fully aware of what he was thinking. Without her on his arm or by his side no one paid him the attention he craved. Seeing Billows seated next to her, his face flushed to a dark crimson, his eyes telling her distinctly that they would have words later that evening.

As usual the women had little else on their minds except family and fashion, the men dominating the evening's conversation with more thoughtful insights and considered opinions well beyond a lady's span of attention. At 9:00 the table disbanded. Three men, each one that many decades older than Jed, agreed to convene in the gentlemen's lounge to continue debating over a good smoke and brandy after accompanying their wives to their quarters and refreshing themselves.

The young man declined, thanking the ladies and Miss

Daisy for gracing his evening, taking his leave of them without affording the feeblest excuse.

Antoine Beauregard stood, stepping aside to wait for his wife to follow. On the deck, returning together to their room, she without warning halted a steward to ask that he kindly bring her a sherry. She wanted to gaze at the moon and the silver-coated sea on a warm summer evening. Antoine, of course, was furious.

"I'm not a child you can send to her room, Antoine. Or an old woman. You should not upset yourself for no reason. You seem on the verge of exploding."

"I won't tolerate this game much longer between you and the Carolinian. He belongs at the boilers, yet you saw fit to dress him and provide his passage at a cost I dare not imagine. By some means scheming to seat him at our table. That was of your doing, wife."

"The ladies very much appreciated his company this evening, as I did. He at least paid each of us a wonderful compliment."

"You deserve the harshest scolding, treating a wandering and ill-bred good-for-nothing with such improper extravagance at my expense. Whatever is in your head, get it out at once."

At that she scoffed. "No. At my expense, with eight hundred of my allowance money. Not yours."

His eyes bulged. "You have clearly lost your mind. I will deduct every penny from your next month's installment."

"In breach of your own contract? I think not. That would make me very well-off indeed, very independent of you, and let's not forget where you found me when you were slumming, Antoine. You never did tell me what you were doing there." She paused for a moment, taking her digestif from the steward's tray. "You should go, Antoine. Your men friends will miss you and I don't want you here a moment longer. I will see you later in the room, if I'm awake. "

"When you won't be as smug, I assure you. I have more to say about this, about the soldier."

Beauregard strode off in a huff, Daisy remaining seated where she was to leisurely finish her sherry. She and Jed decided earlier to forego their third lesson. They would be together five mornings, afternoons and, yes, evenings. With hopefully many more together in his Charleston or her New Orleans. But that evening she wanted to dance and forget she was married before advising her husband later that evening of his forthcoming divorce on the grounds of his constant and cruel mistreatment of her.

Placing her glass on the tray of a passing steward she went to meet Jed and their newly found friends in the clubroom where she danced gaily until midnight with the other girl when the men were engrossed in friendly debate.

Kissing him at her door, her promise was to keep the door unlocked. Despite which Jed remained at his door as she stepped through hers, listening intently and fully prepared to intervene.

Beauregard was sitting in an armchair, a cigar in one hand, a brandy in the other. He stood and went to her, studying her, putting his face close to hers and breathing in deeply. Satisfied, "If you haven't been fucking the soldier where has my wife been until this absurdly late hour?"

"Dancing with Jeddore and friends we met earlier in the day. The evening was amusing and delightful. We agreed we should spend more time together this week, the four of us."

"To dance and do what else, if you haven't yet fully

316

succumbed to the soldier's foul-minded expectations?"

"To dance and laugh and play games together each afternoon, if you must know."

"I forbid you to see him again, wife."

"You're right, Antoine. Tomorrow during breakfast I'll close my eyes."

"I insist."

"That's of no import whatsoever." She poured a small sherry. "I reached the conclusion that the moment I arrive in New Orleans I will be taking a room and hiring a lawyer to apply for a divorce. You have breached the terms of our contract, which did not include beating me, which I expect will be easily proven against you very shortly."

He squashed the cigar, draining his brandy. "I forbid you. We have an arrangement for which you are generously remunerated."

"A marriage contract which calls for love and fidelity, not cruelty and debauchery. I have the bruises to prove the cruelty, which a Southern magistrate will not view kindly in your favour. As for the love, until this afternoon I had a body fully intact to show my doctor as proof of your disinterest in me."

"You fucked him!"

"We made love, twice. As for *your* fidelity and debauchery, I have pondered that question most of the day. Curiously, I never thought to consider where exactly you came from the many times you visited my place of work." She sipped her sherry. "You came from the bathhouse, Antoine, which makes me believe the reason you haven't once touched me is that you are a homosexual."

"Despicable whore!" His fist shot out instinctively, smashing into the side of her head, stunning her, jerking her sideways into a wall. "You will not divorce me! What *I* will do is have the bastard arrested immediately for raping my wife." He was seething, his face distorted and purple. "And make no mistake, when I'm through with him you'll wish you were dead. You will be a whore when I'm done with you."

He punched her hard in the stomach, her body practically folding in two, swinging his arm in a wide arc to strike her against her back. An instant later he lay on the floor, gasping for breath, staring with wide eyes at Jed Billows, bewildered, unprepared for the shoe crashing hard into his face, the bright room instantly black.

Jed helped Daisy to the armchair, clasping her head in his hands, checking her eyes, asking her the day, the year, and his name.

"The best day of my life. The year I want to marry you, my love. I truly do, Jeddore."

"Good. You're fine. And you're magnificent." He poured her a sherry, a deep brandy for himself. "What did you say to him?"

"That I was divorcing him, that I realized he was a homosexual. About this afternoon." Jed knelt to check the unconscious body. "Apparently I'm a whore, Jeddore, a very happy whore. Yours."

"He's not dead. Not yet. More importantly, you are not."

"I won't stay with him. Not now."

"You're right about that."

"Yet how can I be with you, with him in the next room? He wants you arrested, Jeddore, and God knows what else for me."

"You can't. He's sick in the head, Daisy, and not from splaying other men's backsides. He's practiced at hiding what he truly is." Jed put his glass on the trolley, asking for a few moments of quiet to ponder a solution. Although with her husband sprawled on the floor the few minutes seemed like hours. "We must make certain he can't hurt you or anyone else ever again, Daisy. I have the ideal resolution to this dilemma he's forced upon us, very much in keeping with his swagger."

"We can't kill him, Jeddore. Not on a ship, not that I would mourn the loss for a single moment."

"No, we cannot. I've killed enough men, Daisy."

"Still, he deserves the worst I can possibly do."

"Without killing him. I mean to put him where he can't do further damage to anyone else's body or mind, where he can sulk while ruminating privately over his wrongful choices in life." He glanced at his watch: 12:30. "I won't be long. I swear to you."

A few minutes later he returned to her, hurrying into her ensuite reading room where he made all manner of muted noises. Not many minutes later he came out rolling Beauregard's steamer trunk behind him. Beauregard hadn't moved, though his breathing was stronger. That was a good thing, Jed wanted him conscious and coherent in order to fully comprehend his future. Daisy simply sat in awe where she was, puzzled, watching as he worked at slicing several slim perforations into the front of the larger trunk with his army knife before ripping out the entire interior.

"My love, Jeddore, whatever are you doing?"

"I'm giving him air to breath. We can't have him suffocating, can we? We're casting him afloat, alive and as well as can be expected for what he did to you. He boasted enough at dinner of his heightened abilities to surmount the worst possible conditions, to survive every misfortune befalling him unscathed to wage yet another battle." He chortled. "Well, this way he can meet us in New York and prove to everyone that he is not simply a pompous braggart."

She clapped her palms to her cheeks, a girlish yelp escaping her throat. "Perfect! Please let me help you, Jeddore. I must. I am not that badly hurt."

"Getting him there is my job. Yours is to watch for and distract any steward who may happen by. No one else will care if they see us with a chest of drawers."

With the trunk no more than a shell, Jed stuffed Beauregard's mouth with a satin napkin. Together with Daisy they hoisted the body snugly into the trunk, trapping the arms and hands, Jed waiting patiently with his brandy for Antoine Beauregard to fully open his eyes. He wanted Beauregard to be fully aware of his predicament, the way Daisy was aware each time he made her predicament worse. When that happened, Daisy entirely satisfied with his panic, with a smile she bid him fair sailing.

Pleased when closing and locking the front that they could scarcely hear the frantic groans, the couple left the room garnering no attention whatsoever. The port deck was deserted and still, Daisy far from distraught with emotion. She was jubilant, relieved at seeing her husband heaved over the side and into the dark sea with scarcely a splash to mark his arrival.

Returning to her room, Beauregard's entire wardrobe went with Daisy's gleeful enthusiasm through the portholes into darkness, the bits and pieces of his trunk following soon after to litter the sea. Despite being exhausted after her long day, satisfied her room was pristine, she took Jed into his and together they made love.

The next morning in her lover's bed, Daisy lay still to relish the mild throbbing between her legs while Jed showered and shaved. At breakfast the other guests were dismayed to hear of Beauregard's sudden bout of seasickness, his wife explaining the weak temperament of his stomach. He would dine privately in their room for the remainder of the voyage, his weakened state and sickly pallor in unresolved conflict with his sense of manly pride. To their newly discovered and constant companions, Daisy and Jeddore explained her uncle's regrettable malaise less sorrowfully, at last free of his unwanted scrutiny.

Throughout the rest of the voyage Daisy made certain the door to her stateroom's bathroom was closed at mealtimes, returning to the room after each meal she cleared the dishware into the toilet and through the portholes while making sure the bed maintained the appearance of being slept in.

Arriving in New York, the footbridge to the dock lowered in place, Antoine Beauregard was first onto the dock amidst the hustle and bustle of bodies herded together. Mrs. Beauregard, ensuring that her husband was duly accounted for, explained to the purser that he had of necessity disembarked moments before, anxious for terra firma under his unsteady feet.

Later in the day, missing her train that was to carry her and Antoine to New Orleans, she hurried frantically to the nearest police station fraught with worry for his well-being. He had left her at a restaurant where she finally dined alone, assuming he had become lost while searching for a pharmacist. He hadn't been well all week and feared further discomfort brought on by the swaying of the train.

The detective took pages of notes, promising to call her the next morning, arranging for a patrol car to take her with her husband's baggage to the Grand Hotel, secretly sharing her room with a young man who assured her all would be well. A week later, Antoine's disappearance remaining and

321

unsolved mystery, the police were at a loss to tell her what might have happened. Simply too many possibilities existed, not the least of which was the Hudson River considering Mr. Beauregard's penchant for carrying vast sums of money on his person.

Despairing, Daisy left New York by train. The grieving young woman, convinced she was a widow, found solace in the arms of the young man she slept with each night. A month later the police closed her file.

As the months passed Jed found work as a travelling salesman to assuage his deep sense of pride. While Daisy, who adored him and was soon to become a wealthy widow, believed he was being unnecessarily silly by placing too heavy a burden on his shoulders, remained at home to put her affairs in order. Neither one ever mentioning Antoine, Jed not for a single moment wasting his thoughts on Rosemary Sandra or her precious Dominic Drake. They were happy with their new and lavish life, dining and dancing with friends when Jed wasn't coming home late.

On the last day of the year, with her marriage finally dissolved and her husband's assets now fully hers, Daisy hurried home elated to her mansion to tell Jed the most wonderful news that she was free to at last become his loving wife. Instead what she found made her wail and fall to the floor in a heap. With trembling hands she fumbled in her purse for the gun, her eyes blurred with tears.

He was in her bed with a much younger girl, each of them oblivious, each of them groaning the most horrible sounds and glistening with sweat.

"Jeddore," she sobbed, gulping for air, "how could you possibly? I will hate your forever."

The young girl sprang from his hips, screaming out loudly with fright, "Marcus! Marcus!" before she was instantly killed; Jeddore Billows, splattered with blood, howled in his sleep, "Haley, no! I love you! I do. I love you!" before he lay dead.

Chapter Twenty
Marcus Simms & Haley

"Marcus! Marcus!" She shook him gently. "Marcus, wake up."

Jed Billows jerked violently, kicking out with his legs. "Haley, no! I love you! I do. I love you!"

"Yeah, good. That's very nice, thank you. Thanks a bunch. Now wake up, Marcus. You're having a bad dream." She palmed his hair. "Gees, what's happening in there? You're soaking."

"Haley?"

"In the flesh, literally."

He squirmed onto his side, rubbing his face hard. "I'm sorry. Did I scare you?"

"No, you didn't. You worried me. You sounded as though you were crying. God, was I that horrible?"

"What I was seeing was incredibly real. She killed you and I couldn't stop her. I couldn't save you. I felt terrible."

"You felt terrible? I'm guessing not as badly as me, I'm the dead one because of you. Thanks."

He propped his weight onto an elbow. "We're both dead. She killed me too."

"Who did?"

"Some girlfriend, I suppose, since I'm not married. She was pretty upset at seeing us in bed together. And no, you

324

were not horrible. You were fantastic, exceptional. I mean, wow."

"Yeah, to die for apparently." Haley Sands stretched out beside him. "Does this girlfriend of yours always kill your one-nighters in your dreams? This isn't some sort of recurring re-enactment, I hope."

"No. She might have had a bad day and who said anything about one night? I promise, she's not coming back anytime soon. Even if she does, next time I will save you."

She kissed him; he put a warm hand on her bare hip and pulled her closer. "You'd better. And next time meaning…?"

"Tonight. I hope. That okay with you?" He could see she was thrilled, could imagine what she was thinking. He knew exactly what she was thinking, hoping. After a wonderful evening and not enough hours of heated sex he was not making excuses; he was not feeling guilty about cheating on a wife he hadn't mentioned, or an old girlfriend he couldn't live without suddenly reappearing, not a bi-guy out for a thrill with something sweeter, softer and more slippery when wet. He wasn't a jerk and he had a good job. Maybe, hopefully, he was the one. That's what they all wanted to believe, resenting the clock they could never turn back, eager for the moment to scurry and tell their girlfriends they finally snagged a keeper. "That was a direct question, Haley. I would love to see you again, and again."

She shook her head, beaming. "Yes, it's okay with me. Deal. After breakfast, a few dips in the pool this morning and lunch. Unless there's some urgent matter keeping us in the pool, we'll head to your place for some clean clothes. Yours are pretty crumpled. My fault, sorry. Was I too much of an animal?"

"You were absolutely exquisite."

"Anyway, I'm curious. If we're going to try this I need my guy to…"

Her guy? Really? Already? What was up with that? The pool was very definitely a must-do. He needed more closure, more comfort and joy after his horrible dream and because she was vibrant, sex-starved and ravenous after so many months of lonely deprivation. But then he would leave her, as he must. Not ready to start over at forty-eight.

The evening before Marcus sat on his Bourbon Street courtyard veranda. The setting was serene and calming, submerged lighting in the pool casting living shadows onto the trees and tall, elaborately manicured shrubbery. He wasn't interested in a street view, watching a meandering horde of bewildered tourists or a headless parade of semi-inebriated women baring their breasts, and whatever else they felt strangers should admire of them, for the time-honoured prize of year-round 'Mardi Gras' plastic beads made in China. That would come later, near midnight, and by noon the next day their tits and other mid-West blanched body parts would be plastered across the world on social media. He held himself to a higher standard. The oddity was that the most visually stirring, the most charming and the most sober kept their corporeal secrets private.

What he wanted was peace and quiet to ponder his caregiver, his closure and his comfort. He couldn't believe he, Marcus Simms, was forty-eight. He couldn't believe Rosemary Sandra had been gone two years from his life if not free from his haunting memories of her, of her treachery after their many fond years together, tormenting his days and nights, thinking he would very much like to kill her on the day of their perfect and appropriate court date, May 31st. Now that would truly be a day bringing with it cause for celebration, and not in anyone's dreams.

Married, divorced and killed on the same day. Happy Anniversary, *sweetheart*.

New Year's Eve in the core of the Big Easy was not for the faint of heart. The French Quarter would come alive early and remain animated until eventual stupor would usurp an evening of splendour. He wanted and deserved splendour, youthful splendour, the beauty and grace inherent in New Orleans women. His made no secret of his age, the secret was how he forever appeared a fit ten years younger. "Naturally gifted and resistant to stress," he would reply to his girls at the office who had known him twice that number of years. None of them ever thinking to work for anyone else. They adored and admired him. He was their idol, their secret barometer against which all their men past, present and future would succeed or fail.

The Big Easy was also the Big Noise with the deafening clamour each night of jazz blaring from every second doorway and window, painful decibels of high-pitched squeals from the trumpets and saxophones of musicians wearing earplugs to drown out the severe damage they were inflicting on others. The town was also a place of secluded Spanish and Creole-style garden restaurants dimly lit with muted and romantic melodies playing in the background. That's what he needed.

Finishing the JW Blue he went into his room to change from business casual to evening elegant. Despite where he might meet her, he had tickets to the New Year's Ball Drop, a sophisticated end-of-the-evening event in Jackson Square with dancing and midnight fireworks over the Mississippi. So she wouldn't be wearing shorts and bobby socks.

Royal Street was more subdued, a ten-minute walk from his hotel, lined with art galleries, curio shops and chic dining spots catering to an up-scale clientele who would no sooner consume pizza and beer for dinner than they would pitch a tent in the forests of the bayou.

He arrived at a quarter of seven, guided to the corner table he personally chose and reserved the previous afternoon at lunch. He had a view of the entrance, the queue, and all other tables. He ordered a Blue, replying to the waiter that he wasn't yet certain whether he was dining alone. The patio was walled, the evening was clear and unusually warm. Not one of the few women seated were wearing shawls or jackets.

She came in at 7:15, alone, neither striding nor sauntering. An easy six feet in low heels. Hopefully easy. Hopefully alone, at once self-assured and demure. Excellent, he mused. Taller women too often wore flats, instinctively slumping their shoulders, the first indications of low esteem. This one did not. She knew she was attractive and smart with nothing to prove. Not by design she was intimidating to the average man, resented by average women. She didn't care. She didn't want average in her life or her straight curtain of hair wouldn't shimmer as though created from silver and obsidian threads.

Her skin was creamy-white, her eyes sheltered behind black horn-rimmed glasses. She wore no jewellery with good reason: The elegance of simplicity. Her Cheongsam dress complete with Mandarin collar was midnight blue brocade, knee-length with a discreet silver print Marcus couldn't discern. What he could make out were the slits from the hem to her mid-thighs with slivers of dark blue lace peeking out at him. Nothing Rosemary Sandra would deem to wear, not since the rude revelation a few years earlier that fifty was closer than thirty. Not that she couldn't. She wouldn't, a single one-piece taking more space in her drawer than twenty of the imported thongs and Rios that weren't an issue at all through to her thirties. He sipped his Blue, vanquishing the hateful bitch.

She followed the waiter, not scanning the patio. Women that arresting never bothered, fully aware they were the ones passing through the scanner. Seated, she ordered a white wine that came to her before she finished reviewing the menu, the young man acknowledging with a nod that she was in no hurry.

The second hand of his Rolex made 7:30 crucial. No gentleman would dare to leave such an incredibly lovely woman alone in sex-driven New Orleans for five minutes, let alone fifteen. No one as delectable and alluring as her. Never. Nor would she for a moment consider the company of anyone but a true gentleman, a rare twenty-first century species primarily indigenous to the Southeast. She was discriminating, better to briefly forego the best than to readily accept the worst. She was in no hurry.

He stood from his seat, straightening his tie and French cuffs.

"I beg your pardon, madam, for interrupting your peaceful reveries."

She looked up without any particular reason to smile, her female sense of surviving the evening free of bullshit enumerating several reasons in her defense.

"Sir?"

"My name is Marcus Simms, teetering at the uncertain precipices of rapture and misery, the fate of my evening placed entirely in your hands. I am also profoundly hopeful that your enraged husband will not at any moment invite me into the street to demand satisfaction for my being irresistibly compelled to meet you."

"He's not enraged, I assure you. He's divorced, has

been for over a year and probably somewhere nearby this evening hitting on something barely out of her teens. So why aren't you?"

"Because I'm a man of discriminating taste, because I'm standing here wondering why any other man would possibly be such a fool."

"No you're not. You're wondering how to invite yourself to my table or me to yours."

Straight to the point. No bullshit. "Of course I am. Remaining alone at my table when I could be revelling in the company of a lovely woman on an equally lovely evening would make me no less a fool. Particularly this night." She glanced at his tanned hands. No ring, no indentation or mark. "Divorced as well, with fading scars. My ex has the house, I have the mortgage," he grinned. "She suffered from issues of a personal nature a much younger man was able to resolve more effectively than me. Believe me, you'll get over him."

"Do I look disconsolate, like a grieving castoff? Believe me, I'm not. I got a lot more than a house. I'm a lawyer, a very good one. He should have known better."

Marcus knew he passed the thirty-second litmus test with flying colours. "May I sit and plead my case before the peoples' court, Your Honour? Or must I return to my table, my shame and misery the object of everyone's amusement?"

"My name's Haley Sands. And yes, you may."

Marcus signalled over their waiter, asking for his glass and a refill.

She was thirty-six, he was touching forty. Not commenting on her hair was tantamount to gross negligence. The silver pattern on her Mandarin dress which he complimented first was a magpie perched on a tree. She

330

lived in Metairie north of the city where she ran a law firm, he lived in Mandeville farther north across Lake Pontchartrain where he owned an ad agency. She hadn't dated in over a year, nor had he. She had no kids, no dog and no life. Ditto. She was all work, as was he. All she wanted was a nice guy with hair and a good job. He had both, and tickets to the Ball Drop.

Near ten o'clock Marcus gestured for the bill, the couple ambling towards Jackson Square peering into store windows, talking about travel and fashion, avoiding exes and work. At midnight he rang in the New Year clinking her fluted glass and kissing her cheek. Haley rang in the New Year pressing her lips to his and taking his hand. She'd been dry far too long and lived thirty miles closer than him. He'd taken a taxi to the Quarter to prevent his Lexus becoming a park bench or a public latrine, he explained; Haley parked her Jag indoors at the Marriott.

She called the place a quaint home, he called it a fifteen-room mansion complete with heated pool and tennis court. With five hours of preamble behind them, inventing conversation in the living room as a prelude to their frantic and mutual release in the bedroom was totally absurd.

The bedroom was massive, looking out onto a lush garden, the walls lined with modern art and a sixty-inch screen. Haley went into the ensuite bathroom to undress, directing Marcus to the dining room where he would find a selection of malted scotch and chilled Chardonnay for her.

She came out in a floor-length silk gown, taking the wine and kissing him, lounging onto her récamier and patting the space beside her. She wanted the imprints on her body from her stay-ups, panties and bra to fade, telling Marcus that her robe falling from her shoulders seemed more fitting than an inept sensuous striptease after too many years of mundane marriage and too many months of sitting alone in bed reviewing case files. Her independent and disappointing fingers, she too soon discovered, more interested in attending to a client's needs than hers.

She was anything but inept, he assured her.

When the moment finally came, her silk robe became her pedestal, Haley pirouetting gracefully as much for his visible approval as for his palpable anticipation of her. Apart from her miscarried husband, Marcus was the first to see her that naked since law school. She knew she was blessed with enviable good looks, desirable to most men, she simply craved hearing the forgotten words. Which she did throughout the entire night, her mind irresistibly wondering why he had not come into her life a year earlier.
*

Eight years earlier a young New Orleans mother and father set out early on a sunny Saturday morning adventure en route to Biloxi, Mississippi on the I-10 for a weekend getaway with their two little and excited girls. Gambling and theatre for the parents, was the plan, the pool and the beach for the girls. Instead the trip and their lives ended close to home at the city limits.

Antoine Beauregard was twenty-two, a graduate of New Orleans University. He was up and coming, young, handsome and charming. He was at the top of his class, a Valedictorian and privileged. The all-American golden-haired boy coming home early Saturday morning from celebrating four years of gruelling studies. He was three times over the legal limit travelling in the wrong direction, doing one-twenty when his graduation gift, a 70's vintage convertible, slammed into the family's van.

They died in under a second, the DA told the jurors, obliterated, the parents very likely screaming in terror with

332

their final breaths. Antoine Beauregard, on the other hand, was flung several hundred feet and survived. The DA wanted a life sentence for second degree murder, claiming that binge-drinking to three times over the legal limit was as good as loading a gun, that getting into the car was no different than cocking the hammer, that driving into oncoming traffic was the same as aiming and pulling the trigger.

The judge gave Beauregard eight years in the state prison without parole, the combined ages of the children, in his decision agreeing with defense counsel that Beauregard's actions were unintentional, that he would never knowingly or recklessly kill with intent. That, given the inexperience of his years, his exuberance, and the cheering on of his peers, he was ill-equipped to deal with the rapid and ill effects of alcohol.

Marcus Simms wondered how well-equipped Beauregard would be to deal with the ill effects of pentobarbital and sulphuric acid.

He was released in October, taken on at a New Orleans fishery doing the night shift, steam cleaning floors and equipment. No doubt working his way up to the gutting table. He lived alone, shunned by humiliated parents. No kidding, Marcus thought while waiting in the dark. Stinking of fish gut and cheap beer wasn't exactly champagne and caviar. Not exactly every girl's dream.

He had visited the apartment days before. The single room hardly needed a door, except for the fridge where Beauregard kept his free fish bits, beer and pizza slices. He had no clothes other than a pair of jeans, a sweatshirt and work boots, he didn't need any. He went to work and came home in white scrubs and black Billy boots. He had no television, just a radio and a worn sofa, a bed that belonged in a dumpster and a Salvation Army deckchair on the first floor balcony by his empty parking space conveniently located by the bus stop.

The bathroom boasted a toilet with part of a seat, a sink coated with toothpaste spittle and hair, a toothbrush and a bottle of baby oil which Marcus assumed was less expensive than SPF 30. Seemed like Antoine was trying to erase his jailhouse pallor.

Beauregard, he knew, would leave work at six. The plant closing at noon for two days was a non-issue. He would arrive home on the half-hour in the dark, eighty minutes after sunset, Marcus counting down the final five minutes, the final ten of Beauregard's life. Watching the man through the sun drapes shuffle across the parking lot in his oversized boots, Marcus retreated to the bathroom narrowing the opening with a gloved hand.

On cue the single light went on, the door closed, the boots plodded three or four steps and Marcus swung open the door, cloaked in a shadow.

"Hey there, Tony. Nice place you have here."

Beauregard made a loud and raspy 'huh' sound, jolting backwards.

"Saturday night, Christmas Eve in the Big Easy and no gift or girl to unwrap. That's a total bummer."

"What the hell, man! How'd you get in here?"

"The better question would be why I got in. That's your more important issue, Tony."

"Yeah, so why did you, man? And who the hell are you?"

"I need you in the bathroom, Tony. I don't need anyone passing by and seeing this happen." He couldn't resist. "That wouldn't be cool, *man*, for me."

"Seeing what happen, man?"

"Duh! Me killing you."

"What! No!"

"You murdered a young family who simply wanted a memorable weekend, Tony. So, yes, you're dead, *man*. I've got to make things right for them. It's what I do."

"Shit, man. No! Give me a break. I mean, shit, man."

"I know, you've done your time. You're a good man now, fully rehabilitated. Good for you, and the purest Grade-A bullshit."

"No. It was an accident, man. Totally. I was fucking drunk, like fucking totalled. I don't even remember what really happened. I mean, shit, man. We're talking eight years ago."

"No, we're talking here and now. In brief, *man*, you were an arrogant little prick with a rich daddy, a mommy's pride and joy who could do no wrong. At least not until you got yourself shitfaced, *man*, and deliberately slaughtered four people. You had booze for blood that morning and got off too easily."

"Think so? Really? Mother refuses my calls and father's ordered me to keep my distance. He makes more in an hour than I do in a week and he won't give me a fucking dime."

"That's sad, *man*. Like totally fucked-up."

"Nothing's easy about eight years in prison, man. Do you think I went in looking like this?"

Cons all had the same skin tone. White guys were either burnt brown from hours in the yard, or pasty. Some tattooed to appear tough, some not. Black guys either stayed black or took on a chalky-grey pallor. Latinos opted for skin graffiti that served no real purpose on black skin.

Beauregard was pasty. He wasn't the pretty-boy of his yesteryear, Marcus conceded. His head was shaved, a purple scar ran from his left ear to a chin sprouting a sparse Manchurian failure, his left eye was permanently and partially closed and the missing lobe of his right ear was replaced with a gold ring.

Marcus shrugged. "Certainly not suitable for an evening at the theatre, I grant you, Antoine. Although I have seen worse. Like the young man and woman you killed. They didn't look very good when you were through with them. Literally, one second they were young and attractive, both of them in love, and the next they were mutilated beyond recognition. So what is your point exactly, *man*?"

"I did more than my time and I'm still paying. Shit, I had the entire world in my hands, I was going places. Now it's like I'm diseased. My whole life is ruined because of a stupid accident. It's not fair, man."

"Not an accident. You murdered that family. The parents were only five years older than you, the girls too young for school. Their lives were ruined, not yours. You have no life, Beauregard. You're dead. Now get in here and let's get this thing done."

"Think I would have hurt those people knowing what would happen to me in there, or that I would have shit in my pants every day for the rest of my life?"

Marcus chortled. "Shitting yourself is not a very good line of defence. On the brighter side, however, you were never lonely and now you won't be shocked by what happens here next. Seeing you coming at them at nearly 200 feet per second must have been horrific for them. The imagery boggles the intelligent mind, if not yours. For what we know, they shit themselves. I would have."

Marcus stepped into the room, the gun in his hand.

"Fuck that. No way, man!"

"Au contraire, *man*."

336

Beauregard twisted, reaching for the doorknob, his forehead slamming into a wall, wobbling, collapsing to his knees, crashing his scarred face onto the floor. Marcus, pleased with his aim, reached past the crumpled body and flicked off the light.

"Excellent, Tony. Excellent. You're pissing yourself. Good man. The rest won't take long. I would guess under two minutes. The equivalent in prison years to multiple lifetimes condensed into incredibly horrific seconds. Here's the Coles Notes version, so we can get this done." He pocketed the gun, reaching for the syringe, the diffused lighting from the streetlamp adequate for the task at hand. "Pentobarbital, Tony. That's the easy part, or should be. However not this time, not for you. The lifetime part is sulphuric acid, a fifty-fifty mix. Pretty much a standard for me now and, in your case, particularly crime-appropriate: Very fast and very furious. Sort of a victims' impact statement. Otherwise I would give you an extra minute or two. At the rate of speed you were driving you didn't give them much time to think about dying, which was probably for the best. That said, I'm not as considerate as you. So listen up. For the next two minutes, give or take, you are going to bleed pretty much from every orifice. You'll want to scream, and I understand the need. Believe me, I do. I'm not new to this. Yet you won't because you'll be choking on your puke. Instead you'll cry and whimper and squirm, straining enough to pop your eyeballs from their sockets. You'll tear and dig and rip at yourself so frantically that when they find you you'll look like butchered chum, which is sort of meaningful in your case. Don't you think? Best of all, you'll blow out enough shit to fill your boots. So here we go, *man*."

Antoine Beauregard didn't wait to begin his

whimpering, tears dripping onto the floor, his body inert for the time being.

Marcus first plucked the dart from behind Beauregard's neck, expertly sliding the needle into Beauregard's limp arm and thumbing the plunger half way. Then into his jugular to help spread the effects of the dosage, emptying the barrel and stepping quickly to a safer distance.

He had nothing else to concern himself with. He slid the needle into its protective sleeve and the syringe into a pocket as he walked to the sliding doors, suddenly aware that he was hungry and anxious to change from his work clothes. The apartment already reeked of fish gut and within a very few minutes the air would become unbreathable with Beauregard's contents.

He would leave, he had no reason to stay. Beauregard was doing better than expected. He was following procedure, convulsing and twisting, splashing in his urine and tearing at his flesh, conducting an unpleasant symphony of groans and squeals as he was choking and filling his boots.

Marcus walked out into the hall and onto the street. Several blocks later he disposed of his tools. Hailing a cab he went directly to the Doubletree where he changed his wardrobe in the men's room, later discarding his work outfit, shoes and sports bag in the French Quarter as he walked towards Bourbon Street.

*

Her guy? Really? Already?

Marcus cleared his head.

"…not be a clutter freak. The last one believed his entire closet floor was a laundry hamper. Please tell me you know about wash cycles, Marcus."

"I am not a clutter freak, I do my own laundry and I

excel in the kitchen. I employ a home service to manage the more routine household chores."

"Spending two days in a row with a man," she pinched her arm, "and I'm not dreaming. That's a good thing."

He raised the sheet from her hip, humming. "A very good thing from my perspective." He kissed her. "You do breakfast, I'll do dinner at my place. You should pack an overnight bag. No pool, though. Sorry."

Haley beamed, pushing him onto his back and straddling him in a single fluid motion, not waiting for him to auto-react to her warm flesh when she was already primed. She had her day planned and clothes did not factor into the schedule, not with a heated pool and spring-like temps.

Haley Sands was in seventh heaven, deliriously happy. When she wasn't making love with Marcus in her bed she was clinging to his neck in deep water, completely misconstruing his appetite for her, his tender embraces and loving caresses, completely oblivious to the comfort and joy of closure she was bringing to him. She made light of his warnings that she would exhaust herself, depleting her strength with too little or none remaining for their evening. She begged to differ, patting his cheek. If he wasn't weakening, because he certainly was not, how could she possibly?

Nevertheless he won out, as was his nature. With sunset an hour away, the air was beginning to chill. Dressed in fleecy robes they meandered reluctantly into the house, Marcus guiding her, lovingly scolding her for not believing him. She felt drained, feeling sleepy after a day of euphoric sex and intoxicating wine. He would spend the night, he told her. Driving was unwise and he didn't want to leave her. Dinner could wait.

She kissed him, letting him sweep her into his arms and carry her to her daybed off the patio. He kissed her, stepping back to watch as she slipped into a deep sleep. Pleased that she was purring soundly, he returned to the pool gathering the glasses, the wine and scotch bottles. Nothing else was a concern, he was practiced at not touching surfaces or accounting methodically for the ones he would touch.

Inside he went to the kitchen where he washed the lunch dishes, bottles and glasses with her rubber gloves. He went through the bathroom as a matter of habit, satisfied. He was particularly cautious in their bathrooms, seldom spending time in their living rooms. She and the others were all purpose-specific, living rooms were too intimate.

In the bedroom he fashioned his robe into a tight roll before stripping the bed and doing likewise. Dressing, he checked for his keys, wallet and money clip. He checked for more glasses. Nothing. Not that he ever worried about fingerprints, he had never served in the military or otherwise been fingerprinted. Neither he nor Jeddore Billows was on anyone's file or radar and for DNA to become worrisome he would first have to be caught, which was a non-issue. He was simply being as pragmatic and thorough as he was in business. Professional.

He felt good, he felt rested and invigorated. Standing by her side he studied her. She was angelic; they were all sweet and delicate in peaceful slumber. Stepping in closer he leaned forward, tracing his fingertips across her cheeks, kissing her lips. She would never know; she would transition serenely.

Touching nothing as he left her, stepping through the front door into a darkened evening, he sanitized and wiped the knobs with breath freshener and his pocket hanky.

Reaching into his suit pockets for the Marlboros and gold lighter, he paused to reflect on his day. He had a lot of thinking to do, about the bitch in Charleston taking him to the cleaners, the springtime schedule he had ignored far too long, and the fact that one day someone would come after him, set him up.

Flicking the stub onto the street, he walked several blocks maintaining his code.

Drifting into eternal peace, Haley Sands would never awaken.

Chapter Twenty-One
Smithers vs. Williams

The second Sunday of the New Year at 6:58 AM the dim sunlight wasn't doing much to combat the wintry morning chill or Brenda Smithers' miserable mood. She sat fuming in her ten-year-old Acura with the windows up and the heater set midway. She was waiting, for him, again.

Staring into her rear-view, unblinking like a doe transfixed on high-beams, she was well-past being annoyed. She was increasingly and irrationally angry with him, his cavalier attitude towards her and his impudent sense of timing increasingly irksome. Sunday morning in particular, mostly because Princeton was probably peering down from her high-rise sanctum, which was making Brenda feel exposed. Then an unexpected and welcome epiphany, Brenda nodding into the mirror, her lips pursed. She was resolute. She felt relieved, finally rid of him. She could actually whisper the words: She absolutely hated Parker Williams.

She woke that morning at five in the dark, doing ten K on her treadmill and thirty minutes on her Pilate mat. She showered and did her make-up; she drank a power shake and fashioned her hair into a French braid that would survive the blustering wind. She dressed in the shortest flared skirt she dared to wear to the office, a tastefully sheer blouse over a three-quarter lace bra, stay-ups, mid-calf suede boots and a suede bomber with a fleece collar. All new, all bought the previous afternoon with a single purpose immediately following Princeton's unhappy phone call.

Studying herself in the bedroom mirror from all possible angles, whirling her skirt to imitate the wind hammering her windows, she inhaled and blew out a deep breath. Good for him. Jerk. Anyway, he would have seen that and more if he had ever invited her to his home and in-ground pool.

All or nothing. The woman in the mirror was sensational and she was determined, her silver Ray-Bans making her all the more appealing. Determined that if he said the slightest thing to set her off she would request immediate reassignment. She would not spend another day with him. Let the man infuriate someone else every day. She wanted out.

She arrived ahead of schedule on the quarter hour. He would arrive with two minutes to spare, deliberately aggravating her. He would climb nonchalantly from his pretentious Vantage convertible as if stepping onto a red carpet, looking not the least bit smug or self-satisfied; he would smile at her and say all sorts of bullshit nice things, all except one, while striding two paces to her three; he would hold the main and elevator doors for her, his macho thing; he would smile warmly at her, stepping behind her from the elevator to open the last and, that morning, the most perilous door. Screw him. Jerk. She hated herself for being angry with herself, because of him, desperately wanting just once to smack his thoughtless head.

She saw him first in her mirror, the barely audible Aston Martin pulling in beside her. He stepped out smoothly, Brenda certain she wouldn't see a single crease in his Armani suit. She never did. The man was impeccable. He was head-turning handsome, a perfect gentleman, smart and the best at his job. He was better than impeccable, she mused. Parker Williams was fucking wonderful.

She stepped out, not the least surprised that Williams was holding the door, extending his hand to assist her. The one time in any day or week she ever felt his warm and gentle touch.

"Hey, Brenda. Wow. You are dangerously hot this morning. A definite heart-stopper. Wow."

Then try stopping yours, asshole. "I feel like shit."

"Then we'll have to find you a mirror. You are absolutely stunning. You've certainly made my day."

Oh, just fuck off. "This won't be good, Parker."

"All things are relative, Brenda." He swung the door closed, turned and strode toward the building, focused straight ahead on the mirrored doors.

No shit, she thought. Perhaps he wasn't blind after all. She was hurrying beside him. She was constantly hurrying beside him, albeit never before fixated on her own reflection closing in on her, savouring the sensation and the sight of the wind playing teasingly with her skirt at the lacy fringes of her stockings. The thin smile he was wearing made her day. Screw him, because that's all he would ever get, until, a few feet from herself, distracted and seconds too late, her hands shot uselessly downward. Twirling away instinctively, she made her situation that much worse. Not so much his.

"Shit!" she blurted. Shit she was stupid. She was standing in a whirlwind. "Shit!"

He stepped aside, grinning, standing with his Armani

arms crossed.

"I'm not seeing a thing here, Brenda. I swear. My eyes are shut tight." Rare seconds passed. "But can I say one thing?"

She gave up struggling, pushing past him, jerking open both doors with both hands, allowing the wind and Parker Williams a final few seconds of playtime. Once inside her skirt was taking an eternity to fall. She wanted to die. Or, better yet, she wanted to kill him. "Don't you dare say anything that will get you killed, Williams."

"Absolutely spectacular! Wow!"

"You're disgusting," she snarled, marching to the elevators.

"Hey, that was a compliment."

"I don't need to hear shit like that, especially from you."

"You're right, I apologize." He held open the door, pausing, removing his tinted Serengetis. "Brenda, remember one thing before we go in there."

"What now, Williams?" she snapped.

He touched her cheek. "You are the absolute best. There is none better."

What!

The glass doors on the top floor of the glass and steel office building were not decorated with identifying symbols or the agency's name, simply a self-explanatory No Admittance. To anyone mistakenly stepping from the elevator, blindly passing through the doors, they were a call-in centre and the intruders were politely asked to leave.

Beyond the reception area were spartan offices, cubicles and conference rooms occupied most hours of the day and night by sleep deprived investigators and their tireless researchers.

The middle-aged and stern-faced woman occupying the largest and plushest office would appear to anyone at first glance as though she might enjoy chewing on eight-inch iron bolts with her morning coffee. Or whatever else was eight inches that she could find to shred with her bright and perfect teeth. At the moment she was thinking Parker Williams would nicely fit the bill.

Fran Princeton wasn't interested in banter and small talk. She was all business and today she was pissed, royally pissed. She was pissed because her Washington boss and his boss were pissed. With her, because of them, the ones summoned to her office on a Sunday morning as if the school bell had rung and Miss Princeton was not pleased with their homework. Because she was not pleased with them.

She was not a teacher, she was Director of the Collaborative Cold Case Command. The nationwide 4-C based in Virginia, a unit committed to solving the worst cold cases that state and municipal forces chose to leave in the cold, whether for lack of resources or eventual lack of interest. Despite which, despite assigning different teams, 4-C had nothing to go on after seventeen years in seventeen states. No clue whatsoever about the Christmas Killer, except when he would strike next and a sadistically gruesome note left behind free of prints. They didn't care about the ex-cons sent horrifically to Hell; they cared about the young women, all except one found sleeping peacefully and naked on their sofas. Their beds, and the Valcourt woman's hotel bed, stripped of the linen.

The cons they understood. Without exception they got off with kinder sentences than their crimes warranted and he was balancing the scales of justice; the women were another matter. All of them innocent and successful, attractive and single, murdered with clean pentobarbital in their sleep for no better reason than lonely desperation, according to friends and colleagues, and bringing home the wrong stranger.

"Sit," Princeton told them, pointing at Williams. "Williams, you shut your smiley mouth. Smithers, you tell me something I need to hear. Convince me I did not make a huge a mistake assigning a newbie and Mr. Wonderful here to this case."

Brenda Smithers was a petite 5'6" and very cute, not that she couldn't drop any man to the ground in a blink or shoot him between the eyes at fifty feet. Including Parker Williams, her favourite mental target at the range. Her voice was sweet and soft when she was happy, which excluded most days when working in too close proximity with Williams. Today she was neither sweet nor cute, minutes earlier she went from being infuriated to feeling titillated to being completely humiliated while he stood stupidly gaping at her.

He was a jerk, a rich jerk, the braided V-neck sweater and tennis shorts type of jerk. He didn't need to work for a living, she did. She loved her job, when he wasn't making her life difficult and miserable. But he wasn't a thorn in her side any longer. She was free of him. He had crossed the line, making her decision that much easier, and now he was sitting with a silly smirk on his face while she was seated in front of Princeton and the proverbial fan. Why her? What terrible thing had she ever done in her life to deserve him?

They had gone at a moment's notice to witness and photograph each of the last five mutilated ex-cons, leaving the crime scenes after extensive and futile investigations without a single clue other than the ME's report that left them no doubt about the killer's lack of humanity. Prepared each year to remain nearby, to photograph a young and beautiful dead woman one week later.

She was fed up, mostly with him. She hadn't been assigned, she volunteered for the thankless duty after six months with the squad. She hadn't celebrated Christmas in five years, or New Year's, except with him, and the jerk never once thought to buy her a Christmas gift or invite her for a drink on New Year's when all they could do was wait for another Haley Sands to happen. Her life was the purest shit.

She was fed up. She was exhausted, tired of sleeping with the Christmas Killer invading her thoughts and dreams over the past five years like a taunting ghost, a sociopath never made public, fantasizing about his capture and execution as often as she imagined herself sleeping in the arms of Parker Williams. Never certain which was the worst nightmare or the best dream. Not that she loved him, she didn't. Not anymore. She knew everything about him except that, the centre of his self-centred existence, and not knowing whether he was braindead, blind, or just plain dead below the waist made her crazy.

She shrugged the bomber from her shoulders, draping it over the back of her seat, the shock value of her blouse and bra obliterated by her previous impromptu show-all performance. Sitting, she carefully crossed her legs, ignoring their very different reactions.

"Smithers," Princeton leaned over her desk, waving a finger at her agent, "what is up with that?"

"What's up with what?"

"Do not give me attitude. With that. Why am I seeing your perky little breasts and almost all your bare legs?"

Williams leaned to one side, giving Brenda the onceover. "Gee, you're right, boss. A little racy for a serious meeting. And no weapon. Where's her gun, boss?"

You're a complete idiot. "It's Sunday, Captain. I've got a date."

"A date, at seven in the morning?" Princeton asked.

"For lunch. Yes."

"Hopefully not at a family restaurant, Brenda. I mean, really, the kids and all."

Princeton redirected her finger. "Williams, you put your tongue and your eyeballs back in your head." She gave Brenda an approving nod. "Smithers, ignore him. Your outfit is adorable, if not a little too elegant for this place, and hopefully your taste in men is better than Haley Sands'. Speak to me. Tell me something good."

"Haley Sands was no different from the other girls, Captain. She fit all the parameters: Professional, lawyer, really attractive, divorced, lived alone and was found by co-workers on her daybed. She was buried yesterday. We found no indication of violence, not a single clue, and no sheets."

"Yeah. Not the best way to find your lovely boss, boss," Williams cut in. "She came up empty as well. Not a drop to work with. Like all the others, the ME told us she had a good time. Nothing rough, just lots of it."

Fran Princeton didn't smile. "What you're saying is that we wait another year, nothing happens, and somewhere another woman gets herself killed because she's lonely or desperate for love. That doesn't work for me, and soon neither will you two. Not on this case anyway."

"Not a year, boss. A lot sooner. Months, if that," Williams replied. "I've come up with a workable strategy. Drastic measures, that sort of thing."

"What!" Smithers twisted in her seat. "What plan? Jesus, Williams."

"Sorry, Brenda. The idea actually came to me a short while ago, very short in fact, walking into the building actually. I was going to tell you, but then something unexpectedly came *very* up and I was pretty distracted."

"Yeah, I bet you were." Pig.

Princeton let that one slide. She knew full-well how Williams was an incorrigible pain in the butt.

"We should have come up with this at the beginning, boss. Brilliant really."

Princeton sat waiting.

"Brilliant? You? You're brilliant?"

"Thank you, Brenda. It's something not many people know about me because I don't make a big thing of it." He faced Princeton. "This guy in Missouri is slated for release in September, boss. Real SOB. He's done a full twenty-five for walking into a gay bar with an Uzi. He emptied the mag. Killed nine, wounded a dozen more. His lawyer convinced the judge he was wacko, too crazy for the needle. Inside he did half his time in solitary for spooking too many inmates. Especially the bum brothers."

Princeton leaned forward. "And this brilliance works how, exactly?"

"Simplicity at its finest. We don't wait. We cut him loose in March."

Smithers grimaced. She really wanted to smack his head. "The Christmas guy kills in December for a reason. He's patient and he's meticulous. Hundreds of cons get out each month, but he's selective. He's got a criterion. He knows who he wants and why, he knows where they go and he follows them. Then he waits two, three months. Yeah, real brilliant, Williams."

"Ladies, we can get this guy. His victims are all capital criminals, the absolute worst. The problem is the cons never see him coming. They live in the slums and get drunk or do drugs to forget. They relocate, their prison skills go out the window and they get sloppy. The gay basher, Frank Adams, we set him loose on paper but toss him into solitary until we get this guy. No one will care." He paused. Princeton and Smithers waited. "The best part, I take his place. I become Frank Adams and when the Christmas Killer finds me, we nail him once and for all."

Smithers waited a moment, bursting into gut-wrenching laugher, covering her mouth, her face flushed in a deep rouge. Princeton let her, she deserved.

"Are you insane, Williams? You have your nails done and you pay eighty bucks for a frigging haircut. You wake up with a zit and you make an appointment for day surgery. This guy's done twenty-five and I guarantee he looks like yesterday's shit."

He beamed at the compliment. "You are very right, Brenda. As a rule high-end products do require a higher degree of professional maintenance due to their finer craftsmanship and sensitivity to difficult external conditions. Thank you."

She turned to Princeton. "He needs help, real help. He's completely delusional, Captain." She leaned into him, groaning. "Get over yourself, I would have a better chance passing for a con."

He shook his head 'no', letting his eyes travel from her flushed face to her breasts to the sheen of her stockings. "In that outfit, not a chance. More like a con's wet dream, Brenda." Then to Princeton: "I can do this thing, boss. Or we don't get the Christmas Killer, not ever. He's all over the map, probably has fake IDs. He's very good at what he does; thing is, we're better. What we need is leverage, and that's Frank Adams and me."

"Yeah, right. The bodies we find are so mutilated we can't even be certain how he even gets to kill them, as though they let him. Good plan, Williams."

He passed Princeton his dossier on Adams. Finished flipping through the pages, she handed the folder to Smithers.

"The answer is no, Williams. Not because you're insane, because I do agree with Smithers. We simply do not have the financial or physical resources to support a three-month sting."

"Not an issue. I'll share a room with Brenda to cut costs. I mean, really, what the hell? I don't mind bunking up." He glanced directly at her breasts, avoiding her eyes, worried the glare might burn out his retinas. "Especially now. I mean, hello. I'll even spot for dinners."

"Jesus, Captain."

"Forget it, Williams."

That wasn't the answer he wanted. "Tell you what, boss. If I come in here two days from now, passing the test, proving I can do this, I get your approval. Deal?"

"What test?" both women asked.

"My makeover. Because really, this is it. He will keep doing this until he picks the wrong con and he's the one we find twisted and purged on the floor. Do this and I guarantee I will get the guy."

"Conversely, you fail this test of yours and you're off the case. That's my deal. Both of you."

"Agreed."

Princeton pondered quietly for a moment, smirking, a faint snort escaping her nose. "Deal. Tuesday, 8:00 PM. You too, Smithers."

Parker Williams stood, glancing at his watch. He had four hours before her lunch date, 100 feet to her car. He had more on his mind than Frank Adams and rules were meant to be broken. That was his rule.

Brenda remained seated, wondering what depraved thoughts were spinning in his twisted mind.

"Captain, you cannot be serious. Why are you encouraging him when he should be in a bed with restraints? I'm mean, Jesus, look at him. There is no way this will work. He's insane."

"All the more reason for you to be here Tuesday. Now unless something else is on your mind. Enjoy your lunch date." She pointed to Williams. "And take him with you."

"Parker, you go. I have an unrelated subject to discuss with the captain."

Williams understood when he wasn't wanted. Her tone told him 'female talk'. He wished each of them a pleasant day and walked out.

*

Tuesday, near six o'clock, Smithers stepped into her apartment, instantly drawing her weapon at the sound of soft music coming from her living room. She had no boyfriend, her parents were out of state and didn't have a key, and her only girlfriend was on vacation alone at a singles club because screwing around behind his back wasn't Brenda's idea of a good time. Now she was seriously considering booking a flight to forget him.

The man was peering from the window, his feet apart, his hands and arms braced against the windowpane, unaware she was poised behind him. He was tall, 5'11" and fit, the compression tee-shirt defining a slim waist, sculpted arms and back. His arms and neck were tattooed, his head shaved.

"Drop to the floor, asshole! Do it! Now!" Nothing. No reaction. "Fucking do it, asshole! Or lose a leg. Your choice."

He raised his hands deliberately into the air, turning with threatening slowness. A spasm shot through Brenda's arms, jerking them, a horrible gasp escaping her wide-open mouth. He was dirty and sweaty, his skin the colour of ash as if he'd spent his day shovelling coal. His face was covered with stubble and scarred, his eyes dark and sinister, his lips curled into a menacing snarl. A cold shiver shook her body. She was frightened cocking her weapon, reaching for her cell.

"Well hello there, little girl." The guttural sound was sickening. "I been waitin' on you. Nice place you have here. Quaint but liveable. I like it. Like it a lot." He gave her a lewd and appreciative onceover from head to toe, licking his cracked lips. "Damn if you ain't the prettiest damn thing. Whew! We gonna have us a good time, you and me."

He was mocking her. "You have three seconds before I put you on the floor, asshole. Who are you?"

"Well that really hurts, Brenda. And speaking of asses, yours is sensational. Sunday you were fantastic. You were breathtaking. If he hadn't invited you to lunch, I would have. I wanted to."

What!

"Parker?"

"No, Brenda. I'm Frank Adams. Now may I please lower my arms?"

Her body shuddered, every inch of her covered in goosebumps. "No! Parker. This isn't possible."

"Wrong again. What isn't possible is your reassignment. I put the brakes on that foolish notion."

"No! This cannot be happening."

"It is. Princeton had the same reaction. I met her this afternoon, her and five of our co-workers with their guns drawn. Took them awhile to calm down. She also told me you were experiencing a few Parker Williams issues. Discreetly, of course. You know, birds of a feather, that female conspiracy code. Now would you please lower your weapon? I needed your reaction, Brenda. Who knows me better than you?"

She lowered the gun, her shoulders slumping. "Shit, Parker. No."

"The boss was right. You were adorable on Sunday, Brenda. Are adorable. I did not mean to embarrass you, which does not mean I wasn't completely captivated. Whoever he is, good for him. A little cheap though. A lunch instead of dinner? You deserve more."

"Great. All I need for a free dinner is to show you my bare ass. Thanks, Parker."

"You're welcome. At the very least I do owe you a dinner."

"I went home. There was no lunch, no date. I haven't had a date in…for a very long time. And, for your information, those few times I came home alone."

"Then…?"

She sneered. "Then what, Parker?"

Red flag! Danger! Do Not Fuck-Up! "You dressed especially for me? You know, sexy?"

"No, Parker. I did not dress especially for you. Jesus, get over yourself." She holstered her weapon. All or nothing. She sighed, flopping backward onto her sofa. "Okay. Yes, I did. Thanks for making me feel even more ridiculous."

He couldn't resist the sly grin. "How did you conjure up that magnificent wind?"

"That was not supposed to happen, not that way."

"But a little wind was in your plan." He came closer. "Yes? No? Maybe?"

"Jesus, Parker, what have you gone and done? You look like shit."

"Yesterday's shit, as I recall. Precisely as you described Frank Adams."

She leaned forward, her eyes beginning to tear, her voice mournful. "What have you done?"

"The tattoos will fade in a few months, the hair will grow in, the scars and lips are silicone, and the eyes come out at bedtime." He sat across from her. "You didn't answer my questions, Brenda."

Shit. "Yes. Because I needed you to see me as more than a gun and a badge in a pantsuit, that I wasn't a man with tumors on his chest." She sneered. "Good morning, Brenda. You're very lovely today, Brenda. Sleep well, Brenda. Enjoy your vacation, Brenda. I'll miss you, Brenda. Merry Christmas, Brenda. Happy New Year, Brenda. For five fucking years, Parker, without a single gift. Not a single dinner that wasn't all about work, like I only exist in daylight." She pushed herself to her feet. "You stay here." She disappeared into her bedroom, reappearing in seconds, hurling a foil-wrapped box at his head. "And the first time you come to my home, what do you do? You break in. I mean, shit."

"Hey, I didn't go into your bedroom and poke around." He caught the box in mid-flight. "What's this?"

"Your gift from five Christmases ago. It's a gold tie clip engraved with your initials. I didn't know what else to get you after only six months. Then I couldn't give it to you because you weren't with me, Parker."

He unwrapped the box, flipping the lid. "Wow. This is special, very special. Thanks, Brenda. And here I am without a tie. Sorry."

She mimicked his words under her breath, scrunching her face.

Peeling off his cracked lips as he closed the narrow space between them, he lifted her effortlessly from under her arms, pressing their bodies together, pressing his lips to hers.

No way! This was not happening, he was not happening. She was trapped in her nightmare. She wanted to wrap her arms around his neck, to pull him closer, but she didn't. She couldn't, too much in shock or too afraid she was floating in her dream. Shit!

"That felt good. That felt very good." Setting her down, he sat beside her. She looked like a confused schoolgirl, flushed, the weapon and badge on her belt somewhat incongruous to the moment. "To be fair, Brenda, I've got a few Brenda Smithers issues. Firstly, I never bought you a Christmas gift, yet I did give you Christmas gifts. Each year in your name I donated five K to charities. I think that's about what I would have spent on you. Or perhaps I should have given more. Perhaps you'll let me make up for that at Valentine's. I was never with you because at first I didn't want to intrude, you know, being six years older. And, more recently, I believed I was too late. I spent those Christmases like many others working in food kitchens. My way of staying balanced. Ditto for New Years. I mean, who could be in the mood for dancing and gaiety when we knew what was coming within hours?" He examined his clip. "I really do love my gift."

357

"I paid eighty-five on sale." She wiped her eyes. "You never told me. Why didn't you ever tell me? Shit, Parker, five years?"

"Of nights, not days. I didn't want to lose you as a partner. You know the rules. You love your job. At least I could be with you at work, if not everywhere else."

"What are you saying, Parker?" She shook her head, waving a hand towards a cabinet. "No. You get me a drink first, a double scotch. Shit!"

He poured two double shots, sitting a tad closer. "Princeton's agreed to let us work the Christmas Killer together. She knows, Brenda."

"She knows what? What does she know?"

"That you love me, of course. What else? The real reason you wanted reassignment."

"What!"

"Yeah, she saw through all your excuses about me being arrogant, annoying, self-centered, frustrating, a pain in your exquisite ass. That sort of thing. The list was pretty extensive. Brutal stuff, Brenda." He sipped his scotch. "She's right. I can see it now, the glow. All this time I was in love with you while you were living in silent torment. I feel badly about that. You should have told me."

She gulped a mouthful. "You are annoying, Parker, very annoying. You see my bare ass for a split second and suddenly you've loved me for five years? And you feel badly. Really?"

"Really. Except more like ten seconds. It was pretty gusty, and totally awesome. And no. I've loved you for five years, seeing your bare ass made me realize exactly how much I do want you. There's a huge difference. I wanted to tell you all this Sunday while walking to your car, but you had other ideas. You needed some girl time."

358

"What?" She leaned in closer, smacking his bald head. "God that felt good. Really good."

He rubbed the wound, grinning. "I see that."

"This is too weird. Sunday morning I hated you. I did. Now you're kissing me, telling me you love me?"

"I am, yes. I plan to later this evening as well, all evening. As for Sunday, you were afraid for me. I saw it in your face, so did Princeton." He drained his scotch. "On that note, Frank Adams will be released on February 01st, by which time I'll be on-site. We are not rushing into this. We're doing things right. Missouri's DA and the warden have no problem with solitary; they do with the judge. They were extremely amenable. Adams will spend a week unsuccessfully job hunting locally, relocating to Virginia. He'll get a job here at the General, in the boiler-room. His apartment is a three-room on the outskirts of Arlington, my new home until we get him. The audio and visual guys go in tomorrow. I also contacted the national media to ensure everyone knows how bad Frank Adams really is. Wherever our Christmas guy calls home, he's going to hear about this. There is no way he's going to ignore Adams or wait a full year. I'm thinking sometime before April 30th."

"You cannot do this, Parker. It's too dangerous. I won't let you."

He smirked. "Why not?"

She punched him. "You know why not."

"Yeah, I've known for a few hours. I saw the photograph on your desk." He chuckled. "Okay, I did snoop a little bit. But we do look great together. That's why you'll be next door. Princeton's also agreed to a backup team. You're the lead."

"Shit, Parker."

"In the meantime, because I'm not as presentable or as good-looking as usual, I'm preparing a special dinner here. I brought wine." He pointed to the bottle. "Is that okay?"

"No, it is definitely not okay. I've got a stove and an empty fridge, you have a designer kitchen and a heated in-ground which can wait a few hours longer. I cannot wait, and I won't." She pushed him backwards. "Me and you, we gonna have us a good time…Frankie."

Chapter Twenty-Two
Prelude to a Divorce Settlement

Marcus arrived home on the Monday evening to discover that the thickest envelope in his mailbox had come a week earlier from Roger Samuel Rothstone's attorney. She wasn't wasting a moment. She was petitioning him for divorce and using daddy's big guns, the claim asserting negligence and mental cruelty, the threat of violence and adultery. None of which she could prove in court, not yet anyway. Perhaps, he believed as he finished studying the many pages, after he killed her.

Had she delivered the non-negotiable and lengthy document in person then and there he supposed he would have choked the life out of her on the spot. Good thinking on her part. She was demanding the house and its contents exclusive of his personal effects, 100 K annually from Southeast Consulting and, should he at any time sell the company, one-fifth of the negotiated price. She might as well have demanded that he pay her funeral expenses.

The next morning he went to the office, giving the document to his lawyer, confiding in him about her many treacheries prior to Dominic Drake and her secret battle with alcohol. He instructed the attorney to stop her cold. All she was to get was the Lexus. She was a drunk and a tramp. Enough said.

He booked a flight to Aruba and drove to the airport. As agreeable as Charleston was in January he needed and wanted a warmer climate and the serenity of an island setting to digest what was happening, what would happen and when. His greatest worry was the 'when'. The court date was yet to be announced, which his attorney suggested would likely take place near the end of April or May.

He didn't want or need the distraction and inherent demands of hooking-up with a woman. Ten days with the same woman was dangerous, the female mind characteristically confused between the secondary use of one's vagina and the sole purpose of one's heart. He would stay to himself. Which is what he did, returning home richly tanned and decisive, having resolved the issues of timing, method, Drake, his alibi and, above all, his comfort and joy of closure. His ultimate and most ironic closure.

He could not simply kill her and Drake in the midst of an unpleasant divorce. He would immediately become the premier suspect with no alibi anyone would possibly believe, although burying the bitch on May 31st, the day they first met, the day they married, the date of an anniversary they hadn't celebrated in years, was certainly a temptation if not entirely practical.

In particular he didn't appreciate working on someone else's schedule despite his flexibility and having begun his preliminary research at the resort to locate and set up an appropriate target.

His prerequisite was simple: Someone recently released from prison and residing in South Carolina near Charleston. He had many to choose from, the world was a bad place. Most of them petty thieves, punks and losers doing two years or less. Three others were notable: A registered sex offender, sixty-eight; a double homicide, forty-six; and an arsonist, fifty-two.

The arsonist did twelve for cancelling his insurance before burning his house to the ground, leaving his wife, who was filing for divorce, and his kids, destitute. Not a good enough reason. The poor guy needed a break. The wife was likely a bitch and the kids were late teens about to leave home anyway. The double homicide was gang-related, an in-house cleansing and no one cared that he did twenty-five for settling an account. The old guy was another matter. He had gone to Bangkok once too often, leaving innocent kids traumatized and injured, his hard drive burgeoning with digital memorabilia when he was caught that would sicken a healthy mind. Eight years was nowhere near enough.

He was the one, and four to six weeks would allow Marcus ample opportunity to track and set up one Theodore Rumsey.

*

By January 30th, Marcus Simms had Rumsey located and assessed. The target spent his days delivering fliers door to door for pennies per unit, his nights sleeping on street corners and begging for loose change when cots weren't available at the mission. He would be a definite challenge, a challenge that Marcus was about to embrace wholeheartedly.

Paying the price for taking a vacation, he was working late and ordering in Chinese, the flat screen in his office tuned-in to CNN for noise, Marcus occasionally glancing at the screen. This time he wasn't casually glancing, he was staring, reaching for the remote. The image on the screen made his skin crawl. Good. The worse, the better.

For two years since his first major run-in with Rosemary Sandra he struggled with human nature, with being a creature of habit, which, considering his pastime, was far from being a good thing. He was committed in body and soul to a new regimen, a fresh springtime schedule, to not compromising his critical and humanitarian work.

As he listened and watched he sat back, sipping his Blue. He was pleased. Life was good, yet he had invested too much time and effort to forego Rumsey. He wouldn't. Rumsey was set in place to serve a specific purpose, the man decidedly undeserving of a peaceful and natural demise. That he might in fact expire on a sidewalk at a date sooner than later was irrelevant. He would expire when Marcus deemed the moment appropriate. As would Frank Adams, whose release from a full term for the calculated butchery of gay men could not be more propitious. To say the least the hounds, who were most certainly obsessed with tracking down a serial killer, to use their terminology, whose timeline was predictable, would be thrown off the scent.

First Rumsey, then Adams. Perfect. He reached for the phone, leaving a message for his travel agent. He needed a first-class ticket to Springfield, Missouri the next day. Adams would be easy to track. If not from the prison, which was likely, then from the mission, an employment office, or some raunchy low-end titty bar. Cons were predictable creatures. Lifers all wanted one thing: Naked. Young, pretty and naked.
*

Five hundred miles from Marcus Simms, so did Frank Adams, aka Darling, which is why Brenda Smithers was naked lying beside him and softly weeping. He wasn't Parker Williams leaving her to spend the last night of January in the Missouri state penitentiary. He was Darling.

Her darling whom she would not hold in her arms for an entire week.

Gently slipping from her death grip, he dressed quietly into grey cotton slacks, a grey shirt, white socks and thick-soled shoes delivered earlier in the week by FedEx. She watched him. Her man was a multimillionaire and nicer each day, risking his life to save a desperate woman somewhere who would never know about him or care about him, who couldn't wait for her own Mr. Perfect to rip away thirty-dollar panties in the heat of the moment. Because of them he could be worse than killed.

She went to him wearing his robe. "This is for you, darling. The cheapest watch I could find, a prison watch with my name on the back. Don't you dare go and do anything stupid because I'm getting accustomed to you and this place, which I can't afford alone at my paygrade."

He kissed her, strapping the bargain basement watch onto his wrist. "I love it. I love you, and I paid cash for the place. So don't sweat it. I do have a question however."

"What, darling?"

He sank smoothly onto one knee, flipping open the lid of a small velvet box. Inside was a titanium ring graced with a one-caret diamond. "Brenda Smithers, will you marry me, soon?"

Brenda first clamped a hand over her mouth, secondly she burst into happy tears. She lived a good life with no complaints now that she could love him, working hard at a successful career that she loved, but this guy, her man, had brought her to a whole new level of happy.

"Shit! Parker. Yes!" She took the box, not waiting for him to stand. "Shit, yes!" Sliding the ring onto her finger she dropped to her knees, plastering his frightening face with kisses.

"Good. That works for me." He grinned. "In which case I'll see you in seven days at the condo. Our home is off limits until he's dead or captured." Parker stood, taking her hands, kissing each one. "There is one more thing, sweetcheeks."

"What, darling? Like this isn't enough? I mean, holy shit!"

He stepped aside to his bedside table. "This, and don't go all girlie on me, Agent Smithers. It's my will. This place is yours, everything is yours if something happens that might upset our honeymoon in Bali."

"What!" She paled. She knew not to act like a hysterical female. She knew that. She was a frigging hard-ass federal agent who wanted to smother him with kisses and smack his head. "Do I get the jet too?" she tried, forcing a weak smile. "And the Vantage? Do I get the Vantage, darling?"

He chortled. "Yeah, you do, your own for Valentine's. Choose a colour." She punched him, he kissed her. "It's all legal, Brenda, whether you're Ms. Smithers or Mrs. Williams. My lawyer knows everything about you." He checked his new timepiece, kissing her as though for the last time. "The Lear's waiting for me, sweetcheeks. Do not come to the door. That's an order, agent. Bye."

He hugged her, squeezed her bum and walked out. He was not ultra-emotional. She was, about him. He chuckled, closing the door behind him. Sometimes she could be difficult to deal with. He had never killed a man, never had to. That said, as he stepped into a ten-year-old Acura that was his for the duration, there was no fucking way the Christmas Killer's days weren't at an end. Together he and Frank Adams were putting down the son of a bitch once and for all. Case closed.
*

Of all the ex-cons Marcus Simms had wreaked justice upon, Frank Adams was the crème de la crème, a white supremacist dirt bag.

Marcus spent the better part of a week tracking him from the time he left the mission in the morning until, Marcus supposed, the dinner bell was clanging. He was an expert after so many years in changing his appearance, never crossing paths, never taking reckless chances. He just needed Adams to either get a job, a welfare cheque, or get out of town. The latter happened seven days later, the morning Frank Adams boarded a bus bound for Arlington, Virginia.

On the ninth, somehow, Adams landed a job in a hospital allowing Marcus to do real PR work on behalf of Southeast. On the thirteenth Adams left the boarding house he'd been staying in and moved into a furnished rat hole. Satisfied that he had seen enough, Marcus dropped off his rental and flew home to set up his rendezvous with Theodore Rumsey.

*

The three rooms in Frank Adams' furnished apartment were wired for audio-visual, each of them fitted with a Berretta Pico within arm's reach. His fiancée insisted, since she was not required at the apartment adjoining Adams' for several days. Nor would she be invited. The three-man rotating backup team was in place well before Adams arrived. There were no fancy SUVs, no black suits, no Ray-Ban glasses, simply a building housing society's poorest of the poor wearing raggedy clothes and desperate faces. They fit in, the four men cohesively agreeing with annoying smirks that somehow Smithers would not; Brenda calling them all a bunch of macho shits.

Parker had no real idea what the Christmas Killer

looked like from seeing the driver of the vehicle that followed the bus for thirteen straight hours to Arlington. That he was followed was satisfaction enough. When he had exited the terminal building the car was nowhere to be seen. Neither was the killer amidst a few hundred people.

On the fourteenth Frank Adams' shift ended at five. He drove home in the used Acura he'd driven off the lot the evening before, changed from his coveralls into jeans and a V-neck sweater, and drove to Quincy Park in upscale Ballston on the other side of town. Dinner with her anywhere public was out of the question. In any fine restaurant he would stand out like a wart on the Mona Lisa; she understood that, speaking with him several times each day.

On the far side of the park was a sixteen-floor luxury condo building, the top-floor penthouse bought by Parker a few years earlier as an investment property and now a place for Brenda's parents to stay when visiting. He would have parked in one of his two spaces, but his Vantage was parked in one and the other was taken earlier that day.

Walking into the lobby, the security guard stopped him with an open palm, a ready hand at his Taser until Parker enquired with a broad smile about his wife, the kids and their new puppy. The man knew Parker was a cop of some sort, like a director or an analyst or something. But hell, Mr. Williams!

Exiting the elevator, he called her. "Hi, sweetcheeks. Get the flowers?"

"I did. Thank you. Yellow roses, they're lovely." She was pouting. "Shit, Parker our first Valentine's and I'm stuck in a room without you."

"I wouldn't exactly call an eight-room penthouse with a wrap-around terrace and a view of the Potomac a room, sweetcheeks."

"I know that. Where are you?"

"Here, at the door. We're eating in tonight. Happy Valentine's."

Within seconds Brenda's arms and legs were squeezing him, framing the doorway.

Dinner was delectable, Brenda even more so. They made love and they danced, Parker not really sure which was which. She asked when she could join him; he was not doing this without her. The first of March, by which time he would have established a pattern. Good. How was his day job?

She wasn't the only one stuck in a room, he admitted. He actually was working in a boiler room. Good, she told him, he finally had a real job.

Peering across the black Potomac to the bright lights of DC, inhaling the scent of a single rose, she asked with a giggle, "Hey, where's my Vantage?"

Behind her, his arms wrapped around her shoulders, he replied very matter-of-factly, "In the garage beside mine, sweetcheeks. The yellow one."

What!

*

The days were passing by painfully slowly for Brenda Smithers. Although, were she remotely aware of what would too soon shake her entire world, she would have wanted time to stand still as Theodore Rumsey was about to experience.

Conversely, the days were passing too quickly for Marcus Simms. As he had long ago promised his wife, he was allowing his account managers greater latitude with their clientele. He still had much to accomplish and did not want Frank Adams dragging into summer. He wanted things done by early May, latest.

During the last week of February he tracked Rumsey each night to the mission until the 27th when the ex-con's good fortune ran out and he was forced to spend the forty-six-degree night at the edge of an alley huddled between a brick wall and a cardboard box.

Marcus wasn't much into sitting on sidewalks with drunks and druggies. In a manner of speaking he was accustomed to home delivery. He stood across the street on his third Marlboro, believing he would quit for good once divorced, waiting for Rumsey's neighbours to settle in, fall asleep, pass out or stop breathing.

Not certain how things would play out he came equipped with extra darts. He'd never sedated a target from that great a distance and, in the dark, he wasn't taking a chance. The good thing was, he looked like one of them and could replace a dart in mere seconds. Neither was the street a hotspot for hookers and johns and the cops apparently didn't consider derelicts an endangered species. He crossed over at 11:05

Rumsey was 6'2" of skin and bone. Prison had not treated him well. He smelled of cheap booze and poor hygiene. He wore a ball cap, a ski jacket, sneakers and pyjama bottoms, Simms assuming he either sold or bartered his prison wardrobe for a bottle.

Simms held out a lit Marlboro to the man in a gloved hand. When Rumsey looked up, shocked by the gesture, Simms shot him in one thigh, seconds later in the other. In under a minute Rumsey could scarcely sit straight and listen as Simms concealed the gun and squatted beside him, braced against the wall.

"Rumsey, this won't take long. I don't have the luxury of conversation. Suffice it to say you'll be dead in a couple of minutes, two if you're lucky, three if there's a God. You're going to make quite a mess, which appears somewhat relative in your case. You're not yet the worst I've come across, damn close though, possibly second. Unfortunately no one in Bangkok will hear of this which, for you, are equal parts of pentobarbital and sulphuric acid. A new recipe with remarkably pleasing results."

He retrieved the syringe from a pocket, with one hand removing the sleeve, with the other emptying the fluids into Rumsey's jugular. Pushing himself to his feet, he reclaimed the two darts and left immediately.

By midnight he was at home with his work clothes bagged separately in several of the building's dumpsters.
*

Tuesday morning, one day before she was to lead the backup team, Brenda Smithers listened in awe to Fran Princeton. The Christmas Killer was in Charleston. They were instructed to immediately shut down the sting operation and get there pronto.

Within the hour Parker Williams was at his condo peeling off his lips, his scars, and changing the colour of his eyes. They flew commercial to Charleston on the next flight out, bumping disgruntled first-class passengers, his federal credentials and a very attractive Agent Smithers assuaging the flight crew's fears. Upon arrival they were met, they viewed the corpse, they spoke with the horrified ME and photographed the relatively spotless crime scene. And then what?

"Nothing, boss. Nada. That's my entire point," he complained over the phone. "What the hell good will it do staying here and waiting for him to kill some woman? We don't know how he picks them up, we don't know where. This time we don't even know when. He had a thing for

Christmas and New Year's. Now what, maybe Good Friday? We don't know. We never will. The fact is she's going to die whether we stay here or not and when she does Smithers can fly in and out the same day to officially connect the dots and take over the case from the locals. But she won't find anything. We never do."

"What does Smithers think?" Princeton asked.

"Nothing at the moment. She's too busy puking. This one was as bad as Beauregard. The guy percolated big time, looked like a cheap bag leaking poutine. They're blocking off the street to clean the sidewalk. Pretty gruesome stuff. Anyway, Smithers does agree with me."

"Then you get her to a nice hotel and put her to bed." She coughed a curt laugh. "I do not believe I said that."

"She's still working to resolve a few Williams issues, boss. Apparently I'm a work in progress."

"She's not the only one, Williams."

"Boss, he's coming for me. I can feel him. He will not let me slip through the cracks. He won't. He knows where I am, not where I could be anytime soon. He will not chance losing me."

Seconds of silence.

"Then do it. Recall the team."

"Yeah, about that, boss. They're pretty much still in place. We left really fast to get here. You did say pronto, boss. I guess I sort of overlooked the order."

"I bet you did, Williams." Silence. "In which case I'm ordering Brenda to smack your head. Or I will."

Fran Princeton disconnected.

*

Late Tuesday morning, March 07th, Jeddore Billows flew from New York City to Charleston, South Carolina on a tight fifteen-hour schedule that would include lunch and a late-day meeting.

Monday Marcus Simms spent the day in the Big Apple with clients until late in the evening, Tuesday he had breakfast with one client and spent what remained of the day conversing with others, confirming luncheons and dinners. He was understandably eager to get her divorce over with, travelling and putting in more hours to occupy his mind. Strangely, he found himself thinking increasingly each day of Wendy. Truly, he confessed with a snort, when hadn't he thought of Wendy in years past picturing her alone in his bed or between Rosie and him?

He didn't believe Rosemary Sandra's impromptu fable about two playful ladies and a coach. Wendy was too classy a lady to play touchy with a loser. She was drop-dead gorgeous, as attractive to women as to men and not as tightly wound as her best friend. She had no need of a coach. Neither did Rosemary Sandra. She despised sports. That she was divorcing him to marry a low five-figure basketball coach cut a deep wound, in spite of the fact he was happy to be rid of her, rid of the Rothstones. Tuesdays, he knew, were game nights. A mid-thirties semblance of a man eking out a living by bouncing a ball with kids, plying them with drinks after each game, earning their adoration and confidence with Cokes and Pepsis. More importantly, Rosemary Sandra would be home alone until nine.

She would arrive at half past five. She would drop her keys onto the marble planter at the door and pour a glass of red wine from a decanter in the cabinet near the stairs that she would climb to their bedroom. She would hang her purse on the hook in her walk-in. She would sip her wine, putting the glass on her vanity before stripping in front of her full-length mirror, twisting and turning, bending and stretching, to ensure from every angle that she was ever perfect for the coach. She would sip more wine while clearing her face of day-old make-up before applying a fresh layer for the coach. Then, being March and dark, she would slip into a teddy or tap pants, fur-trimmed slippers and a long silk robe the coach couldn't afford in his dreams. Or she would have.

"Fuck!"

"Good evening, Rosie. It's been a while. Not that I haven't been thinking of you, sweetheart."

Her arms locked over her breasts. "Fuck, Marcus! What the fuck!"

She practically leaped to the towel rack, stumbling, clumsily wrapping herself in fleece.

"Nice to see you looking good, Rosie. Very good indeed." He sipped wine from the crystal goblet he'd filled from a bottle of Pétrus, savouring the aroma. "Still hitting the gym, I see. Good for you, staying in shape for the young guy."

"You're breaking the law, Marcus. Get out, right now. In fact, just fuck off."

"I'm not staying long, Rosie. We're going to have a glass of wine, talk rationally about a few things, set things right between us, and I'll leave you with a different perspective on life. That's all I require of you."

"That won't happen. Dominic will be here in minutes. He'll kill you for doing this to me."

"Not on game night, he won't. Besides, I'm not here. I'm in a New York hotel room working on a proposal." He pointed to her glass. "Bring your wine into the bedroom. Now, Rosie. Let's get this thing done."

She did, passing him. "You are in such deep shit, Marcus."

Marcus went to the bed, drawing back the duvet,

flinging it onto the floor with the pillows. "No, I'm not. You are, to a very great extent. Finish your wine."

"Marcus, what are you doing?"

"I'm stripping the bed. I won't sleep in some other guy's DNA. And I told you to finish your wine. Please do so, unless you require my help."

She did with two gulps. Not because of him, because she needed to calm herself. "Get out, Marcus. You are totally insane coming here. This is not going to happen. We're divorcing. We are completely over. This is not your home anymore."

"Yes, we are." He went to her, taking her glass, waiting, suppressing his amusement. A dream was coming true. "Sit, Rosie. You're beginning to sway. I'll explain what's happening as I go along."

He guided her to her futon before taking a new duffle bag from what used to be his walk-in, now lined with shorts and Dockers, tee-shirts and two department store suits. He stuffed it with the sheets and her wineglass, covering the mattress with a top sheet from the linen closet. He put his goblet on the coach's night table, helped her to stand, tore away the towel and carried her to the bed where he dropped her as he would a sack of whatever else he would soon discard.

"To be clear, Rosie, this is strictly work-related. Like a wolf urinating to mark its territory. Please do not confuse what comes next with any desire on my part to relive our vital past. Truth be told, I do not like you Rosemary Sandra. This is simply something I must do in order to maintain a high standard, to maintain a protocol that others will expect of me."

He reached into a pocket for the condom.

"Marcus, please don't," she managed, her head lolling

sideways.

His sweater and shoes lay by the bag. "Speaking is not requisite to the evening, Rosie. In fact I would prefer that you don't. You really have nothing to say that I want to hear. You're sedated. I want you to relax. " His slacks dropped to his ankles, stepping from them to remove his socks. Neither was flair requisite to the evening. Pushing his straight-backs to the floor he went to the bed. He eased apart her legs and grinned, making himself ready. "I can remember when this part was automatic, Rosie, if not a pleasant nuisance very often. No offence. It's me, not you. And the condom, well, I suppose I never previously thought of you as a sewer."

Her "no" was a wretched whimper. She was trying in vain to squirm, to raise her arms, to close her legs. She couldn't.

"Now usually with my comforters we do this over a few hours, a few glasses of wine. In a word, we enjoy ourselves. This evening however I'm more concerned with appearances."

He pushed himself into her, forcing his mind elsewhere, disinclined towards tenderness. Ten minutes later he jerked out, drying her eyes with the edge of the sheet. Tears were not part of the equation. He went to his slacks for a second condom, dropping the first into the bag before finishing his wine. He repeated the process twice more with single-minded urgency before dressing and refilling his glass at the wine cabinet, satisfied thus far with his evening.

He carried her limp body to the futon and went to her closet. Selecting her sexiest dress, taking a garter from a drawer, stockings and a thong meant to arouse from her laundry basket, he dropped them onto the floor near where she lay.

Adding the damp sheet to the bag he went again to the main floor where he turned off the lights, put on his gloves as a matter of habit, and sat patiently waiting. He'd been in the house an hour and fifteen minutes. There was nothing inside that he either wanted or needed to see or take, except the house itself. He wasn't even particularly hungry after his exhausting expenditure of energy, having eaten at a restaurant where he wasn't recognizable an hour after exiting the airport.

Dominic Drake, Marcus pondered, was an hourly worker. He began each day at nine with a different gym class each hour until three, with an hour for lunch and court practice from four until five when he would arrive home for dinner at six. Except Tuesdays when would leave the little lady alone and come home late to her from playing with the boys.

Dominic Drake walked in precisely at nine.

"Sweetheart, baby, your big guy's home." The door closed, the lights brightened the room, then: "What the hey!"

"Good evening, big guy." Drake's head pivoted left to right. Why did everyone do that? "She's upstairs resting. She's had a rough day…big guy."

"Simms?"

"Yes, Simms, who won't be staying long. My flight leaves at eleven. I simply require a little cooperation on your part, a touch of the dramatic, if you would be so kind. And, truthfully, it's the last you'll see of me."

"Simms, what did you do to her?"

"What do you think I did to her? I fucked her, three times. But don't get excited. The experience wasn't memorable for either one of us, pretty much one-sided, actually."

"You bastard."

"Not the convincing drama I need, big guy. This is where you rant and rave and come at me with a vengeance, enraged that I raped your benefactress. She actually warned me that you would kill me. So what's your problem, big guy? Leave your balls on the court?"

"Fuck you." Drake lunged forward, twisting violently, crashing against a sofa and coffee table, staring dumbly at the blue and red dart protruding from his chest.

"That was appreciably better, Drake. Thank you. The sedative is potent and works quickly. Don't fight it. That's about all you have to know. I'll spare you further details, which is an undue kindness you should be grateful for."

He left Dominic Drake as he was, climbing the stairs to the bedroom where Rosemary Sandra lay sleeping. Her eyes were dry, her breathing shallow, not the least aware of the needle sliding into her forearm. She died peacefully, for appearances and no other reason, when what he truly craved was to drive it into her chest and watch her decay. He closed the light.

Downstairs he dropped the syringe into the bag along with the empty wine bottle and his glass. Dominic Drake was inert, the strain in his eyes defining his inner turmoil and fear. Marcus kneeled by his side, gripping his arm.

"This will merely put you to sleep so I can finish my discussion with her and leave. You'll be together with her very shortly, Drake, I promise you. Good night."

As Dominic Drake was dying, Marcus Simms dropped the second syringe into the bag, turned off the lights and left.

By the time Jeddore Billows boarded his flight, Marcus had disposed of the bag and its contents in various airport men's rooms. He arrived at his hotel near two in the morning, greeting each of the reception staff by name.

Chapter Twenty-Three
Wendy, Comfort & Joy

Marcus understood what would come next after his Wednesday breakfast meeting with a client. The school would call the house wondering why the coach wasn't dribbling balls in the gym and Rosemary Sandra's office would phone at some point throughout the morning wondering whether she was still in love with herself. Someone would eventually go to the house where two cars were parked and call 9-1-1. The police would arrive, figure things out with the help of neighbours and go hunting for the guilty husband, discounting words of admiration and high praise from his girls at the office who adored him. Because spouses were always guilty. Until hearing caustically from Beverly Benton that he was practically 800 miles away, thereby stumping their narrow mindsets.

His cellphone buzzed on cue Wednesday while he was at lunch with a client, though Marcus Simms never answered his phone unless he was alone and free to speak privately. He returned Beverly's call at 1:30, his agitated secretary passing him directly to the detective in charge. The preamble was curt, Marcus audibly stunned by the news of his estranged wife's murder in his home.

They wanted him in Charleston that very evening for questioning; a federal agent was also flying in to interview him. He disconnected without a further word to cancel what remained of his week.

*

Brenda Smithers flew commercial into Charleston, Parker Williams upgrading her to first-class. Fran Princeton wasn't wasting tax dollars on a predictable murder that would accomplish nothing beyond linking otherwise unrelated cases.

She went first to the morgue where the reception was decidedly lukewarm. The lead detective did not like the little federal woman with a gun and a badge meddling with his case.

She viewed the bodies and spoke directly with the ME. His lab would have an initial report on the cause of death by morning. She advised him that she would also require a copy of the report and that further analysis by his lab was unwarranted. The cause was pentobarbital injected into Simms' arm sometime after intentionally bringing home the wrong guy for whatever reason. Possibly to ignite something with her live-in. The boyfriend was a bonus, in the wrong place at the wrong time. Or, more likely, paying too high a price for shacking up with the wrong woman.

The detective abruptly cut her off. The murders were obviously a crime of passion, the jealous husband the probable perp. Simms claiming he was in New York didn't mean squat.

She thanked him for his concern and input, stating for the record that the husband was innocent, briefly explaining the correlation between the wife and Rumsey who were not her killer's first victims.

Also, she was not meddling in his case file. She was relieving him of it entirely. The double victims and Rumsey were part of an ongoing federal investigation that was

381

about to end. Enough said. As for the husband, whether Simms was estranged or not, the body could be released to his preferred funeral home whenever. He did not orchestrate her death. She brought this on herself, tragically, by playing a dirty and dangerous game for whatever reason. Rosemary Sandra Simms would serve no further purpose.

Brenda arrived at the Simms residence near eight, not long after Marcus himself who was in the process of being interviewed. The lead detective had forewarned the cops with him to expect her, Agent Smithers summarily dismissing them. She wasn't interested in out-dated suppositions.

She went through the bedroom, the walk-in and bathroom without Simms. Nothing was different. Not the bed, not the strewn clothes, not the pristine crime scene. Shit, was he good.

In the living room Simms' mood was pensive more than quiet, feeling devastated more than saddened that such a terrible thing could take place in his home.

"Two years, Agent," he replied. "We didn't like each other very much, waiting too long to resolve irreconcilable differences. Until we married her life was privileged and spoiled. She was daddy's little girl, everything handed to her by overly indulgent parents who confused love with luxury. That never changed. My upbringing was somewhat more plebeian, more balanced. Everything you see here, my company and her lavish vacations, her wardrobe and car, evolved from gruelling hours and sacrifice that she had major trouble dealing with. Unlike her cushy nine-to-five position, she didn't get the work ethic."

"And Mr. Drake? Was he her first episode?"

"No. She had others, I'm certain she did. Wendy would

know more about that than me. Wendy Brighton, they were inseparable buddies. She knows more about Rosie than I ever did." He gave Smithers the particulars. "As for Drake, he was a loser, an opportunist. For her, a diversion. Simply put, he was younger. She had this chronic fear of growing old, of losing her looks. I didn't mind him. Jealousy is after all a function of love. In this case indifference obviating both. However I never wished her harm, Agent Smithers. People change, they move on. What makes this much more horrible is the brutal rape."

"Mr. Simms, she was not raped. The sex was consensual. The coroner's official finding. Her body showed no signs of violence or trauma other than mutually aggressive enthusiasm. That's how he works. The killer selected her. From the clothes I saw on the floor, her dress which is far from office attire, she was either at a bar or a restaurant hopeful of someone's attention other than Drake's for whatever her reasons. This was not a random act. Your wife went out to meet someone and she did. And she's not the first. His victims are historically single, very attractive and lonely. Why she acted that recklessly is a question we cannot answer, particularly knowing Drake would be home sometime that evening. Possibly he was no longer enough for her. As you mentioned, she was accustomed to the good life. That's a difficult thing for us humans to give up. He *was*, however, a first. The killer has never before murdered an innocent intruder."

"My God, he's done this before?"

"He has. And he's very thorough. Not only does he not leave evidence, he takes crucial evidence with him."

"What happens next, Agent?"

"You're still legally married. Call a funeral home. I've released her body."

"That's it?"

"Yes. We know you didn't do this. I've terminated the local investigation. When I leave here I'll speak with her parents, Drake's, and I'll call Ms. Brighton. Tomorrow I will speak with the school and your wife's office."

"To what end, if I may ask?"

"Profiling. Each victim gives us a little bit better insight into his thinking and mindset." She stood. "I wish I could tell you more." She extended a hand. "Good luck, Mr. Simms."

"Naturally I've cancelled my New York trip. I'll be available this week whenever you need me."

"That isn't necessary. I'll be leaving tomorrow. Your wife's death is officially a federal case file, a cold case regrettably."

"That does seem cold, Agent."

"What I can tell you, Mr. Simms, is that we are not giving up on this killer. We will get him. He knows he's close to being captured. As do we, when I will personally call you and the Rothstones for, at the very least, closure."

Brenda drove to the Rothstones next. Roger Samuel was livid, his wife inconsolably grief-stricken.

What made working the Christmas Killer different from other 4-C files were the survivors.

Ex-boyfriends and husbands, along with current and presumably dismal lovers, were consistently emotionally detached. They would express sadness and disbelief, but they never wept or succumbed to hysterics. The Rothstones, as with all other parents, were both the exceptions and the most difficult to interview.

Brenda Smithers was far from callous, yet she had no reason and no interest in sugar-coating the reality. Their privileged and naïve daughter went on a hunt for novelty too scantily dressed for a woman alone and, inexplicably, brought home a stranger, a sophisticated sociopath, when she must have foreseen the evening ending badly with Drake.

The Rothstones didn't want to hear Agent Smithers dispassionately casting despicable aspersions on their daughter's pure reputation. Rosemary Sandra was a decent and good girl. Unquestionably Drake was a dreadful error in judgement, a lamentable under-achiever and hanger-on, forced upon her out of desperation by a negligent husband. Simms was the truly culpable party, Roger Samuel Rothstone insisted, for the despicable fashion in which he treated her. That their daughter was so hastily being dismissed as a cold case and forgotten was intolerable and unconscionable. And what the hell was 4-C? The governor would hear of this. Be damned certain of that, he exploded.

Brenda didn't like them. Neither was she easily intimidated, barring the recent event in her home that nearly got her fiancé killed. She left them with a simple "go ahead. We really are not concerned with governors. He will simply tell you what we tell him, that we do not dismiss anyone." After which she went to Drake's family where the opposite was true.

Their son refused to heed their constant warnings and apprehensions. He was such a good-looking young man, Mrs. Drake told Brenda, with such a good future doing what he loved best.

The Simms woman was older and came from affluence her son could not compete with. She was advantaged and thought herself superior. Everyone knew the Rothstone name. Dominic was being used by her to facilitate the woman's divorce and to bolster her already conspicuous vanity. Once divorced she would have without question discarded him to seduce someone better suited to her high and mighty social circle.

"She was neither a decent or good woman, Agent Smithers," Mrs. Drake told Brenda. "She was deceitful and impure. I can scarcely imagine how her poor husband must feel. I pray for him as much as I do for my son."

"The blatant whore killed our boy, Agent Smithers. That's the short of it, whoring wantonly with an absolute stranger while expecting our Dominic at any moment," Mr. Drake added, struggling with tearful emotion. "I'm a God-fearing man, miss. That's the God's truth, but on my life I would have joyously cut the whore's throat to save my Dominic."

Brenda commiserated with them to the extent her professional dispassion allowed. Then she left. Giving any hope whatsoever with promises of eventual capture to grieving parents was useless, if not entirely misleading.

Near eleven she called Wendy Brighton, apologizing for the late hour, asking permission to drop by for a brief conversation. Otherwise they could speak in the morning. This evening by all means, Wendy agreed, thankful she had not been left out of the investigation.

"They were a mistake, Agent Smithers. He and Rosie came from very different backgrounds.

He married Rosie because she was very attractive and, let's be honest, broken in. Not for the family's money. That was never a question with Marcus. In fact, his unwavering independence was an ongoing irritant to Roger Samuel. As for Rosie, she married him for the same reasons and because she emphatically did not want kids. She never did. She was terrified of being scarred, amongst other reasons, and the Rothstones are all about family. Her father took years coming to terms with her adamant refusal to continue the family name. If he ever has. His one failure was never having a son, never an RS junior."

"A marriage of mutual convenience."

"From day one. They should have grown into each other, but they never truly did. She was all about appearances and who better than Marcus? I mean, the man's a dream. The problem was, while he worked hard at success travelling the country, tirelessly working all manner of hours, Rosie worked to fill her days behind a desk with tons of assistants who were probably better qualified than her. But they didn't have Roger Samuel for a father. I loved her deeply, Agent Smithers, but that was Rosie. She was a wealthy man's daughter."

"Mr. Simms told me you were best friends."

"We all were at one time, before he became too focused on Southeast. The three of us met in college during Marcus' final year. He stood out, and he stood alone, completely unaffected. Good with fashion and the ladies. He was a nice guy, Agent Smithers."

"Was, Ms. Brighton?"

"I took Rosie's side." Wendy shrugged. "Easy to do, I suppose, when hearing one side of a story. I haven't seen Marcus in over two years. I'm kind of sorry about that. I have missed him and, really, we could use each other's company. I just didn't feel good getting stuck in the middle."

"And Dominic Drake?"

"A bad match. I didn't like him. He was forever prancing around her like a puppy dog. I mean, the guy was a high-school coach, which I don't mean to sound elitist. He was light years out of his element, didn't know how to carry himself. Personally, Rosie screwed up big time with him. Marcus is a super guy, a true gentleman. He flies first-class everywhere, he wears thousand-dollar suits and drinks Johnnie Walker Blue without being full of himself. The man is completely well-grounded. I mean, be honest, Agent Smithers, would you leave a man like that?"

Brenda chuckled, softly. "No, Ms. Brighton, I won't. I waited too long for him to grow a brain. But will you now, see Mr. Simms?"

Wendy blew a stream of warm air from between her lips. "At the funeral, yes, when I can at least see him ignore me. I won't blame him. He'll have every reason to snub me. I've treated him terribly for no reason."

"Somehow I don't believe he will." Brenda stood. "Personally, I like the guy. Thank you, Ms. Brighton."

"Will I hear from you again, Agent Smithers?"

"When I catch your friend's killer, yes you will. You've been very helpful." Brenda's smile was warm. "Good luck with Mr. Simms."

As a depleted Brenda Smithers walked into her hotel room, dropping onto the bed and digging into her purse for her cell, Marcus Simms was finishing another bottle of Pétrus and would sleep in his own bed for the first time in two years.

Parker Williams answered with the first buzz.

*

The following morning Marcus called a funeral director after first removing all traces of his ex-wife and Drake from his home. He gave possession of his beloved Rosie of twenty three years to her parents at the chapel on Saturday, three days following the gruesome discovery, as painters were busy at his home and a recently hired design and decorator team was at work reinventing the interior.

Notable mourners were the Rothstones and Wendy Brighton in the front pew opposite his where he sat with

Beverly Benton. Many others of his staff were seated behind them. The women, aware of Rosemary Sandra's heartless betrayal of their boss, his lengthy separation and pending divorce, wiped their eyes admiring him. With all the suffering and indignity he was made to endure, he could still weep quietly for such a hateful and loveless woman. The men were all of the opinion that he was a nice guy, a gentleman who navigated around the best looking women with enviable ease and confidence. If he wasn't already, he would not take long to regroup and find a younger and better replacement. Most of them betting on the ever bubbly and beautiful Beverly who believed her boss was her life source, her sole reason for being. If he hadn't already.

Gathered behind the Rothstones was an assembly Marcus neither knew nor cared about. Neither did he outwardly acknowledge her parents who patently loathed him, particularly since the previous day when Roger Samuel went to his daughter's home to collect her most personal and prized possessions that his grieving wife would henceforth preserve in a curio cabinet. He learned instead that Marcus had donated her clothing, her china doll collection and her jewellery to a charitable outlet, her books to a local library, and her Lexus, that Marcus had paid for, to a neighbour's kid. Which was true. He simply omitted telling the old man that the 'outlet' and the 'library' had four wheels and a serious trash compactor. What he *was* able to give them however, and would, he conceded while standing at the door, were her ashes and the funeral director's invoice.

When the service was over the mourners dispersed en route to hors d'oeuvres and an open bar that Beverly planned for him in a ritzy hotel lounge reserved for the send-off. She did her best for Marcus, for his reputation, not his undeserving ex, Beverly and Marcus the first to leave by limousine in order for Marcus to properly receive his employees and the Rothstone horde at the semi-formal wake. Later in the day the same limousine would deliver the patient and hopeful young woman to her home alone.

Now that his divorce was no longer an issue, Beverly had no reason to worry what others would say. She wanted Marcus Simms in her life, not his name on her paycheque. At the very least she wanted a reasonable chance at loving him as he loved her most nights in her fanciful dreams.

The disconsolate Rothstones and a tearful Wendy remained behind to receive the freshly sealed urn that Mrs. RS wanted placed immediately in her new cabinet. Last to arrive at their daughter's farewell, they had no understanding or sense that their seating beyond sight of Marcus was not unintentional. Beverly took very good care of her boss.

Interrupting his conversation with her, excusing himself from her company, he stood and went to where he noticed Wendy near the main entrance speaking into her cell. Seeing him coming near, she feigned disconnecting and waited.

"You must hate me, Marcus." She hugged him. "You should hate me. I've treated you terribly for too long."

"I would never think to hate you. How are you, Wendy?"

"I'm dealing with it. You?"

"My head's a bit of a dead zone. Am I sad? Yes, of course. Am I grieving? No. I'm not that forgiving. The past two years have been too brutal."

"In part because of me." She put a hand lightly on his arm. "Marcus, I want to be your friend again. We need each

390

other to get through this."

"I would like that, Wendy. Thank you. I would like that very much. Perhaps in a few weeks, when the shock of all this wears off, we can have a quiet dinner and talk."

"At my place. I plan on crying a lot."

"We'll cry together. But Wendy, one question, please. And please be honest because what's done is done. The wounds are healing."

He didn't have to ask, she could tell by his eyes. "Rosie was always popular with the boys, Marcus. Long before our college days. Marriage didn't do much to calm her inherent obsession with attention. Yes. She was a flirt and she was a cheat. Please understand the difficult position she put me in. I'm sorry, Marcus, but Dominic was not her first escapade, neither were you. You simply met her criteria for both escaping Roger Samuel's influence and causing him the most indignation. You didn't care about daddy's name or his money. What's worse, you made the big league without him." She tried forcing a smile. "I loved her, Marcus, but you placed somewhere in the middle of a long line. I am sorry."

He chuckled. "Now I am too. This send-off is costing me fifty K." He put a hand gently over hers. "As much as I once loved her, Wendy, the last two years pretty well convinced me that I married the wrong girlfriend. I can't tell you how being with you today brings me such comfort and joy. I know that in a few weeks we will both feel so much better. In fact I guarantee we will."

Chapter Twenty-Four
A Tribute to Marcus Simms

Marcus Simms sat in his study Sunday afternoon pensively swirling a JW Blue, pondering events of the previous day, his past and his future while staring at the priceless ten-dollar bill tinged with discoloured blood that once again hung rightfully on his wall. Sleeping with Wendy in the coming weeks was a given and long overdue, Marcus fully cognizant of the implicit consequence. She was ready, probably had been for years. He certainly was, wanting her in his bed since first seeing her, then too committed physically to Rosemary Sandra Rothstone that long-ago summer to act on his urges.

Not that she wasn't as much of a whore as Rosie. She was, for years each invitation to dinner or the theatre requiring introductions to a new and improved lover. She was no one to talk. Picturing them together intimately came easily to his mind. They were whores, each other's constant shadow, so what would the difference be? He shrugged, refilling his glass. He would ask her. Why wouldn't he?

He practically envied Jeddore Billows as much as he would miss the man who of necessity, he decided, he would soon unwillingly sacrifice. Rosemary Sandra and Wendy weren't the only inseparable conspirators in Marcus Simms' life. Jeddore Billows had been an integral part of his existence for thirty years, waiting in the shadows for just such a day. He was forty-eight, living on borrowed time unless he soon brought dramatic change to his life beyond a dead wife.

Marcus Simms exemplified every characteristic of a Southern gentleman and the integrity of a successful businessman. He was respected in the community as a leader, a leading citizen, proof to anyone that perseverance and hard work are their own rewards. He wanted to become a multimillionaire and he did. Jed Billows' determination to succeed made that happen. Jed Billows saw the good in him and made Marcus Simms all that he had surely dreamed of becoming.

He hadn't thought of his mother or his father in years. Nancy Billows was very pretty, her body youthful and firm, enviably proportioned, unblemished and smooth despite her difficult farmyard chores. She was also, at age thirty-two, an untiring and willing whore. Popular with wandering strangers and local townsmen alike, she was the county's best known secret. Jack Billows, a year older, was a habitual alcoholic who reasoned that letting the wife fuck strangers in their backwoods ramshackle home when she wasn't distilling gin or toiling in the yard was preferable to him working. When he wasn't drinking, Marcus remembered, the poor excuse of a human was kicking the shit out of young Jed who that year was fifteen.

May 31, 1987, he remembered, was deathly hot, steam rising from the ground after torrential rains as the sun was still hovering over the tree tops. Sweat trickled down his back, his hands too slippery to properly grasp the shovel that was dripping with the wet shit of cows and hogs. He had a month left in his schooling, anxious to find work in town since more schooling was a painful and recurring

393

dream beyond his reach. He would never travel, never see the world. He would never know more than he did. He was a bright boy with an aptitude for learning, good with numbers and words, but his father, sitting by the front door with a jug between his legs and a crisp ten-dollar bill peeking from the pocket of his soiled shirt, wanted the extra money the boy would soon bring home.

His mother had just gone into the shack with a new visitor, scarcely waiting until she was past the door to undo the buttons of her housedress under which she was instantly and entirely naked. He was a pompous and pretty boy in a fancy suit who at once scoffed at seeing Jed with his ragged trousers stuffed into thick rubber boots that were ankle-deep in foul-smelling slop. He had heard through the grapevine about the gifted young whore and her many unabashed ministrations and had hurried eagerly from Columbia in his shiny new car to wet his cock for the first time ever inside Jed's mother.

Jed didn't mind menfolk balling his mother. Most summer evenings well before dark, as his father was drinking himself into a deeper stupor, Jed would watch her in secret from behind his bedroom window, watching her climb deliberately in and out of the tub in the yard with her tits and her ass bare, soap suds clinging to the curly brown hair between her legs as she stretched and twisted to towel herself dry. Jed quite certain that his spying wasn't really a secret. Often he would watch her keep her private parts clean and fresh for her 'friends' as he sat on the porch in the middle of hot summer days, making himself believe she was not his mother when Nancy would smile at him and hold out her towel for Jed to dry her back. He understood why all the men liked her. Most nights he and Nancy were the last images in his youthful mind as he made himself ready for her and waited for the sleep that would make her more real.

What he did not like were the other boys at school taunting him, wanting their thirty minutes with his mother before she was too old. The girls were worse, promising they would never marry any boy like him to become a whore like his mother. At those unkinder words Jed would sneer and pay them no mind. At least his mother was not a liar. Everyone knew those girls were being poked by the boys, all of them whores like his mother. At least his mother was bringing home money.

He remembered dropping the shovel into the slop at his feet and going to the shiny new car, opening the door and sliding onto the bench to share the shit on his boots with the condescending city fucker balling his mother. He remembered being dragged out roughly by his hair and thrown to the ground, cowering as his father lashed out at him cursing, kicking his legs, punching his face and his head, yelling that because of Jed he could well lose the ten dollars. He remembered his father marching towards the shack, yelling at Jed that he best be gone far beyond sight when he returned if the stranger inside refused instead to spend another thirty minutes or more freely sticking the wife.

Jed Billows was big for his age and sturdy. He stood six feet, his body lean and hard from taking on the most arduous and unpleasant tasks in the yard to spare his mother. He remembered hearing himself yelling "never again, pa!" He remembered scrambling to his feet and reaching for his shovel.

He remembered going into the shack, his mother's all too familiar giggles and squeals and the men's grunts he would hear through his bedroom walls when the weather or the dark made working outside impossible. He remembered the naked boy trapped between her legs frantically pounding her, sucking on one tit and squeezing the other. He remembered watching them, his mother's laughter and the glee in her eyes. Most of all he remembered her scream, both their heads jerking, both their heads exploding into the air.

He waited an hour for his father to regain consciousness that early evening, standing near the doorway, stepping back as his father burst through the door in a blind rage, intent on killing his son, the man stopping dead in his tracks at seeing Jed cock both barrels of the shotgun. An instant later the man's head came clear off from under his chin, the body jerked into the air, the lifeless arms flailing as if striving to regain its lost part. Marcus left the corpse where it lay sprawled, where it would lay gripping the gun's barrels until morning when the bright light of day would hide the raging flames as he ran out of breath to a neighbour's farm for help. In the meantime, he had much to accomplish.

He wasn't afraid, not then, not any day thereafter. First eating a thick sandwich of ham and cheese to sustain him throughout the day, he filled the house with all the kerosene and tinder he could find, dousing his mother, his father and eighteen-year-old Marcus Simms with gas from the tractor and truck.

Unscrewing the tag from the rear bumper of Simms' fancy car he buried the menacing plate deep in the woods before stuffing the gas tank with paper and laughing as he struck the match.

By the time help did arrive, young Jed winded from his frantic race and afraid, his eyes reddened with tears, the shack was a charred heap. Two of the bodies inside were found fused together, a morbid sculpture he was not permitted to witness, while the incinerated and headless corpse on the floor grasping an empty shotgun told the story of a drunken husband gone mad.

Jed told the sheriff everything he knew. His father, hearing his mother laughing and giggling, stomped into the house fiercely angry that the man had overstayed his minutes and demanding more money. The next thing he remembered was his mother's heightened laughter. Moments later he heard the gun blasts, one then another, and his father rushing out. He remembered his father beating his face, yelling at him to stay put, then his father burning the car and running into the house wailing like a crazy man. He never came out.

The man with his mother must have been very bad, Jed explained to the sheriff, wiping his face. He was as old as his late thirties or more, likely as not running from the law in a car stolen from some rich folks. The car had no tag, he pointed out, could be that's why his father went out of his mind and killed the man.

Young Jed watched as the bodies were carried away under white sheets, the sheriff assuring him the county would attend to the burials. When everyone was gone, the men in the pumping truck determining the fire was extinguished, Jed squatted in the middle of the yard to examine his work. He was pleased, and he was excited. The bad man, he knew, the worst man in his life was his father. The hate he felt for Jack Billows was intense; no less intense than his nightly torment brought on by vivid dreams, dreams of an appealing and enticing young whore he could never in his life touch the way they all did.

He was glad they were all dead just because he thought to climb into the rich fucker's car with shit on his boots, thankful to Marcus Simms for coming by when he did.

Assuring the neighbours who were first after Jed to witness the horrible scene that he was alright, that he simply needed a short while alone to say goodbye to his home, he promised the older and fretful couple that he would be at their home well before the dinner hour. He hugged the woman and gripped the man's hand, thanking them for wanting to take him in and care for his needs.

Instead that very afternoon Marcus Simms, in a clean shirt and trousers and with over 300 dollars and his driver's permit in his pockets, began a thrilling journey into the anonymity of Charleston, South Carolina. He would learn all that he could and become the man that Jeddore Billows was certain in his heart he would become.

Jeddore Billows, now three years older than the previous day when need be, went with him into a brighter future with a blood-stained ten-dollar bill in his pockets and written proof of his unwanted birth, where thirty years later he put Wendy Brighton from his mind to consider the future of one Frank Adams.

Chapter Twenty-Five
Till Death Do We Part

Jeddore Billows boarded his flight to Washington Dulles International Sunday, April 09th, at seven. From Dulles he would drive to Arlington, Virginia where he was booked downtown for two nights.

Marcus Simms would not wait much longer to bring about that dramatic change that would ensure the continuance of his humanitarian work. He couldn't, his meeting with Frank Adams suddenly more urgent. He was unexpectedly and seriously distracted, without warning catapulted into a difficult situation the previous Friday when clear thinking was the most essential element to his success.

Rosemary Sandra was laid to rest four weeks earlier, after being dead to him for two years. That truth, he would never deny. What he could not get his head around were those very words coming from Beverly Benton. He hadn't dated since then, since the decisive day Rosemary Sandra converted his home into her private whorehouse. Discounting occasional and professional female companionship that was purely requisite to the male need and mutually gainful to both parties while out of town on business, he was not interested. Those women, at least, were honest. But that Beverly Benton would out of the blue invite him to her home for a 'candlelight' dinner the following Saturday visibly stunned him, bringing an expectant smile to her lips. He happily accepted, of course, as though her invite was commonplace. A simple dinner between friends, when in fact the softly veiled ultimatum left him feeling exposed and weak. Refusing was not an option, not that he wasn't entirely aroused by the prospect.

They had worked together for twelve years, now she wanted to sleep with him. Candlelight was a statement, never synonymous with a handshake and a peck on her cheek at the end of a delightful evening. This was serious. He didn't want to lose her, certain that he would either by declining her invitation or inadvertently disappointing or humiliating her.

He wasn't getting married again, that ship sailed and sank off the coast of South Carolina. That was the dilemma. He had no concrete idea what she wanted, and asking her would have made him appear blind or stupid. Worse, asking her would have required hiring a new secretary.

Being romantic with her, taking her to bed after their many years of banter at office parties, working lunches and dinners with clients would seem tantamount to him making love with a sister. Thoughts of laying between her warm legs, of gazing into her liquid eyes, of kissing her soft lips were one thing; knowing he might actually do all those wonderful things terrified him.

Of course he often thought of her that way, like every other healthy male at the office. She was spectacular, witty and smart, 5'10, her body a glorious gift to the eyes and eleven years younger than Jeddore which didn't seem to bother her. Not to mention that Easter weekend would certainly require more than flowers and a grand cru. Worse, he couldn't ask his secretary to buy the gift.

As much as he tried he could not expel her from his thoughts. Apart from her staggering good looks Beverly was a gigantic shit-bomb about to detonate. Ordering another airline scotch he reclined his seat to confront her as he would approach any other impending disaster.

Two hours later, intellectually exhausted, stepping from the Jetway at 9:05, Jeddore Billows believed in his heart he had diffused the bomb that was not Beverly at all. Rosemary Sandra's true mission in her idyllic life had gradually evolved into methodically ruining his. Even in death she was relentless in her resolve to frustrate his work.

Beverly was not the problem, Rosemary Sandra was. She was to have served a dual purpose: Firstly bringing him freedom of her, secondly bringing him the comfort and joy of closure from Theodore Rumsey. Drake he never cared about, the coach was purely a well-deserved pleasure. Yet now, thanks to Beverly, he understood that he badly needed closure from his wife. That, unlike the others who came before her, she would forever haunt him. He realized that, because of her undying and baseless deep hatred of him, he would forever require the comfort and joy that only someone who truly did love him would freely and unconditionally bring to him.

*

That same Sunday Mrs. Smithers was elated to hear from her daughter, barely able to speak through her tears, her husband commenting over her shoulder into the receiver that she damn well took her time about it. She wasn't getting any younger. And why did she wait so damn long to share the news with them, what was wrong with the man?

Brenda's mother would not hear "no" for an answer. Her daughter was getting married in June and she wanted to meet the young man straightaway, her husband asking

401

plainly what the urgency was all about. Did she go and get herself pregnant?

Brenda did her best to bow out, stopping in mid-sentence, her eyes and mouth gaping. Parker was waving corporate boarding passes. They hadn't taken proper time to themselves in months. A few days from work would do them good, give them balance. Besides, the team was in place and nothing would happen without Frank Adams. That's what he told Fran Princeton.

And that's partly what Brenda told her mother. She would be home in a couple of hours, with her fully intact fiancé, dad.

Brenda disconnected, punching him. She barely had time to pack. Shit! Their flight was scheduled for mid-afternoon. Princeton agreed to Parker using 4-C's corporate jet on the QT if he reimbursed all costs. He wrote her a cheque. What! They would arrive in Dallas for dinner with her parents after checking into the hotel. He wasn't much into loving his fiancée in her parents' home, Brenda asking with a furrowed brow how he would even know that…darling.

The Smithers lived in an upscale gated community. He was an oil executive who disliked his daughter living in a mid-range apartment and driving a vehicle better suited to accessorizing a junk pile. He wasn't a snob, he simply loved his daughter and wanted the best for her which she could not afford on a cop's salary. His wife worked as an organizer for a non-profit family centre and hated that her daughter's workday required carrying a gun.

Beverly was unmistakably reticent on the phone with her, not answering any of her questions about the young man she was marrying. She was fit to be tied all afternoon, fussing and fidgeting around her husband and her home, finally driving him from the house until later in the day. He didn't know anything more about this Parker Williams fellow than she did. And how the hell could they get there in a couple of hours out of the blue?

They did. Brenda and Parker arrived near seven in a limo, Mrs. Smithers clamping a hand to her mouth at seeing the extravagance from her window, waiting under her husband's watchful eye until the very last second to scurry to the door where she shrieked and stumbled into her husband at seeing her lovely young daughter in the arms of a frightening Frank Adams.

She was scarcely recovered later in the evening while listening to Brenda's wedding and honeymoon plans since shoptalk was very much off-limits, clasping her hands to her chest when Brenda with giggles finally showed her mother digital photographs of the real Parker Williams sitting in the passenger seat of *her* yellow Aston Martin, and on the terrace of their penthouse where her mom and dad would be staying for the wedding, and at the poolside of her stately new home. Mr. Smithers commenting that Parker must be on excellent terms with the bank.

"Something like that, Stan."

*

Monday morning in Arlington was wet and damp, a light drizzle and dark skies making the day unseasonably chilly and unpleasant.

Marcus, arriving early at the apartment, saw no sign of Frank Adams leaving for work. He saw no sign of him any time during the day at the hospital, nor at day's end when Adams, who was clearly short on disposable income, should have gone home. Returning each hour until midnight, Adams' apartment remained darkened.

The next morning was clearer and brighter, the sun

making the inside of Adams' apartment impossible to see. Marcus arrived an hour earlier, tired from lack of sleep and the frustration of not knowing. Did Adams lose his job? Did he move to a cheaper and worse place, if that was even possible? Was he sick? Or worse, was he prematurely dead?

In desperation he called the hospital from a motel payphone, hoping for an underling to pick-up, sanitizing the receiver with mouth freshener and his pocket hanky that he would later discard.

Adams wasn't at work, he was told. Apparently he called in sick or took a personal day or something like that, bud. Hold-on. Yeah, that's it. Took a day off, bud. Call back tomorrow.

He didn't think so, fully appreciating why the helpful fellow worked in a boiler room.

All Marcus Simms needed was ten, maybe fifteen minutes. He had already assessed Adams, the man wasn't a huge threat. Men like him seldom were unless holding an Uzi in a defenceless crowd. Ten minutes, in and out.

Parked on a neighbouring street he waited until early afternoon after walking past the building a few times wearing a jacket, then not, driving by twice in his sub-compact rental, passing by again in a taxi. He was satisfied, he was ready.

Dressed in jeans, an oversized hoodie pulled over his cap and dark glasses, he went in through the broken main entrance. He selected the proper pick from the seven in his German-made kit, working with the precision of a microsurgeon, separating the driver and bottom pins until hearing the shear line click and the tumbler turning. Twenty breathless seconds: A lifetime.

Inside he paused, checking his watch. He was surprised.

The place was reasonably furnished. The living room looked like one, most everything chipped, scratched or faded; the bedroom had a bed and a bureau that was near empty, and a closet that was empty. The separate kitchen was minimalist Salvation Army with a circa 50's table and chairs, the bathroom one step better than what Adams had left.

Marcus did a three-sixty. The kitchen door directly faced the entrance with a good twenty feet between them. To one side were the patio doors, to the other the bed and bath. He decided on the kitchen and left.

*

Next door two men were slapping their knees, good-naturedly cursing Parker Williams for being bang-on as usual. They had the man on video, most of him anyway. The Christmas Killer's twisted smirk was all they needed to see. Christmas was coming early to Arlington, Virginia and Fran Princeton.

*

Brenda and Parker spent long days through to late Tuesday with her parents, staying at a local hotel, the Smithers very content not to bother with restaurants when Parker suggested dining out Monday evening. He didn't understand their reluctance. He did have a suit to wear, he assured them.

Finally capitulating to public opinion, he volunteered to prepare dinners that evening and the next, Brenda suggesting very strongly to a doubtful mother that she should let him. She also correctly assumed that her personal connoisseur would be doing lunch the next day, mildly miffed with him for answering his cellphone during the midday meal Tuesday despite his profound apologies to his hostess who was taken aback by his palm smacking the table and his animated, "Yes! Yes! Goddamn sonofabitch! Yes!"

Mrs. Smithers jerked in her chair, Mr. Smithers for an instant seeing what he hoped was not the real Parker Williams.

Brenda instantly reached out to him, worried. "What, darling! What is it?"

"I was right, Brenda. I was right. That effing sonofabitch is mine." He cleared his throat. "Excuse me, Bella, just some very good news from the office. Work stuff, very mundane really."

"Parker," Stanley cut in, leaning into the table, "if the news is that good and so mundane, please explain to me and Bella why our daughter has lost all her colour."

Parker smiled. "Stan, I'm better at my job than I am in the kitchen, our little girl here is and will be perfectly fine. This is *my* party, mine alone. She's not invited until the other guest leaves."

Brenda smacked his head. God he could be so annoying. As good as he was, and he was, he did not have thirteen combined Dans in three martial disciplines. So there, darling.

Flying out late that evening, Parker promising Bella that his scars and artwork would be gone long before the wedding, Stanley gave Parker an extra-long onceover while he hugged his daughter at the private gate, whistling under his breath as the couple waved a final goodbye from the steps of the Lear Jet.

"Bella, girl, by all appearances your daughter has done as well as you."

Bella Smithers took her husband's arm; he didn't see a mother's tears staining her cheeks. She was worried for Parker. She just knew something terrible was about to

happen.
*

Jeddore Billows returned that evening to Charleston where Marcus Simms left a message with Beverly that he was flying out the next morning to Miami. He *was* looking forward to dinner with her on Saturday. In the meantime she was to call him in the event any situation beyond her comfort zone would come across her desk, which he doubted, which meant otherwise do not call me.

He spent Wednesday through Friday on South Beach, alone, soaking up the sun's curative and cosmetic rays. He had to be certain beyond the slightest doubt that he could go through with her, transforming fanciful thoughts into true and meaningful love. He wasn't fully convinced, though he was certain that if he failed the Saturday litmus test he would lose what little he did have of her.
*

Saturday he arrived at her condo at 7:00 with a thirty-year bottle of Pessac-Léognan in one hand and a twelve-year Riesling in a stainless steel cooler in the other since he had no idea whether red or white was appropriate. He had considered flowers, changing his mind at the last minute. Too romantic. Instead he bought her a week for two in the Canaries, departing in three weeks. Enough time for her to figure things out or for him to find a new secretary; either way, he would have some explaining to do at the office.

She opened the door to her boss who was standing straight in linen slacks, a long-sleeve silk shirt with the cuffs at mid-arm and Cole Hann tasselled loafers. She had said casual, and any attempt at appearing relaxed, suave or sophisticated would fail miserably.

Beverly spent the day at her spa for the head-to-toe treatment. Her dark brown hair was long, hanging loosely over a breast; her wrap-around silk evening gown was floor-length, held in place with a single bow at her waist and seductively décolleté exposing the glimmering swell of her other breast. Her sandals were patent leather, three inches; she wore no nylons and Marcus didn't have to wonder what else she wasn't wearing. As glamourous as she was, he could not resist sensing that he was walking into her lair and not her home.

"Hi, Marcus."

He was expecting something resembling her usual "Good morning, Marcus" or "Good night, Marcus." Even a warm "Good evening, Marcus," the "Hi, Marcus" somehow making the Canaries seem much closer.

"Bev, you are incredibly radiant." He inhaled a deep breath. "Wow, not in my wildest dreams."

"Well, that's good to hear, Marcus." She stepped aside, smiling. "At least you dream of me."

"I do, day and night. As part of a long-standing office fraternity and, this evening, the most honoured member." He held out the bottles. "I wasn't certain, Bev. I believe they're both quite passable."

"Thank you, excellent choices. Come in and sit. I hope you like 60's crooners."

He did.

The living room was tastefully appointed with twin sofas, a coffee table and a cushioned bench by her window, soft recessed lighting, a sound system and sensual yet discreet wall art. Two-fingers of Blue were in a crystal old-fashioned on the table beside her untouched vodka martini, leaving him no doubt whatsoever that he was in her lair and pleasantly trapped. Sitting beside him with less than a hand width between them, her gown separated to expose most of her crossed over thigh. Not noticing or commenting was ludicrous. The woman was determined.

He reached for both cocktails. "I feel as though I've owned a jewellery store, Beverly, and for too long ignored the most precious stone in my collection. Thank you for opening my eyes."

She leaned in closer. As he would often say, "All or nothing." He only ever called her Beverly whenever he was completely serious or very upset.

"I was tired of waiting, Marcus. The first ten years were hard enough, the last two were horrible. I can't work with you anymore, Marcus, not unless I'm more to you than a secretary and a firewall. It's too hard. In fact, I have until Monday at end of business to give Harry Pendleton my decision. I am that serious."

He grimaced. "Beverly, please do not mention that cretin's name to me. Had I for a moment suspected..."

"You would have done what, exactly?"

He reached into his shirt pocket. "I would have done this long ago." He passed her the flight vouchers. "One week in the Canaries. A private villa with no interruptions and no work on pain of death, just you and me if I live up to your expectations this evening. I'm sort of a nervous wreck sitting here, like a schoolboy who hasn't studied properly for the upcoming exam." He sipped his Blue. "You are absolutely exquisite, Bev."

She studied the vouchers. "Is this for real, Marcus?"

"Us? Yes, if you're still interested after three more weeks with me. The vacation is yours either way."

"No separate rooms?" He shook his head 'no'. "Does that mean you're staying with me tonight?"

He put a hand to her bare thigh. "Or lose you to Pendleton? Yes, I'm staying."

No smile, simply piercing eyes. "Is he the only reason,

Mr. Simms?"

"I've wanted this for a very long time, Bev. I'm staying for us, months or years overdue."

"Good." She leaned closer still and kissed him. "Now we're both nervous wrecks." She put her drink on the table, standing, reaching out. "I think I have to dance with the boss before I sleep with him, Marcus. This evening is a bit more than a little hug and a luncheon on my birthday."

Dinner began with fried boccocini drenched in a spicy tomato sauce, a seafood salad of shrimp, scallops and mussels on a bed of shaved ice. The main course consisted of grilled salmon filets served with roasted potatoes, fresh greens and a delicate Riesling. Dessert was a pleasantly warmed, deliciously fragrant and delectable Beverly Benton served with occasional sips of Rémy Martin on a bed of satin. The cheeses and Pessac-Léognan could wait another day.

Wakened by the morning sun Marcus lay as he was, searching his mind for the slightest doubt, the weakest regret. What he found was that everything about Bev felt right. He felt good, revitalized when he should have felt drained, depleted. He felt good about Rosemary Sandra, whispering a final goodbye to her as he twisted in the sheets to face Beverly Benton who was standing at his side with coffees.

"Last night was incredibly sexy, Bev." He chuckled. "You were, are spectacular. You must have read my mind. How many times have I imagined you standing in panties with your dress crumpled at your feet?" He took a long moment to absorb her, grinning. "I'm thinking we should have a lingerie day at the office. It occurs to me that I have never hired an unattractive woman. It would be good for morale." He sipped his coffee. "Very good, I believe, if my male imagination serves me well."

She shrugged. "Okay, boss. I'm good with that. When?"

"Yeah, boss." He blew a stream of air from between his lips. "That's a memo I have to send."

She curled in beside him. "I'm glad I got tired of waiting, Marcus. I'm happy, very happy. And since when do you write your own memos. I'll take care of the girls who will naturally hurry to tell the men. Then *you* will deal with *them,* Mr. Simms."

"I'm glad I thought of the Canaries instead of flowers." He sipped his coffee and kissed her. "Pendleton? Really?"

*

No one at the office was surprised. The women all giggled, hugging and kissing Beverly; they wanted to hear every sordid detail. The men knew better than to ask, all of the opinion that he was one lucky bastard, the boss agreeing. Both Beverly and Marcus agreeing they would wait until after the Canaries to make life-altering decisions.

Friday, the 21st, Beverly booked his flight to Richmond, Virginia and his hotel room, from where Jeddore Billows drove two hours Sunday evening in a rental to Arlington. Monday morning he followed Frank Adams to the hospital, he entertained a client at lunch, and he watched from a street corner as Adams stepped from a bus and disappeared into his building at day's end. Later, parked across from Adams' balcony, he watched a single shadow behind the curtains until the lights went out at midnight.

Tuesday Adams left for work at 6:45, arriving for his shift near eight, after which Marcus met a client for breakfast at his hotel and another for lunch. By 3:30 he was dressed in newly acquired shoes, slacks, a sweater, and a jacket that held the syringe, lock kit, and a new gun he thoroughly tested the day before that he preloaded with a fresh dart and CO_2. He stepped nonchalantly into the apartment at 4:00. One second later a flurry of excitement and anxiety erupted next door.

*

"Brenda," the man called out in a hoarse whisper, "get over here. Serious shit's going down. He's back. The sonofabitch is back."

Brenda Smithers hurried to the screen. Her mouth instantly went dry remembering Parker's less than humorous prank in her apartment. The man in Adams' living room was dressed in black, his eyes covered with glasses, his head with a long-billed cap. As in all other cases he was drawing the curtains, closing doors that might pose a problem, create an unwanted issue, tossing an overnight bag onto the kitchen floor. She reached for her cell, Parker answered on the first buzz.

"Parker, he's here. He's setting up. He's here, Parker."

"What's he doing?"

"Shit, Parker, he's getting ready to kill you. That's what he's doing. Shit."

"The guns, has he seen the guns?"

"No. He's in the kitchen checking angles, checking how open or closed the door should be. Thus far no gun, but he's got a bag."

"Good. I'll be home at six. See you then, sweetcheeks. Thanks for the update."

"What! Screw you, be home at six. We have him. All we need is the fucking needle. Please do not do this."

"We've been over this, sweetcheeks. Do not get your tiny panties in a twist over this. What we need is him trying to kill Frank Adams. Frank Adams, not me. And, hello, I am the best." He chortled into her ear. "Otherwise you wouldn't want me."

"Shit, Parker."

"Six, precisely, sweetcheeks. And things have to playout. Is that understood, Brenda?"

She did, she had to, wanting to smack him. Disconnecting, the men with her ignoring her last three words, she called Princeton who reminded her calmly that "Parker Williams, Agent Smithers, and those men in the room with you, are my very best agents."

She disconnected, sitting with the men, gluing her eyes to the screen, wondering how they could sit impassively slouched in their chairs watching the Christmas Killer as if he was, she didn't know what, a single-minded sociopath who had murdered thirty-six people.

The killer didn't sit; he didn't walk around or look into drawers, the fridge, the bedroom or bathroom. He'd done all that previously. When he wasn't in the kitchen doorway he was at the patio doors standing motionless, frightening her more each moment with his aloof patience. At 5:50 he went to the kitchen, kneeling at the bag, removing his glasses and cap. Standing, he stretched, reaching into his jacket, unaware he had stopped Brenda Smithers' heart.
*

"Holy shit!" She blurted, grabbing for her phone, the men framing her wondering what the hell. She was cursing, Parker wasn't picking up. "Parker, do not go into that apartment. Do not. It's him. He's Simms, Marcus Simms. He's in the kitchen and he's armed." She ran to the windows, stamping her feet. Parker was stepping from the bus, checking his watch, completely unperturbed.

He stopped, checking his phone, smiling. Looking up he saw Brenda jabbing her phone with a finger. He waved and blew her a kiss, his brow furrowing. She was flipping him the bird. She was royally pissed, silently enunciating for him to "answer the fucking phone." He assumed.

Parker Williams heard the message. Nodding, he gave her a thumbs-up before walking into the building. The men with her understood the tirade. That's precisely why 4-C had rules in place. Women were consistently women first.

At 6:00 Frank Adams walked into his apartment. At 6:00 one man beside Agent Smithers increased the volume, the other widened the view. The third man was wiping sleepiness from his face with a damp towel.

Adams closed the door, forgetting to flip the lock. Hanging his windbreaker on a hook, he slumped against the wall facing the kitchen. He was exhausted after a long day. Rubbing his face hard, he looked up.

"Frank Adams, pleased to make your acquaintance. And thank you for being punctual."

"Who the fuck are you?"

"Not really important. The better question would be, why am I here, waiting for a white supremacist dirt bag. The answer: Nine murdered gays."

"Fucking queers. So what? You one of them, one I missed? Fuck you."

"Hardly. Simply a concerned citizen doing the little he can to better a failed justice system. The judge must have been somewhat of a homophobe himself to let you off as easily as he did."

"Twelve of twenty-five in solitary ain't exactly a joy ride, mister."

"Possibly not, but we digress. Don't we? I'm not here to debate your sense of social cleansing. I'm here to make things right. Those twelve other men you shot are still in wheelchairs. I don't see that the judge clearly understood the depth of your savagery." He raised the gun, coughing a laugh. "No. Nothing as quick as a bullet, nothing like the splattering of an Uzi. How pedestrian would that be? This is a sedative to make my work easier and your imminent passing somewhat more meaningful to your surviving victims and the families."

The dart shot from its chamber, slamming into Frank Adams' upper chest, knocking him hard into the wall, dropping him precisely where Parker Williams wanted.

Brenda's gun was in her hand, the key in her other in case Parker tripped the lock, hating herself for not trusting him. Not giving a shit.

"Stay where you are!" Agent Williams shouted.

Brenda blurted, "No fucking way!"

Simms said, "I'm afraid that would be counterproductive, Adams."

Adams dropped his head to the floor, watching his killer toss his gun into the bag, watching as Simms took a syringe from his jacket, taking extreme care to slide the sleeve from the needle.

"One part pentobarbital, one part sulphuric acid. The Pento puts you down, the acid inspires an immediate sense of regret, Mr. Adams." He glanced at his watch. "Three minutes, give or take, depending on your general well-being. You are about to experience the worst depths of hell, Frank Adams."

The killer came closer. Adams' eyes were distant, staring past him. Then directly at him, plucking the dart from his chest with a cavalier smirk as he would a petal from a flower.

"Yeah, I've seen your work. Sick shit. Seventeen other bad guys and seventeen innocent women, excluding your wife and Dominic Drake. Do I have that about right, Marcus Simms?"

Simms stopped dead, stumbling. What?"

"That's right, Markie. You're done. You are totally fucked. We got ya, Markie. Smile. You *are* on candid camera. You took us a while, but goddamn you are done."

"Or you are, whoever you are. Murder is a strong word, I prefer appropriate justice. As for the women, they were all whores. Each one of them deservedly dead, my ex-wife the worst whore by far."

Marcus Simms lunged forward, partly diving with his thumb on the plunger. Parker Williams sprang up, gripping the man's wrist, Brenda Smithers, far ahead of her team, throwing open the door.

Simms and Parker were struggling, their faces and arms strained, the syringe jerking indecisively between them. Parker slipped a leg between Simms' kicking out the left, his back taking the brunt of Simms' fist as he gripped Simms' right wrist with his other hand, the two men sprawling to the floor when strength was at once the deciding factor. Simms was strong and fit, Parker was strong and trained by the best, though Simms was not surrendering, Smithers' team blocking her. Men would always be men first. That she was their lead didn't matter. They instinctively knew what Parker wanted. He did not need a conflicted female getting in his way.

"They were evil, rapists and killers," Simms groaned, struggling.

Williams already knew that.

"I needed to kill all the whores. The bitches, all of them whores. You do not have to do this, you do not have to die."

"No, Simms. But you do." Parker Williams grunted in a strained whisper that no techie would ever distinguish on the recording. "As you said, appropriate justice. In your particular case immediate justice." He heaved his full weight to one side, pinning Simms' arm. "Now! Now!"

The closest team member rushed in, sliding on his knees, wedging his weapon between Williams and Simms, shoving a protective hand hard against his friend Parker while putting two ten-millimetre rounds into Marcus Simms' chest. Simms jerked once, his eyes flared open and he died.

Another agent with Brenda ran to capture the rolling syringe, another rushing in with both hands to help Parker stand. Brenda pushed him away almost as quickly, she needed to hug and punch her fiancé. She wouldn't cry, not in front of her team. She just wanted to kiss him, to love him and to smack his stupid head.

"Shit! Parker. I mean, holy fucking shit!"

He grinned. "Hey, what's up? I love you. I knew this would work out. No problem. But really, sweetcheeks, honestly, so much for your concealed Berettas."

The three other men were grinning. Sweetcheeks? Really? They nodded. Oh yeah, really.

Fuck the team. She hugged him and kissed him. She didn't care who saw. "You got him, Parker. You got him. I'll call Princeton. Shit!"

Chapter Twenty-Six
Marcus & Jeddore

Marcus Simms died at age forty-eight, Jeddore Billows died at forty-five. Marcus' home was stately and elegant, recently more masculine in its design. Everything was neatly in its place, everything top-end yet understated. Everything about the man spoke simplicity and finesse. The man had style.

Further investigation revealed that another privileged Marcus Simms went missing in South Carolina on May 31, 1987 and was never found. Presumed dead after very little had been done to locate him. They also went through the computer on Simms' desk under a framed ten-dollar bill where they found Beverly Benton and Wendy Brighton.

Jeddore Billows ran from his home on his fifteenth birthday from a difficult life after his mother and father were found incinerated in their home, Mrs. Nancy Billows with another man attached to her in bed. No trace was ever found of him. Jeddore Billows and Marcus Simms both quickly went cold and stayed that way.

Searching Billows' Charleston condo, Agents Smithers and Williams found a state-by-state listing of stores selling high-powered dart guns, a collection of pentobarbital vials and vials of sulphuric acid. His closet was lined with tailored suits, shirts and ties, Italian shoes and imported

418

French loungewear. His dining room boasted enviable wines, Johnnie Walker Black and Blue, high-priced vodkas and cognacs. Label for label what they found at the Simms residence. They also found his computer where they discovered scanned newspaper clippings alluding in detail to the May 31st, 1987 double murder-suicide and two boys who went missing at the same time.

"Shit, Parker. Billows killed Simms at fifteen. Shit!"

"Looks that way. The cops got it wrong. Country hicks. Who woulda thunk? The father didn't kill anyone. He might have wanted to, but his kid got to him first. Too bad, Billows changed a lot of history. The mother was a whore bagging Simms for a measly ten bucks, so he killed them. Who knows, maybe he was jealous of the rich kid. Maybe *he* wanted mommy. Lots of boys like their mommies a little too much. Then he killed his old man for kicking the shit out of him, set the place on fire and took off. Thirty years ago, especially in these parts, anything was possible. Give the guy credit, from a mid-teen bubba to a multimillionaire sophisticate."

At the Rothstones, the strain of his grief made worse at hearing who really raped and murdered his daughter, and how, Roger Samuels' face discoloured to a deep purple. He gazed despairingly at his wife and died, inadvertently and posthumously gratifying Jeddore Billows. Wendy Brighton, hearing the truth of her best friend's death and of Roger Samuel's passing, hearing the truth of Marcus Simms and realizing what could well have happened to her, collapsed onto her sofa in anguish where and when Agents Williams and Smithers left her inconsolable after readily consenting to her wishes.

The next stop was Southeast Consulting that would close forever that day. The women wailed and screamed, hugging each other, hearing how their handsome and charming boss was a serial killer, that he had killed that many innocent women, his wife and her lover. The men went into the conference room to pour everyone full glasses of expensive booze and got drunk. Their lucrative careers were at a standstill.

They were ordered not to contact Beverly Benton who had left early. Doing so would be considered…"Well, just don't do it," Parker Williams suggested.

Beverly opened her door upon seeing their shields and calling Fran Princeton to verify their authority, curious what federal agents would want with her.

When they were seated Brenda began, "Ms. Benton, if you have something to drink, do that right now. We'll wait."

"Are you serious? What is this about?"

"I am serious. We'll wait, Ms. Benton."

When Beverly returned, she sipped Rémy Martin from a snifter, Brenda encouraging her with a discreet hand sign to finish up. She did in a gulp, feeling nervous, becoming agitated.

"Ms. Benton, Beverly, I'll get straight to it. This is *not* good news. Early yesterday evening, outside Arlington, we killed Marcus Simms as part of a sting operation for the murder of thirty-four people, Rosemary Sandra Simms and Dominic Drake. He died quickly while attempting to kill Agent Williams with a drug that's used for executions."

"What?" Beverly sat stunned, trembling. She dropped her glass, wringing her hands. "You killed him? That's ridiculous. He wants to marry me."

"I killed him, Ms. Benton. His real name was Jeddore Billows. Some thirty years ago he also killed his parents and the real Marcus Simms. And yes, he was trying to kill me believing I was someone else. We've spent seventeen years searching for him. He killed bad guys, one each year. Then seven days later like clockwork, for some reason consistently at Christmas and New Year's, he would murder an innocent woman after flirting with her, probably entertaining her, and finally having what we believe was consensually aggressive sex."

"He wants to marry me."

"Then, Beverly," Brenda cut in, "you are an extremely fortunate woman. He set a pattern and sociopaths very seldom stray from their established behaviours. You are very fortunate we got to him. If I were you, the first thing I would do is cry, cry a lot. That's what I did last night. Then take a few days, go somewhere. 4-C is right now authorizing your corporate bank to allow funds for your staff's counselling. None of you will be getting over this anytime soon. As for Southeast, it's finished." She put a hand to Beverly's knee. "Beverly, can I call someone?"

"Are they at the office now, my staff?"

"Yes," Parker replied, reaching for the glass. "Many of them probably, and understandably, in dire need of taxis for the drive home."

"Agent Williams, Marcus attempted killing you last night?" He nodded. Beverly glanced from Brenda to her glistening ring. "I am very happy for your lovely fiancée that he did not. You said seven days, at year's end. That answers many questions, resolves many frustrations, except why I loved him for such a very long time." She sighed deeply, squeezing Brenda's hand. "Congratulations, Agent Smithers."

"I'm so sorry for you, Beverly."

"May I ask a favour, Agent Smithers, Agent Williams? Would you kindly take me to them, to my friends at the office? I believe they need me and I'm a little shaky right now."

"Certainly we will, Beverly," Parker replied, Brenda suggesting she might want to freshen her make-up.

Parker stood as Beverly Benton stood. She offered them something from the bar while they waited. She would need a few minutes. Brenda said "no, thank you." Parker went to where she pointed, wisely choosing the Rémy Martin over the JW Blue and Black he and Brenda had seen in both men's homes.

Two days later without the least ceremony, Marcus Simms and Jeddore Billows were cremated, his remains personally emptied into a landfill by Wendy Brighton.
*

June 24th was a Saturday. The sky was a deep blue, cloudless, and the wind knew better than to spoil her day. She was the most dazzling bride of all time in a strapless midnight blue gown that fell to satin blue sandals. Her stylish updo was crowned with a sapphire tiara, her one hand cradling a bouquet of delicate red roses, the other hand adorned at her wrist with a slim silver and sapphire bracelet. That hand rested on a proud Stanley Smithers arm.

At the altar Parker Williams stood by the one best man he could think of, a good friend, the man who didn't piss around saving him from becoming a molten mass. No one cared that he was dressed in a deep blue tailored suit, a Mediterranean-blue shirt and sapphire-blue silk tie. No one except Bella Smithers who hadn't heard the entire story from her daughter. He wasn't important. The day was all about her.

Kissing her father before he stepped back, Stanley willingly and happily losing her to another, Brenda passed her bouquet to a beaming and teary-eyed Fran Princeton, stepping to her handsome groom's side. His beautiful hair had grown in; his eyes, no longer dark and menacing, were sparkling with love, his sensual and smooth skin clean and tanned as he clasped her hand in his.

Then a deafening hush enveloped the hall that Brenda's deliriously happy mind was oblivious to. She was with her man.

"Do you, Parker Williams, take Brenda Smithers to be your wife, to have and to hold from this day forward, for better or for worse, for richer, for poorer, in sickness and in health, to love and to cherish her from this day forward until death do us part?"

"I do."

"Do you, Brenda Smithers…"

"Shit, yes!"

Other Mystery – Suspense - Thriller Novels
By Doug Booth:

The Viewing Room
The 4th Man
The Madam
Family Lies
Mother's Pearl Dagger
From Inside Her Bedroom
The Feast of Tombola
Deferred Prejudice
The Hunt for Gilligan Rose
The Fatal Diners' Club
Silent Conviction
A Christmas Killer, Comfort and Joy
Pariah In the Mirror
***

No One to Tell(A Creative Non-Fiction)

www.ingramcontent.com/pod-product-compliance
Lightning Source LLC
Chambersburg PA
CBHW020504260626
47156CB00006B/1848